TRAPLINE

An Allison Coil Mystery

TRAPLINE

MARK STEVENS

MIDNIGHT INK
WOODBURY, MINNESOTA

FIRST EDITION
First Printing, 2014

Book design and format by Donna Burch-Brown
Cover design by Lisa Novak
Cover images:129460/Dale Robins/ iStockphoto.com; 57478434/
    Taylor S. Kennedy/National Geographic Collection/Getty Images
Editing by Connie Hill

Midnight Ink, an imprint of Llewellyn Worldwide Ltd.

Library of Congress Cataloging-in-Publication Data

Stevens, Mark, 1954–
  Trapline : an Allison Coil mystery / Mark Stevens. — First edition.
      pages ;   cm. — (An Allison Coil mystery)
   ISBN 978-0-7387-4164-2
1. Hunting guides—Fiction. 2. Reporters and reporting—Fiction. 3. Colorado
—Fiction. I. Title.
   PS3619.T4914T73   2014
   813'.6—dc23   2014019594

Midnight Ink
Llewellyn Worldwide Ltd.
2143 Wooddale Drive
Woodbury, MN 55125-2989
www.midnightinkbooks.com

Printed in the United States of America

ACKNOWLEDGMENTS

Many thanks to private detective David Keil, who offered hours of insight. "America's Secret ICE Castles," an article published in *The Nation* by Jacqueline Stevens and the documentary "Lost in Detention," written and directed by Rick Young and aired on *PBS Frontline*, offered inside looks at national issues with immigration and incarceration. Rachel Maddow's coverage of issues with private prisons generated fresh leads and insight. *Illegal: Life and Death in Arizona's Immigration War Zone*, by Terry Greene Sterling, provided excellent details as did *The Death of Josseline: Immigration Stories from The Arizona Borderlands*, by Margaret Regan. Frank McGee of Colorado State Parks & Wildlife answered many, many questions about wildlife and criminal investigations in the woods. And Renee Rumrill, well, I wouldn't be here without you and thanks also for your sharp eye on the manuscript.

To my late pal Gary Reilly, thank you for planting the seed for this story. This was your idea. Thanks to my friend Ralph Beall for pointing me to Richard Connell. Editor Shana Kelly's big-picture insights and thoughtful analysis of the story were golden. Suzanne Gluck and Eve Atterman, thank you both for your enthusiasm for Allison Coil as a character and for several critical ideas for this final version of the story. Thanks to Stephen Singular, Barry Wightman, Mike Keefe, Allyn Harvey, and Mark Eddy for detailed readings. Mark Graham, thank you for your support and advice over the decades and for a thoughtful take on this story. Thanks also to the entire Short Story Book Club—Ted Pinkowitz, Susan Fox, Dan Slattery, Parry Burnap, Laura Snapp, and my wife, Jody Chapel—for tackling the tough job as beta readers. Many thanks to my three girls—Jody, Ally, and Justine—for their unwavering support and enthusiasm. Deep thanks to the ever-strategic Linda Hull (for obvious reasons) and many thanks to Terri Bischoff, who has done so much as an editor to champion good mysteries everywhere and who helped shape this story in particular.

ONE:
SUNDAY NOON

THE ASPEN TREES STOOD like students at a new school. Nobody wanted to get too close. The sun washed Lumberjack Camp in a gold-green bath. Allison Coil wished she had a camera. Even better, Allison wished she had the time and inclination to store and savor the thousands of killer shots she could have snapped over the years that she had basked in the seasons, particularly late summer and fall, in the Flat Tops Wilderness of Colorado.

"You don't shoot pictures either, do you?" asked Allison.

"What do you mean 'either'?" said Colin.

"Well, I don't," said Allison. "So you'd be either."

"You never did?"

The grove that marked Lumberjack Camp stood a quarter-mile across an open meadow. They rode single file on the narrow trail, Allison on Sunny Boy and Colin on the ever-dependable Merlin.

"Not really," said Allison. A pocket-size digital was back in her A-frame but she couldn't remember the last time she'd used it. "Plenty of mental photographs, some real prize-winners. I need to figure out a way to download them from my brain, frame them, and enter the big-money contests."

"If you figure that out, you might be a rich woman before you sell your first picture," said Colin.

They were meeting up with William Sulchuk, a businessman from Glenwood Springs. Allison reminded herself *William*, not Will or Bill. He went out of his way to urge use of the full name. He had become a regular late-season client and he had a knack for bagging trophy bulls.

William Sulchuk had called two days earlier and asked a favor. He wanted to come up to the wilderness with his daughter Gail, who had turned thirteen and was now ready, he believed, to learn how to hunt. He thought an hour or two of exposure with a real-life outfitter and hunting guide might rub off. When Allison had told him she planned to be up on the Flat Tops, they agreed on Lumberjack Camp around noon. William would have three other friends in tow, all with teenage offspring.

If all went well, they would utter their *hi-how-are-you's*, talk a bit about scouting for elk, and be on their way.

"Not in another place, but this place," said Allison.

"What?"

"Not in another hour, but this hour," she said, turning around with the sure knowledge that he would be giving her a whacky look. She was not disappointed. He screwed up his face like she was speaking Greek.

"Happiness," she said. "It's a Walt Whitman line. The 'Leaves of Grass' guy. Today. It's a gift."

"Gifts are good," said Colin, playing along.

"Happy as those aspens in the sun," she said. A neat line of eight horses stood at the camp's hitching rail on the outer edge of the aspen grove.

"The trees. Are happy?" Colin liked playing the backwoods hick.

"How could anything so beautiful not be happy?" she said. "It's impossible."

The horses suggested humanity, but the grove looked otherwise empty.

The fire ring consisted of uniform rocks the size of soccer balls. A twenty-foot section of a well-worn fir tree formed the official camp sitting log. Allison dismounted at the same time as a childish squeal pierced the quiet and alerted her to a cluster of pint-sized human forms on the far side of the trees.

"Apparently the children have all eaten their parental units," said Colin, climbing down from Merlin. "We're next."

He looked around, faux suspicion on his face.

They were eight weeks shy of their second full year together. Allison still relished Colin's casual strength and boundless outdoor talents. His latest phase involved primitive hunting skills—stick throwing, snaring, and experiments with the atlatl, the prehistoric arrow-slinging weapon. Colin's Colorado roots ran deep. His mountain roots ran deeper. His middle name could be "Indigenous."

"I see no boiling pot of water. Unless they are all carrying machetes in their teeth, I think we have a chance," said Colin. "I'm already questioning the parenting skills of this man you call William, however."

She had rehearsed him on the *mmm* in *William* and he emphasized it.

There were two boys and two girls, all in unsoiled hunting garb. Their serious expressions were laced with a hint of dread. Three went back to look at whatever they were watching, but the fourth, a girl with dirty blond hair tied up in pigtails and easily the tallest among the four, greeted them with worried eyes. She had a long face, perfect patches of delicate freckles on her cheeks and studded diamond earrings that looked real. Allison knew she lacked any expertise. Something about the girl reeked of plush bedrooms done up in girlish pink. A whiff of sweet perfume like strawberries hung in the air. Out here, wearing the scent would have the same effect as running around in the woods carrying a boom box on your shoulder blasting hip-hop. She wouldn't be sneaking up on any animals anytime soon. She reminded Allison of herself at that age.

"I'm Gail," she said.

"And I'm Allison and this is Colin," said Allison, shaking hands.

Gail's eyes were the kind of blue that would no doubt make men weep for decades to come. She might be thirteen but her father apparently didn't object if she added three years, or six, with makeup.

"What's going on?" said Allison, noting Colin's fixation. No doubt it had been many moons since he had spotted such a rare species as well-kept, upper-middle-class American Female Teenager, especially up close.

Gail took a breath. She'd been holding something in. Being asked to use words required tears to accompany the narrative.

"They're up in the woods," said Gail. Her chin vibrated.

Allison put an arm around Gail, who willingly took the comfort.

"They are up in the woods," said Gail, taking another run at maintaining composure. "I was up there with my dad. We were … My dad … mushrooms …"

The sobbing hit full force.

"A body," said one of the two boys bluntly. "Nasty. And we all saw it first."

Gail's sobs deepened, perhaps at the further indignation.

4

Allison asked the other three for their names—Sophie, Joey, and Henry. "But Hank is better."

"He's on his back," said Hank, who had stepped up with an air of casual indifference. "I mean, his face is pretty gross and stuff, but from his chest down, I mean. It's gone."

TWO:
SUNDAY NOON

As the sidewalk tightened and the crush of followers grew, Duncan Bloom elbowed his way to the front, not wanting to lose sight of the candidate. *That* would be a cardinal no-no. The throng had grown tight with fans and bystanders and tourists caught up in a rock star wave of excitement. The crowd bulged out onto the road and police worked to keep one lane of traffic open.

Autographs, handshakes, hi-how-are-you's.

Repeat. Smile.

Bloom took notes and a picture with his cell phone. Visual notes.

Tom Lamott, the center of attention, wore a white golf shirt with the campaign logo over faded jeans. The golf shirt hinted at country club. The pants said weekend dad. He stood six-three. His head bobbed in the stew of humanity. The overall frame was lanky—maybe two hundred pounds. His healthy color and relaxed smile belied the fact that he had survived a grueling primary fight to represent Colorado in the U.S. Senate as a Democrat.

Across the street, a band of silent protesters stood vigil. There were six in this group, the third such band Bloom had spotted on Lamott's walk down Grand Avenue.

"Duncan?" The voice came from behind him, along with a gentle tap on the bicep.

His profile of Trudy Heath had earned Bloom a statewide award for feature writing. For multiple reasons, Trudy was hardly an unknown before Bloom wrote about her. The Denver papers and a few national outlets had followed the story of how her ex-husband had murdered two guides and rigged hunts for high-end clients. Trudy, who had been confined to her house due to an untreated case of epilepsy and who had been kept in the dark about the ugly side of her husband's operation, emerged like a butterfly from the dark cocoon.

She was now watching her regional celebrity rise through the explosion of her regional brand of herbs, pestos, and other natural food products. Bloom had written a piece marking the three-year anniversary of the arrest of her husband, George Grumley, and a few shorter pieces about her role leading the green movement in and around Glenwood Springs. Bloom had written a catch-up profile on Trudy and had met and interviewed her boyfriend and business manager, Jerry Paige, and thought he had made friends.

"How are you?" said Bloom.

"Good," said Trudy. "I had to hear Tom Lamott myself. Something more than the news clips, you know?"

Trudy Heath glowed with a woodsy charm. She exuded quiet confidence. You looked into her eyes, insanely white where they weren't creamy brown, and you found yourself thinking about green vegetables, plump tomatoes, and life as a vitamin vacuum.

"Mind if I quote you?"

Trudy smiled. "Not this time, okay?"

"Sure," said Bloom. "How's Allison?"

In Bloom's brief time in Glenwood Springs, no feature assignment had lingered longer than the Trudy Heath profile. First, for meeting Trudy and absorbing her grounded, serene view of the world. Second, for meeting the mysterious and slightly more inscrutable Allison Coil, who had dropped in during the lunch Trudy had prepared in her part-greenhouse cabin-cum-house on the edge of the Flat Tops. For Bloom, the sight of Allison made him want to know every scrap of her mind, heart, and flesh, and how those elements came together to form this intriguing woman from the wilderness, who might have been bred from some magical concoction of tree bark and horse sweat. The day lingered in his memory like a gift from another world, where concerns of the big city didn't interfere. Certainly Allison Coil had sprung whole from the Flat Tops and he tried to hide his surprise when he learned later that she had emigrated from the big city.

"She's fine," said Trudy. "She's up there somewhere today, doing some scouting," said Trudy.

"I'd love to go riding with her sometime," said Bloom. The thought of having a shot at Allison Coil had stayed with him for weeks. He hadn't sensed a half-encouraging smile from her, but the fantasy stuck. He was in good shape and a series of Denver girlfriends had enjoyed his company. Now that he had moved to the high country, mountain hikes kept him fit and trim. He let his brown hair grow shaggy between haircuts and let his wardrobe reduce itself to blue jeans, a series of pullovers, simple shirts, and running shoes. His last girlfriend, a lefty lawyer who worked on water issues, told him he could have passed for Tom Hanks' younger brother. Basically, that told Bloom that his everyday-okay appearance only meant he might get his foot in the front door.

"I'm sure she'd take you," said Trudy. "It's a matter of setting something up. But not for another story, right?"

"Just for fun," said Bloom.

The throng crammed in around the Doc Holliday Tavern, where Grand Avenue climbed the bridge over the Colorado River. Lamott stayed on street level, heading to the footbridge that paralleled the vehicle traffic bridge. Lamott's itinerary, the one e-mailed to all reporters, noted that Lamott would make a statement here, at the base of the footbridge, before heading over, alone.

"Does he do it for you?"

"He's impressive," said Trudy.

"What is it about him—can you put your finger on it?"

Trudy mulled the question, raised her neat dark-brown eyebrows, a shade darker than her hair. Her features were delicate but she looked like she could handle anything, including long days digging and turning soil. "His ideas seem so grounded in the way this country works—helping to fix problems, not getting sucked into the shrill yelling matches."

Bloom said good-bye to Trudy and wedged his way closer to Lamott, who had made his way up on a step of the footbridge.

Lamott held up his hand and the crowd grew quiet. Somebody handed him a microphone connected to a portable amp.

Every detail covered and right on time.

"My name is Tom Lamott and I'm a politician. You know there are two kinds of politicians, don't you?" He paused, smiled. "Yep, two kinds. The first kind can talk nonsense on any subject under the sun. The second kind don't need a subject."

Lamott launched into his canned speech. Bloom had heard every talking point through YouTube videos and coverage in the Denver papers. Lamott laid out his vision for embracing Mexico as a neighbor, treating them like a neighbor.

Crowd about half Hispanic.

Lamott's campaign challenge involved turning out the vote in November, but his team had already shown enough organizational skill that Republicans were petrified.

Lamott reached the end of his five-minute stump spiel. He paused, looked around, smiled.

Crowd quiet, attentive. Usual themes. Boyishly confident.

Bloom had read the next section of Lamott's speech online. *Ad nauseum.* It was the sensation, all the rage. It had landed Tom Lamott a mention in *Time Magazine* and the *New York Times* and, of course, Univision.

Lamott started speaking in Spanish.

It wasn't broken, token foreign language. His Spanish had depth, nuance. Bloom had spent a summer in Cozumel and had soaked up as much conversational Spanish as anyone, but when Lamott spoke in Spanish, the accents and inflections seemed natural.

This isn't Kennedy's Ich Bin Ein Berliner. *This is a politician who wants to communicate.*

"Nobody is saying the United States of America should abandon the English language," said Lamott. "Hardly."

Lamott smiled. He watched the statement sink in.

This was all said in Spanish, but Bloom could follow along with the script e-mailed ("please keep the Earth in mind should you choose to print this document") in advance.

"But to work with each other—and I would suggest that the United States and Mexico not only must work together, but that we rely on each other—we must understand each other. And what better way than to speak each other's languages, I ask you?" Famously, Lamott had learned every lick of Spanish in his middle and high school years at a public school, the Denver Center for International Studies, and then the University of Colorado, where he had double majored in Spanish and Political Science.

Ronald Reagan brought down the Berlin Wall. Tom Lamott wants to bring down the tortilla curtain.

A photographer draped with a bundle of cameras around his neck stood two stairs up and behind Lamott, snapping away.

"Thank you, Glenwood Springs," said Lamott. "Thank you for your hospitality. We all know there are challenges today—primarily economic—and we must work together to repair what's broken. We can do that if we work together, if we find common ground and agree on a plan. I know words are easy. The work is hard. But if we're committed to do it, we can find a way."

No script. Metal water bottle in one hand. Audience rapt.

Briefly, Bloom thought Lamott caught his eye. And Bloom wondered if Lamott knew that the reporter who had hounded him in Denver now worked in Glenwood Springs.

"If you want to see conditions deteriorate with your neighbors, you build higher fences, point fingers, and make up scary scenarios that play on fears. I believe we can do better. Come November, I hope you will give me a chance."

The immigration "problem" had faded as a front-burner campaign issue with fewer immigrants making their way illegally across the border—lower birth rates in Mexico, for one, and scarce jobs in the United States, for two. But hatred simmered.

Wild applause. Whoops like a sporting event.

Again Lamott seemed to look over and nod in Bloom's direction.

No matter what had happened in Denver, Bloom would treat this day like any reporter covering any campaign stop. He considered himself pretty good at burying the hatchet.

"Now the campaign manager wants a few pictures of me on the bridge. I need a few minutes alone up there. Again, thank you to each and every one of you."

He respects his audience. Or fakes it extremely well.

Standing in the throng of Lamott's supporters now, Bloom thought he could feel the city turn, ever so slightly, on its collective heels.

Lamott's official media spokesperson, the young and stunning Stacey Trujillo, who had first greeted Bloom when Lamott stepped off his bus back in Sayre Park, gave Bloom a head nod as if to say "follow me." Bloom wedged his way through the crowd and up the pedestrian bridge.

"Just wanted to make sure you've got all you need," she said.

"Is it like this everywhere?" asked Bloom. "This kind of a turnout?"

"It's insane," she said. "In a good way."

Over the first part of the bridge going north, steel mesh siding rose about twelve feet on both sides. You could walk over the Colorado River and then the four lanes of Interstate 70, but you couldn't jump and kill yourself and you couldn't throw any crap over, either. The northern half of the footbridge had a railing of more or less regular waist-high height and more mesh from the grade level up to the railing. You could jump, Bloom supposed, but you'd land in the parking lot of the hot springs pool and at least they wouldn't have to put boats in the water to fish you out.

Ahead, Tom Lamott posed, smiling and then not smiling, leaning on the rail and then standing more erect, arms folded over his chest.

The photographer took pictures at a rapid-fire pace, from fifteen feet away.

The first bullet smacked metal near Lamott. A sharp *zzz-ting.*

Bloom ducked, put his arm up in a gesture of useless reflex. The sound alone was mean and violent.

Stacey let out a yelp like she'd been goosed. The photographer froze.

The second *zzz-ting* struck closer to Bloom than the first. Bloom's skin prickled. Stacey yelped again.

The third shot had the *zzz* but no *ting* and Bloom heard Lamott cry out like he'd been punched. His white golf shirt blossomed bright red at his shoulder.

The fourth shot caught Lamott as he buckled and he spun. He crumpled and rolled, ended up on his back.

Bloom grabbed his phone. Password in, phone button pushed. *Don't blow this.*

He dialed, flattened down. He tried to crawl under the asphalt.

Bloom looked out through the mesh and up the river, scanning. There was nobody on top of the train station. The river looked normal. He crab-walked over to Lamott, stayed low.

"911 Emergency. May I help you?"

A woman's voice. Calm.

Stacey sobbed. Bloom stared out through the steel mesh, searching for anything out of place in the riverside bushes or woods that covered the slope in the far distance, upriver.

The rip in his shirt offered an ugly window into Lamott's upper chest—blood gushed from the cavity and raced down his neck. The blood pooled black behind his head. Between pulses of red fluid, a shattered bone, most likely clavicle, revealed jagged edges. The sound coming from Lamott's throat was a dry rasp. Agony. Shock. His mouth was frozen open in horror and disbelief. Desperation filled Lamott's eyes. Lamott's look might have been the same if he was falling backward off El Capitan.

"Are you there?" asked the voice in Bloom's ear. "Are you there?"

THREE:
SUNDAY AFTERNOON

"YES, BUT THAT WAS after I found the sticks," said Gail, who had taken a breath. "A pile of brush and stuff. I didn't see at first what was underneath."

Allison looked at Colin, sure she could read his thoughts.

Mountain lion.

Tact suggested that you didn't utter the deduction out loud unless you were prone to yelling "fire" in a crowded theater.

The odds of a mountain lion attack were about the same as plopping a penny into a slot machine in Black Hawk and watching it transform itself into a thousand dollar bill. There were mountain lions all over Colorado—at least every part of the state west of the Front Range. Sightings were rare, attacks few and far between.

Allison ran her internal range finder and imagined an elk walking at the tree line. It would be a long shot and beyond most shooter's capabilities, especially uphill, but some nuts would try. She figured six hundred yards to the forest's edge, all uphill.

As much as she had been scanning the tree line where the foursome had been looking, she hadn't spotted any human activity.

Colin pointed to where a man emerged from the woods. The man peered through a pair of binoculars.

"He's checking on us," said Hank. "That's my dad. He wants us to all stay here in a group until they come back. Every few minutes, he comes out."

Allison wondered if Colin might stay behind to keep the kids calm, but knew better than to ask.

"I'm coming," said Colin.

Had her thoughts always appeared in instant script on her eyelids or scrawled across her forehead?

Allison picked out an indirect route to avoid dense sections of waist-high brush. Peak wildflower season had ebbed, but the undergrowth lit up with yellow touches—sunflowers, daisies, and alpine buttercups. The torch had been passed from the July cornucopia of columbine, blue flax, and fireweed, though some hung tough. The official start of fall waited in the wings, nearly a month away, but its harbingers were right on cue.

The man with binoculars was Larry Armbruster. He was bald, medium height, and his hunting camos probably fit him twenty pounds ago. His chin was home to a wild goatee—long and untrimmed—and the rest of his face sported thick stubble. "Pleased to meet you," said Armbruster. With no apparent chit-chat skills, he led them thirty paces into the woods.

The ground had been well trampled. Finding a mountain lion track—or the tracks of bear or anything—would be a challenge. Nonetheless, Allison preferred to stare at the ground and not at the destination, which emitted a gut-tossing odor. Colin jammed mouth and nose into the pulled-close collar of his jean jacket. Allison used the crook of her elbow.

It didn't help.

"Not the afternoon we had planned," said William Sulchuk. No greeting. The odor made talk unappealing. The less breathing, the better.

William Sulchuk was a sturdy six-footer. His hair was conservative corporate under a Denver Broncos cap. He wore a faded jean jacket over dark blue jeans and simple hiking shoes, nothing fancy. The whole presentation said affable, cool—if a bit too put-together.

William introduced Allison to the other two in the group—Arthur "but everyone calls me Dusty" Brock and Neil Goodwin. Brock had a moustache that looked like it had been a fixture for decades. He was dark and squat. Goodwin stood back and waved from a distance as a greeting. Hunters came in every shape and size, but other than Larry Armbruster these guys all looked like they expected to hunt and hike or camp grit-free.

Allison introduced Colin and then Armbruster headed back to the ridge to check on the young ones.

"The kids tell you?" said Sulchuk.

"Got the general idea," said Allison. "The dispute about who spotted it first is not going to be settled anytime soon."

If mountain lion had been the killer, he had feasted first on the legs. There wasn't much left. The head and torso were completely mauled but the shape of the flesh and one intact ear gave plenty of indication of the human form.

The body had come to rest on its right side. The man's left arm ended at his wrist. The right arm underneath protruded at an impossible angle back where no arm could go without being disconnected from its owner. The man's shirt sported no discernible color or style. There was no clear indication of intentions to hunt. A camouflage pattern on a jacket, for instance, might have helped. The shirt looked like it had been wet and then dried. His torso had turned a sickening

16

brown, the same swampy color produced by combining all the finger paints in first grade. His jaw gaped open, his eyeballs were history. Perhaps a snack for a lucky crow. Flies feasted and dense knots of maggots dined where the torso came to an abrupt end. A layer of grit and loose sticks covered the body, but the handiwork was sloppy.

How many people on the planet were so inured by death or a corpse they had no reaction to it? Embalming fluids, silk-lined caskets, and giant flower displays were all designed to soften the grizzly details of what happens to the body when the motor stops ticking. When the death was violent, like this one, the transformation from complex breathing life form to decomposing mass of ex-*Homo sapien* was lightning-quick. The wilderness treats a human's demise the same way a busy highway treats road kill. With indifference.

Allison pulled her phone from her jean jacket, waited for the device to channel its inner coffee.

She wanted wildlife officers on the scene as soon as possible, with a houndsman in tow and a couple of Treeing Walker hounds to pick up a scent. She wanted the coroner's analysis. She wanted the body examined for every scrap of animal DNA, whether it was mountain lion or bear. Sticks and other detritus that the animal had used to cover the body needed checking for DNA and saliva. She wanted the whole scene studied in exacting detail for stray animal hairs and saliva around the wounds. The flies and maggots and birds and other critters, depending on their size, could consume the rest of the corpse in days. Every minute counted.

"Wildlife officers are going to want to track this cat—as soon as possible," she said. "You don't want a cat out there that's had success with a human. I've got no cell, by the way, at least from my feeble rig."

"We tried, too," said Sulchuk. He seemed oddly untalkative.

The three fathers stood back in a semi-circle. They looked defeated and indifferent. She turned to look back through the trees to the ridge. Armbruster had his back to them, binoculars glued to his eyes.

"Triangle Mountain," said Colin.

"Probably the closest spot," said Allison. "And only reliable about half the time, when the sun is just right."

Allison led the way back to the open sky at the top of the hill. The foul cloud from the half-corpse seemed to follow.

"Any chance you packed a tarp?" Allison asked. "A blanket? A sleeping bag we can sacrifice?"

"Day trip," said Sulchuk. "We've got nothing that big. And if the cat comes back?"

A gentle breeze sliced through the woods at their back as they stood at the top of the open hillside. Arthur Brock and Neil Goodwin started working their way down.

"If the cat comes back while we're gone, we'll have less of the body to work with," said Allison. "I've got that spare poncho rolled up behind Sunny Boy's saddle. I'll take my chances on the rain—even if it looked like a downpour coming, we've got to keep the critters and birds off. As much as possible, anyway."

Armbruster volunteered to retrieve the poncho and headed off.

"Any point in taking a picture or two?" said Colin.

Back at the body, Allison and Colin stood on opposite sides of the half-corpse, taking pictures one-handed. Evidence had been trampled by the four children and now, in all, six adults. Allison stared off into the woods, wondering which way the cat had run—if it was a cat—after hiding its cache.

"No matter how he died," said Allison. "How long do you think it's been?"

They were walking back to Lumberjack. The shadows from the ridge behind them had grown longer.

"Two days at the most," said Colin, who appeared to have given the question some serious analysis.

"Not a big guy," said Allison

"Hard to say for sure," said Colin. "Given the legs. Or lack of."

"Give me your impression. Head size, shoulders."

"Compact, maybe. But I wasn't taking notes," said Colin. "I was trying to breathe."

"Anything seem odd to you?" said Allison.

The mental movie clip in Allison's head ran in a loop. Victim's point of view, walking through the woods or up the broad hillside. Was he a hunter out scouting? While the clothing on the half-corpse was all one blotchy bloody color now, it didn't appear to be camo. Hiker? Any sign of a backpack, day pack? Hat? Maybe a fisherman headed to a favorite hole? With what fishing pole?

"Not really," said Colin. "But I've known guys who have spent all their lives in these woods and never seen a mountain lion in person or a mountain lion kill. Tracks, yes. But that's it."

Possible victim types in the Flat Tops in August comprised a short list—hunter, hiker, camper, fisherman, horseback rider, what else? Maybe a stray scientist.

"Unusual, sure. But if he was hungry," Colin. "Every attack is calculated on some primal instinct. The lion figures his odds and starts to chase—or not. You?"

"Nothing looked right to me," said Allison.

"Really? Nothing?"

"There's some other story going on," said Allison.

"Why so sure?"

"I can't put my finger on it," said Allison. "A feeling. I can't picture it happening."

"Happens so rarely, how do you know what to picture?" said Colin.

"Just going on gut," said Allison. "So you think it's possible?"

"Hungry lions happen, stray hikers happen," said Colin. "And possible covers a lot of ground."

FOUR:
SUNDAY EVENING

She knew the cop.

"You still live up Sweetwater Road, back in by the Flat Tops?"

"Same general area," said Trudy. Sometimes being recognized was good for the business. This wasn't a good time.

"What brought you down?" He was a city policeman, not a sheriff's deputy.

"Same as everyone else," said Trudy.

"You were close to the footbridge?" said the cop. "When he went up?"

"Right there," said Trudy.

"Did you see him get—"

"No," said Trudy, cutting him off. "I was lower, down below. I was going to walk over to the hot springs so I was waiting for the bridge to clear. But no."

They were sitting on two metal folding chairs, face to face. The cop's name was Gary Lemke. She remembered him from high school. Lemke had greeted her warmly.

He was short and stocky. He had brown-red eyebrows and a ruddy round face. After hours and hours of witness interviews, he didn't seem a bit worn out.

The police had taken over the train station—inside and out. Boxes full of packaged snacks and bottled water appeared like an airdrop into a third-world disaster zone. There were reporters, news trucks, a First Aid station, and more cops than Trudy would have guessed worked on the entire Western Slope. The initial burst of panic—when the throng of Lamott's followers flinched and gasped as one—had given way to a trained bureaucracy doing its thing. The whole city remained on lock down.

"Did you hear anyone at all during the day say anything crazy-sounding or angry?"

"Nothing," she said. "Everybody knows about the freaky protesters. Spooky."

"Did you notice anything at all?" said Lemke.

Most everyone had pointed to a spot further east, up the river.

"No," said Trudy. "I looked this way, didn't see anything."

"A rooftop?" said Lemke. "A window?"

"Not really," said Trudy.

Lemke took a couple of notes, but they couldn't have been much.

"When are they going to open the bridge, do you think?" said Trudy.

"Not up to me," said Lemke. He smiled.

Trudy had planned to have a late dinner waiting for Allison and Colin. They were probably back, making do on their own. She settled in for a wait. Her problems were minimal compared to the police effort to find the shooter.

"It's been a long few hours," said Trudy. "Is there any word about, you know—"

"From what I heard, it's going to be touch and go for a day or two," said Lemke. "Good the hospital was so close."

At the image of Tom Lamott on the brink of death, Trudy imagined tubes in his mouth, doctors hovering. She found herself wiping away a tear.

"I remember you from high school," said Lemke. "You were a year ahead of me."

The comment caught her off guard.

"Sorry to say I wasn't paying much attention back then," said Trudy.

"Probably not too many would have pegged you for future entrepreneur—and quite successful at that, am I right?"

Did this mean the official stuff was over? Lemke's posture hadn't changed.

"I feel lucky," said Trudy. "Things have been going well." The last big publicity splash, which generated another spike in sales, included a full-page article in *Sunset.*

"My mother swears by your marinades," said Lemke. "On chicken. Slapped on the grill—that one with basil and garlic, incredible. And I've got a couple of sisters who have each taken up gardening because of you—homegrown vegetables, fresh herbs. You are like their guru."

Trudy didn't know what to say.

"So let me ask you this," said Lemke. "Don't you employ Mexicans?"

Trudy felt the accusation like a knife slipped between her ribs. Trudy's burgeoning business in West Glenwood stood at a crossroads between regional label and national brand. They had their own greenhouses and contracts with others across the Western Slope, too. A food processor in Grand Junction followed her recipe and packaged the sauces for distribution. The market for her fresh herbs, cross-branded with the sauces, showed staying power. Her produce stands hopped. Investors hovered.

"Sure," said Trudy.

"So you must have a strong opinion. I mean, on this whole issue."

"I think the issue has gone way out of control," said Trudy. "I liked Lamott's approach."

"Because it helps you keep cheap labor," said Lemke. His gaze tightened.

"We do everything by the book," said Trudy. "If an identity card doesn't match up, we let them go."

"For the rest of us to deal with," said Lemke. "You know things have changed in Glenwood Springs. It isn't what it used to be, the drugs moving through here, coming up with the brown tide. It ain't the intellectuals wading across the Rio Grande."

Trudy squirmed. She thought of her crew and how hard they worked. They were natural gardeners and savvy mechanics. They spread a warm family feeling throughout her operation. They cared about efficiency and floated ideas to improve the work flow.

"You have to realize," said Lemke, "that if employers only hired people they knew—not strangers on the street, especially if they don't speak English and especially if you don't know where they are really from or how they got here, that we wouldn't be having any of this crap going on. These fights."

"I can't fix who lives here," said Trudy.

"But you don't have to hire them," said Lemke. "You hire them and they send the word. Soon, the brother is here. The uncle. Even with the economy in the shitter up here, it pays better and life is better. Their kids sit next to my kids in class and you ought to see the contortions the school goes through to help these kids learn English."

Trudy kept thinking about her workers, her team. She tried to think if any skilled white gardeners had applied when she posted jobs.

"If I were you, I'd clean up my act. You know, check. Make sure."

"What do you mean?" said Trudy.

"You know exactly what I mean," said Lemke. "Go through your stuff, your records. Make sure everything really is on the up and up."

"What are you telling me?" said Trudy. "That someone's coming?"

"It's always coming," said Lemke. "Now might be a good time to make sure your nose is all-American squeaky clean."

In a daze Trudy headed back toward her pickup, parked eight blocks south of downtown, halfway back to Sayre Park. A caravan of news trucks had overrun the street by the train station. Television reporters stood in a row. Each reporter had his or her own spotlight.

The traffic crawled crossing the river. A cluster of flashing lights blasted the rise to the east, on Lookout Mountain trail. Spotlights lit up the forest like the spaceship descending in *Close Encounters*. If that had been the sniper's perch, it would make the shot in Dealey Plaza look like the one in Ford's Theater.

Trudy snaked her way through town and came up to speed on the interstate. The pickup climbed Glenwood Canyon, following the tight curves in the road.

Was Lemke's warning for real?

Was it based on *anything*?

The pickup rambled out of the canyon and the traffic sped up. Trudy slowed at the Dotsero exit, ducked back under the interstate and followed the road north, into the black summer woods.

Her thoughts returned to the footbridge, those surreal seconds that had already moved into a section of her memory where all thoughts and all the associated sounds, smells, and sights would be kept in a hermetically sealed container for as long as her heart kept beating.

The planning that must have gone into those seconds of action—and the cold-hearted nerves behind the trigger—gave Trudy a shudder.

She cracked the front window, tasted the cool night air. A freight train ambled along on the far shore of the pitch-dark river, heading in the opposite direction. Piercing squeals of steel on steel floated across the night. Her headlights caught a porcupine scampering across the road. From the rear, the porcupine was a headless ball of spikes. It looked perfectly alien and terribly alone.

FIVE:
MONDAY, EARLY
MORNING

DUNCAN BLOOM STARED AT his newspaper's website. The first bit of instant history was in the books.

"Dem. Senate Candidate Lamott Shot Downtown."

It was 2:38 a.m., a grueling fourteen hours since the shooting. The cops had so little information that most of his first piece was all from eyewitnesses inter-mixed with reaction from political and civic leadership.

The newspaper had thrown everything at it that they could, but the big boys from New York and L.A. were already here or on the way, landing now at Eagle-Vail or DIA, speeding along the interstate with all their presumptive access and armies of producers, fact-checkers, investigators, and sources.

A bottle of red wine served as dinner and drinks in one convenient container, supplemented by a package of gas station peanuts, hours ago, and a granola bar grabbed from the abundant stash of supplies where the police set up shop at the train station. Given the paucity of edibles in his carriage house, rented from an active, bright-eyed widow, the wine would have to do.

It was three blocks straight up Lincoln Avenue to the scene that was now putting Glenwood Springs on the national news map. Bloom lived at 10th Street and Lincoln. The floodlights and police were buzzing around 7th Street, by the river, and up in the woods to the east of Lincoln Avenue on the base of Lookout Mountain. From the window over the kitchen sink that faced north, the glow that rose from the police encampment looked like premiere night in Hollywood. The people who lived in the houses smack next to the scene would need sleeping pills tonight. For Bloom, sleep wasn't on the agenda.

Bloom scrolled to a number on his cell phone and hit redial. The big boys were coming, but Bloom wasn't about to choke on their exhaust. This was his story, this was his town. He'd been right *there* for Chrissakes.

The moment Lamott fell defined surreal. He stewed about those split, fragmented seconds over and over. He had already played them in his mind a thousand times. He relived them as he interviewed witnesses. He relived them as the cops interviewed him. He was treated like any other witness put through the drill at the train station. Bloom knew four shots for sure, but there might have been more. How did he know if the first shot didn't miss the bridge? He didn't. Trudy Heath was at a nearby interview station, being grilled at the same time.

"Officer DiMarco," said the voice, no tinge of excitement.

"How ya doing?"

"Better question for you. Not every day you're kneeling over a man with bullet holes."

"All instinct," said Bloom. "Who's running the show?"

Deputy Sheriff Randall DiMarco was the nephew of Bloom's landlord and had been an even-tempered source. In Denver, it had been a challenge to get to know cops as individuals. Up here, it was possible.

"State moved in—CBI, FBI, governor's office, you name it. We ran the show for about the first six minutes."

"Are you where you can talk?"

"In my cruiser, taking a break," said DiMarco.

"Out at the scene?" said Bloom.

A radio squawked on DiMarco's end. "Does it matter?"

"I'm sure it's a cluster fuck," said Bloom.

On the TV, one fuzzy, over-enlarged video from a cheap camera caught the attempted assassination. A teenage girl had been standing on the train station platform and accidentally recorded the moment. She'd been shooting a video of her sister. You could make out Lamott and his entourage on the footbridge, then a minute of posing for pictures and then the ugly inevitable. Some video editor had highlighted Lamott with a circle of light and Bloom could see himself, a vague figure moving toward Lamott as he went down.

"What about the photographer?" said Bloom.

"Which one?" said DiMarco.

"The professional."

"You think you've thought of something we haven't?"

Bloom sipped his wine. It was his fourth glass but he felt oddly sober.

"Did those shots have anything interesting in the background? Are you looking at those?"

DiMarco slurped a drink, likely a Diet Mountain Dew, snapped his nicotine gum. "I gotta get back to looking around in the dark for nothing."

"So they showed something."

"I don't know every detail of the investigation."

"You would have heard a tidbit if it was good," said Bloom.

"It's possible," said DiMarco. "But I didn't. Are we off the record or on?"

"Off," said Bloom. "If I need something to quote, I'll tell you."

The Garfield County Sheriff's office seemed competent and most of his encounters with individual cops had been civilized.

"If anyone has picked up a trail, I haven't heard," said DiMarco.

"Don't you think you'd have something to go on by now, some breadcrumbs?"

"Don't mention food to me," said DiMarco. "And I'm not exactly in the inner loop."

Bloom pictured the Lookout Mountain trail in mid-August. It was no hot spot like Hanging Lake, halfway up Glenwood Canyon. No signs drew tourists. The barely-marked trailhead started behind a house with a clothes line and small flower garden.

"That trail heads up over the top," said Bloom. "To the east."

"Don't try to play cop," said DiMarco. "Right now the cops and detectives in Glenwood Springs outnumber the citizens of this hamlet about two to one. We've got angles coming out the wazoo."

A jolt caught Bloom like one of those flash headaches that make you wince and then goes poof.

Through the mayhem of the last twelve hours, he had forgotten the phone call.

"Hang on," said Bloom.

"I'm hanging," said DiMarco. "But actually, I've gotta go."

"No," said Bloom. "I might have something."

"Don't jack me around."

"I'm not," said Bloom, his mind flashing back and his whole body coming alive like he'd touched an electric fence. "I had a wacko on the line this morning. This guy wanted to double-check the times of Lamott's schedule for the day. Said he was a freelance photographer."

"Time was this?"

"After I got to the office. Little after ten."

"He was focused on the footbridge?" said DiMarco.

"Everything, really," said Bloom. "Start to finish, the whole campaign stop."

"How long was he on the phone?"

Bloom stood up, energy rekindled. The work phone stored records of inbound calls.

"A minute, two maybe," said Bloom. "Hard to remember but not long."

"The voice?" said DiMarco.

"Deep," said Bloom. "But chit-chatty like an excited tourist."

"Name?"

"I don't remember it or if he said."

"Hang on a second," said DiMarco.

They had printed details of Lamott's planned campaign stops in the paper. Not much had changed in terms of timing or logistics. Was there some other detail the caller had been after? Bloom wracked his brain. The swirl of events was thick. Bloom recalled the routine note-taking prior to the shot and his brief chat with Trudy Heath. That calm moment put the alluring Allison Coil, Trudy's pal, back in his thoughts in delicious fashion. Then there was Lamott's canned speech and he had followed Lamott up on the bridge. And then everything was a blur and he was swallowed whole by the whale-sized moment and plunged into a dark, busy blur of questions, digging and writing that had consumed the last eight hours. He knew it was the biggest news event he had ever covered. The steps were all the same as every other story, but the intensity factor was off the charts.

"Your office closed?" said DiMarco.

"I can get in."

"You going to need us to have a warrant?"

"We're cooperative," said Bloom. "If there's nobody down at the office, I'll call and check with the upper-ups. I suppose this can't wait until morning."

"No," said DiMarco. "Time is the enemy. And she's growing fangs."

SIX:
MONDAY MORNING

MORNING CRACKED OPEN THE day.

Allison walked the well-worn path from her A-frame across the open field to Trudy's place, tucked next to a grove of trees but in a spot that could catch sunlight during the day, at least in the summer. Colin led the way on the narrow, winding path that cut through the field.

A finger of smoke rose from Trudy's chimney. There wasn't a hint of a breeze. The agenda was simple—lead authorities to the torn-up body near Lumberjack Camp. Sulchuk and the others all had commitments and couldn't return to the site.

They had managed to raise a cell and contact the police around 8 p.m. The 911 dispatcher had been thorough and detailed when Allison made the report, passing her off to someone to go over all the particulars again. The cop mentioned the shooting in Glenwood Springs and that explained why they were so short-handed. Allison couldn't imagine it. The news explained her dispatcher's somewhat harried state. The half-corpse was bad and unsettling enough—Allison still felt certain that the mountain lion scenario held no credibility—but trying to imagine the attempted assassination was a double whammy.

"Smell anything yet?" said Allison.

"Bacon," said Colin. "The fake stuff."

"I'd eat a picture of bacon," said Allison.

"I'd eat the camera before it took the picture," said Colin.

Regular grocery store trips had not yet become part of their domestic—Allison hated the word—routine.

"One of us is going to have to maybe settle down and get that damn little house in order," said Allison.

It was a running joke. Theirs was a match made deep in the woods and it worked. One of the reasons was that they both shared the notion that keeping house, cleaning house, repairing house, enjoying house, or thinking house was low on the list of priorities. It was nice to have a bed, for all the reasons it was nice to have a bed. In fact, the loft bedroom and spectacular views of the broad field and mountains to the east were now permanently part of the imagery that went with the memories of making love with Colin. The bed had become theirs, not hers. Beds were good things and Allison was also generally in favor of a roof, especially in winter, but all the rest of what came with the term "house" was vastly overrated.

Especially if you had a neighbor and friend whose talents in the kitchen were both innate and refined.

The kitchen hummed. Two cats lay about, completely unexcited by the guests. Batter bolstered with fat blueberries dripped from a spoon in gooey dollops onto a cookie sheet. Trudy aimed each dollop with care.

"Scones," said Trudy when Colin asked. "To go with poached eggs and broiled tomatoes."

"No bacon?" said Colin. Trudy shot him a look and a smile. "What I meant to say was *yum*."

Colin liked to balance his intake of organic ingredients with a healthy portion of animal fat. You can lead a cowboy to bean sprouts, but you can't make him chew.

Trudy poured coffee and they quizzed her for her version of events. Allison shook her head repeatedly, finding it hard to imagine being so close to the shots.

"Couldn't sleep," said Trudy. "I kept thinking about all the little things I could have done. You know, to make it all come out differently."

"The cop sounds out of line," said Colin. "Way out of line."

"That was the capper," said Trudy. "He probably thought he was helping me. Maybe he knows something, but he was so dire."

Allison recalled the timid woman she had met when Trudy was still married to George Grumley, who ran a wicked world of rigged hunts behind Trudy's back. Allison had knocked on Trudy's door the first time they met and had found a meek flower child with little experience in the big wide world. In the end, Trudy had played no small role in helping learn the truth about her husband's racket and it all came out, including his role as a double murderer, when the sheriff and the prosecutors were finally done. Trudy had shaken the experience like a snake shedding a skin. She would always broadcast more femininity than Allison—her curves were better—but she'd added confidence to the mix and the time she spent in the fields and gardens had added a glow to her beautiful skin, which she tended carefully with organic sunscreens. Trudy was wary of synthetics at every turn. The face Trudy once kept hidden behind too-long hair was now open to the world. She had lost a bit of the flower child earth woman and had gone with a look that was sleeker, but she still oozed all things wholesome and healthy.

They sat at a breakfast booth with oak benches and matching shoulder-height backs and a table worn and stained with character. There was room for six, three to a side, but Allison and Colin sat close, thigh to thigh. Over Trudy's shoulder, a greenhouse jutted out and away from the house, bursting with herbs and plants.

A small TV on the kitchen counter was tuned to CNN and Allison could see the images from Glenwood Springs and what appeared to be a well-seasoned, well-travelled male reporter recapping the news. The sound was low but from the occasional word she picked up there didn't appear to be any fresh developments.

"Candidate's Condition Stable" said the banner at the bottom of the screen.

In Trudy's organic food, plant, herb, and cat emporium, the television stood out like an electronic pimple, but Allison knew Trudy liked to stay up on all the news. She was a reliable source of information on pending issues from Denver to Washington. Trudy's updates about the world gave Allison a fleeting sense that she didn't live completely in a black hole.

"Kerry London," said Trudy.

"What?" said Allison.

"You're staring at him," said Trudy.

There was something oddly familiar about the reporter.

"Strange to see Glenwood Springs on national news."

"And Kerry London too," said Trudy. "He goes everywhere and now he's right here. He's sort of the master of disaster—earthquakes, hurricanes, and, you know, chaos. He always seems calm. Worried, but calm."

"And familiar," said Allison. "But back to you. I can't imagine you do anything but operate by the book."

"If *you're* in trouble," said Colin, "every business in Garfield and Rio Blanco counties needs to be checked. There are Mexicans everywhere, and most of them do the work Americans don't want to touch."

"Maybe," said Trudy. "But he scared me, made me feel bad."

"Hell, he's the one who is probably scared," said Colin. "The cops I've known don't mind blaming others."

Colin had taken out his atlatl, a foot-long beauty he had been refining all summer. He was making a grip with leather shoelaces, wrapping the leather tightly. The shaft of the weapon glowed with a golden sheen from the steady polishing and sanding. The notch was perfect. Colin could whip an arrow at such speed that she couldn't follow its flight. He had fashioned three perfect oak arrows with duck feathers for stability. The points were honed to an exquisite sharpness, like X-Acto blades. She liked watching Colin bear down on a problem, refuse to give up, and make the step-by-step improvements until everything was just-so. In other words, perfect.

"I've got to re-check the whole staff," said Trudy. "Maybe it's a good thing. For my own reassurance."

"You're going to let someone go?" said Colin. "Just because their paperwork isn't all together? If you do, they'll find work somewhere else is all, somewhere right down the street, most likely."

"I keep having images of a raid of some sort, like that nasty raid at that meat packing plant a few years back, the one that was in the news for weeks," said Trudy. "They had all the buses waiting, went in and snatched workers right off the line, shipped 'em off."

"That was in Greeley," said Allison. "Kind of an ironic location. I guess the Utopian vision isn't working out."

"It's not like it's okay to be here if you're not legit," said Colin.

Colin put his atlatl aside, mopped up a bit of egg yolk with a last bite of scone. Trudy looked lost in thought. CNN switched to a volcano erupting in Chile, hundreds dead in the resulting mudslide that buried a rural village.

Allison itched to get going. She had lost a day of scouting and prep work. There were tents to clean, camp gear to sort out, authorities to escort to half-corpses.

Some thought chewed in her guts, but it remained safe and secure in that part of the so-called brain where good ideas turned to mush. Whatever the notion, it may as well have been written in the most impenetrable code ever devised by the CIA and buried in an ironclad vault with no doors a thousand feet down on the dark side of the moon. Allison had tried concentrating on it. She had tried ignoring it. Why they hadn't yet invented some sort of implant to record every thought—some device you could rewind in case you missed something—was another indication of a world gone lazy. Whatever the idea, it had to do with confirming her point of view about the half-corpse: no mountain lion was involved in his demise.

Allison's cell phone chirped. She didn't recognize the number.

"Allison Coil?"

The voice was male, young and chipper.

"Yes," she said.

"Brad Marker, Garfield County Sheriff."

She glanced at the wall clock over Trudy's sink. One minute before 7:00 a.m. Five stars for promptness.

They discussed meet-up times, horses, pack mules. Marker's team would be six all together, including the county coroner and a wildlife officer from Colorado Parks and Wildlife, who would also bring a houndsman and his three best Treeing Walkers. Allison would charge the standard daily fee for the horses and, with a thumbs-up from Trudy, provide lunch for the whole crew. They'd put that on the bill. Marker had some experience riding. He was just leaving New Castle, where he lived. They had two hours to get ready.

Allison checked her watch. By the time they got back to the half-corpse, it would have been exposed to the elements for an additional twenty-four hours.

"Now what?" said Trudy. "What happened?"

Allison gave Trudy the highlights. Trudy was rapt, uttering only an "oh my" at a couple of appropriate moments.

"So where are the rest of the legs?" she asked.

"Probably a pile of shit in the woods by now," said Colin, always cutting to the chase.

"If it was a cat," said Allison.

"It's still a possibility," said Colin. "If he was slight and not too tall, a mountain lion—a hungry mountain lion—might have taken the chance."

"Not exactly the kind of reassuring story you want to see out there right before all your hunters start arriving, is it?" said Trudy.

"It won't take them long to clear the mountain lion scenario," said Allison. "And they'll figure out the name and if he was alone in the woods."

"He must have been alone," said Colin. "Nobody has reported anything."

"Haven't heard anything," said Trudy. "Maybe it's not news until it's been a couple days. Unless it's a child that's wandered off. "

"Think for sure it was not a child," said Allison.

"Thanks for that," said Trudy.

"And I still don't get what makes you so sure about what it's not," said Colin.

The look from Colin suggested she dial up a dose of humility. Colin, no doubt drawing on the experience of his extended family of outdoorsmen, had more experience in the woods. Maybe she didn't want to think about a mountain lion around her camps—a lion with a taste for human would complicate matters considerably. By day's end, they'd have a better idea. Maybe she should back down.

"Just going on everything I feel," she said. On the other hand, maybe she should stick with her guns. "And what I saw."

"You're guessing," said Colin. "Not like you."

"No squabbling," said Trudy. "I won't have it."

"I wouldn't call it a guess," said Allison.

"Well, you're jumping ahead."

"You'll see," said Allison. "Wait. Observe. Discover."

Of course it was absurd that the former city girl was attempting to school Daniel Boone Jr. His faint, fake smile said he knew it.

"You can show the cops all the ways you're right, but it sounds like I'm staying here today," said Colin. "I see that worried look in your eye."

"All the prep for the hunters coming in," said Allison. "You know."

"We went over the list three times yesterday," said Colin. "Think I got it. Clean, fold, straighten, organize, clean, count, sort, and clean some more. And feed the horses."

"And don't forget to clean," said Allison. "Sharpest outfit in the West, that's what we want."

Trudy stood. "I suppose I've gotta get down to Glenwood and go through my records. Make sure the paperwork for my crew is copacetic."

If everyone was as respectful of the law as Trudy, there would be little need for policemen, prosecutors, judges, or tax auditors. Trudy was a speed-limit queen. She did well with boundaries.

At the rate Trudy's business had bloomed, the center of gravity in the culture might be shifting. You didn't just buy Trudy's products, you bought into a culture of eating well, of doing things the right way. A bottle of anything from Down to Earth in your grocery cart was a signal to yourself and the world that you understood that eating well was an active choice and that it went hand in hand with the idea of community togetherness. Like Birkenstock sandals or Tom's of Maine toothpaste, the product shined a light on the user as a thoughtful citizen of the planet.

"I know you'll square things up right with your business, even if there is a problem," said Allison. "And I doubt there is one."

"What if I have to let somebody go—just because their paperwork isn't right?"

"Cross that bridge when you come to it," said Allison. "And you'll do it in the most humane way possible."

Trudy looked quiet. She'd gone deep inside herself, still reeling. "I want to go back a day," she said. "And start over."

SEVEN:
MONDAY, MID-DAY

ALLISON SQUATTED IN SANDY rocks and bunchgrass at the top of the ridge near the half-corpse. The summer sun warmed her cheeks. Behind her up the slope and under the cover of the woods, three Garfield County Sheriff officers and the county coroner busied themselves with measurements, photographs and a careful examination of the body.

She slowed her breathing, played statue. She watched the tops of a fireweed flutter under the spell of a gentle breeze. She quieted her mind. At least, she tried. She wanted the cops to be done, wanted the body picked up and packed up—she wanted their conclusions oh, about an hour ago.

She stopped naming the individual plants and flowers. She let them be as the living things that they were before human beings came around and tried to order and organize the world. *King Philip crossed over France going south*. Kingdom, phylum, class, order, family, genus, species. Her father had taught her the first mnemonic. She preferred the ones her high school girlfriends giggled about, *King Philip came over for good sex.*

No order to anything. *See. Feel. Sense. Absorb.*

She moved five slow steps north, squatted again. Her working theory was rickety but as good as any other. If it was an animal attack, the only two truly eligible critters were bear or mountain lion. If it was one or the other, her theory went, the closest stand of woods were their likely cover. Allison planned to follow an arc that should have intersected where the animal would have raced out of the woods and where the attack would have happened. She hoped to come across some feline or ursine track or, better yet, some indication that she needed another line of thinking.

She faced the open valley. Lumberjack Camp plopped in the middle of the otherwise treeless bowl like a pin cushion at the bottom of the town water tank.

Allison scanned the ground again, overlapping each view in the grid. Marmot tracks? She'd seen plenty. These were about seven inches apart, a right and a left. A V-shaped print with four elongated toes. The fifth vestigial lined up like a forgotten finger.

Allison moved again, squatted. What she wanted to see was a paw print or scat from something feline. Uncovered scat would be the real prize, suggesting the cat was comfortable, moving and working on its own turf.

Five more steps, another squat, another moment, another chance to ice-down the percolating brain and live in the moment, to expand her thoughts and senses so she could pick up what was happening for hundreds of yards—or a mile or ten—around. A deer could do it, why couldn't she? An elk could do it, why couldn't she? Coyote radar had a hundred times her sensitivity, why couldn't she channel that power, if only for a minute?

A daisy. A sunflower. More fireweed. A scattering of lupine.

The lack of evidence matched the lack of a credible scenario. If it was a mountain lion, which the stick and brush-covering business suggested, then the attack, if confirmed, would send a shudder deep down in the bones of every hiker, camper, or outdoorsman in Colorado. In fact, she should be quaking in her Ropers, the new black pair she'd been breaking in for the season and which, in fact, looked as good as they felt. The same ones that would now leave a nifty track for some other mammal or insect tracker to decipher. But she wasn't afraid. No quaking. The only mammals in the Flat Tops that gave her pause were the ones that came up this way with rifles, alcohol, and a mad desire to channel their inner Teddy Roosevelt.

Five more steps. Here, some vole scat but no vole tracks, the soil too firm to collect an impression. Or maybe you'd need to be another vole to notice.

Three more squats, three more mini-vistas of wildflowers, scrub, and rock in their wonderfully random arrangements. If the attacking beast hadn't come from the woods, he or she had to have come running across a half-mile or more of open expanse, as unlikely as a Colorado aspen grove suddenly becoming the home for a troop of howler monkeys. This wasn't the Serengeti, where predator and prey interacted in big bloody widescreen Technicolor smack in front of every Range Rover full of safari-esque tourists, this was the goddamn Flat Tops where beast-on-beast takedowns, when they happened, took place off-screen like a movie script carefully crafted to earn no more than a PG-13 rating. Humans were common here and many carried rifles or bows. Thus the term *heavy hunter pressure.* All the big mammals in the Flat Tops faced the consequences of hunting season and all the big mammals, as a result, were champions of avoiding human contact except during the rut, of course, when sexual urges overrode every other instinct and a 700-pound elk could be manipulated like a horny virgin.

Allison climbed back up to the top of the ridge. The trio of deputies lifted the half-corpse onto a sheet of plastic. It was wrapped with care, placed in a body bag and then into an oversized saddle bag on Eli, her old reliable mule.

The threesome pulled their masks over their heads in unison. They packed up trowels, knives, scissors, forceps, evidence bags, glass vials, measuring tape.

"You have an inquisitive look on your face."

The speaker was the most talkative of the bunch, lead deputy Brad Marker. Allison had fallen into easy conversation with him on the ride up. Marker had been a deputy for eleven years but had transferred from New Mexico two years ago.

"I'm that obvious?" said Allison.

"Don't think we have anything conclusive," said Marker. "Tom?"

Garfield County deputy coroner Tom Potts couldn't have been a day over thirty. He wore mirrored Aviator sunglasses and a plain baseball cap. Besides being truly circumspect and inscrutable all morning, he had complained about his back on the ride up and issued leave-me-alone vibes from the first moment. Not much about him said sports or outdoors. Allison stood a couple of strides uphill so they were eye to eye.

"Going to be a simple case of undetermined causes until we send the parts out," said Potts. "There's a wildlife forensics lab up in Wyoming that handles all these cases."

"Mountain lion?" said Allison.

"Can't rule it out," said Potts. "We've got all the sticks and stuff that was moved around to cover him up—might be animal hair that shows up in there somewhere, or on the body itself. And maybe the DNA analysis. We have a long way to go."

"Was there anything on the body—an ID? Did he have a wallet— anything?" said Allison.

"What was left of his pockets were empty," said Potts. "He wasn't carrying much or wearing much."

"What did you find?" said Marker, almost as if he was trying to spare Potts.

"Lots of wildflowers and some marmot tracks," said Allison. "So, mountain lion?"

"I'd like to see the legs," said Marker.

"Doubt that's going to happen," said Allison. "See any bite marks?"

"He's going to need cleaning up," said Marker. "I can't tell the difference between the original attacker and post-mortem eaters. No major puncture wounds on the back of his neck, though, and that's where mountain lions like to attack, no?"

Marker's stiff-jawed inconclusiveness didn't help. Allison wanted closure and certainty or new theories to stir into the mix.

"But can you picture a mountain lion?" said Allison.

"More than a bear," said Marker. "We'll have to see if the dogs pick up on anything."

With the half-corpse moved, the houndsman made his way up the slope with his two best dogs, who strained at their leashes. The houndsman had a reputation as one of the best mountain lion trackers on the Western Slope. His name was Sal Hickman. His black Stetson was well-worn. His tired face and the ungainly white whiskers on his neck suggested he was at least sixty. He walked with an awkward gait, as if one knee wouldn't bend right. His brass belt buckle featured a relief of a mountain lion leaping, teeth bared.

"And it doesn't matter if I can picture it," said Marker. "Stranger things have happened. A mountain lion will eat anything from elk to grasshopper so a good old slow-moving guy is really just another option. Hey, for him, it worked."

There wasn't much arguing with fact-based reason.

"Experts will get a better look in the lab," said Marker. "This guy's too much of a mess right now to tell his story without help."

Hickman let his dogs go with a "hunt it up" command. Marker gave him a walkie talkie. The dogs circled, all-business. Noses scraped the ground.

"You had maggots all over the body," said Allison, "which means it's not a fresh kill—those eggs take at least eight hours to hatch. And there would be birds that would come in to graze and there's some evidence of birds and their droppings but not as much as you'd think."

"True," said Marker.

"And no drag marks," said Allison. "If it was a mountain lion, he would have dragged the body and this guy looks like he fell out of the sky."

Marker sighed. "Lots to consider."

The dogs headed off and Hickman followed on his horse.

Back at Lumberjack Camp, they sat around the fireless fire ring. Trudy's sandwich concoction went down without conversation. Whole wheat baguette with cucumber, bean sprouts, tomatoes, and some sort of olive tapenade that served, as Trudy put it, as a binding schmear. Tasted like heaven to Allison. If the guys were expecting roast beef, they were likely disappointed. But no complaints were uttered. They were joined by a Colorado Parks and Wildlife officer, who had circled the site on his own and had taken dozens of photographs. He was the seasoned type, with curly gray hair and black eyes. His uniform was spotless and, among all those who had come on this mission, he looked the most like a cop, with his full belt and holstered gun.

They chatted about the shooting in Glenwood Springs. Marker didn't know much. The others didn't say much.

"Still waiting for our first solid lead," said Marker. "But I've been out of touch, obviously, since I climbed on the horse this morning. They could have it all wrapped up by now, you never know."

Marker's walkie talkie crackled to life.

Allison couldn't make out Hickman's garble, but Marker got the gist. "How much farther you going?" he asked.

More static and garble, but Hickman's upbeat tone was clear. The dogs had lit on something.

"Okay," said Marker. "Take it as far as you need or as far as you can."

Allison's stared at Marker in disbelief. "What?"

Marker put down his walkie-talkie. "He's on the trail of a live one," he said. "The dogs are on a tear."

"A cat? A mountain lion?" said Allison, feeling the jabbing sting of humiliation. She imagined the smug look on Colin's face when he heard the news.

"Sal's specialty, as the whole valley knows," said Marker. The implication was clear.

The men packed up their lunch trash, stretched. They were all content to be sucked into the groupthink. *Must have been a mountain lion.* It wasn't hard to pick up on their relief. One lit a cigarette, exhaled clouds against the blue sky.

"Well, the hot pursuit of a live cat might settle things down," said Marker. "And that will let us pour everything we've got into the looking for the shooter in Glenwood Springs. We really didn't need this distraction and, as a matter of fact, we better get."

"What about Hickman and the dogs?" said Allison.

"He could be gone for hours," said Marker. "If he gets the cat, he'll bring it out and we can cut him open, see if we can find the other half of our victim. Put this baby to rest."

The sun told the time. Just past two. Maybe she'd stare at the sun until she went blind, protect her from any future temptation to jump to conclusions.

Marker and the others checked their horses and saddles. Allison tied Eli's lead rope to the tail on Marker's horse—rope once around the tail, fold the tail, three more loops, lead rope under the wraps and pull tight, leaving an easy-release loop in the knot. Eli knew the drill.

"Wouldn't you rather have it sorted out and done?" said Marker.

"Did I say something?" said Allison.

"It's in your scowl," said Marker.

"Just thinking," said Allison. Wanted to say, *you don't know a scowl.* Wanted to say, *you presumptuous jerk.* Ground her teeth together instead. "Thinking everything it might mean, what I'm going to tell all my hunters this year."

They stepped out into the open meadow and pointed their horses toward the trail. Nobody needed a guide now.

"You all go on ahead," said Allison. She was bringing up the rear, behind the mule.

"What?" said Marker.

"Know the way?" she said.

"Sure," said Marker.

"I've got a few more hours, or at least two. I'm going to hang around."

"And do what?" Marker said it like a distrusting father.

"Might scout a bit," said Allison. "No point in wasting the day, now that you've got everything."

And maybe help the houndsman if he ends up coming back this way. She wanted to see the dead cat draped over Hickman's horse. She wouldn't be satisfied until she saw with her own eyes and directly from the cat's guts that the lion was responsible for the demise of the half-corpse.

And besides, she didn't want to stare at Eli and his sad cargo all the way back to Sweetwater.

EIGHT:

MONDAY, MID-DAY

"THAT'S THE GODDAMN PROBLEM right there."

The cream-colored van bore scars. Bloom guessed mid-1990s. New Mexico plates.

Just another traffic stop.

Three cop cars.

Bloom counted seventeen passengers, then counted again to double-check.

Sitting cross-legged. Quiet. Obedient. They have accepted their fate. They are used to this.

"Can you believe they were all packed in that one van? On a day like this?"

DiMarco muttered. He wouldn't want to be seen consorting with a journalist. But it was DiMarco who had alerted him, ten minutes ago.

The van had been pulled over in the parking lot for the stand-alone, mid-valley restaurant Dos Hermanos, once the semi-swank

Mt. Sopris Inn. The shell of the restaurant and its long-abandoned parking lot attracted only weeds and dust. The Mexicans sat on concrete parking bumpers that hadn't been used for years.

Dos Hermanos. More than "dos."

Somehow, he would work that into the lead paragraph. He might need to find out the precise date the restaurant was closed for a tasty detail.

The lights on top of the cop cars flashed. Engines idled for the AC.

"What's going to happen to them?" said Bloom.

DiMarco was average height with a dark complexion and permanent stubble. Bloom guessed he was pressing fifty. He was deliberate and savvy. He wasn't in charge and didn't want to be. His nose was fleshy and had a sloping tip.

"One-way ticket back for every one of the passengers," said DiMarco. "Up to the feds. Unless one of 'em suddenly coughs up a legitimate ID. About the same chances that one of them can recite the Pledge of Allegiance."

"The driver?" asked Bloom.

They were two strangers talking to the breeze, not each other.

"Whole different story right there," said DiMarco. "He'll be arrested, booked, and we'll try everything we've got—human trafficking for sure. Not just a federal crime anymore."

"Where were they headed?"

"The driver is remarkably unforthcoming right now," said DiMarco. "That'll change."

Four young. Late teens. Rest are older. Two women. They look comfortable, cool, despite heat. One says something, smiles.

"Heading to Carbondale?"

"Or Aspen," said DiMarco. "Dishwashers, landscapers, painters—waltzing into the country like they run the place. A thousand get through for every one we stop."

"Why did they get pulled over?"

"Imagine how low the rig was sitting with all these people inside," said DiMarco. "It was dragging ass."

"This ain't Arizona," said Bloom. Some Colorado legislators had tried a similar law, but it had failed.

"Illegal U-turn," said DiMarco. "Don't get your tighty whities in a knot. Officer said he could hear voices in the back, had the driver show him the cargo."

A decent news story. Worth ten or twelve inches of copy, maybe more. In the wake of the shooting, ironic at least. Hard to imagine fitting it in with everything else Bloom needed to get done, but with the *Dos Hermanos* bit, this would practically write itself.

"Where do the illegals go?" said Bloom.

"Federal holding," said DiMarco. "ICE on the way."

Immigration and Customs Enforcement. Bloom had done stories on a big ICE raid at a meat packing plant in Greeley.

Bloom fought off an undertow of fatigue. The wee-hours meet-up with the cops at the newsroom hadn't taken as long as he had predicted. A telephone technician quickly isolated the number from the strange caller. Bloom didn't love the idea of the cops seeing all the numbers from other sources, but what could he do? What could the paper do? The independent editor had prepared a statement in case some left wing journalism professor threw an editorial hand grenade, but they had the cops' agreement that they'd keep the newspaper's role out of the narrative.

"Anything new on the main event?"

"There's a noon press briefing," said DiMarco.

"I'm aware. Did the phone number lead anywhere?"

DiMarco stood straight, cranked his shoulders around like he needed a stretch, returned his gaze to the gravel. "The number was one of those temporary phones, pre-loaded with minutes, you know?"

"I know them."

"That's the bad news," said DiMarco. "No name goes with the number, you know?"

"If you paid by credit card?"

DiMarco gave him a sideways look that said *think about it.*

"Okay, probably not likely," said Bloom. "What's the good news?

"Who said there is good news?"

"You implied it. The bad news, good news thing. One follows the other."

Another van, solid beige and spit-shine new, pulled into the parking lot. This one had windows and side-folding doors. There were no markings, but it screamed government business.

Three dark sedans wheeled in behind it and suddenly the parking lot was a busy hub of intergovernmental authorities sorting out roles, rules, laws, and egos.

"My work here is done," said DiMarco.

"The good news?" said Bloom.

DiMarco looked squarely at Bloom, for a flash. "You still got my back, right? Protect me?"

"All the way to reporter hell," said Bloom.

"The phone was activated yesterday morning."

One by one, the Mexicans were interviewed and loaded into the newly arrived van.

"And?"

"And the company that sells these phones distributes ninety percent to convenience stores all over the state."

DiMarco paused, proud of this nuance. One of the Mexicans, a man with a wrinkled face and dejected eyes, stared out at them from behind the window.

"Do we know which store?" said Bloom.

"No," said DiMarco. "But we can find the stores that sold a phone yesterday."

Bloom spotted a flaw in the logic. Just because the phone was activated yesterday didn't mean that was the day it was purchased. Everything else about the assassination attempt was obviously tight. Why would they have made this slip?

"A little sloppy," said Bloom. "Correct?"

"The kind of slop we need," said DiMarco. "And like."

Besides the sick notion that he might have been on the phone with Lamott's shooter—or one of the accomplices—there was also the question of whether he could write today's article since he was now part of it. That might be a journalism no-no in the big city but couldn't be helped in a two-reporter town.

"How long is it going to take?" asked Bloom.

"To what?"

"I assume you're checking all the store cameras in all the stores from Grand Junction to Denver where a phone was sold yesterday," said Bloom.

DiMarco shrugged his shoulders up, held them there for a second. "Maybe. All this consorting with the cops must be rubbing off. You're wearing your Dick Tracy hat."

Bloom ignored the slight. "How long do you think?"

"Today," said DiMarco. "Maybe tomorrow."

"And nothing more from Lookout Mountain?"

"You think you can keep squeezing me until I run dry?"

"So you're still coming up empty. Don't worry," said Bloom. "I gotta go talk to the feds—do my job."

"Understood," said DiMarco. "Keep in mind we wouldn't be here today if the feds had done their job in the first place—protecting our fucking borders. None of this would have happened."

NINE:
MONDAY AFTERNOON

THIS TIME SHE RODE Sunny Boy all the way up the ridge. She tied him to a tree and went back to stand in the same spot where she had been with Colin the day before, when they had looked down at the half-corpse for the first time.

Indignation wasn't a mood she relished. Fused with her stubborn streak, it would be a grueling afternoon. She knew not to fight the gathering cloud. It was better to stomp through the emotional muck—muck she'd proudly produced all by herself—than ignore it.

Allison pulled her cell phone from her jean jacket pocket and dialed up the pictures she'd taken before the sheriff's men and the coroner played Pick-Up Sticks with the tinder and wood scraps that had covered the half-corpse.

Again the picture sent the same odd signals but Allison couldn't grasp the specific idea, like rain that evaporated before it hit the ground.

Three times she circled the site in concentric circles—ten, twenty, and thirty yards out from where the half-corpse had been found. No drag marks.

She walked back and forth across the slope that rose up from Lumberjack Camp—hundred-yard-long sweeps. She moved quickly, scanning for anything undisturbed, broken brush or wildflowers.

Near the northern end of her last sweep, she spotted a set of parallel and faint tracks, subtle indents about three feet long in an exposed patch of dirt. Each was slightly wider than her thumb. The two tracks were about 18 inches apart. Straight, parallel lines. The indents were carved in a layer of loose grit on top of the hard-baked dirt. Something had been rolled or dragged. No tread. The tracks followed the line she would have followed if she was walking uphill and headed to the spot where the half-corpse had been found. She followed down the slope and found another set, even more subtle and only inches long but oriented in the same direction as the first.

Again back at the first location, she snapped a photo with her cell phone from a variety of angles, but the tracks didn't have enough relief to show up on her crappy device. One good breeze or rain shower would destroy the tracks. Maybe the detail would emerge once uploaded to a computer. She stared at the tracks, felt her anger rise. From the moment she'd found Gail and the boys at Lumberjack Camp, nothing about this scene had seemed right, no matter what the houndsman claimed.

She retrieved Sunny Boy and walked him to the edge of the ridge.

"Had about enough?" she asked Sunny Boy. "Eager to get?"

Sunny Boy shook his mane.

"I know—frustrating, isn't it?" she said. "But I think what you're thinking—we've got something fishy here."

Allison realized the earth had, in fact, maintained its rotational speed and not even this once had put her needs for a bit more daylight over its boringly predictable habits.

She walked around to Sunny Boy's uphill side—the easier to climb on—and spotted three riders on horseback heading east to west. They were on the trail that formed the spine of the valley floor far below. Sunlight caught them flush, heightened the detail. Allison dug for her binoculars. She and Sunny Boy were in the shade of the mountains and likely hard to spot. But what did it matter?

They were almost out of view, rounding a bend in the long flank of the ridge where she was perched. All three horses were nose-to-tail.

The lead rider wasn't merely tall or wide, he transformed what appeared to be a regular-size blond sorrel into the stubby runt of the litter. The way he sat on the horse—an odd, uncomfortable-to-watch melding, like he was the first man to ever try it—was painful to watch. His horse would remember this day and Allison hoped it was only one. The middle rider was on a dark bay and the third rode a brown-and-white paint. The third rider carried a rifle with the butt down on his thigh. "It's archery season, boys," Allison said out loud. Even if the rifle was replaced by a butterfly net, their energy was dark.

Riding with a rifle out in the open meant they expected to need it in a hurry and that meant, of course, that it was loaded.

Three horses, three men, three saddles. They had two hours of daylight left. With some groups in the wilderness, you wouldn't think twice because they looked ready. That's really what the woods came down to, be *prepared.* These three were ready for nothing but the sun to shine.

Allison went back to the middle rider—something different about him.

They were almost out of view. Their pace was steady but unhurried. They hadn't looked up or around. The middle one looked smaller, even slight. His head slumped forward and his hands grabbed the horn on the saddle. He wasn't actively riding. His posture suggested defeat and Allison had the thought, but more of a sharp sensation, like the lightning-quick pain from a mean cramp, that he was captured prey.

TEN:
MONDAY AFTERNOON

TRUDY HEATH'S VIEW OF Down to Earth was probably not how they taught you to think about profit and enterprise in business school.

She cared deeply about the business. Up to a point, she wanted it to flourish. A strong regional brand would be plenty. But soon it could lose its personality and it could morph into one of those other labels that had vaulted from regional specialty to bland, ubiquitous national nothing.

For now, Down to Earth clicked along. They did well in Meeker and Craig, to the north. They were well known in Paonia, Hotchkiss, Delta, and Grand Junction in a broad arc to the south and west. Their distribution reached Eagle along the I-70 corridor to the east. She had resisted the staff's push for Montrose, Ouray, Telluride, or maybe even Durango, but she might cave. Basically, the heart of western Colorado was the market for now. She had teamed up with a local distributor—filling up space on trucks already making their rounds—so she didn't feel any less green or any less local. In fact, she pictured her business with a bit of wonder and awe. It was like trying to figure out precisely how shoveling coal into the engine of a locomotive would propel steel wheels down the tracks.

It didn't compute. She tried to imagine all the transactions that had to happen—retail transactions, cash and credit cards changing hands. Phone orders, online orders, one bank account dipping while another—Down to Earth's—rose. People must have been telling each other, because no advertising had been bought. She'd been lucky with well-placed newspaper articles, glowing ones, and that was that.

The organization mushroomed like one of those videos on the nature channel that condense three weeks' of growth for a morel into thirty seconds. She had found the sweet spot of demand and product. But it wasn't really her. She'd given the green light on a new bottling contract in Grand Junction. She had okayed a new, expansive greenhouse plan in a field halfway to Rifle. But the man behind it all, the man who had come crawling back contritely, sheepishly, sweetly, gently—he had given her a month to pause and reflect—was Jerry.

Jerry Paige.

He said all the right things, apologized from the heart and removed the pressure, said he didn't want to lose her as a friend. Of course, five minutes later, after a kiss, they were all tangled up and laughing and how could she not grant a big old governor-size pardon on the spot. His crimes had been misdemeanors of the heart, of unchecked zeal. This was after the fallout, when he had done his over-the-top and too-pushy speech in front of the school board, embarrassing the whole erstwhile band of reformers and causing the team and its agenda to implode on the launch pad.

But weeks of space and quiet was plenty of time for Trudy to realize she hated loose ends, despised grudges and loved closure. Especially closures with Jerry, who was an excellent physical companion.

As the business blossomed, Jerry had offered guidance and suggestions and before she knew it he assumed the role as the unofficial manager of Down to Earth, the new company borne out of The Growing Season, Trudy's line of pesto products and marinades. The pesto and marinades remained hot items, but now Down to Earth sold organic fresh herbs, organic produce, gardening equipment, soils, mulch, shrubs, trees, bushes, ground cover, birdhouses, and a whole line of sculptures and other outdoor decorations created by local artists. Down to Earth conducted classes for the home gardener. Down to Earth encouraged the home gardener to take care of herbs and produce them at home, so they no longer had to shop at Down to Earth. It was anti-selling and in some crazy way it worked.

Down to Earth had promoted a corporate giving campaign akin to Ben & Jerry's. They had the "we're different" vibe of Paul Newman's line of grocery items. The brand oozed organic street credibility. Shippable products danced off the shelves of Whole Foods and similar stores with barely a promotional blink. Jerry had a sixth sense for negotiations and hiring. Her staff, in fact, had grown and she had met everyone at one point or another. But she couldn't really say whether their paperwork was all in order, whether the feds wouldn't frown. Or worse.

The day after the shooting in Glenwood Springs, the view from the highway made it look as if even more media had arrived. Trudy could only glance. Going sixty on the tight curves by the hot springs in Glenwood, she wondered if she would ever see the footbridge without thinking of Lamott and the blood. It wasn't the memories, it was also the sounds and the nausea that went with thinking about Lamott and the inconceivable anger behind whoever pulled the trigger.

Trudy steered off the highway and looped over the bridge through downtown, heading south to her headquarters in a small business park, the Valley View, seven miles south of downtown. Down to Earth was squeezed in between an electric supply company and a used car lot. The green-gray building sat up along the highway, directly across the Roaring Fork River from a sprawling golf course and down the hill from one of the Colorado Mountain College campuses, to the east. Inside were cubicles for the staff and the guts of a warehouse with all the stuff of their business—bottles, soil, herb pots, hoses, lumber, planters, shovels, rakes, fertilizer, seeds, packing materials.

Jerry sat at his desk in an open-door corner office. Trudy was surprised to see him, alone, given the number of times she had pictured the sheriff or federal immigration authorities poring through her files or lining up her workers, giving them all the third degree.

Files flopped open on Jerry's desk and steam floated up from a mug of coffee at the ready. His look was grim, but she didn't want to know. Not yet.

A kiss, a hug, and she poured herself a cup of tea in the kitchen, an unoccupied cubicle nearby.

"Bottom line," said Trudy.

"We have issues," said Jerry.

"I thought we confirmed every match," said Trudy. "Or tried to."

"We're waiting on about seven, maybe more. The socials didn't match at first. At least, the system kicked them out and now we are supposed to have the employee contact the Social Security Administration, to see if it was a typo or some other clerical error."

"Out of how many employees now?" Trudy hadn't kept up since they passed two-dozen. Jerry knew the needs and knew how to hire.

"Thirty-nine," said Jerry.

The number scared her—all the promises bound up in each paycheck.

"Last time I checked—" said Trudy.

"I know," said Jerry. "New greenhouse over in West Glenwood, we bought a bottling plant in Rifle, plus running around the maintenance work. It's all labor."

"Have we told these seven what they're supposed to do now?"

Trudy felt she had dropped a ball she didn't know she was carrying.

Jerry's prematurely gray hair was pulled back in a tight pony tail. He checked the hair tie's tightness as a security tic. He wore checked flannel shirts, favored prints in green. He was taut and lanky underneath, his yoga ritual unchanged for years. The casual appearance and physical health belied the business intensity. "They won't do it," said Jerry. "They won't contact authorities. So why ask?"

"Because we're supposed to," said Trudy. "At least the responsibility would shift to them, right?"

"For a while," said Jerry. Despite being two years younger than Trudy, he came across these days like the one with the wise old head. According to the calendar, she was coming up on forty but when Jerry focused on business, he looked half way to fifty. The sparkling whites of his brown eyes, behind ever-present bifocals, revealed his inner youth. "A month or two. And then we're supposed to let them go."

"But—"

"But what?"

"But you always have a plan."

Jerry smiled, but it was a weak version. "You know me too well."

Jerry tapped his pen, wobbled his head like he was weighing an offer, and held her gaze. His in-the-moment quality was one of his strengths.

"You know what we're up against," said Jerry.

"Well, everything," said Trudy. There was a well-respected grower in New Castle that had distributed across Colorado for years.

"The only thing we've got going for us is brand loyalty," said Jerry. "Our products are good, but we cost more. We're up against the high-tech greenhouses in California, Mexico, and the Caribbean. Fresh herbs are being air-freighted from Peru and Israel, all that mineral-rich water for the Mediterranean herbs."

"Ours taste better," said Trudy.

"And we got lucky," said Jerry. "The whole buy-America, buy-Colorado wave. We're riding it."

"Where are you going with this?" said Trudy.

"Where I'm going is we've got to protect what we've got. You don't want to put all this at risk." Jerry had a touch of professor in his soul. Maybe too much.

"So how?"

"Subcontracting," said Jerry.

"I've seen them go over this on television. It's not right."

"I know," said Jerry. "And I know what every other business does—but have the subcontractor set up first."

Between Officer Lemke's warning and this shaky plan, Trudy felt oddly trapped. Every thought was woven like a braid with the dread born yesterday at the base of the footbridge.

"A subcontractor buys us arm's length," said Jerry. "Separation."

Jerry paused. He knew he was gaining headway.

"You look like you've got one more thing to say," said Jerry.

If there was a scale for measuring inscrutability, Jerry was a lightweight—an open book.

"Why do we have to do their job for them?"

"Whose?" said Trudy.

"The *government's*," he said with some snap. "They're the ones not protecting our borders. Why should we have to play defense for them?"

For the first time since her seizures stopped, following the successful temporal lobectomy that had ended her days as an epileptic, Trudy had the sensation of fog and floating, of seeing everything through a thick mist. It wasn't hard to imagine the whole business going *poof* like a gust from a hurricane doing its thing on a birthday cake candle. But these weren't seizures. Those had been fixed through surgery after George's exit to state prison.

"You should have seen the look on the cop's face," said Trudy.

"He was reacting to the moment," said Jerry. "Cops think they know how to fix everything. Part of their nature."

"But if we go to a subcontractor, or try to set one up, that will be so obvious. They would all be working for us one day and then working for somebody else the next and still doing all the same stuff in the same places."

"It might have to be done gradually—start with the maintenance crew first."

"And let them go?"

Jerry gave a shrug. "What's the difference if we make the move or if ICE forces the issue?"

Trudy pictured the conversations with the employees—breaking all the bad news, how the word would spread. "They depend on us," she said.

Jerry shrugged. "A job is not a lifetime guarantee."

"You've already decided," said Trudy.

"I'm suggesting," said Jerry. "But you have to figure they all know each other, passing tips around. Not often you get a heads-up. We got lucky again."

"I wouldn't even know where to start," said Trudy.

She had slowly given over control to Jerry. He knew the books, the online banking, the passwords, the cash flow, the payroll, the contracts, the debt. She signed papers as he explained. There was good communication and everything checked out. Things they ordered showed up. Except for the wonderful, lounging sex—Jerry didn't care for quickies, preferred to relax naked or with few clothes on and talk for a while, see what developed and repeat—Jerry could have been her most trusted brother. She had turned into another chapter of herself and how she had behaved around George. She demurred. She wasn't evaluating hidden dangers or preparing for them. She played second fiddle. Or played for another band. It was hard to admit. Allison would never have lost control.

Maybe it was the shock from yesterday's event, being right *there*, but she realized suddenly that she was about to tear up.

"They're so loyal," said Trudy.

"Most," said Jerry. "We've had turnover. It's not like old company towns where you see them at Little League and the grocery store and church. We don't know them, not really."

Jerry took off his wire-rims, wiped the lenses with a tissue.

"We didn't promise them anything except pay," he said. "Work comes and goes; they come and go."

Jerry put his glasses back on.

"However, there's a situation going on now. Alfredo Loya. Usually when someone slips back into the twilight, it's not too big a deal. They seem worried this time. Someone called back to Guańajato where he's from and he hasn't turned up."

"Where did he work?"

"Wherever we needed him. He could fix anything—pumps, mechanical stuff—and he can do it fast. A real knack."

"How long has it been?"

"Last day here was two weeks ago, but it's not like I can go poke around and try to pick up his trail. He's just gone."

Now the tears came, trailing down her cheek. A couple. She had so much to do, so much she would do. She didn't wipe them away.

"Is he one of the ones, one of the ones without a matched social?"

"Yeah," said Jerry. "He's one of the seven."

ELEVEN:
MONDAY AFTERNOON

THE POLICE STAGED THE media briefing at the gazebo shelter in Sayre Park, not far from where Lamott first stepped off his campaign bus before his long meet-and-greet stroll through town and his appointment on the pedestrian bridge.

Sheriff Allen Marrs handled the news conference flanked by deputies, City Council members, the mayor, and a bevy of state and federal types whom Bloom had never seen. Today, they were props. It wasn't hard to imagine the cluster-fuck cop meetings and, without anyone in custody, the tension.

Facing the scrum of media, Sheriff Marrs looked tired. He was smart not to shave. You didn't want to show up looking like you'd thought about primping. Marrs had a high forehead, dark eyes, and a moustache that curled down at the corners.

The main theme was reassurance. Sheriff Marrs was seasoned enough to follow the script, which was fluffier than cotton candy. He used lots of words, but added nothing new.

Every possible resource devoted to the manhunt.
We have leads but I can't go into detail.
Glenwood Springs is a safe and caring community.
We urge anyone with information to step forward.

Reward funds have been established for the successful prosecution...

No mention of the disposable phone.

Bloom had been in big media hordes in Denver and this one was right up there—national and Denver crews, national and local print reporters, Grand Junction, Spanish-language news stations, magazine writers. On the national news scale, the attempted assassination of a U.S. Senate candidate rated a nine or ten. The immigration theme would make Glenwood Springs a trough for media feeding for weeks and months to come. Editors were making notes to do anniversary stories. For Bloom, the teeming pack of reporters brought back the old days of Denver, the occasional flare-up of news that drew the outside buzzards.

This first wave brought the high-powered reporters with access to private jets and staff to help with logistics. Waves of others were moving out, the army of grunts. Bloom wanted to work alone but also relished the challenge. This was his town, his story. It might not be a bad time to outwit his old Denver-based cohorts.

The general working theory rested on the idea of shots coming from somewhere in the first few hundred yards of trail that led up Lookout Mountain.

There was a trail to the top of a high knoll overlooking the confluence of rivers, but it was lightly travelled and mostly by locals.

The possible escape routes numbered two.

The first escape route would be the trail up and over the Lookout Mountain peak. Perhaps the shooter quickly transformed into a backpacker and walked innocently away. He might be still walking.

The second escape route would be straight down through the scrub to the streets on the eastern edge of Glenwood Springs.

If the up-and-over theory was correct, the shooter would have had a healthy head start and, obviously, he didn't have to stay on the trail.

The cops preferred the mingle-with-civilization theory and they indicated that somebody probably saw the shooter escape, but didn't realize it. They were urging everyone who might have been hiking or driving in the area to recall everything they had seen.

Bloom thought one other theory was being overlooked—a variation of the return-to-civilization theme. What if the shooter came down the hill but hopped over the train tracks and went down to the river to a waiting kayak or raft? Maybe there was too much exposure—the river would take the shooter right under the footbridge—but recreational kayaks and tourist rafts were common.

Distance was the big problem with Lookout Mountain as the shooter's perch. The reports so far had settled on 500 yards. The distance would depend on the height of the shooter's precise location on the hill, which sloped up and away to the east. For every foot of elevation the shooter might have wanted, he had to add four or five yards more distance. The shot wasn't impossible, but it would require skill, practice, and balls the size of grapefruits.

The questions from the reporters made it clear that this was the over-arching consensus, that someone, probably a lone gunman, had known enough to plan the shot and was one helluva shooter with sophisticated military-esque or at least special hunting gear. And, most likely, a bug up his ass about immigration.

Or, at least, hated Tom Lamott.

With the media beast fed and as the questions grew lame and repetitive, Sheriff Marrs thanked everyone and walked away. Reporters tried to worm their way in for one-on-one time, but they were waved off. No individual spoon feeding allowed, only mass distribution of the dry breadcrumbs they'd been asked to swallow.

"Hey, stranger."

"The one and only Kerry London," said Bloom. "Don't you have a flight to catch?"

The man hug was quick. Kerry London looked like he wasn't used to the Colorado altitude or the summer heat. He was short and a bit tubby. He had an unlikely television face—more nosy weasel than handsome fox.

"Looks like I better rent an apartment," said London. "Maybe a long-term lease. I didn't hear anything that makes me think they have a hot lead. Do the local cops know their way around a case like this?"

London was the ubiquitous newshound for NBC. He could cover a messy celebrity murder in Miami one day and mudslides in Puerto Rico the next. London spent less than a year in Denver on his meteoric rise to the network, but he had been a good friend.

"They're getting a shitload of state help," said Bloom. "You know I'm not based out of Denver anymore, right?"

"Oh no," said London, surprise on his face. It would have been nice to think that Kerry London would have spotted the Duncan Bloom byline on *The Glenwood Springs Post-Independent* front page this morning. "You're the last reporter that should have been shown the door."

"A kind sentiment."

"And now?" said London.

"I can walk home in about five minutes from this spot," said Bloom. He pointed generally to the north. "Or five minutes from the office downtown."

They were walking back to Grand Avenue, but London stopped in overly dramatic fashion.

"Right here?" he said.

"Coming up on two years."

"You've got the inside track."

"Ideas, at least," said Bloom.

"I'm sick of parachutes," said London. "Barely enough time to get acclimated. Speaking of which, how long does it take to get used to this thin air?"

"A week or so. It's only 5,700 feet, a bit higher than Denver. We could go hike Mount Sopris or haul up into the Flat Tops, jack you up another six or seven thousand feet. Then you'd feel it."

"No thanks," said London. "Lucky you—you're actually in town long enough to know the ins and outs and you're completely adapted to living at elevation in an oxygen-free zone."

London's faux jealousy amounted to a kindness. Bloom tried not to think about London's network salary. Deep down, Bloom knew he wouldn't switch places. Airports, road food, hotel rooms, strangers.

"So what are the local cops really saying?" said London.

"You got something to trade?" said Bloom. Bloom was unlikely to cough up anything, but he could make a flake of fool's gold flash in his palm if London was willing to barter.

"Me?" said London. "I'm a big zero up here. Come on, you probably owe me anyway."

"Nothing from the feds or FBI?"

"Nothing," said London. "Look, when I say 'local sources tell me' on my live shot tonight, you'll know it was you."

"I'm bone dry," said Bloom. It wasn't true, but that was Bloom's prerogative. "The cupboard is bare."

"I get the picture," said London. "Hope you don't mix your metaphors when you write."

"Funny," said Bloom. "A TV guy who knows the definition of metaphor."

London smiled. "I plead guilty."

"Speaking of prose, I've probably gotta get back and start writing." The network boys always got a jump on this kind of story. With federal agencies moving in, Bloom wouldn't know one federal face from the next. He might suddenly be disconnected to the power center of the investigation. "How long are you going to be around?"

"Few days at least," said London. "The whole country is watching this one, you know."

"I think the cops know it," said Bloom.

"I covered some of that Arizona law," said London, "about making it easier for cops to stop possible illegals. The people out there who hate illegals really fucking hate illegals."

"We got our share," said Bloom.

"So you think the killers are local?" said London.

"Somebody had to have known the possibility of using that hill for cover."

"Helluva shot," said London. "Seems they would have found something up there in the woods. Floodlights like a Hollywood premiere."

"I've told the cops they need to bring in a real tracker," said Bloom. "Someone who can spot shit, literally, in the woods. If the shooter was on that hill, they might need someone who knows the woods, not the city."

"Or maybe Devo," said London. "I see he's back up there somewhere with his grubby band of devolutionists. Everyone knows he makes his home in the Flat Tops."

"But still nobody knows exactly where. He must have some ingenious underground network to get his videos in and out, the video gear and supplies. He's a hit, though."

"Ever meet him?" said London.

"Of course not," said Bloom. "Not that I haven't tried. Wrote a whole feature about him and talked to some people who met him. It was like trying to put together a story about Bigfoot with a sit-down over the campfire."

"If we settle in for a long siege here in Glenwood Springs, I might have to put together a quick feature on Devo. More elusive than Sasquatch, a modern throwback shunning technology. I've got one of my producers trying to find his pal with the ultralight that ferries the videos in and out. We're trying to send a message that we'd like to come up and do a profile, spend some time with him."

Bloom had a hard time imagining how Kerry London had time to do anything else. Squeezing in the Devo story was a stretch, but he had remembered hearing about a guy named Ziggy from Paonia who drove over McClure Pass once a week to fly his ultralight into the Flat Tops and make runs for Devo. The rumor was that Devo's flock was closing in on forty fellow devolutionists. The story idea was a good one and Bloom wished he had thought of working through Ziggy.

"And if there's time," added London. "Between snooze conferences I gotta work on my book."

"Book?" said Bloom. London reminded him of the old phrase, *if you want something done, ask a busy person.*

"Project I've been working for quite some time. There was this plane crash in New York, at LaGuardia. Right on takeoff. You remember it. Thirty-one passengers died, the rest were in the harbor, big mess."

"I remember it," said Bloom. "Who doesn't?" He had an instant hunch he knew where this was going. How had London triangulated things so quickly?

"Lawsuits over de-icing and payouts."

"Remember," said Bloom.

"I'm going to publish a look back. It's called *Seven Seconds.* I'm interviewing all the survivors. There was some real heroism that day, people who fished others out of the water. It was one of the first big stories I covered. Plus, there's what happened with the legal payouts, how people fared. And one name comes right back to this area. In fact, her name popped up on a Google alert last fall around the same time as Devo's. I've been meaning to get out here. She's got an outfitting business."

"Helluva project," said Bloom, a bit in awe and more than a little jealous that one of the most ubiquitous reporters on television would also have a long-term project making steady progress. Smart to have several back-burners simmering.

"I think it's going to be good," said London. "Lots of angles."

"Let me guess," said Bloom.

"You know her?"

"Sure," said Bloom. "I've met her. But I can't say I know her. Allison Coil."

TWELVE:
MONDAY EVENING

AFTER HEARING THE RUNDOWN of her day, Colin was kind enough to focus first on the three oddballs on horseback.

"He looked like a prisoner?"

"He reeked of it," said Allison. "His shoulders, his head. His whole body slumped."

"You're positive?" said Colin. "Even from that distance?"

It was late. She had arrived back at her A-frame after nine. Colin had heated a pot of pork-less posole, poached from Trudy's freezer, and he had opened a bottle of organic red wine that carried Trudy's stamp of approval.

They stood side by side at the counter, a few swallows of Cabernet left in their glasses.

"Your alarm has sounded," said Colin.

Was that an accusation or an observation?

"Wish I'd been the one to find the body," said Allison. "And that I'd been there before all the commotion and activity. And I wish the cops had the manpower to focus on this."

"But you said Hickman's dogs lit up," said Colin. "Isn't that enough?"

It would serve her well to down a slice of humble pie in Colin's presence. She should choke down a big hunk of the stuff and leave no crumbs on her lips or chin. She should wipe the plate clean and maybe take a second helping. But the idea didn't sit well. She had told Colin about the faint tracks, but he didn't seem persuaded. The overriding point was the fact that Hickman's hounds, based on the last report anyway, were hellbound. She should concede defeat, but couldn't find the words.

"I can tell when you're all tangled up," said Colin.

"Really?" Was this the second time today a guy would try to interpret the look on her face? "Tangled up? Tangled up how?"

Colin wasn't ready for a challenge. He shifted on his feet while she stared him down. His open, always-eager expression didn't fare well when he was criticizing others. He looked down and she stared at the cute raisin-size freckle near his left eye. Hickman's hot trail had earned her the right to listen carefully, but Colin wasn't one for rubbing it in.

"I can tell you're being pulled in a few directions—and not wanting to go along with what's turning up. Hell, the houndsman was your idea—you knew one would be needed from the first second. You get credit for that. You practically designed the whole investigation within a few minutes after we climbed the ridge the first time."

She waited, gave Colin's thought space. Treated his comment with respect.

"You don't think it's odd?"

"There's always odd stuff out there. And you know that better than anyone," said Colin. "And now you've got cops and the coroner and a top-flight houndsman all over it so maybe—"

He didn't have a specific suggestion for her but filled the gap by lifting his glass into the void.

"Maybe what?" She chugged her remaining wine, started thinking of all the reasons to open another bottle. "Maybe forget it? You're saying I should just let *whatever* happen, let the chips fall?"

"No," said Colin. "And I know you'll do what you have to do. But the cops have it covered—at least, they responded quickly and we've got hunters coming in. Were you thinking about chasing men on horseback all over the Flat Tops?"

The thought of the three men on horseback, whose presence had been the visual equivalent of nails on a chalkboard, gave her a shudder. Colin was likely right that she shouldn't pursue them as a rogue ranger, but she didn't want anyone else, even Colin, defining her world.

Or limiting it. Or telling her how best to watch out for the Flat Tops. Was the issue boundaries? Since moving to the Flat Tops, she was perfectly happy to stay put. Anything but the city. She left the Flat Tops only when absolutely necessary. But limiting her choices within the wilderness? Not likely.

The issue was more than this low-broil feud. The issue had been rearing its head for weeks. What clock or calendar enabled the thought was a complete mystery. It was a sticky thought with gripping power and it had squarely to do with Colin: the "what next" question.

The Flat Tops were supposed to put an end to the "what next" questions. For the first stretch of years of her new life in the woods, there was no path, no road, no course, no objectives, no career, no arc. None needed. Surviving the accident had smashed every measure that once appeared to matter. She was happy to heal and happier to dig in her heels and declare a new home, particularly one with the magical power of The Flat Tops.

If she could, she'd order an instant lumpectomy on whatever part of her brain dredged, without her permission, through the thought patterns of her previous life. That sentimental bit of bitchy brain tissue scoured for those pointless questions she used to pose. It refused to forget that she had moved—and moved on. The question grated like the two-note cry from a bully Blue Jay. "What's next?" "What's next?" "What's next?" Staying with Colin meant, or so the active theory went, that she would remain in the Flat Tops forever. Colin was a man of the woods. His whole family was of the woods and the outdoors. His blood was tree sap. He was gun smoke, gutting knives, and hunting grit. He was a fine catch—and he wasn't going anywhere. She wouldn't leave Colin as long as she stayed in The Flat Tops—she knew that much. But the "What's next?" drumbeat toyed with the part of her sensibility that, at some point in time, had preferred that the horizon and the landscape change from time to time. Until lately, status quo was heaven. She suddenly had a desire to see around the corner and quietly loathed herself for not being able to shut the question down. What more could she want?

Perhaps the mild disagreement over the half-corpse was her way of testing a new space with Colin, but even that didn't make sense. The disagreement with Colin and her clear thoughts about the mountain lion bit was based on her years in the woods, nothing more.

Allison put the last touches on cleaning up the kitchen and stood outside for three deep inhalations of cool night air.

Colin was already stretched out in bed when she went upstairs. There was a look in his eye, perhaps encouraged by the wine or the desire to affirm they were playing for the same team. She wasn't opposed. Maybe some physical love would re-prime her heart, which had been running cool since the stop at Lumberjack Camp.

Even in August, nights in the Flat Tops came with a purposeful chill, and even though the heat from the woodstove kept the upstairs loft toasty, Allison preferred the window open so she could smell the evening breeze and hear the occasional coyote. Come morning, a chickadee or raven might provide the morning alarm.

"You're still thinking you should have followed them," said Colin.

"If you had been there," said Allison. "We'd still be on their tail. I was tempted. They didn't have any stuff with them, you know, gear. Anything."

They were lying on their backs, shoulders and hips touching under the thin wool quilt, legs entangled.

"But they could be camping," said Colin. "Or scouting. Did the guy with the gun look like he was part of the posse in an old western with Clint Eastwood? You know, like Josey Wales. 'Are you going to pull them pistols or whistle Dixie?'"

"Josey Wales?" Allison had never seen the movie.

"His best line is about Kansas. 'There are three kinds of suns in Kansas—sunshine, sunflowers, and sons-of-bitches.'"

Allison laughed. "These guys were sons-of-bitches, trust me."

"We could always go back to that area, check around Lumberjack, see what the elk are up to and see if we stumble into anything."

Colin rolled on his side to face her, let a hand fall on her stomach. He made slow circles around her belly button with a finger.

"You're not curious?" she said, doing her best to ignore his touch.

"Couple of whack jobs in the wilderness," said Colin.

His finger stopped circling and took up a new course, moving back and forth below her belly button, about an inch above her underwear. Back and forth.

"At least I'm not as hard to read as you are," said Allison.

"I'm a closed book," said Colin. "Impossible to decipher." His hand ran a quick scouting mission to check her breasts, a cursory inspection each, and then returned to its teasing pace below the belt line.

"Big word, decipher," said Allison. "You sure you didn't go to college?"

"Not that I recall," said Colin.

"Do you think you would have remembered?" said Allison. "You know, college is a school where you pay money to enroll and you might have stayed in a dorm or a frat house and spent all your free time drinking beer and chasing girls?"

Allison pulled her hips up ever so slightly, encouraging his wandering hand.

"Really don't think so," said Colin, playing the dumb witness. "The chasing girls thing, is that a course where you get credit?"

"Not exactly formal credit," said Allison. "Although I think you're earning some now."

"But what's credit good for now?" said Colin. "I'm not working on a degree or anything."

"You're always working on something," said Allison.

The fingers took a tentative dip beneath her underwear and then he flattened his hand, the palm moving in slow circles. Warm fire bloomed inside her and she let out a moan.

Colin flipped the covers back. She loved the sensation of being covered and gently smothered. Protected. The weight of him, somehow, added to what little she brought to the equation and she enjoyed the additional flesh like it was her own. He kissed her and she kissed back, hard. She felt even smaller in his embrace, loved the power in his shoulders.

He leaned up and tugged down on the only bit of clothing she ever wore to bed. She reached down and grabbed him, hard like granite.

"Got a condom, big boy?" she asked.

He flicked her underwear away. "For my tongue?" he asked.

"Yes," she said. "Protect me from all those big words."

"Funny," said Colin. "I wasn't planning on doing any talking. None whatsoever."

THIRTEEN:
TUESDAY MORNING

THE KNOCK ON THE door was like an electric shock. It wasn't Allison, who always rapped gently as she opened the door and started making herself at home. This knock wasn't "hello." It was "man outside."

Trudy put down her bowl of dough for lemon rosemary biscuits, felt an odd flutter of panic wobble inside. She headed to the door, trying to remember the last time she had a surprise visitor and attempting to squelch the thought that this was the beginning of the crackdown on Down to Earth.

Standing outside was a cop. A sheriff's car sat in the driveway and the man was in full uniform, his dark green shirt crisp, his badge shiny like it was straight from the silver mine. He smiled, but only in a polite way.

"Allison Coil?" he said.

"Um, no," said Trudy. "Everything okay?"

"Just the largest manhunt in Garfield County since Ted Bundy slipped out of jail. Other than that—"

"I mean, with Allison—"

"Far as I know," said the cop. He had a thick moustache, a head shaped like a pineapple with prominent jowls.

"She'll be here soon," said Trudy. "For breakfast. Expect her shortly."

The cop introduced himself as Deputy Sheriff Robert Chadwick. He was dressed for a summer morning in the city, not the mountain chill. He had two sips of coffee and was admiring her plants and greenhouse, or at least pretending to, when Allison and Colin arrived, looking every bit like a couple of college kids in mid-crush. Trudy did the introductions.

"Something to do with the body we found?" said Allison. "Is there an ID?"

"No," said Chadwick. He was standing near the kitchen table and making a point, perhaps, of not leaning on anything. "I heard about that. I believe they're getting him into a location where they can do all the processing, you know, all the analyzing."

"Nobody reported missing?" said Allison.

"Not to my knowledge," said Chadwick.

"Nothing in the news either," said Trudy. "All pedestrian bridge shooting, all the time."

"And what about the houndsman, come back with anything?"

"I heard his dogs got confused," said Chadwick. "Something like that."

"Confused?" said Allison.

"Lost the trail at least," said Chadwick.

Allison shook her head. "If there was a trail," she said.

Colin shrugged. "It happens, you know."

To Trudy, Allison looked unperturbed by the presence of the cop. But Trudy wouldn't mind if Deputy Sheriff Robert Chadwick didn't stay long. Normally hospitable and open to feeding all, including strangers, Trudy wondered if the cop could sense her chilly reaction or if this was all some sort of trick. She passed around coffee, her hands less steady than she would have liked. Something about a uniform in this kitchen made it seem like the whole cavalry was here.

Since the shooting, in fact, she'd felt tense and nervous. Guilty. She couldn't stop connecting the shooting with her business. If even one of her workers had falsified documents and was in this country illegally, wasn't she part of the problem? Where did the responsibility of her business end? They weren't living in San Diego or El Paso, they were smack in the middle of the country, surrounded by large states. How was she to know who was legitimate? How much effort was she expected to spend on screening employees? But she felt selfish for even having such thoughts. Compared to the Lamott family and their grief, her discomfort was minuscule and irrelevant, wasn't it?

Chadwick took a minute to take in the room, with most of his focus on Colin, who always looked younger than his real years. "Wondering if I might have a word alone," he said, "Maybe outside?"

Allison looked around. "With me?"

Trudy felt a flash of relief, but just as quickly realized the cops might need to triangulate some details with her best friend and neighbor.

"Yes," said Chadwick.

"It's all fine right here," said Allison. "These two know everything I know. And besides, I don't need privacy to answer a question as long as you don't need privacy to ask it."

Chadwick took a breath. "We need your help," said Chadwick. "Some of your time."

"My supplies in that department are low," said Allison. "What is it?"

Colin sat down at the kitchen table, in the booth. Allison stood leaning against the counter, her coffee cradled high in both hands like a sacred, rarely-held crucible.

Chadwick held her stare. "We'd like you to do something but we'd also like you to keep it to yourself, you know, if reporters are around, if there are questions down the road."

"Have to hear first," said Allison. "I need the whole picture."

"It's the shooting," said Chadwick. "We need your eye."

Trudy realized it was Chadwick who was nervous. He was out of his element. Besides the fact that cops didn't usually ask for help, Chadwick was probably thrown off guard by having this conversation in front of Allison's friends.

"Me?" said Allison.

"You've got a bit of a reputation," said Chadwick.

Allison turned to look at Colin, who shrugged. Trudy caught a flash of a mischief in Colin's grin, playing innocent. "What exactly do you need?" she asked.

Chadwick took a sip of coffee, gathered his thoughts.

"We need you to look around in the woods. Where the shots were fired."

"Where you *think* the shots were fired?" said Colin.

Chadwick shifted his gaze to Colin. "All the witnesses pointed up there."

"There's nothing?" said Allison. "No sign anyone was there?"

"A few things, maybe," said Chadwick. "A few homeless people make camps up there in the summer so it's not exactly pristine wilderness."

There was no way Allison had time for this request but it tugged at her urge to keep order.

Allison looked at the floor, her coffee, Colin. "There are better trackers out there than me," she said. "I know a guy from Craig who can follow a spider's trail on a fresh slab of slate."

"Your name came up," said Chadwick. "You're here."

Allison turned to look at Colin, who shrugged his shoulders as if to say, "It's your call, boss."

"We have so much to do," said Allison. It was a general statement for the room.

Trudy dropped dough on a cookie sheet, six biscuits in all. She slid the sheet into the oven and chopped some bits of broccoli and goat cheese into a slow-cooking pan of scrambled eggs. Tried to mind her business.

"I know your season is coming up," said Chadwick. "We can have you back by sundown. All-expenses-paid ride in my cruiser down and back, even set you up with lunch."

Allison studied Colin for a clue. Trudy knew she'd do it. Trudy knew that Colin knew she'd do it.

Chadwick looked like he was waiting for an invitation.

"Have a seat," said Trudy. "There's plenty."

Chadwick waited a polite second, then sat. "Very kind," he said.

Having a cop in her kitchen was agony. His presence resurrected every bit of residue from her ex-husband George. When he was caught and his racket exposed, the cops had spent days around his business and her house, sorting through every document they could find and grilling her about her role and knowledge of his affairs. The cop today brought it all back, the younger and more naïve Trudy who had been trapped or, she saw now, had chosen to trap herself. Ever since George had been arrested and since the surgeries had put an end to her seizures, she imagined her life as two chapters, barely in the same book. She had been pleasantly surprised—shocked, really—to learn you could restart your life. Now the cops and the possible problems with her business made her think she'd screwed up and she wanted to put everything back, live in her bubble without city, state, or federal entanglements. Trudy imagined a swarm of cops pulling up to her nursery, cruisers skidding to a halt in the dirt parking lot, her workers in a panic or making a run for it. She didn't consider herself prone to paranoia, but maybe Chadwick also intended to keep an eye on her? Keep her under surveillance while the others poured through her files? Why else knock on the wrong door?

"I'll give it a shot," said Allison. "Help out if I can. As you can tell, I'm a bit worried it's not exactly fresh ground at this point. That body that was pulled off the Flat Tops yesterday—same problem. Too busy around there for too long, just a big mess."

"Understood," said Chadwick.

"On one condition," said Allison.

"Name it," said Chadwick.

"You keep me up to date on processing that body, the half-corpse. Animal hairs, DNA, saliva. Anything."

"Okay," said Chadwick. "I think we send that kind of lab work to an animal forensics crime lab in Wyoming."

"I want the results as soon as the other cops and the Colorado Parks and Wildlife have the results," said Allison. She wasn't being overly forceful, just clear. "I want it to be like I'm in on the briefing. Do we have a deal?"

"Far as I'm concerned," said Chadwick.

A muffled chirp sounded from the pocket of Allison's jean jacket. Allison looked at Colin. "Do we have any clients from 212 area code? New York?"

The phone rang again. Chadwick peppered a plate of scrambled eggs, using Trudy's hand grinder.

"Not that I know of," said Colin. "But maybe. When was the last time you checked your e-mail?"

Allison rolled it around. "Good point," she said. And then: "Hello?"

Chadwick attacked his food, fork tines jabbing into his eggs and pinging off the plate like he needed to kill it, too.

Colin ate with a leisurely approach. His eggs were drenched in hot sauce and dusted with pepper. He was the most civilized cowboy Trudy had ever met. He moved deliberately, never forced a moment.

As she listened, Allison stared straight down at the table, cell phone to ear. Allison shook her head, shrugged her shoulders, slumped back in the booth. She listened, said the occasional "yes," "no," "most of the time" and then, "not until tomorrow." She listened for another long stretch. "We've got horses, sure, and they'd be our standard rate for a day each and you're welcome to come up tomorrow and go along. We're probably going to scout or check on our camp sites, sure." Again, another break as she listened. Finally Allison went over directions and final logistics. And hung up.

"These are going to be two of the greenest flatlanders we've ever taken up," said Allison. "But it can't hurt business."

"Who was it?" said Colin.

"It was that reporter," said Allison. "The one we saw on TV, the same one I sort of recognized."

"Kerry London?" said Trudy. How could Allison be so relaxed? Kerry London was one of those reporters Trudy had followed for years, popping up everywhere there was severe weather, odd accidents, weird child disappearances, bizarre manifestations of humanity. It was almost a game Trudy played—where would Kerry London land today?

"He said while they're out here on the shooting they wanted to sneak in a quick story on the energy boom," said Allison. "And they want some wilderness video and an interview with an outfitter. Unless something breaks on the story and he gets assigned to leave, he wanted to call in the next day or two and come up and ride for a couple hours, so it looks remote and high up, which isn't hard, and we'll be done. Easy peasy, national advertising."

Trudy put down a biscuit and eggs for Allison.

"Just so long as you're not talking about anything you're doing for us," said Chadwick. "He's about the last guy we'd want you relaying anything to. In fact, none of you know about my visit."

"You don't need to worry," said Trudy.

"Yeah," said Colin quickly, his mouth full of toast. "Not an issue."

Allison shrugged. "What they said."

The morning gathering occurred only a couple or three times a week. When hunting season was in full swing Trudy could go for weeks without seeing Allison or Colin. The meal was a time she cherished and she thought about how much more she'd be enjoying it without the cop. She tried to look on the bright side, decided finally that Chadwick's mission involved no ruse.

Colin took a bite of biscuit. "By the way, how did Kerry London get your name?"

"I don't know," said Allison. "I didn't ask."

FOURTEEN:
TUESDAY MORNING

Population 9,000, Glenwood Springs couldn't afford more than two full-time reporters. A network of freelancers helped fill the newspaper with copy to make it at least appear to be well-rounded, but Duncan Bloom and his counterpart in news reporting were the two main engines for words and daily fodder.

Of course not every city council or school board meeting led to a compelling news story, but there was usually something that somebody else cared about and Bloom always had his antenna up for any clash of political values. For the most part, however, the city leadership was in lockstep, although the school district had stepped up lately and started to talk openly about its challenges, particularly in the area of teaching all these Spanish-speaking students—the ones whose parents moved to the Roaring Fork Valley to work in hotels, restaurants, landscaping firms, roofing companies and wherever the labor was hard and the pay was marginal or worse. The school district superintendent, an energetic woman with big-city savvy, had made the reading and writing skills of these children—now a quarter of the student body—her central issue. Her campaign had raised the ire of the city's old guard and gutter-living racists maintained a steady volley of vile vitriol—letters and blogs, comments at public hearings. By openly embracing the issue, the superintendent had at least moved the city's awareness forward. Spanish-speaking parents and Spanish-speaking kids are here, she said, and they need school. Bloom had written about a concerned parent who didn't care for an elementary school's class project on September 16—*Diez y Seis*, celebrating the Mexican War of Independence—because she claimed that when you're in the United States of America you don't teach about Mexican holidays. That kind of mentality hadn't gone away. If anything, the battle was more pitched and more pointed, though Bloom didn't get the sense that Glenwood Springs dwelled on the issue. The newspaper had made a conscious decision, partly due to Bloom's steady persuasion, that highlighting the whackos, particularly individuals, only added fuel to the fire and wasn't a good use of limited space to print.

Now, however, it was time to go converse with the haters.

Tom Lamott's shooting changed everything.

Immigration was *it*.

Or was it? A fleeting thought nagged at Bloom. The hot-button immigration issue might make everyone think the trigger was pulled to send a message about national policy.

But Bloom had seen Lamott's temper.

It had been four years. At the time, state senator Tom Lamott represented a heavily Hispanic and upwardly-mobile district in west Denver. He sponsored high-profile, risky legislation and spoke glibly on a variety of topics. He was the newspaper's go-to guy for a good quote and frequently visited the newspaper's editorial board meetings. Golden boy.

He had married a Hispanic woman who had graduated with honors from the University of Colorado and the University of Denver School of Law. She worked on environmental issues. Their Democratic blood was thick. They had two adorable children. Television cameras and reporters were Tom Lamott's friends.

The story had started with a leak that suggested there was another version of Tom Lamott behind the scenes.

All three tidbits passed to Bloom had to do with Lamott's outsized temper and abuse of power.

First, Lamott had humiliated a junior staffer for an innocent mistake over the schedule. He had yelled at him, almost nose to nose, and the young man quit the same day.

Second, Lamott had met privately with the principal at the school where his older daughter was now in kindergarten and had demanded that his daughter be placed with the more experienced of the school's two kindergarten teachers, one of the best in the district.

The third item required the most digging.

Tom Lamott, the tip suggested, had fought hard for a friend to be awarded a contract through the school district in Denver to provide educational consulting for a trio of schools that had underperformed for years. The schedule and phone records would show, the tip alleged, that Lamott had phoned the superintendent repeatedly to exert his influence and that Lamott had threatened to turn up the state's oversight heat if he didn't get his way.

The tips confirmed what Bloom had long suspected, that's Lamott's ego was overly ripe. Lamott's spiel carried a distinct whiff of bullshit.

Bloom made inroads, developed sources. He made up reasons to interview possible sources and then casually mentioned what he was really after. While some of the confirmations were off the record, Bloom felt like he had enough to present to Lamott and get his reaction. His editors debated it. Not all were in favor, but Bloom was green-lighted to seek Lamott's reactions.

The interview didn't last long.

"I really can't believe a newspaper of your stature would put resources into this kind of a topic," Lamott had said. He was so cool it was as if he'd been told everything ahead of time. "My only statement to you is that you have completely false information on all three counts and I am not going to give any one of them the time of day. I have better things to do."

No story ever ran. The editors backed off.

Bloom hadn't laid eyes on Lamott again until yesterday.

Was it outside the scope to think Lamott had other enemies who might have a motive for a completely nonpolitical reason? Bloom needed to check back with some of his old Denver sources, see if Lamott might have prompted a rattle from an entirely different type of snake.

Sitting at his desk in the small newspaper offices off Grand Avenue, Bloom made a list of ideas for stories. The list went into a daily e-mail to his editor and to his fellow scribe, a just-the-facts kind of reporter named Marjorie Hayes. Never one to question and never one to read much beyond official news releases and public relations come-ons, Hayes was a Chamber of Commerce dream. She never questioned motives and maintained a surprising ability to turn every story, no matter how rich and complex, into something two-dimensional. She knew everyone in town and was never piqued or dismayed by government decisions or commercial business plans. All plans were progress.

Today, she looked exhausted and worn out. She sat at her desk making her way through the papers from Denver, Aspen, and Grand Junction—all online—and she wasn't saying much. Her assignments since the shooting had been all reaction, basically stories with a litany of quotes capturing the mood of the town and its civic, business, and religious leadership. It was one of the quotes that had struck Bloom as odd.

"Quick question," said Bloom.

"Sure," said Hayes.

"This quote from this guy at the Chamber of Commerce," said Bloom.

"Troy Nichols," said Hayes, "the one on the board."

"That's him," said Bloom.

"I can't remember what he said," Hayes said.

That alone was odd, given the content, but it was further proof Hayes' approach to the job was to organize information, not ponder its meaning.

"Down toward the end of the story," said Bloom. "Want me to read it to you?"

"Sure," said Hayes, who hadn't so much as turned slightly from her computer screen. She was wearing a simple summer blouse with a green paisley print over a too-tight jean skirt. Her short curly hair, a reddish gold, looked recently re-colored. She was tall, slightly plump and never looked too comfortable in the office chairs and modest desks that constituted office space at the *Post-Independent*.

"Okay, here goes," said Bloom. "Here's what he said: 'When you claim to have all the answers, especially on such a volatile and incendiary issue as immigration, when you come into a town like Glenwood Springs, you are walking into the crossfire and people do feel strongly. For some, this is an extremely personal issue and they feel that being lax on immigrants is being un-American and threatens our way of life. I'm one of those. It's true. Every citizen has to do their part. These people are breaking the law. Case closed. Of course nobody condones what happened, but there's a certain inevitability to the shooting too.'"

Bloom stopped, let the quote sink in.

"What about it?" said Hayes.

"From a Chamber guy?" said Bloom. "Did he say anything more? Did you happen to press him?"

"On what?" said Hayes.

"Inevitable?" said Bloom. "Did you ask him what he meant by that?"

Hayes never pressed anyone on anything. Statements were swallowed whole, then regurgitated in ink. Hayes wandered into journalism as a curiosity, not a calling. She could have just as easily taken a liking to selling real estate or baking cupcakes.

"He just sort of said it," said Hayes.

"Gotcha," said Bloom, who knew not to come on too hard. He was still the untrusted one. Hayes knew enough people in town, he had quickly realized, to quietly spread doubt about his talent and attitude. "Did he happen to say anything else?"

"I don't think so," said Hayes.

"Did he say it kind of angry or just nonchalant, if you know what I mean?"

Hayes sat back, folded her arms across her chest. If she'd been offended by the suggestion that she'd missed something, Bloom couldn't tell.

"There wasn't any real mustard on it," said Hayes.

"Know anything about him?" said Bloom.

"He's been around," said Hayes. "Owns a distribution business or something."

There were few types of stories better than pots calling kettles black. Bloom wondered how much a trucking business might rely on cheap labor.

But *inevitable?*

It almost meant Lamott had it coming.

If anything, Bloom would have pounced on the comment, played it up. You could see a quote like that making national news, having Troy Nichols on a talk show like Bill Maher or Rachel Maddow, being sliced and diced.

"You get the feeling that the shooting must have been someone from Glenwood Springs?" asked Bloom, trying to lob the question over with a friendly "let's chat" vibe, not an indictment of the town.

"No," said Hayes. "Hadn't considered it, really. What an awful thing to think about."

Yes, thought Bloom, and even worse, an actual awful thing really happened.

Right here.

"Maybe I'm off," said Bloom. "Lamott wins the primary last Tuesday. He spends Wednesday doing interviews and making appearances along the Front Range, thanks his campaign staff. They announce the Western Slope stops on Thursday. He hits Colorado Springs and Pueblo and then comes up through the San Luis Valley on Friday and he stays all the way up in Leadville, half-hour stops here and there. So the Glenwood Springs stop is more full-blown walk-and-talk event, not a whistle stop."

Hayes had leaned back in her chair and turned to listen.

"The campaign had approved the Glenwood Springs stop but didn't put out the details of his walk until mid-day Friday. And, of course, they post it on his website—"

"In English and Spanish," said Hayes.

"Correct," said Bloom. "And they even mention the pedestrian bridge thing, the photo shoot. They have it listed to last five minutes on the itinerary."

Bloom stopped to let it sink in, see if Hayes saw the same issues.

"You'd have to know this area fairly well to recognize, you know, the opportunity," said Hayes.

"You see," said Bloom. "That's kind of the way I'm thinking about it, too. Unless the shooter was looking at every campaign stop, every public appearance and every schedule and every town for the right configuration."

Hayes' look suggested a glimmer of understanding.

"Maybe not someone we know," said Bloom. "Someone connected to an organization here. It must have taken a few people to pull this off."

"Organization?" said Hayes.

"Maybe they call themselves something," said Bloom. "A loose network. A hate group."

"Hate group?" said Hayes. "Here?"

"Do you think it's possible?" said Bloom.

"Actual hate groups?" said Hayes.

"Just a thought," said Bloom. "I'm sure the cops are talking to everyone who has ever thought a mean thing about illegal immigrants. Somewhere in that group is a guy with some seriously bad-ass sniper skills who owns a long-range rifle."

Hayes said "hmmm" in a distracted way and shook the mouse to her computer as if it was dead, not asleep.

Hayes' sudden interest in her computer was likely due to the approach of Chris Coogan. It wasn't as if reporters couldn't shoot the breeze, but Coogan had been pushing Hayes to turn up her productivity. Hayes bristled at Coogan's editing style on a number of levels and resisted his coaching with disdain.

"Ever going to let me know you and Lamott had history?" said Coogan.

"I've got history with lots of folks," said Bloom.

"This particular *folk* came to our city and you covered him," said Coogan. "Think it was important you told me you once tried to chew his ass?"

"Who called?" said Bloom.

"Is that important?" said Coogan.

"It seemed irrelevant until yesterday," said Bloom. "At least, in my mind. Never published a word in Denver. Somebody called?"

"Yeah," said Coogan. "The campaign wanted to make sure, since there are now going to be many stories to come, you know, that we had options in case your bias started to show."

Bloom didn't have to look to know that Hayes was enjoying this, pretending to ignore it at the same time.

"No bias here," said Bloom. "Got bigger things to work on than that."

"Do yourself a favor," said Coogan. His tone was stone cold. "Keep me in the loop on everything. *Everything.*"

"Got it," said Bloom.

"And what now?" said Coogan.

"Mulling that," said Bloom.

"I got one suggestion," said Coogan. Suggestion meant directive. Bloom indulged Coogan, who had five fewer months in town that he did. He was another refugee from the big-city newspaper meltdown. In Coogan's case it was Albuquerque. During his short stint at the editorial helm of the *Post-Independent*, Coogan showed an unbridled passion for anything that involved mayhem and strife.

"Shoot," said Bloom.

"I want a complete breakdown on who is calling the shots from the investigation side," said Coogan. "And I want to know if our local cops, the city and county, think the investigation is being handled well. No doubt they're feeling flattened, steamrolled. There's got to be tension."

"Probably true right there," said Bloom, who generally liked to keep editors on his good side.

"Maybe go in with a bit of a pretense," said Coogan. He was in his mid-fifties, had curly light brown hair and a ruddy complexion. He ran hot and hyped-up. He wore wire-rim glasses a bit too large for his face. "Maybe go in looking to profile the lead agents. Tell them we want to know who's running the show, make them feel a little flattered, you know, and then get inside their heads, find out what they're thinking."

It was hard to picture any of the cops taking a break from their work to talk about themselves, but Bloom kept that reaction to himself. Coogan's idea machine was theoretical, out of idea books or stolen from journalism websites like Poynter. With the national layer of bureaucracy now involved in Glenwood Springs, highlighting the inevitable pissing match over turf and tactics held about as much interest for Bloom as running down to cover the local elementary school bake sale.

"I like it," said Bloom. "I'll put that in the mix."

"Are you heading out?" said Coogan. Asking how soon Bloom was heading out was his passive-aggressive way of saying *get the fuck out of here.* Hayes was gathering her things, making it obvious. She could probably take a bite out of her stapler like it was a peanut butter sandwich.

"Momentarily," said Bloom. "Couple of calls to make." A true statement on any given day, at any given moment.

"I want to crawl up inside the cops' heads and download every scrap," said Coogan. "The more you think about the shooting, the more you think about the organization it took and the planning, some amount of teamwork. Very short notice for the event itself—"

"I was saying the same thing to Marjorie—"

"Almost like a terrorist cell, a terrorist cell of deep, racist hate," said Coogan.

Coogan pulled assumptions from air thinner than the atmosphere around Pluto and he expected reporters to thank him for the insight. Bloom preferred to connect the actual dots, from one fact to the next.

Coogan drifted off, leaving Hayes unscathed. It was hard to imagine what absorbed Coogan's time. Coogan made himself available to the publisher, who was pressured on a daily basis to deploy a reporter for some PR puff piece or pressured for the opposite reason, to steer the reporters away. The walls between advertising and editorial space, in theory, kept the two from inter-mingling. In this newspaper, the walls were wet tissue. Bloom hadn't directly changed or altered any story due to external influences, but he knew you didn't propose stories that would harm the reputation of the Hot Springs Lodge, which was practically the town's cash drawer, or the banks or the key Chamber of Commerce types of businesses. You didn't.

Bloom was nobody's circus monkey, but he was still in the process of ingratiating himself into the community. Denver was a small town in some ways, at least among the civic and business leadership, but by comparison Glenwood Springs was like one of those spooky caves that carried a whisper from one end to the other like the whisperer's lips were close enough to lick your hammer bone. There was a layer of dug-in town leadership that called the shots. Provoking the wrong individual—no matter how innocent—might mean Bloom would be quickly out on the streets. In that case, Bloom would never know what hit him. Or why.

And then what?

Then, nothing.

Being bounced from Glenwood Springs would be journalism's way of saying *adios.*

FIFTEEN:
TUESDAY MID-DAY

It was a world-class shot. Allison had heard tales of longer shots, but those targets were elk, deer, or the occasional bear or moose—not a human. The added wrinkle here was the wind coming out of the canyon, over the right shoulder of where the shooter had allegedly stood. Or sat. Or something.

"Is it six hundred yards?" said Allison.

"Within a few," said Chadwick.

"It would take somebody with solid experience," said Allison. "Anything beyond a gentle breeze over that distance, you'd be clueless where the shot would end up."

"Agreed," said Chadwick.

And then there was the elevation and adjusting for the drop.

"What did the wounds say about angle?"

All the way down from the Flat Tops, Chadwick said they wanted her to look at the scene without the cops' vision of events bouncing around in her head. So he hadn't said much about the case. The only conclusion Allison could draw was that the cops didn't have much. Or didn't have anything.

Allison had fought back a rare case of nerves as they approached the scene, side-long glances from the cops and officials as the sea parted to make way for her inspection. The air had been thick with doubt. If Trudy had been there, she would have lost count of the black auras and clogged throat chakras.

"Six or seven degrees north of horizontal," said Chadwick. "He was above his target, but not by much."

"Plus the bullet drop," said Allison.

"Correct," said Chadwick.

"Were there any strays?"

"Four," said Chadwick. "Two hit the steel decking on the Grand Avenue bridge deck behind the pedestrian bridge to the west. Those two bullets are most likely in the water, but they left a mark. A third bullet was in the rear quarter panel of a southbound late-model Chevy pickup, a carpenter on his way to a job in Aspen. The last bullet, though of course we don't know the order, was on the front bumper of a northbound minivan, family of five from Alamosa on their way to the hot springs pool."

"A spotter," said Allison, almost without thinking it through. The first two shots had likely hit the cars, then they adjusted and hit the decking and adjusted again. "How you'd pick up the misses without a spotter is beyond me. No dirt or dust to kick up, no idea how to adjust."

"It's a problem," said Chadwick.

"And how many of the shots hit Lamott?"

"Two," said Chadwick. "One high in the chest, one in the shoulder."

The hill they were standing on was steep. The pitch was walkable, but you'd want to hold onto a branch or something for stability. The ground was rough. The trees were sparse, but two were substantial enough to climb. The space between trees consisted of bare dirt and scruffy bushes and grasses that looked sad and beat-up.

Allison squatted on the trail, tried to calm her breathing like a sniper. Her thoughts buzzed in a swirl that started along the lines of "what the hell do you think you are doing here?" to "make this quick and be on your way" to "maybe, just maybe, you can help."

"Suppressor?" said Allison. A few hunters preferred to shoot with a suppressor because they cut down on noise and saved their ears.

"The witnesses said the noise was kind of muffled," said Chadwick. "More of a tick-tick-tick."

"So yes?"

"That's our supposition at this point," said Chadwick.

"How many heard them? How many pointed to this area?"

"Four solid witnesses," said Chadwick. "We got a guy right down below the hill, he was out in back of his house painting this new trellis, said he hadn't heard that sound since street fighting on the way into Baghdad during Desert Storm. He knew instantly what it was, though at the time he figured the shooter was someone who picked an unsafe place to test a gun."

"But he isn't sure," said Allison. "Really sure."

Chadwick shook his head. "Not with suppressors. They throw sound like a ventriloquist."

"Good one," said Allison.

"Thanks," said Chadwick.

There was a non-cop side to Chadwick. He was more teddy bear than grizzly and his eyes hadn't gone jaded and accusatory.

"So you're going by bullet angle?" said Allison.

Allison propped an imaginary rifle like she was sighting it, right elbow jabbed into right thigh, left elbow resting on left knee. The grade was so steep that her left leg didn't come up high enough to hold the rifle level. Or steady. To be reliable at this distance, the weapon would have carried some weight.

"The shooter wasn't on top of the train station," said Chadwick. "The angle from there would have been too much from the side."

"How about that apartment building on this side of the train station?"

"The angle still isn't right," said Chadwick.

"But you checked it?"

Chadwick let out a heavy, slow sigh.

SIXTEEN:
TUESDAY MID-DAY

BLOOM KNEW SOME OF the country's best newspaper reporters—real writers with long-form journalism credentials and book credits under their belts—were moving in to investigate the investigation, always a winner, or to start laying out pieces to prove that Glenwood Springs harbored the kind of mentality that could have bred the assassin. Bloom could write these fill-in-the-blank pieces now. But the pressure was on, to not lose the local edge.

The ideas percolated—more than a few directions to head.

There were two local gun clubs—one a couple miles off I-70 closer to Glenwood Springs and one in Basalt, about halfway to Aspen. The Basalt shooting range had been in the news due to neighborhood complaints over noise. The facility was run by a sporting club and leased public land. They were under pressure to build enclosures. The club's website mentioned nothing about long-range rifles and, besides, Basalt was a good fifteen miles from Glenwood Springs. Too much time to risk.

But the search engine coughed up a name in connection with the club. The name was Lee Kirbinowicz, a prominent and vocal member of the club. The name turned up in letters to the editors from the *Post-Independent*, *Aspen Times*, and *Carbondale Sun*, too. Kirbinowicz was a busy beaver producer of opinion, vehemently anti-immigration.

The Glenwood Springs Gun Club was promising, too. A map on its website showed the road from the highway back into the range and then another map showed the layout of the range, with distinct areas for trap shooting, rifles, handguns, and archery. It looked more secluded, which might be more inviting to whackos.

He would have to check in with the cops, not only to please Coogan. There was another formal news briefing at noon and he had to call DiMarco, to find out what was really happening. Bloom had spotted a strange item in the morning paper about the discovery of a dead man in the Flat Tops. It was odd how the item had been under-played. It wasn't an everyday occurrence, after all. DiMarco might have a lead on that.

Another idea was to track down Troy Nichols and ask him to elaborate on "inevitable." If he retracted the statement, easy story. If he defended it, he could call up any Lamott supporter and extract a reaction in a counter-quote.

But all story ideas seemed subordinate to thinking about the shot. The whole matter of the long-range shot appealed to Bloom's inner boy and he knew the place to satisfy his desire to see what skill was required.

YouTube.

One video showed a bunch of guys plunking a Pepsi can from 900 yards, shouts of "yee haw" and high-fives when they hit it. In another, a military weapon took out an Afghan "rebel" from 1,800 yards. More than a mile. And a bull moose, standing on the shores of a broad river in Alaska, was felled from 800 yards. That video's comments section included discussion about the use of a ballistics calculator and, of course, the inevitable epithet-filled anger lobbed back and forth between hunters and animal rights activists, who were sure the moose had suffered, given the inability for the shooter to quickly administer a kill shot, or even to determine if one was necessary.

Certainly the combination of an angry anti-immigration zealot and talented long-range marksman would limit the pool of suspects in Glenwood Springs to no more than, say, three. Throw in the new factor, a man stupid enough to buy a disposable phone and use it in connection with the shooting, and you're down to one.

Two more story options occurred to Bloom.

One, follow up on the ICE process. Where did those illegals get taken? Where are they now? What were the rules?

Two, do what Coogan wanted. Get as close as possible to the cops and see what he could glean. Given the high-stakes nature of the situation, any local cops he might know were probably under strict rules about making eye contact with media, let alone conversing.

But maybe he'd relied too much on DiMarco. Maybe the cops were using DiMarco to monitor *him*. He wouldn't stay long at the scene where all the cops were converged up on Lookout Mountain, but he wanted to get a true flavor of the investigation scene and, if possible, find out why the hell it was taking so long to get on somebody's tail.

SEVENTEEN:
TUESDAY, EARLY
AFTERNOON

"ALL THE WITNESS STATEMENTS pointed right up here," said Chadwick. "We had a team in the apartments and there are investigators who favor that as the site. But they cleared it."

Allison studied the apartment building, knew she needed to see it up close.

For appearance's sake, she tried lining up her imaginary shot but she couldn't find a comfortable position. The grade was so steep she almost slid downhill. Some hunters used bi-pods to steady a long shot, but the best position she could imagine would have been lying prone. Except with the steep downhill, it would have been an impossible position, head down a couple feet below your toes. Your head would need to be tilted so far your neck would break. And if your neck was made of rubber your downhill arm, the left, had no support.

Allison stood, made a show of stepping carefully down the hill, as if she was trying to spot tracks. The summer heat had baked the dirt so it had as much give as a brick. An orange plastic tag hung limply off the tip of a fir tree that had seen healthier days.

"What's that?" asked Allison.

"The exact elevation as the pedestrian bridge," said Chadwick. "Straight across."

The optics were deceiving. Allison would have sworn on a stack of GPS devices they were still ten or fifteen feet higher than the bridge, maybe more.

She stepped past the tag and studied the ground and bushes and weeds and grasses. Chadwick stayed behind. At the base of a dilapidated fir, no more than sixty feet tall and looking windblown and weary, she wormed her way through the low-hanging branches and climbed as far she could. The top of the tree was too dense, too thick and the branches had not been cut, nicked or disturbed in any way. The idea of a tree stand was one last notion that might put the hill back on her list of possible places where the shooter had taken cover. But why would a sniper want the trouble of dismantling a tree stand? The load would make for an encumbered getaway. Besides, these trees were too flimsy to guarantee a rock-like perch.

Allison let herself down. "Anyone see anyone leaving?" Chadwick was back up the hill so she had to raise her voice.

"Nothing credible," said Chadwick. "Someone thought they remembered a black old-model Buick screaming down 8th Street shortly after the shots, but we found the Buick and the couple had a fight, you know, that kind of thing—the wife was getting out of the house. A fight over finances, what else? We also thought maybe the shooter would have taken off up the trail up Lookout Mountain. There were a dozen hikers on the trail up that day, including a couple of runners and nobody saw anyone suspicious or anything out of the ordinary."

Back at the cop's base camp near the head of Scout Trail, Allison kept her gaze up and square, looked others in the eye. By previous agreement, Allison drifted over to Chadwick's car while he quietly reported the details—specifically, the lack of any new details—to a higher authority. Leaning on Chadwick's car, sipping a bottle of water she had plucked from a communal cooler, Allison hoped he wouldn't take long. The plan was to go down to the apartment building in a low-key mode, not drag the whole entourage along. She might be wrong about the rooftop, but if the sniper had stood or squatted on the hillside, he was one of the most skilled sharpshooters in the state, hands down.

Allison pulled out her cell phone and found William Sulchuk in her contacts.

Yes, Colin, I'm getting all tangled up.

He answered immediately and they exchanged quick greetings. He didn't seem surprised to hear from her.

"Just wanted to see how Gail is doing and let you know they've got the body off the Flat Tops," she said.

"Well, the Sunday outing is not Gail's favorite topic," said Sulchuk, "and not sure she slept much the first night."

"I'm sure it's not easy," said Allison. There were images from the Long Island Sound she'd never forget. Pictures were one thing, lifeless flesh was another.

"What did the cops think?" said Sulchuk.

"Not much," said Allison. "And didn't say much, either. No jumping to conclusions, that sort of thing."

"No ID?" said Sulchuk. "Any idea if he was a local?"

"No," said Allison. "They've got the body somewhere being processed and who knows maybe there's a missing-persons report that's a match. The cops told me they have an artist working on a sketch of his face. You know, using what was left."

"The morning paper had a small item," said Sulchuk. "Buried, given everything else that was going on."

A man emerged from the sea of uniforms, but he was too scruffy to be with them. He was ten steps away. Allison wanted to put her head down and slip into Chadwick's car. He walked right up to her and Allison turned slightly, gave him the universal index-finger indication to wait.

"By the way, you're pretty sure the body didn't get disturbed in any way—before you got there?"

"What?"

"Were you up there when they found the body, with the mushroom hunters?" said Allison.

Sulchuk paused. "I don't get what you're asking," he said.

"Gail said all the kids were up there looking for mushrooms," said Allison. She hoped Sulchuk would fill in the blanks.

"Yeah, we were all in the general vicinity and then Gail screamed and we all came running. We were all right there."

She wanted Sulchuk to feel free to embellish the story, maybe mention something about why everyone already seemed so tense when she and Colin had arrived, but Sulchuk didn't bite.

"Well, we'll see what the cops come up with," said Allison.

"Yep," said Sulchuk. "Not exactly the experience I had planned for Gail—but that is the big old outdoors. You never know."

Allison said goodbye and hung up, still unhappy with the pictures in her head from how the whole scenario happened—finding the half-corpse, standing around, and how the adults had all left the kids at Lumberjack Camp.

The guy waiting was a reporter—the same guy who had been in Trudy's kitchen writing up a profile months ago.

"Allison."

She remembered him—the strong, thoughtful face, the deep-set eyes—but not the name.

"Duncan Bloom," he said. "We met at Trudy's house, if house is the right word. Her greenhouse."

"I remember," said Allison. She smiled and guessed she looked about as sweaty and strung out as a junkie.

"How are you?" he said.

"Mostly hot," said Allison. "But fine."

Allison reminded herself: *he's a reporter*. He'd written a beautiful piece about Trudy, captured her essence, but he was a reporter. "So they took you to the spot?"

There was no sign of a notebook. A pen was clipped to the pocket of his shirt.

"Not for me to say," said Allison. "Better ask the ones with uniforms."

"The police are saying diddly," said Bloom. "Lots of words, but it's fluffier than the down on a baby goose's butt."

Another reporter, video camera on his shoulder and microphone in his hand, was jogging across the street.

"I bumped into Trudy before the shooting," said Bloom. "Minutes before."

She didn't want it to look like she was giving him any information and stepped away. "I don't mean to be impolite. I can't talk."

The reporter with the video camera held out a fuzzy gray microphone fatter than a bottle of wine.

"This isn't an interview," said Allison. "We're acquaintances." She gestured to Bloom.

"What did you find?" said the cameraman, ignoring her assertion.

"You'll have to ask the police," said Allison. "I'm hired help."

She said it calmly and with enough sincerity that the cameraman looked instantly deflated. He turned and drifted off.

"Cops are a stone wall," said Bloom. "No cracks."

Allison let the comment hang. The cops didn't have much to tell themselves, let alone anyone else.

"So this was a favor?"

"Least I can do." He wasn't bad looking at all. He looked bookish, had a thoughtful air. "The whole town is hurting."

"They seem pretty stumped," said Bloom. He had wavy dark brown hair and he was maybe three inches taller than Colin. Bloom looked strong through the shoulders, too.

"You're not trying to get me to confirm—"

"No," said Bloom. "Look." He folded his arms, leaned back against Chadwick's car. "That day I spent with Trudy last spring was one of the finest days of my life, work-wise anyway. I'm not going to burn you or Trudy to grab a two-bit quote for a story."

"Do you even have to mention I was here?" said Allison.

"I'm afraid I'm not in control of that," said Bloom. "When the cops don't make progress, the media can get a bit ornery, you know, and they track every move the cops make."

Chadwick emerged from the throng of milling cops and crossed the street, eyeing Bloom suspiciously. He gave Allison a "let's go" head nod, climbed in behind the wheel of his car.

Bloom had his business card ready. She stuffed it in a back pocket.

"Here's what you can do," said Allison. It was a hasty thought. She hadn't completely processed it. "A body was found up in the Flat Tops two days ago. Badly decomposed—"

"We had it in the morning paper," said Bloom.

"Come on," said Chadwick, suddenly on her shoulder. "No reporters."

"Stay on it," said Allison. "See if they come up with an ID, anything useful. If you hear anything, if it's not too much trouble, call me or call Trudy."

She gave Bloom her cell number. "Sometimes I'm out of range up there, but leave a message. I'll get it."

Bloom looked happy to have an assignment. "You were there when they found it?"

"Time to go," said Chadwick. "Unless you want to walk."

Allison leaned in close to Bloom, half-whispered. "Stay on the cops about that body from the Flat Tops. The whole town is focused on the politician and I get that. But this one has got something to it, too."

"Do what I can," said Bloom. He gave a quick smile. It was more than she could have hoped.

EIGHTEEN:
TUESDAY AFTERNOON

THROUGHOUT THE "DOWN TO Earth" store and farm, well-scrubbed young white girls worked side by side with Mexican men. Every job was a group effort. Jerry insisted on team work, no strict division of labor. An employee's personal skills might help determine the right job at first, but cross-training was a big theme.

Their roadside stand west of Glenwood Springs, just off the highway, was the size of a two-car garage, with the herbs, seeds, bedding plants and produce displayed on a series of shelves and tables around the perimeter. Local honey. Local eggs. Bedding plants. Books and magazines. The stand was where customers shopped and milled about, but they were welcome to tour the five greenhouses behind the stand, too.

A customer service ethos had taken over Trudy's crews, including how the stand was run and how visitors were treated. Customers were cooks and gardeners and green thumbs who liked to ask questions, learn something. Trudy's theme was "keep it simple." Plants, herbs and flowers, and vegetables all knew what to do. They'd been growing in a wide variety of environments long before the invention of fertilizer. Trudy pushed for organic. But it was more than that, too. She promoted going rustic. She was growing home crops with the same attitudes as farmers from the 1930s, before things got complicated. Grow a winter crop to improve the soil. Use simple tools like a good grab hoe for the vast majority of your needs. Don't over fertilize, don't over water. Listen to your soil and sunlight, let it tell you what it wants and watch what thrives. Her new push was promoting self-fertilizing gardens, where the goal was to build a self-sustaining eco-system that required minimal external interference. The idea emphasized care of the soil as a living organism and managing the ecosystem so the garden could take care of itself. Tricky in the semi-arid Glenwood Springs climate, but it could be done.

Deep down, though she would never say it out loud, Trudy believed herbs, flowers, and plants all fared best when they weren't guarded by helicopter parents who buzzed around over every new shoot or who were alarmed by any slight flaw in a textbook growing environment. To most gardeners, she wanted to say, *relax.*

Now, she tried to give herself the same advice. But with the missing worker and the clear warning from the cop, it hadn't taken hold.

Trudy followed the path around back and headed toward the third greenhouse, where Juan Diaz was working. Jerry had recommended Diaz as someone who knew the Loya family and who could provide an update, if there was one.

Juan Diaz was working with a crew of five harvesting Thai basil, each plant being plucked whole, including the roots and some dirt, and placed in a loose plastic wrapper. The basil grew in beds at waist level to make for painless harvesting. Trudy loved the serenity of a well-maintained greenhouse, all the plants in neat rows, happy to be together. She savored the rich aroma of loamy soil and the soft pungency of the Thai version of basil, lacking that sweet note of the regular variety. It packed a more workmanlike punch.

Diaz had an easy smile. His "hello, how are you?" greeting was all-American English, not a hint of accent. He was a third-generation native of Rifle. He had spent two years at Colorado State in Fort Collins before coming home to help plump up the family income. The crew greeted her with familiar smiles. Spanish, an underground currency that didn't allow her to barter, flew quietly.

Diaz had earnest, kind eyes. His skin was creamy brown. He stood with his arms crossed like a confident athlete who had run for an hour but hadn't broken a sweat. He had powerful forearms and a broad chest in a compact frame. He looked like he could work all day.

"Alfredo hasn't turned up at home?" said Trudy. "In Mexico?" She tried to make it sound less like an investigation and more like a conversation.

"True," said Diaz. "They call home every day to see if he's turned up."

"Who calls?"

"His brother," said Diaz. "Tomás. Very worried. He saw him last. They were out fishing early one morning. Somehow they got separated and Alfredo was picked up, taken in a van."

"Where was this?" said Trudy.

"Glenwood Springs," said Diaz. "Right downtown."

Diaz turned to the crew and spoke rapidly in Spanish. Trudy only made out "Alfredo," "*casa*," and "*dónde*" in the stream of words. One of the women replied softly.

"They live in a mobile home park," said Diaz.

"And where's Tomás now?" said Trudy.

Diaz hesitated. "You would know better than me."

"And Alfredo would have said if he were heading back to Mexico?" said Trudy.

"Tomás and Alfredo were twins. Close twins."

"And Tomás hasn't reported it?"

Trudy knew it was a dumb question before she finished it.

"No," said Diaz. He was kind enough to pretend she was savvy about these matters. "You don't go to authorities. And since the shooting, even more so."

"I want to talk to Tomás," said Trudy.

Diaz turned again to the women and Trudy waited through a rapid-fire exchange. The women looked uncertain.

"They don't think there's much to do, except wait," said Diaz.

"But it's been two weeks," said Trudy.

Another fast exchange, the women waiting for Diaz to finish before responding. She sensed a tone of assurance.

Diaz turned back. "No cops."

"Just me," said Trudy. She turned directly to the women and somewhere from deep inside her memory the word "*solamente*" flashed. She tapped her chest.

NINETEEN:
TUESDAY AFTERNOON

CHADWICK DROVE SLOWLY. HE turned right at Bennett Avenue and north toward the river. He hung a quick left on the frontage road and stopped, the train station straight ahead to the west.

He was agitated about something, maybe her chatting with the reporter. Whether Chadwick thought this was a crazy theory or a worthwhile step, Allison couldn't read it. The vibe among the cops was sour and black. Chadwick had caught the funk.

The building in question was Glenwood Manor. The architecture was straight mid-1970s. Faux stone, small windows, blocky construction. The manor's super rode up the elevator with them to the top floor, the sixth. The elevator moved at a speed so slow Allison was sure that it was affecting the time half of the space-time continuum. The super stared at the floor indicator lights as if he was unsure whether four followed three. He stepped into a hall that had all the charm and warmth of a New York City hospital.

"Police have already come by," he said. He was a tired, rail-thin man with overly-slick hair and a gaunt face that gave him away as a lifelong smoker. His name was Harry Long.

"But they weren't here for more than a few minutes," added Long, "And the roof, well, it's pretty rare to go up there, although we had a company up here doing a patch three weeks ago. We had water working its way in after heavy rains. Never understood a flat roof, never will."

Long led them down the short hall to an unmarked door, opened it with a shove. The room held mechanical gear. A built-in ladder of ten rungs led to a hatch in the ceiling. "A few of the tenants use the roof for tanning and small parties," said Long. "Nothing too wild."

Allison climbed up, following Long's instructions on how to swing down the hatch door.

The access door brought her up on the southeast corner of the roof. The shooter, if he had been up here, would have perched on or near the northeast corner, the spot closest to the pedestrian bridge and the only corner with a view in that direction.

The roof was surrounded by a low wall about 18 inches high, an ideal height to rest a rifle. Best of all, the only witnesses who could see anything on the rooftop would be higher on Lookout Mountain, a squirrel in a nearby tree or a circling hawk.

The surface was cream-colored and had the texture of medium-grade sandpaper. Windblown refuse from nearby trees and other crud from the sky were scattered about. Bits of trash. Cigarette butts. Black sealant created a three-foot-wide ring around the outer edge, like bad bathtub scum. From a distance, anyway, a man could easily disappear into this blackness, lay low, and scope the bridge.

The roof's sheeting material was soft enough that it might have picked up a man's footprint, but only the general shape and not any detail from the tread.

"Does anyone come up here?" Chadwick had followed up behind her. He must have read her mind.

"I come up after storms to check for puddles and once a month or so to have a look around," said Long. "We had a travel photographer come up here not too long ago—Colorado Western history book he was working on. What he said, anyway."

Chadwick was a jump ahead of Allison. "How long ago?"

"About late July, I believe," said Long. "He didn't end up taking any pictures. Just scouting."

Would somebody make such detailed plans to take out a politician before they knew they would even make a stop in Glenwood, let alone walk across the bridge? Didn't seem likely.

"He was legit," said Long. "I Googled him later. Big ass coffee table books and stuff like that. Cost more than a month's groceries for one copy."

Long retreated, said something about a broken toilet. Allison led the way to the northeast corner, setting the pace of a hung-over sloth. Each step produced a muffled crunch. Allison worked to let the moment take over. It was a process of subtraction, of telling every stray random oddball thought to fuck off. There were plenty of thoughts and they all wanted their time at the surface. They all tried to wave flags or do jumping jacks. One after another the thoughts kept flying. She forced her mind to now. *To here.*

She took a breath, slowed some more.

Chadwick gave her space.

She scanned everything left, right, back—and step. She inventoried each non-roof item—stick, bird poop, dead leaf, recently clipped stick, pine needles, a tuft of hair, most likely squirrel. A gum wrapper, faded and baked into the surface of the roof. A bottle cap, also carrying years of wear.

The black perimeter came into view on the edges of her peripheral vision. Would the shooter have scrambled away quickly? Did he move fast? Drop something? Had he been lying up here? For how long? Did he hide his gun, somehow, until it was time? Did he have a two-way radio? Was someone radioing Lamott's progress on his walk through town? Relaying a countdown of sorts? Was he lining up the shot?

For how long?

Allison looked up at the pedestrian bridge. This shot was much tighter, cleaner than the one from Lookout Mountain. A shooter would still need a scope but the angle was good and the height—slightly above the target—was perfect. The spot on Lookout Mountain had a major drawback—the issue of stray hikers or joggers who might remember a man or men with a major piece of artillery taking dead aim at a target in the thick of civilization. This spot offered cover.

Would someone in the apartment building have noticed a stranger with a rifle, rifle case, or any other gear sizable enough to conceal one? Maybe. On the other hand, a couple of avid hunters could rent here so the sight of a rifle case was nothing to get excited about.

"Shots were how far apart?" Allison studied the rooftop, didn't turn around.

"Three seconds," said Chadwick. "That was the average, thereabouts."

In the corner, sitting right on the edge of the light-colored roofing material was a piece of straw, like a bristle from a broom. Maybe the sniper flew off the roof when he was done. Or maybe he brought cleaning supplies with him. Another straw was nearby, its tan woody hue a shade darker than the backdrop. Allison didn't touch it, but if she had to guess she would say they were synthetic. She pictured the shooter lying up against the corner, shells ejecting, having a plan to conceal the rifle and then also having enough other gear so there was a plausible scenario for being up here in case of a stray sunbather or making-the-rounds super. How much lead time would you want or need to pack up, cover up?

Again Allison studied the pedestrian bridge and spotted a man walking who turned to stop and look over the train tracks. Three seconds between shots? It was enough time for a spotter to call adjustments and pull the trigger, but the spotter would have to be damn good. It was easier to picture one man, shooting solo with a helluva scope.

"Evenly spaced?" said Allison.

"Three close together," said Chadwick. He had moved closer behind her. "A longer pause, a second longer, and then the final shot."

Allison flashed back to mid-day Sunday. Bright sun, clear skies. A hawk circling high could have seen Lumberjack Camp and the pedestrian bridge in one turn of the head. Lumberjack Camp was eight miles north and 4,000 feet higher.

Allison lay prone. Her short arms didn't provide enough height to hold a rifle above the lip of the building but any average-height man would have no such challenge.

Walking slowly back to the rooftop hatch, Allison counted the paces with a normal stride. Thirty three. She wondered if the shooter would have run. If he had taken time to pack his gear. A shooter this good would have been in charge of his heart rate. Experienced, confident.

"You look like you've got something," said Chadwick.

"Maybe," said Allison.

The grinding hum of the elevator cab offered the sole indication they were moving.

"Where are we going?"

Was that hope in Chadwick's tone?

The yellow lamps counted down the floors with excruciating agony. Adrenaline gnawed at Allison's guts. The elevator doors parted like they were made of marble.

Outside, Harry Long sucked so hard on a cigarette that he might be trying to kill it. He was chatting with two women, both approaching senior citizen status if not already there. No doubt Long had primed the pump on the building grapevine. Their chatter came to an abrupt halt as Allison led Chadwick to the northwest corner of the building. Trudy would have known the precise names for the two shrubs at the corner. Allison guessed boxwoods. The shrubs guarded the corner. Each ended a row of three. The green needles were splotched with rust and the trunks grew from dusty hardpack that looked as nourishing as concrete. As landscape decoration, they failed miserably in their role. Allison had the urge to send Trudy on an emergency rescue mission, maybe take them back to their home in the woods. The shrubs were eight feet high. It was possible she'd need a ladder. Allison tucked herself in between the brick wall and the line of shrubs on the north side of the building. There was enough room to move without bothering a needle.

The bullet shell was resting gently like a gold ornament on an outer branch, at eye level.

"Hello," she said to herself. The moment came with a bit of satisfaction along with all the hard, grim reality.

"One shell right there," said Allison, emerging from the shrub. "Maybe others. Looks like a .308 to me but that's just a guess. At that distance, I'd say 165 grains plus or minus 15. I'd check everything on the roof for prints. Were the bullets boat tail?"

Chadwick sighed. "Son of a bitch," he muttered.

The lead engines of a freight train rumbled past, heading up the canyon. The growl forced Allison to speak up. She put her back to the tracks and the street.

"I think the shooter used a broom, too, after he was done. There might be a broom up on the top floor somewhere. Check it for prints, too, unless it's been used lots since the day, you know, since. I can't say but I think it'll be a black matte finish on the rifle, nothing reflective, and he probably used flat-shooting bullets to minimize drop. A helluva good shooter and he either knew someone in the building or he had a good ruse to get inside or he figured out the access code to that cheap security touchpad door buzzer."

Chadwick was already pulling up the square microphone attached to his shirt, asking some lieutenant to respond. "Son of a bitch," he repeated.

"Can I get a ride back?" said Allison. She had five minutes, she figured, before Cop Nation descended on Harry Long and Glenwood Manor.

"Just let me tell our building super friend over here that his world is about to get turned upside down," said Chadwick. "And then we can go."

She was so focused on Chadwick's words through the train's rumble that the presence of a third person, suddenly standing so close, almost made her jump.

Duncan Bloom. He looked up the street where the first cop car rounded the turn. Then Bloom looked up at Glenwood Manor.

"What's going on?" said Bloom. "Are you thinking Lamott was shot from up there?"

TWENTY:
TUESDAY AFTERNOON

THE STORY TOOK AN hour to write, fingers only a second behind the brain. This one was all Duncan Bloom's personal observation, of the cops moving like bees swarming to a new hive. All the reporters saw it, but he would be first in getting a solid story up on the website.

The police had gone for forty-eight hours looking in the wrong location.

Bloom couldn't be that blunt, but close. He was beginning to think of things to do when he was done writing, like use the reverse phone directory and call every resident at Glenwood Manor.

It wasn't hard to imagine that someone in the building might have been an accomplice, unwitting or not. The investigation was back to square zero, as an old Denver editor liked to say. Bloom always liked the image of a square zero—something you couldn't picture. It was worse than square one. You were screwed.

When the phone rang, Bloom thought about ignoring it, but that went against every fiber in his reporter bones.

"Go easy."

DiMarco.

"Just the facts," said Bloom.

"You can soften them."

"I don't write for NBC or the *L.A. Times*," said Bloom. "Are you making a hundred of these calls? Think they'll listen? Can someone tell if the apartment building was even considered, checked, analyzed?"

The edge in his voice surprised him.

"This isn't that kind of call," said DiMarco. "You'll have your chance to ask those questions."

"Anything on the convenience store and the temporary phone?"

Bloom leaned back in his chair, hit save on his computer, looked around the newsroom. Marjorie Hayes sat up straight, hands poised over her keyboard like the first day of typing class. She stared at a blank screen. White wires descended from her ears to an invisible iPod. She was partial to old-school Johnny Cash.

"Matter of fact," said DiMarco. "We found him. He's a big-time fan who wanted a chance to shake Lamott's hand. Showed us the autograph he got. He was by Doc Holliday's bar before Lamott went up on the bridge. Took a selfie, as they call it."

Bloom silently lamented the loss of a lead that he hoped had gone right through his telephone. "You sure this is an immigration thing?"

DiMarco paused, but not too long. "What are you saying?"

"You focused on the idea that this is immigration-related violence, a hate group or something?"

"We need a suspect first and then we'll work on motive," said DiMarco. "How you going to play this?"

"I'm not *playing* anything."

"It's where you give credit—to the woodswoman or to the cops for bringing her in."

"I think most people care that you're on the trail," said Bloom. "The town wants a suspect in a bad, bad way. The whole state. The whole country. Give us something to work with."

DiMarco paused. It felt odd to have him on the run.

"Believe me," he said. "Every cop feels the pressure, rookie to chief."

"Is that why you called, to help me select the attitude in my prose?"

"Just wanted to see if you're going to keep the editorial page where it belongs," said DiMarco.

"Appreciate the counsel," said Bloom. "Maybe if I'm a good boy, at least in your mind, you might owe me a favor down the line."

"Now we're dreaming," said DiMarco.

"Okay, I'll give you a chance to show this is a working relationship. You know about this dead guy they brought down from the Flat Tops?"

Since the chat with Allison Coil, Bloom had this fleeting fantasy of somehow winding his way to her doorstep, developing a friendly relationship. At least for starters. He was good at being friends first. It wouldn't hurt to know someone in the hunting and outfitting business. Bloom imagined the chances were pretty close to zilch with Allison since he possessed no horse, hunting, or outdoor skills—but Allison Coil hit that sweet spot between cute and beautiful, with her confidence and toughness binding the whole package together. Didn't every "woodswoman" crave a city boy?

"Know of the body," said DiMarco. "Being processed. We've checked against missing persons reports and nothing lines up. Going statewide next, see if we can get a bite. Probably a hiker got caught by a storm or zapped by lightning. In fact, I heard something that it might be a mountain lion kill. Wouldn't be the first."

"Not every day," said Bloom.

"Think a broad daylight assassination attempt is a bit more out of the ordinary," said DiMarco. "Up in the woods you got wild animals, dumb hunters, and then the whole easy-to-do fuck-up category called lost. That's child's play. Open to all."

"I want to know if you get an ID," said Bloom. "And I got another question."

Bloom knew he wanted to hit 'send' on his story in five minutes, but didn't want to miss the opportunity.

"You're at your quota," said DiMarco.

"The van the other day," said Bloom. "Where do the illegals get taken?"

Bloom needed the mental picture filled in. When the unmarked ICE van arrived, it was like a shadow government had been waiting in the wings and pulled back the curtain to stage its own bit of legal theater. Bloom wanted to make sure he hadn't been memory-zapped like the citizens in *Men in Black* who inadvertently witnessed alien creatures.

"Aurora, Colorado, USA," said DiMarco. "At least as far as I know. Trust you know it."

"You're hilarious," said Bloom.

Aurora hugged Denver's eastern border. It was a sprawling, complex suburb. "There's a detention center there," said DiMarco. "And if they can't produce the right paperwork, it's a swift bus ride back to their mama's tortillas and home tequila."

"They get taken straight down the highway to Denver, just like that?"

DiMarco paused, almost like he wanted Bloom to answer his own question.

"You're resourceful," said DiMarco. "All that big-city training. As soon as you're done tearing us apart, it'll give you something to do."

TWENTY-ONE:
TUESDAY AFTERNOON

THE DAY WAS NOW an abbreviated version of itself.

Allison walked through and around the barn, thinking she could feel the sun sink with a hard clunk as each minute ticked by.

It was four days until archery season opened and there was an overwhelming list of chores to plow through. All the "to-do's" revolved around the barn and the horses and the camp gear. She reminded herself that any semblance of stress was entirely self-inflicted.

Trudy's car had been gone when Allison passed her house and Colin was taking a string of three pack mules to Lumberjack with weed-free hay. Jesse Morales, another of her wranglers, was out in the field sewing up two small tears in the canvas wall tents while they aired out. After a season of woodstove smoke, cigar smoke, and indoor cooking of animals and fish, then being packed away for months to marinate, the canvas needed the full spa treatment. There were saddle bags to patch. Fly rods needed a tune-up. Tackle boxes needed a spruce-up, too. The barn needed cleaning. The vet was coming tomorrow for routine annual check-ups on half of her twenty-two animals, including vaccinations. One propane stove needed its jets cleaned, another needed an hour with steel wool and an energetic elbow. Running down the mental checklist of chores, Allison kicked herself. Her cell phone had developed a nasty habit of deciding on its own to freeze up at particularly inopportune times. When it happened, she may as well have been holding a rock. If she had been thinking, the morning would have been a good time to swing by the phone store in Glenwood Springs, but she'd forgotten. Now, it would take an extra half-day round trip, all for the most techno-centric item she kept.

To Allison's mind, an outfitter offered hunters ten essential things. First, horses to ride. Second, horses or mules to carry loads of stuff. Third, the know-how to load and balance the animals. Fourth, the outfitting permits. Fifth, a guide to help glass and stalk if you felt you needed it. Sixth, a cook if you wanted to be spoiled. Seventh, horses or mules to help you pack out your kill. Eighth, food planning and menu prep. Ninth, someone to explain all the state rules, if needed.

But when it came right down to it her main business was the tenth item: putting hunters on their prey. Most of what hunters paid for, she could control. The only thing out of her control was the wildlife.

But how could she stop thinking about the half-corpse? Now that the police were on the right track at Glenwood Manor, she wanted the half-corpse to move up on their priority list and she wanted to call Chadwick again, to express some impatience. She wished she had given names to Duncan Bloom—names like William Sulchuk and Larry Armbruster to see if anything registered.

Her cell phone sounded, string chimes that might sound good in a *zendo*. Trudy had picked the ringtone.

"Allison, it's Kerry London again."

One fear she'd had since leaving Chadwick was that her name would be splashed out, that reporters might want her analysis of the cops and their work.

"Yes," said Allison, going for indifferent. She really didn't have time for Kerry London's needs, either.

"It's a beautiful afternoon and we were wondering if today might work, maybe later this afternoon, come get some shots of the area up there, do the interview we talked about."

"Well, I—"

The slight delay in the connection, which wasn't good on the best days, failed to give Allison a chance to wedge herself in.

"The sunset light in the mountains, homes, and the ranch and everything," said London. "Might be perfect."

"You can't get very far up in the time that's left and I've really got my hands—"

"We don't need much," said London. "Don't really need to go very far. It's the way of life we want."

Maybe an all-nighter of cleaning and organizing would give her a chance to catch up. The pressure from energy development really hadn't eased and she wanted to show what was at risk.

"Know the way?" said Allison.

"GPS loaded," said London. "We're actually already out of the canyon and just turning off the interstate right now."

They had answered their own request to come visit long before she had answered the phone. Presumptuous? Shit. She thought she might have two hours alone while they packed up and headed out but now she was down to about forty minutes, max. She could kiss the daylight good-bye.

TWENTY-TWO:
TUESDAY AFTERNOON

TOMÁS LOYA DIDN'T KNOW a lick of English. He stood as he was introduced to Trudy and stayed upright, tucking his hands far up into his armpits. He spoke with his head down. Anguish filled the room. Tomás knew Diaz. There was a comfortable familiarity between them.

Tomás poured three glasses of tap water, carefully turning the water off and on for each glass. Trudy liked him instantly. He smiled politely through his nerves.

They were on Teakwood Lane in the Riverside Meadows mobile home park on the west bank of the Roaring Fork River across from downtown Glenwood Springs. Trudy had never seen the mobile home park. At least, she'd never let it register. There was pride in the neighborhood. The landscaping was maintained. Inviting mini-patios were perfect for watching what little of the world came down this way. The interior of the Loya home was bright and smelled of onions and cinnamon. A pot simmered on the stove. A small crucifix was the sole item on the wall above a red-topped kitchen table.

"He's leaving tomorrow," said Diaz. They had chatted, Trudy trying to pick up the flow.

"Where?" said Trudy.

"Home," said Diaz.

"His brother is missing *here*," said Trudy.

Diaz shrugged. "There's not much he can do."

"Any more brothers or family here?"

Trudy heard "*otro*," "*familia*," and "*aquí*" in Diaz's question.

Their conversation was being watched by two women who sat side by side on a small couch. One was sewing an elbow patch on a jean jacket. The other watched and fanned herself with a section of newspaper.

"Just the two brothers," said Diaz. "At least, in this country."

"What does he think happened?"

Tomás launched into a long story and looked like he was concentrating. The Spanish flew. Diaz probed whenever he need clarification.

"He was there," said Diaz when Tomás was done.

"He was where?" said Trudy.

"Sometimes they fish in the early morning," said Diaz. "There's a spot down along the river, by the bridge. They have good cover. They were walking back when Alfredo realized he had left some string and bait back by their spot. Tomás waited while Alfredo went back. Tomás could see Alfredo come back up on the road from their spot when a van pulled up behind him and stopped. There were two men and they grabbed him."

Tomás watched Diaz while the story was recounted, nodding occasionally.

"A police van?"

"Unmarked," said Diaz. "He made a big point of this. A blue van. Plain."

"*Sí, azul*," said Tomás.

"New?" said Trudy.

Diaz shot a question at Tomás, who replied carefully.

"Newer," said Diaz.

"Did they talk to him first?"

It was mid-afternoon and plenty warm outside, close and stifling inside. Tomás' forehead shined with sweat.

"Not for long," said Diaz. "A few seconds."

"And then what?"

"And then the van drove away. It drove right past Tomás, who hid in the thicket along the side of the road."

"Did Tomás by any chance get a license plate?"

Another rapid-fire exchange. One question, one answer. One follow-up question, another answer.

"The van was going fast," said Diaz. "And Tomás was of course scared. He looked at the last second. Only half of it, CL9. If not 9, then 7, but he's pretty sure it was 9."

"And Alfredo lived here?"

"Yeah," said Diaz. "Here."

Trudy felt as ill as Tomás looked. "How is Tomás getting home?" she said.

"There are ways," said Diaz. "There's always someone going. People know. Small cash payment here, help out there. Help load, help drive. It's not hard."

Glenwood Springs was where she'd been raised, but standing in this motor home with Tomás Loya and the two women on the couch, Trudy had the strange sensation she'd stepped into a parallel universe that coexisted through some trick of intergalactic physics. She couldn't be standing at a much lower elevation and still be in Glenwood Springs, unless she dug a tunnel under the river.

"He needs to stay and help." Trudy heard a desperate edge to her words.

"Needs?" said Diaz.

Tomás must have caught the drift. When he spoke, he shook his head with authority.

"What do you think he's going to be able to do?" The new voice was from one of the women, the one who had been sewing. She put down her work. She stood slowly, as if she hadn't been fully erect for a week. It didn't feel like a hand-shaking moment. "He needs to go home."

Her English was clear but the words were steeped with a thick Mexican accent. Her hair was pulled back in a long braid.

"*Sí*," said Tomás.

"One brother is enough," said the woman, sharpness to her gaze. Her brown eyes revealed warmth but she looked worn down, too.

Behind a closed bedroom door somewhere down the short hall to the bedrooms, a baby fussed.

"Tomás' daughter," said the woman. "Three months."

"Oh my," said Trudy.

Tomás didn't budge at the sound.

"Yes. One brother is enough," she repeated. "No place to go, nobody to tell. Nobody."

Trudy remembered what it was like to live in a delicate bubble of uncertainty, the years before her ex-husband's unraveling. Before she had met Allison. Before doctors found the part of her brain that randomly decided to convulse and misfire of its own volition. Those years had been like living in an earthquake zone, not knowing if any moment the earth would crack and you'd suddenly be free-falling toward a hot ball of fire.

"I know it's hard," said Trudy. "But there are people here who realize this isn't right."

"People are scared," said Diaz. "Very scared."

"The hatred gets all the attention," said Trudy.

"Tomás?" said one of the women, the one sewing. The Spanish flew between them, the woman dominating, instructing. Trudy thought she heard one question in the mix and Tomás paused, pondered a response. Finally the woman turned back to Trudy.

"What are you going to do?" asked the woman. "If he stays?"

Tomás looked as scared as if she was holding a shotgun on him right now. No fully-formed plan had yet jelled, but Trudy knew Tomás' story was worth more in Glenwood Springs than if he took it with him back to Mexico.

"We need his story," said Trudy. "We need to tell somebody what happened."

The woman shook her head. "And who is going to listen?"

"I have to figure that out," said Trudy.

The baby's sobs ramped up to full-bore bawl.

"Tomás wants to go home, but he also doesn't want to leave his daughter," said Diaz.

A door opened and the volume of the scream doubled. The mother was as white as a freshly painted picket fence. She might be twenty-one, she might be eighteen. She bounced her crying baby carefully in both arms. She came to Tomás' side as if it was the only place she belonged. The baby wore nothing but a diaper and a pink bow in hair so short Trudy wondered how the bow stayed in place. The pink bow matched the highlights in the mother's blonde hair. The baby's skin was a beautiful light chestnut. In one seamless move, Tomás scooped the baby to his shoulder. The baby took two more furtive sobs and decided all was right with the world.

"What's going on?"

The young mother had a gold nose ring that looped tightly around her left nostril like a clamp. Her eyes were amber, her hair was straight. It was clear she was bonded with Tomás, but there was no ring on her left finger.

The pint-size kitchen felt cramped. Trudy fought the urge to step outside.

"This is Miss Down to Earth," said the woman. "She's here to help."

TWENTY-THREE:
TUESDAY DUSK

FOR LESS THAN AN hour, they shot scenes around the barn. Allison brushing down and saddling up Sunny Boy, who knew it was a show and behaved like he hadn't signed his contract.

Allison handling a call from a client, a request to add one more hunter to this weekend's first bowhunting party.

Allison riding up the trail. Yes, toward the sunset.

They didn't go far. They need "flavor," "a bit of color," London explained. London's cameraman was at least fifty and sported an unapologetic paunch. He needed help getting up on his horse. Allison figured even the hour on horseback would take a burning toll on the cameraman's hamstrings.

London was a good sport. He cracked dry jokes and started the laughter with his own over-the-top cackle, his eyes closing and his mouth excessively amused by a bad pun. "The horse is a very stable animal," he said assertively, then waited for the rim shot and let loose the laugh.

For the interview, they sat on two boulders that were off the trail from the first ridge west of the barn. They could see the barn, the lone bit of human construction in a vast sweep of forest. The barn was already in the shadow. They sat in the fast-dying shards of direct sunlight and London asked her about why wilderness areas are so important, why she is so concerned about the energy development on the Roan Plateau, why people who would never visit the area should care. Allison kept her answers simple. All the points came easily.

"You can't go back," she said. "If you destroy the wilderness, it stays destroyed. It could take centuries or longer for nature to repair the damage and by then who knows what impact there would be on animals, the fish, everything. We owe it to ourselves to preserve the wilderness. We owe it to the animals, too."

Allison thought of Devo, who was back in the Flat Tops somewhere, more determined than ever to lead mankind back to the nineteenth century, a time period he believed was the last time the vast majority of Americans were tough and capable.

London gave some invisible signal and the cameraman switched off the gear.

London sighed.

He looked overly serious, like he might be readying a joke. He pulled a stalk of grass and chewed the tip. The cameraman cleaned his lens with a small white cloth but, oddly, wasn't packing up.

"True confession time," said London. "You weren't chosen at random."

Allison thought: *Carve that on my gravestone.*

When the time came, of course, she wouldn't be taking up space in a hole in the ground. She would be dust, scattered to the wind from high on a Flat Tops summit like Dome Peak or tossed to the breeze over Trapper's Lake. Trout chow.

London sighed. An acid twinge nipped at Allison's guts.

"I haven't been entirely up front with you," said London. His face contorted in worry like a nervous teenager asking out a girl on a first date.

"The interview is over, okay?" said London. "We are in fact doing a story about the Roan Plateau and the risk from natural gas development, etcetera."

How could a human heart, still lacking key information, decide to hit the panic button?

"That was all legit," said London. "And by the way you were fantastic. Now I want to ask you about a separate project."

London sported a permanent smirk as if nothing was too serious that it couldn't use a cynical jab. Now he tried to eat the smirk up from the inside, furrowed his brow, stared at the ground.

"It's about the airplane crash," said London. "I'm writing a book and—"

"No," said Allison, on her feet faster than she thought possible. "No way, no how, doesn't matter."

"Hear me out," said London. "I've been working on this project for years."

"You can keep working without me."

"You don't even know what it is."

"I don't *need* to know what it is," said Allison, already turning toward Sunny Boy. She took three steps, stopped.

Turned back.

"It doesn't matter. Doesn't matter a lick what it is. If you want to ask me questions about anything that happened before, during or in the long period after, the answer is no. And it's not *I'm sorry, no.* It's no."

"It's a book about the lives on that plane," said London. "It's part tribute, to those who survived, and those who didn't. It's about how key people reacted and how they were able to act and think in extreme circumstances—"

"Save it," said Allison.

"There are survivors who credit you for getting them to shore, for making sure they overcame the moment, for minimizing panic. The water was—"

"The water was what?" said Allison, already furious at herself for taking the time for the media distraction, furious at Kerry London for the ruse, furious at herself for being in this spot. London's prodding forced her to flash on the images from those surreal moments, when something taken for granted and ordinary and routine flipped dark and frightening, when a moment of dread—collective dread among all the passengers, they all felt the plane struggling for altitude—turned black. The earth had leapt up, something it wasn't supposed to do, and delivered an awful smack. And everything came apart.

Allison gasped, recalling.

"It happened. It's over. Done. You asked. I said no. I know I'm unnecessary—"

Surely every of one of her fellow passengers had focused every ounce of mental capacity on one question: *how do I survive this?*

"Well, actually, you played a major role," said London.

"Please," said Allison. "It doesn't matter what any of the others are saying. This isn't for me. You're taking an accident and exploiting it to line your own pocket. I think re-victimizing the people who went through it, making them relive every moment is flat out wrong."

"Just looking to portray the best of human character in challenging circumstances," said London.

He appeared relaxed, unconcerned. Worming his way to this moment had been the hard part. Everything else was cake. Allison felt utterly betrayed.

"Besides," he added. "Nobody else has reacted this way."

A short, sharp breath forced its way past her tightened mouth.

"I'm getting on my horse and I'm going back down," said Allison. "If you want to ride, I strongly advise that you not say one more word about this. If you do, I'm taking my horses with me and you two can walk. Your choice."

London looked at his cameraman. If he looked sheepish, it was only a touch. The cameraman put his fists side by side and made circle motions like he was holding the reins at full gallop.

"I think you've made it clear," said London. "But can I ask one more question without being told to go take a flying leap?"

Allison stared at London. His eyebrows were in the up position, all anticipation. He was used to getting his way.

"I've got a million things to do," said Allison. "All of them better than this."

"One question," said London.

Allison held his pseudo-innocent gaze. "Make it quick."

"If the book helped others—and by the way all the profits from the book deal would go to the nonprofit that works on improving airline safety—if it helped someone else in any small way, in how to act, how to survive the most challenging situations, wouldn't it be worth it, to give up a little bit of—"

"Of what?" Allison snapped. "Privacy? Were you going to say *privacy*?"

London stood. Maybe he'd seen a monster. "Yes," he said.

"Just because we've been through something doesn't make it open season on what we might think or say. It was an accident. Some of us happened to survive. I can tell you one thing—we feel incredibly fucking fortunate. There are no words for how I feel. You have all of time and the entire world of tragic accidents to do what you feel you need to do with your premise, your *theme*. Find someone else. I survived, I reacted. I did what I did. You feast on carnage. You smell blood. If someone will cry and remember, if you make them go through the whole experience again, re-live every freaking fucking moment with the cameras zooming in, hoping for a tear drop or a flood, that's what you're after. You don't care about privacy." Her words came steady and sure—she required no extra emphasis. "You don't know the meaning of the word."

London's expression hadn't changed. He looked a bit like he might have enjoyed the tirade. But he kept his mouth shut as she turned and went to retrieve Sunny Boy.

She piled recriminations on herself for the distraction, for not staying focused, for everything.

"Okay," muttered London behind her back. "Guess the answer is no."

TWENTY-FOUR:
TUESDAY EVENING

THE VIGIL WAS ORGANIZED by a loose confederation of immigration reform groups, some from Denver. Bloom spotted two buses from New Mexico, one from Arizona. A prayer circle had been held the night before, but this one was going to be the big one. For show.

The day had already been a monster, but the pint-size staff at the *Post-Independent* had been told they would be stretched far beyond normal hours to stay on top of the rolling story. Bloom didn't mind. He felt the adrenaline, relished the challenge.

The idea was to follow the route Tom Lamott had walked before he was shot, from Sayre Park down to the footbridge, but it was hard to imagine how this swarm would make its way to the pedestrian bridge in an orderly fashion or in any way confined to the sidewalks.

Half Hispanic, half white.

One thousand people? At least. The park, a full city block, is packed. Milling throng.

Candles flicking like fireflies.

Nearly breezeless.

Bloom found a pickup truck where the white candles emerged from stacks of cardboard boxes. When you want to find organizers, Bloom knew, you look for the mess tent or supply wagons.

Luis Tovar was right near the center of the action, but off to the side of the core activity. He was a barrel-chested man with a round face, puffy cheeks, and a white-gray, carefully groomed moustache. Bad knees forced an ungainly walk. His years as a high school and college wrestler had taken their toll. Surgery to fix them hadn't gone well.

Tovar was the voice of calm among Hispanics in the valley. He lived in a big house downtown with his wife and two girls. He commuted to Grand Junction, where he was the thoughtful History and Hispanic Studies professor who preferred context and dialogue to demonstrations. Reporters had him on speed dial for a good quote. He said what the establishment liked to hear and not necessarily the flame-thrower comments that lefties hoped he would deliver.

"Señor Bloom," said Tovar. "*¿Cómo está?*"

Tovar held an unlit candle. Around him, a tight circle of friends and supporters mingled and chatted quietly, mostly in Spanish.

"*Muy bien,*" said Bloom. "*¿Y tú?*"

"*Bien,*" said Tovar. "But very much wishing we weren't here. Your articles have been good, by the way. And I heard today a major shift in the police work, changing the place where the shots were fired. News alert on my mobile from the *Denver Post* and they credited the *P-I.*"

"First time for everything," said Bloom.

"A hunting guide helped them?"

"It didn't take her all that long, either," said Bloom, happy again to think about the sure presence of Allison Coil. "Maybe they are getting closer now."

Tovar smiled faintly. "Let's hope," he said.

"What are you hearing?" said Bloom.

Square, silver-rimmed glasses added to the professorial air. His black hair was streaked neatly with rivulets of gray. A cotton Guayabera shirt, white on ivory embroidery down both sides, topped clean blue jeans and brown sandals. His attire nodded to Mexican heritage but it wasn't in-your-face.

"Everything," said Tovar. "And nothing. Nothing new."

"What would you say is the general attitude among the Hispanic population, you know, about the shooting?"

Bloom hated the question as soon as it was out. He sounded like a rookie.

"There is no general attitude," said Tovar. "There is no Hispanic monolith. We don't move in lockstep."

Tovar had a way of stating things that didn't make it sound condescending or patronizing.

"But this was a jolt, make no mistake," Tovar added. "This was a mini 9-11 and I mean only in terms of ugly message, of course, not the scale of the horror."

Not the scale of the horror.

A thousand white candles sending one message.

The mass of protestors headed out but Tovar stayed put. Bloom felt the urge to go with the crowd, decided to linger.

"Look at the history of immigration," said Tovar. "At least, look at the history of immigration policy in this country. Look at the number of mixed messages, enticing immigrants one decade—sending them back the next. Look up the Bracero program. Look up investor visas. Look up Operation Wetback. Look up the Border Industrialization Program and on and on. Welcome mat put out, welcome mat yanked away."

Bloom remembered doing a college paper on Benjamin Franklin and recalled he had argued against immigration from Germany because he didn't think Germans could assimilate. "So what are people saying tonight?"

Tovar mulled a response. A young female protestor suddenly stepped up and touched her burning flame to Tovar's cold wick.

"*Gracias*," said Tovar with a smile. He dropped the grin, thought some more. "I suppose more than anything that our hearts are with Tom Lamott, what he stood for. This is a vigil, but we don't want any vigilantes, if you know what I mean. We don't want to point fingers."

Those funneling from the park into the thick mass of the walk itself kept strolling by, candles flickering, but Tovar made no move. Bloom told Tovar about the ICE vans, the group of Mexicans whisked away.

"Like street sweepers cleaning trash," said Tovar.

"Who knows where they are taken?" said Bloom. "That's what I don't get."

"Is that the story you want?" Tovar smiled broadly, looked sideways at Bloom. Light from the candles made Tovar's teeth glow. They were razor straight, blindingly white. One was capped silver. "You really want to go up against the big boys?"

"Don't people know what happens?"

"In some ways," said Tovar. "It's racial profiling on steroids. And it used to be that the immigration people were one function, one agency by themselves. And now they are all merged under one big house, with Homeland Security. They can punch your ticket back to Mexico in less time than it takes to snap on the handcuffs."

From everything Bloom had gathered, Glenwood Springs was tolerant on the issue of illegal immigration. There were pockets of radicals, but you didn't get the sense that this issue was a driving force in the business community or among political leadership, not that there was much difference between the two in a small town. In any town.

"Nobody minds?" said Bloom.

"I wouldn't say that," said Tovar. "But the mood has shifted and I think many know what they are up against, so there is a bit of acceptance. All the security paranoia, you know, it's all rolled into a big ball with the terrorism issues."

The throng spilled over into the street, television cameras and photographers and reporters following. Traffic crawled.

"Shouldn't there be a process—a process everyone knows about, a process we can see?" If he was really doing his job and if he was really intended to compete with journalism's best, Bloom wondered, should he be gathering such marshmallow opinions?

"Sure," said Tovar. "Of course. Some are back home in Mexico before their families here even know they're late for dinner. Not quite, but that's the way it seems."

"So where?"

"If you see another of these vans, don't let it out of your sight."

"You got that right," said Bloom.

"There are those here who have been through everything. Someone might be willing to talk, but you have to understand the level of trust in your public institutions. That includes newspapers, of course."

"Our ratings are better than Congress. And maybe lawyers as a whole." Bloom smiled to show the sarcasm.

"Take comfort in that if you must," said Tovar.

"You are not walking tonight?" asked Bloom. "Or are you waiting to bring up the rear?"

Tovar sighed, looked around. "Only an observer tonight. Watching and thinking."

"I want to meet these people, the commuters," said Bloom. The vigil was at a crawl. "I have this feeling there would be anger. Some outrage. People being snatched off the streets, suddenly captives and no due process."

"Now I see your problem," said Tovar.

"Problem?" said Bloom.

"Okay, your perspective," said Tovar. "You think of these people as taxpaying American citizens who are legal residents, that they understand they can fight for something here to change, that they have a voice to advocate for something,"

"No," said Bloom. "I believe government and the justice system should be open and every individual should have a chance to have their case heard in open court."

Tovar held his candle in his beefy fist and the light flickered off his broad face.

"You think these illegals feel comfortable," said Tovar. "But every step in this country—every minute—they watch out. They are on alert. They are all in prison even before they are picked up. It's not that big a transition."

TWENTY-FIVE:
WEDNESDAY MORNING

"I'M CALLING TO SEE what you've come up with. What anyone has come up with."

She had reached Chadwick on his cell phone after a series of aggravating chats with clerks and other cops who had to be cajoled into making the effort to locate an individual officer in the middle of what was still a high-alert situation.

"Still no ID," said Chadwick. "No one has contacted us, either. And the sticks and that stuff that covered the body is on its way to that lab in Wyoming and I'm not sure we can—"

Allison cut him off. "The more I think about it, the more I know there's something wrong with the whole picture, the whole mountain lion scenario, everything about it."

Certainly her credibility was in reasonable shape, given the bullet shell in the bush.

"I can place a call."

"And can you find out if there's any information on the body? Anything?"

She turned Sunny Boy to face the early morning sun. She'd left at dark, her system on overdrive and her head chasing itself in ugly circles, one furrow of recriminations for letting herself fall into the reporter's trap and another for how she'd treated him.

"Sure," said Chadwick.

"This hasn't been setting right all along."

"I would think the ME would have something soon," said Chadwick.

"What's soon?" said Allison. An awkward delay in the signal. "But this guy was a person, too—and he was a person not that long ago. Somebody was expecting him."

Had she sounded pushy? Not a bad thing.

Allison said good-bye, thanked Chadwick and turned off her phone. She might check messages soon, she might not. She'd made the call because she had to. The rest of the day was built for maximum solitude and minimum civilization.

Sunny Boy walked like he was wearing ankle weights, looking for the right gear. Maybe he was channeling her heavy, black vibes. She'd give herself another couple hours of brooding before challenging her heart to open up. She wasn't ready. She wanted to wallow in her shit. It had been a long night. She tried a large tequila and then a second that was more like a double and then another. She insisted on sex, which Colin happily obliged, and she insisted on talking afterward, not falling asleep. She told Colin about Kerry London and Colin listened and asked questions, but he didn't get it, not down deep. A second round of romping with Colin, this time even sweatier and more determined. More goal-oriented. Love was in the room, but it cowered in the corner and didn't ask to be recognized. Colin had to know this session wasn't about him. She took control, stayed on top, used his shoulders for grips, buried her nose in his warm neck, helped herself to as much as she could take. The sex was selfish and gritty. She still couldn't sleep. She'd spent an hour on the couch. Colin slept soundlessly. Chamomile tea had the same effect as espresso. She spent another hour outside on the mini porch, watching the stars and letting them blur into personal constellations, *all the fire-folk sitting in the sky.* Gerard Manley Hopkins. One of her father's favorites. It surprised her how the line came roaring back. *Down in dim woods the diamond delves! the elves'-eyes!* Too many exclamation points for the moment. There were no elves off in the woods. She couldn't feel their eyes. She kept seeing Kerry London right before he said the word *airplane.* He may as well have cut out her stomach with a ballpoint pen.

Flake-doves sent floating forth at a farmyard scare!
Ah well! it is all a purchase, all is a prize.

When she had finally accepted the sleeplessness, an hour before dawn, she slipped out quietly and left a note: "I'm scouting. Will you and Jesse clean today and start putting together a supply list? P.S. Tell Trudy I'll catch up with her tomorrow. P.P.S: I love you. P.P.P.S: I promise to let you run the show next time. Thanks for being my punching bag."

Now, with the morning sun to her back, she was paying the price. The morning sun lit up the scenery like a spotlight. Normally these moments were worth a week-long cleanse at a health spa, but not today. Her tequila-woozy head didn't appreciate having to process any visual information and it fought the same running banter of crap from the London face-off.

She let Sunny Boy trudge, didn't push him.

It was Wednesday morning. The hunt started in three days.

Allison had one group coming in that wanted to move immediately up to higher elevation to get acclimated and start scouting. They were six guys coming from Oklahoma City. They would hunt for a week. All six had drawn cow tags and, based on the steady flow of e-mails, all six expected to go home with freezer meat. The success rates during hunting season suggested otherwise, but they were welcome to their fantasy. Allison felt like she would be doing her job if she gave them either fresh sign or a close look at the actual prey.

The second group was from Davenport—not too far from her childhood home in Cedar Rapids. Allison had come recommended. The client was a professional friend through her father's teacher networks in Iowa. Their expectations were a bit less bloodthirsty. She wanted, instinctively, to work harder for them than the pushy crew from Oklahoma. Even if neither group managed to take a shot, Allison knew little ways to click up the comfort level for the Iowans, make the food and service top-notch.

Allison worked to focus on one thing, tried to focus on giving her mind a single track.

Elk.

Elk could vanish by the dozens, en masse, in fresh snow in October. It was if every herd had a bull that practiced Santería. He could sneak up on you and spit some foul chemical-laced substance on you that made it impossible to see any four-legged mammal over 500 pounds. Elk were tricky and supremely skittish this time of year, and the only thing that made August or September hunting possible, of course, was sex. The ability to call an elk in close—close enough for a bow and arrow, anyway—made late-August hunting possible. Finding them without calling them in, which Allison planned to do, would require luck, a sharp eye, and a clear head.

As for the last ingredient, she didn't expect to get back to equilibrium for weeks. It was as if Kerry London's question had triggered an earthquake and she was left to wobble, knee-deep in rubble. She had carefully assembled the house where she lived—the mental house. It was a simple place, function over form or beauty. More than anything, it kept strangers at bay. Enough time had passed that there were whole long stretches—first a day, then two, then maybe a whole week—when the airplane crash had lost its power. When she could almost believe the events didn't happen. When they must have happened to a previous incarnation of herself. Whenever she had chosen to think about the airplane crash recently, it was her choice to pull it down off the shelf and hold it in her arms, see if it sparked rage or sadness or, occasionally, nothing. It was her story, her event, her details. Time helped. The Flat Tops had helped more. The new scenery, so utterly devoid of machines and machinery, kissed her daily with the sensation—no, a deep-down-in-the-bones truth—of rebirth. That it was possible. After years now, the airplane crash was finally parked in a well-guarded place and nobody was going to come along and make her spill it all over the page or convulse for the cameras. Nobody. And she resented the hell out of Kerry London's baffled expression, which implied she should thank him for the opportunity to go public.

Ugh.

The trail cut straight up a grassy knob to a high ridge line ahead, the view beyond obscured. Lumberjack Camp was less than an hour away and at that point she would need to decide on her options to go look for elk or their sign.

Either one would work fine.

Anything would be better than thinking about Kerry London and his hideous, self-assured smirk.

TWENTY-SIX:
WEDNESDAY MORNING

Pesca. Rio. Van azul.

A thin bead of sweat formed on Tomás' upper lip and his hands trembled. He looked to Diaz for reassurance. He pointed down the road to an innocuous spot and said, emphatically, *allá*—where he was waiting when he saw the *van azul*.

Duncan Bloom was respectful, patient. He smiled, gave Tomás space. Tomás talked about his upbringing in Chihuahua. The family business was a bakery. When he talked about his mother, tears formed and Tomás had to take a breath. Trudy realized the enormous risk he was taking, the trust he was extending.

Bloom asked for personal details about his skills and interests. Again Tomás fought hard to keep it together, with only partial success.

"A gold mine," said Bloom to Trudy. Diaz listened in. "What I really need is the blue van, of course, and where it went."

Bloom looked up and down the road, as if it might reappear if they waited long enough.

"Now what?" said Trudy.

Bloom put his pen in his pocket, his notebook in a back pocket. He was wearing faded blue jeans and a simple red short-sleeve shirt. He folded his arms, leaned on the hood of his scruffy green Camry, the hood splotched white where the paint had lost its battle with the sun.

"In the 1920s, Congress passed a series of immigration laws and at the time Asians were among the excludable aliens, except the Japanese," said Bloom. "Been reading up. You look back, it's a mess—laws jerking policy one way and then the other."

"The laws don't seem clear now," said Trudy.

"So Alfredo worked for you?" said Bloom.

"Yes," said Trudy. "But—"

"Don't worry," said Bloom. "I want the whole story, not the surface. Not this sliver. The question is where in the hell do they go?"

"Denver?" said Trudy.

"One person in a van all the way to Denver?" said Bloom. "Expensive cab service."

Bloom produced a palm-size camera, shot pictures of Tomás from behind—hiding his face—as Tomás pointed down the road to the spot where Alfredo had been nabbed. Tomás was a stiff model. He looked tired from the interview and uncertain.

Lingering probably wasn't a smart idea. Curious drivers would notice them and her truck, the company logo.

"Can you start in Aurora?" said Trudy. "See how they arrive? Look for vans?"

"Maybe," said Bloom. He studied the road again, looked up and down. "I could ask if Alfredo is being held in the system. At least that would confirm that was the destination—the ICE system. It's worth a shot. I just can't imagine seeing your brother snatched from the streets—no surprise he wants to get the heck out of here."

"But he's dealing with leaving his girlfriend and daughter," said Trudy.

Bloom froze like he was playing a game of statue. *"What?"*

"A baby," said Trudy.

"I can't believe I missed that," said Bloom. "I must be losing my touch."

Bloom re-engaged Tomás and Diaz for another round as Bloom soaked up the details.

"And you would leave your baby?" asked Bloom. "No problem?"

Tomás welled up and his eyes glistened and he started speaking.

"His mother can't afford to lose another son," said Diaz, when Tomás was finished answering. "He'll come back when things settle down. If things settle down. He feels terrible. He is torn. *Indeciso.*"

Tomás wiped his eyes on his sleeves, turned away to fight more tears.

"I want to meet her," said Bloom. "Your girlfriend. And I want to meet the baby, too."

Diaz translated. Tomás' eyes were still moist.

"No names. Girlfriend or baby," said Diaz.

"*Sí*," said Bloom. "Same rules."

"It's okay," said Trudy. Her instincts were solely based on how Bloom treated her when he wrote the profile. His auras were blue—good principles and maybe some psychic talent. Bloom cared. She remembered him sitting in her kitchen, how he settled in, made the transition from professional to person before her eyes.

Tomás took an unsteady breath, muttered to Diaz.

"He doesn't want to put his girlfriend in trouble," said Diaz.

"It's to show how this impacts families," said Bloom. "That families are being ripped apart, that babies will grow up without fathers. And it's about our two countries. About getting along. It's what Tom Lamott was saying."

Bloom followed Trudy's pickup, with Tomás and Diaz on board, to Riverside Meadows, a quarter-mile south.

Tomás went inside to smooth the way while Trudy, Bloom, and Diaz huddled under a tree. A skinny calico cat stepped out from a gap in the wood skirt that covered the gap between mobile home and ground. It promptly plopped down on a patch of grass in the shade. A distant air conditioner whirred. The sun felt as if it had decided on a day trip to visit the moon.

It suddenly occurred to Trudy that Tomás lived in the same community with the same roads and buildings but had to go through the day with his head down, hoping to stay invisible. It was half a life, or less.

"I've got a question for you," said Bloom.

"Okay," said Trudy. "I guess. But not about my business."

"No," said Bloom. "Allison."

Trudy waited. Every time others mentioned Allison's name, Trudy knew they wanted a piece of her friend.

"Yes?" said Trudy when Bloom failed to fill the void.

"Is she around?"

"I don't keep close tabs," said Trudy. She wished Allison had a permanently embedded GPS. There had been times when Allison disappeared for days.

"I'd like to talk to her about what she found up on the building," said Bloom. "The roof. That's all. Plus, it would be nice to come up, if you want to know the truth. To look at the sky up there. Down here, you almost feel like you're in a hole. The day I spent with you and Allison—well, it's locked in my memory forever."

Trudy knew how guys looked at Allison.

"We're not gate keepers for the Flat Tops," said Trudy. "But I doubt Allison would talk about what she did for the police. I can ask her—"

"Please," said Bloom.

Tomás' girlfriend stepped from the mobile home and sat down on the middle of the three-step entrance. Tomás followed. She wore a white T-shirt with an oversized basketball across the front. A white cap with a large visor shaded her face. Bits of hesitant female Spanish floated across the still, hot space. She held the baby in a thin white wrap.

Candy's expression was inscrutable. She stared off and on at Bloom. This should be a simple yes or no, Trudy figured, but the back-and-forth between Tomás and Candy lasted longer than she would have expected.

There was an unexpected hiccup. Something had changed. Trudy felt like she was intruding. Candy peeled the wrap back like a banana and revealed the top of her baby's head, kissed her gently.

Tomás headed their way, head down.

"Something's up," said Bloom. "Though you don't need a translator to tell you that."

Tomás fought off tears. But he was smiling, too. He took a deep breath, blew it out with puffed-up cheeks, put his head down and then he was beside them, gathering himself. He gave a fist pump at mid-chest like a coach exhorting a team to do its best. Despite the tumble of emotions, Trudy sensed the bottom line was something good. Underneath it all, Tomás looked relieved. He gave the news in two rapid-fire sentences to Diaz, who replied with a one-word question.

"*¿Aquí?*"

Tomás took a breath. "*Sí,*" he said.

"It's Alfredo," said Diaz, summing up. "While Tomás was out with us, Alfredo turned up. Last night he was out, alone. He was hiding and running. He was being held somewhere. He really needs a doctor and he is very, very afraid."

TWENTY-SEVEN:
WEDNESDAY, MID-DAY

LATE SUMMER RASPBERRIES HUNG on the bush, dabs of bright and pale red. Allison grazed her way around the edge, ate enough to call it a light meal. Juice burst in her mouth, a delicate balance of tart and sweet. The berries could have used a bowl of vanilla ice cream. She wished she could pick a few pints and bring them to Trudy for jam or compote.

It was high noon. She'd seen elk sign, but nothing fresh.

Actual elk? *Nada.*

Actual deer? Double *nada.*

Any mammal worthy of a hunt? She may as well have been scouting in Times Square.

When she had passed Lumberjack Camp an hour ago, she had stopped for a long stare, using the vista up the hill as a movie backdrop and imagining chase scenes playing out, scenes from National Geographic specials, the ones she watched as a kid with cheetahs flashing across the African savannah, streaking low and so fast the background was an indecipherable smudge of green grasses. The scenes had scared the crap out of her. She'd cover her eyes whenever the cat leapt at the wildebeest or other frightened prey of the day. The ten-minute stare down of the area around Lumberjack produced no such imaginary documentary that was credible. It was all science fiction, B-grade stuff. At least the mountain lion problem and the half-corpse question had taken her mind off Kerry London and his evil proposition.

Back on Sunny Boy, she worked her way out to the broad east-west plateau.

East would take her back past Lumberjack and offer a straight return to Sweetwater in plenty of time to check on progress around the barn. West, more scouting.

Allison chose south. A rocky high point beckoned. The ridge jutted into the valley like the prow of the *Titanic*. She tied Sunny Boy to the largest tree in a small thicket of aspens. An animal trail snaked up the treeless east side of the high knoll. The valley floor dropped away. Allison let her thoughts tumble and drift.

The half-corpse drew the most hits, with the rooftop of the apartment building a close second. She observed the ideas from a distance, found a way to not let them gnaw.

Blue flax dominated the route up, other than the usual green smudge of late-summer grasses. She inhaled with her eyes. If a wildflower bloomed on a hillside and nobody was there to see it, was it really color?

The ridge top was no wider than a country road. The opposite side dropped farther and steeper than the one she'd climbed.

The knife edge narrowed down to sidewalk width at the prow of the rock ship. The view opened her heart. The view was real and the view cared nothing about her trivial woes. She didn't exist. The view sent the same message it had delivered when she first plunged into the Flat Tops. *You ain't nothing.* She was meant to be here, at this spot and at this point in time. She would look for elk, sure, as soon as she took in everything else.

She wondered what this spot looked like as the mountain ranges crumbled, as seas moved in and receded, as the land masses took after each other in their slow-motion demolition derby. Basalt from volcanic eruptions formed the Flat Tops, but the geological violence that shaped it was impossible to picture. If the resulting evidence of their clash was this beauty, and its dense kaleidoscope of nature, let a million more battles commence. What was impossible to accept was that the scene before her was changing, evolving still. That the continents were relaxing between rounds in their respective corners, getting water squirted into their mouth and their cuts patched while they waited for the next round in the ring. She was watching evolution. Time ticked. Sand dripped. Rocks eroded. Gene codes cooked, stewed, adapted. The universe, said the experts, was flying apart. In three billion years, this would all be ice. Somewhere out there were elk, deer, big horn sheep, bears, coyotes, rabbits, porcupines, chipmunks, squirrels, mice, voles, beaver, muskrats and every kind of bird and waterfowl that enjoyed a lush, elevated alpine climate and a hundred million or billion bugs at the bottom of the food chain. Her kind of melting pot. But Allison's view was wonderfully inert, a still-life landscape for some future painter to add the life forms. How could 30,000 elk hide so easily? Or 80,000 deer?

The sun was high, set to braise. Late summer days at elevation in the mountains rarely carried the ferocity, say, of the New Jersey shore boardwalk. Allison thought she could sit there all day, the air temperature matching her skin.

What about this thing called work? If human activity was low, there was always the possibility of spotting elk out for a graze. She popped a Fig Newton like a happy pill and scanned the broad valley through binoculars, encouraging any brown, four-legged mammals to move a muscle. Nothing. She lay prone, her forearms stiff like iron pipes. She looked a mile down the valley. She inched her way along, trying to accomplish in minutes something that might have taken hours on horseback.

If she got lucky.

The vast view overwhelmed her. It sank into her marrow. Her whole system smiled. The scene was either pure design or pure art, take your pick. Or maybe some magic combination of both, a seamless marriage of expression and purpose, of soul and brain. Surely the vista couldn't be improved. It was a life-giving, life-producing valley that spoke to her like the finest music, the most moving art. It confirmed her humanity and at the same time, made her thoroughly forget it.

Was she being selfish? Greedy? The question towered up over her like a sudden dark cloud. Coincidentally, Allison noted the shaft of a blue-black thunderhead that had encroached on the otherwise unblemished western horizon. The cloud appeared to be an alien renegade, an interloper who drifted into the wrong party on the wrong block in the wrong city on the wrong planet. It looked fat and loaded.

"Scram," said Allison.

The thought ground into her—the happy loner was by definition selfish. She was keeping all this to herself. She had re-wrapped herself in a precious cocoon and wasn't going to allow one strand to come unraveled. Colin fit fine inside her tight little world because she had found him there. Trudy fit fine inside her tight little world because she had found her there. Trudy belonged, a natural student of the earth.

All other would-be intruders had to be checked at the door or go through the kind of months-long physical and mental shakedown that would scare away even the most determined suitor. By definition, she was selfish. Snarling at Kerry London had proved the point. She was so determined to keep her world intact and she was so dead set on getting herself drunk on Flat Tops serenity as frequently as possible that she was really no better than a desperate junkie, a gun in one hand and a knife in the other, guarding her last score.

The big question ahead was if she could open up to strangers. If she could commit to Colin, if she could imagine bringing a child into this scary, frightening world and being responsible for its well-being, if she could reconcile with the city and all its crazy crap.

Choosing to ignore the dark blotch on the high horizon, Allison aimed the binoculars along the edge of the forest, where the open meadows gave way to dark dense timber. She scoured the nooks and crannies, the transition areas. She willed elk from their hiding. She drilled holes through the dim corners with her X-ray vision. Soon, she would have to return to Sunny Boy and the less efficient method of scouting from bush to bush, tree to tree on horseback.

Out of the waves of green and brown, a flickering orange-red dot.

Flickering orange meant only one thing. Flickering and dancing orange confirmed it was the one thing. With her naked eye, the dot didn't register. Had her survey position been an inch to the left or right, the dot might have been obscured by a tree. The dot was more than a mile away, maybe two. It was hard to gauge its size, but at least it wasn't growing. And that meant it was being tended and that meant campers or scouts and human activity and that meant the odds plummeted for seeing elk or deer in this stretch of the Flat Tops.

Allison scrambled down quickly, no melancholy good-bye to her precious view. Sunny Boy was happy to see her—ears gently forward, a relaxed whinny. His ears said it: *what's next?* They rode up the throat of the valley, a wary eye on the darkening cloud, now producing intermittent flashes of jagged white cracks that connected ridge and cloud. The flashes were silent and carried no clout.

"Stay put," she told the storm. "Or, at least, hold your horses."

As if in spite, the air cooled and the treetops swayed like they'd been kicked in the gonads. The light dimmed. Allison caught a whiff of smoke. She tied Sunny Boy to a thick fir. Now that she was near the orange dot, she had the gut-grab sensation that she didn't like the firestarters. But since the fire was a fire and she wanted to make sure it was being tended and didn't pose further risk, she was obliged to investigate. It was her duty, given the badge she'd pinned on her chest and the silent oath she'd administered to herself.

The fire sat in a neat fire ring, minding its own business. Its flames were waist-high, bending a bit to the oncoming wind. No Hollywood special effects expert could have created a more typical, well-groomed campfire. It must have been recently fed or tended, but the camp looked empty. No pots or dishes rattled in the small canvas wall tent. If someone had gone to the trouble of building the fire, then why wasn't it being used or enjoyed? The camp looked old and well-worn, but it wasn't on Allison's radar. It was fifty yards off the main valley, tucked away. Private. Every bone in her body said get the fuck out.

But there was the fire, ridiculously perky and cheerful, waiting for a circle of hunters or cowboys and bottle of Wild Turkey or Patrón Silver, her new favorite.

"Help you?"

The man stood by the opening to the tent, but Allison hadn't seen the flap open.

"Saw the fire," said Allison. "Going down the valley. Saw the fire back in here."

"Hiking?"

"My horse is—" She gestured over her shoulder with her thumb. "I've got a horse. Saw the fire."

"Fire's not going anywhere," said the man.

"I can see that," said Allison.

And in my permit area, she wanted to say.

The man was a beefy six-footer. Even so, his head was disproportionately large with thick curls of gray hair and matching muttonchops. His cheeks could have been stuffed with acorns. His jaw was slack and his mouth didn't look like it ever closed. He wore a navy baseball hat with a round insignia in white but it was too small and too far away to read the words. It had a quasi-military look. He wore green camo pants, thick brown boots and a maroon pull-over, the sleeves yanked up to his elbows, revealing weightlifter forearms. He could probably pick her up one-handed for a chat like she was Fay Wray.

"We like it neat," he said. No offer of an introduction.

"Do I hear female?"

A second man from the tent was taller and had gaunt cheeks and pinched, deep-set eyes. His blue-jean jacket had a large American Flag patch over the front pocket. He wore a black baseball cap that said "iPack" in the same font as all the Apple gear. His neck was heron-long.

She didn't like the camp. She didn't like them. She also didn't like the fact that they had both managed to quietly emerge from the tent and she hadn't heard a grunt, a fart, a cough, a clang, a step, or a word. She hadn't interrupted a Buddhist sit. They weren't opening the hand to thought. Every follicle in her scalp buzzed with alarm.

"You're a long way from home," said the second man. Was he implying he knew who she was?

"On horseback," said Allison.

"We've already covered this," said the first man. "She's got a horse around here somewhere. Guess he's shy."

Allison did a fast-scan check of the camp. No bows. No quivers. No black powder guns. The ground around the tent looked well-trampled. Steady use had pushed the forest back. She saw a hitching rail and turned slightly to double-check—it was a double-wide rail with room for ten or a dozen horses. The apron of dirt around the well-trampled camp was, in fact, covered in horse tracks. Two horses stood at the rail for now. A crooked blaze gave one horse a lopsided-look. A small star dotted the forehead on the other, a chestnut Spanish Mustang.

Sunny Boy opted right then to issue a call of boredom or alarm, a forceful but distant whinny. Maybe he'd known she was studying other horses.

"There's your guy now," said the second man. "Why did you tie him up so far?"

"No reason," said Allison. "Just wasn't sure what this fire was all about. I guess I'll be on my way."

The men were inert. There wasn't a welcoming gesture between the two of them. Maybe she needed to leave before someone else arrived. Their beefy silhouettes didn't reek of *Brokeback Mountain*, but the thought flashed. The inhospitable undertones reeked of conspiracy, not love.

"Glad to see the fire has an owner," said Allison. "You guys have a good one."

Allison had the distinct feeling that the tent held another warm body or two, that they were guarding something or somebody. Backwoods etiquette wasn't exactly in the well-established protocols of say, a White House dinner, but she'd venture to say that in the chapter covering chance encounters it was considered polite to offer coffee, water or a scrap of something edible. Staring and glowering were likely listed as *don'ts*. Allison got their message, no semaphore decoder needed.

To add to the chilly reception, the sun blinked off. It wasn't a slow fade. It was if someone had turned down the Flat Tops rheostat setting from noon to dusk with a twist of the hand, no different that dimming a dining room chandelier so mom could walk in with the birthday cake all aglow. The accompanying chill was instant. Wind cut through the woods with a cold bite and the flames in the fire pit cowered like a scared puppy. Embers fired horizontally across the camp like red bullets. The sky went black.

The men didn't flinch.

Allison wanted to peek inside Tent Sing Sing but had the sensation it would be easier to penetrate Fort Knox.

"Something's moving in," said Allison.

"Or already has," said muttonchops. Maybe he liked good news.

Allison gave a two-finger salute from the brim of her hat and instantly felt like a dumb cliché. She turned to head back, ignoring the holes being drilled in her back by their stares. She scanned the ground before the bare dirt gave way to forest floor. There were plenty of horse tracks but there were smaller, equally distinct marks too.

Canines.

Everywhere.

TWENTY-EIGHT:
WEDNESDAY, MID-DAY

As far as Bloom was concerned, being inside was progress, but not enough. He sat with Trudy at the small dining table. One of two women buzzing around—Bloom wasn't clear of their relationship with Tomás—had brought him *horchata de melon*. The tasty drink had a hint of vanilla and lime but it couldn't counteract the heat of the mobile home.

Tomás played the role of shuttle diplomat, scurrying between the kitchen and the back room. Bloom had yet to see Alfredo, but the scraps of information from Tomás, doled out in bits and pieces, were plenty vivid. Bloom knew he wouldn't write a word or trust a word until he had seen Alfredo in the flesh.

But he couldn't wait all day.

Twice he had punched off his cell phone when Coogan had called. Bloom texted his reply: "Heck of a lead. Will call soon."

Coogan expected tight communication. Bloom was taking a gamble. If the cops had a breakthrough and were about to announce something, Coogan was screwed. His only other option would be to instantly inject Marjorie Hayes with hard news skills and hard news touch. So, really, there was no other option.

Police bulletin or not, he didn't want to stop watching Trudy. Her entire essence focused on the health of Alfredo Loya. Bloom knew the phrase "give your undivided attention" from dozens of grade school teachers, but he now knew precisely what that phrase meant. Trudy did one thing at a time. When she spoke, words flowed from a calm center. Her mood owned the room. Alfredo Loya trusted her. Tomás trusted her. Tomás' girlfriend Candy was the last to fall under her spell.

From what Bloom could gather, Tomás' girlfriend knew someone who knew someone who knew a doctor who could come to help. Tomás' girlfriend wasn't going to settle down until Alfredo was receiving medical care. Still, Trudy kept calm. She was the first visitor escorted back to see Alfredo. Maybe they thought she could sprinkle some magic dust on his wounds.

Bloom waited, wondered if he was making a mistake. Should he call Coogan? Check in? Tell him what he'd come across? He was torn—with the police now working every angle imaginable from every resident in Glenwood Manor, it would be easy to miss a breaking story if he stayed with this odd tangent. But Alfredo had a story. Every instinct told Bloom to stay put.

Surely how he handled this situation today could help him get invited to Trudy's kitchen again and possibly manage another encounter with the enigmatic Allison. Trudy would be his ticket. Possibly. And if nothing else he would have Trudy's friendship. He didn't want to overlook that possibility. But Allison Coil was the one he wanted to unlock.

"It's not too bad," said Trudy. Her expression hadn't changed. She smiled like she was greeting a long lost friend. "Bruises, a sprained ankle, not severe. Exhaustion more than anything."

Bloom nodded, made sure she was finished. "I need to talk with him directly."

"I explained," said Trudy. "With the girlfriend's help, of course. Right now he's scared. He feels cornered."

"I need ten minutes," said Bloom. "Maybe fifteen. Of course I'd like more, but that would be enough for starters."

"He won't be here long," said Trudy. A moment of genuine concern flashed across her face. "Tomás figures they'll know to come here, to look for Alfredo."

"Who?" said Bloom.

"The people who picked him up," said Trudy. "Alfredo said he was in a jail of some sort with others, too. People were giving orders. It was organized."

"I need a few minutes," said Bloom. Already the story was writing itself in his head.

Bloom's cell phone rang.

"We're thinking of taking him up to my place," said Trudy.

And what if Alfredo' captors were legitimate, some official branch of ICE? Or similar? Then wouldn't Trudy be aiding and abetting?

"I'll take my chances," said Trudy, who must have read Bloom's mind. "Something isn't right."

"I want to talk with him before you move him," said Bloom, ignoring the phone. "I can't come to your place. Not today or tonight, anyway."

"Let me ask him," said Trudy.

Bloom glanced at his Caller ID. Coogan.

"Yes," said Bloom, standing and letting himself out of the mobile home. He stepped down three metal steps to the street and the heat. Two boys kicked around a soccer ball, taking aim at imaginary goals on the asphalt.

"Cops are holding a big-deal news conference right now on the steps of City Hall. How far away are you?"

Five minutes, thought Bloom. If he had a bridge or a zip line straight across the river, even less.

"I'll swing by there as soon as I'm finished," said Bloom.

"Where are you?" Coogan's voice snapped with authority, a certain *pissed-offness.*

"I'm outside the door of a guy who was picked up by ICE or by someone and tossed into a holding cell," said Bloom. "He's illegal—undocumented, anyway. And he escaped. He's going to tell me the whole story here in two minutes."

"Cops have a person of interest," said Coogan. "We need all the details on the website eight seconds after the news conference ends."

Maybe Kerry London would let Bloom view the whole raw footage from whatever the cops had to announce. Maybe DiMarco would tell him if this was a genuine lead or pure smokescreen. Maybe his ass was in a sling or halfway out the door and he didn't know it.

"I'm on it," said Bloom.

"*The Denver Post* has already sent out a news alert and the *New York Times* has a teaser on their site," said Coogan. "I will not be the caboose on this fucking train."

Coogan was ramped up, but he said it with all the matter-of-fact narration of a civil war documentary on public television.

The line went dead.

TWENTY-NINE:
WEDNESDAY AFTERNOON

Turned toward the barn, Sunny Boy perked up.

Sunny Boy was about to be seriously disappointed.

Allison made it look good. In case she was being followed or watched, she did everything by the book for a quarter mile, then stopped and went through a long exercise of pretending to adjust the fit on Sunny Boy's saddle, all while catching glimpses back the way she had come, to see if she had company.

Nobody.

An Engelmann spruce made for good cover and provided a post for Sunny Boy deep under a broad canopy.

"Looks like rain, big fella," she told him. "Maybe worse."

She tied a halter hitch, sure that the sight of it was giving Sunny Boy the lone horse blues. The sky scowled.

The wind at ground level was steady. It was cooler, stiffer. August in the Flat Tops was only August when it wasn't performing dynamite impersonations of September or October. On the Flat Tops, the season blender was set to puree.

The key was to maintain a bearing. She had kept careful track of distance. She needed to cruise along a parallel track in the woods back to asshole muttonchops and his buddy and get the real story. Allison had seen a hundred hunter camps and met hundreds of hunters. She had never met a twosome as dripping with secrets.

The woods were clean and open, as if the forest floor enjoyed regular maid service, all swept and tidy. No blow-down timber to hurdle, no creeks to cross, only serene stretches of well-spaced spruce and fir, a soft carpet of pine needle droppings and mulched-up tree detritus. The smell was seductive.

The first rain drops suggested it was best to stay focused. The drops were cold and intermittent. They exploded around her feet like sniper fire. Her jean jacket took a couple of hits, her hat took a dull, wet *thwack*. The water bullets bordered on hail. As soon as she thought the word, pea-size marshmallows started dancing off the forest floor and pinged her hat with purpose.

Hang tight, Sunny Boy, she thought. *Hang tight.*

She slowed. Her internal GPS suggested she was getting close. Something about the change of the slope, the mix of trees. She was nearing the place where Sunny Boy had been abandoned the first time. Open valley to her left. She found herself crouched as she ran, head low like she was bracing to bash a brick wall. The hail spat thicker and she told herself she'd take no more than twenty minutes. More than that would be unfair to all horses everywhere.

Allison slowed to a careful walk. A patch of aspen felt familiar. The view through the woods clouded up in a wet, white misty gauze. A tank crashing through the woods at full torque probably wouldn't be heard amid the pounding shrapnel from the sky. By comparison to the heavy artillery, her footsteps were like a squirrel doing a grand plié. She couldn't hear her own footfalls amid the ground level thunder.

Hail—good for sound-proofing her approach, bad for boosting the chances that muttonchops and his sidekick would be outside doing much of anything.

The camp popped into view. Had the men been standing around the fire, which was struggling to retain its dignity, she would have been easily spotted. But the camp was empty, the formerly dirt hard pack apron around the fire pit now layered in white like an oversized doily.

The hail relented. For a moment, at least, calm was restored. The outer ring of the storm had passed, but there was more to come. She stepped back into the woods and found cover, laying low behind a lodge pole with Sumo-respectable girth.

Rain replaced the hail. Steady, but not as threatening.

Fifteen minutes more in this spot, ten back to Sunny Boy.

Home for a late dinner and then raid her stash of tequila and she'd thank the crew for their hard work and no doubt on the return trip she would spot fresh elk trails or maybe the real thing and no doubt her day would feel like a complete success, including the part where she figured out what these backwoods assholes had in mind and including the part where there was a speedy report back from the cops about the half-corpse and all would be revealed.

"It's over."

The voice was male and the words were uttered simultaneously as its owner stepped from the tent.

New guy.

He was dressed for a U.S. Marine assault of Corregidor and vastly overdressed for a hunt—or any camping activity—in Colorado in August. Complete fatigues, head to toe. Baseball-style cap with a long camo brim. Black boots.

"Ten minutes of bluster," he said for the benefit of others inside the tent. "We're fine."

Allison brought up the binoculars. The hat bore the same insignia as what she'd seen earlier. This guy had a solid nose familiar to a dozen Mediterranean countries but the first one that came to mind was Greece. A proud nose. His skin was dark. He wore sunglasses that fit tight to his face, narrow strips of lenses no wider than fat Band-Aids but green-black and shiny. With her high school trigonometry and a wild-ass guess, Allison put him at six-two and 225 pounds. Fit, not fat.

"Let's wait. No rush." Not every word was crisply enunciated, but that was the gist of what Allison had heard. And her sense of it was confirmed by the retort from the man who had come out to check the weather.

"Come on, Dillard, get your ass out here. It's over and done. Like springtime all over again out here."

The man took three steps to the fire and gave it a sideways karate kick, stirring up the struggling embers in a hornet's nest of swirling red flecks. One fact couldn't be disputed—the camp was well-established. Undergrowth doesn't get obliterated in one week or two of trampling around. The camp was neatly hidden, too. It was deep enough within the forest to be hard to be spot by the occasional passerby. Then, why the fire? Maybe they'd gotten cocky.

"Just a passing little hail deal, Dillard. Let's get a move on."

Dillard was muttonchops. "Thought the world was ending there for a minute or two," he said.

"Fuck it, man, it's only hail. Always sounds like hell. It's over."

Allison didn't have to look to know the sky was still cast-iron black. She doubted the man's primary occupation was meteorology.

Allison dropped the binoculars. Dillard carried a bow in his left hand. It was camo green and gray. It was one of those compound bows that looked fiendish and overly complicated. Dillard strapped on a pack and a quiver that appeared full.

Where was Mr. American Fat dude? How come he hadn't come out to join the weather forecasting? He couldn't have gone far.

Five more minutes…from now, she told herself.

Horses were good at waiting. Boyfriends, too. Could she step away from the camp as easily as she arrived? A minute ago, it was as loud as a jet engine, not that she cared to think about jets. Now it was as quiet as a country road at dawn. Her exit would have to be a model of stealth.

"Go check and see if they're close," said not-Dillard. "Bring the binos."

Allison couldn't see any eye-rolling, but she could feel Dillard's reluctance to take orders. The first man kicked the fire while Dillard went back inside the tent and, a minute later, returned and headed straight out of the camp on the opposite side from where Allison watched.

Her heart thudded. Her lips and tongue dried at the same rate as a snowflake in the Sahara. Not-Dillard stared at the fire, didn't bother to look at the sky above, which had the same patina as, say, coal. She should slip away now and spend the rest of the night admonishing her paranoid brain.

Or not. What could be observed so far wasn't illegal, bad or in any way reportable. The way her alarms raged, like fireworks, was a different story

Dillard wasn't gone long. He was trailed by two drenched cowboys on horseback in full body slickers. They dripped water and their horses looked like they they'd come through a car wash. On a long tether behind the horses were four dogs on a group harness. All muzzled. And all equally soaked. All the dogs were a breed, or mix, that Allison didn't recognize. Maybe a bit of Bloodhound in their droopy ears and wrinkled snouts. Maybe a bit of Walker in their determined, eager looks.

If there was anything sinister going on, the dogs were the only indication. Dogs don't hunt without snow and tracks. Dogs don't come with hunters in archery season. Dogs are unpredictable, make noise. They aren't necessary. They don't help. The dogs added to the bizarre platter of issues that turned Allison's stomach sour.

Five minutes more? From now?

It wasn't likely they were about to stand around the fire and discuss the rest of the day's planned activities for her benefit.

The two new men were cut from the same stock as the fatigue-clad nameless dude. One was white and he had the pink-pale complexion of a purebred Scandinavian, complete with diamond-blue eyes visible only with the aid of the binoculars. The second man was as brown as the first man was white. Allison raised the binos again to double-check the Hispanic features—a broad, round face with full cheeks, black eyes and thick dark eyebrows like two fuzzy caterpillars. Allison guessed he was fifty; a bit of gray dabbed his hair below the wet cowboy hat. The new white guy mumbled something Allison couldn't hear, although the general tone berated the others. Something about complaining about the storm.

It started to rain again—a solid shower—and a fresh round of squawks erupted from the foursome. Dillard headed to the tent and the others weren't far behind. Dogs, too. That made four grown wet men and four wet dogs in one medium-size canvas wall tent. Allison could only imagine the disarray and the stench, particularly after one or two inevitable cigars were torched.

The show was over. Allison stayed low as she backed away from the camp, but didn't wait long to stand up and start heading back, picking up her pace in the pouring rain. She chose her return route by feel. She ran to make up time or at least create a good impression for Sunny Boy when she arrived. Surely being out of breath would show she cared. She didn't want him to think she'd been dawdling.

The spot where she thought she'd left Sunny Boy must have had an identical twin, although it was odd that the exact match would exist so close—almost as if an adult had his doppelganger living next door. There was the same indent. There was the same pattern of trees. She was expecting to see a large brown mammal—and thinking about how to respond to his recriminations—that at first she didn't see the stub of cotton rope, dangling there as if the tree had a white, braided and flaccid penis. The rope had been neatly chopped, perhaps the work of a hatchet. As quickly as she processed the fact that the Sunny Boy was gone, she realized they might be watching and waiting for her, too. She flinched and ducked, quickly darted back into deep cover.

No shot came.

Allison slowed to a walk and waited, turned and looked again.

Nothing.

She sat in the woods, stared out at the broad and empty valley in the distance.

She waited, watched. Waited some more. Listened. Stared. Took a breath. When nothing moved, she slipped back to the spot where Sunny Boy had waited, studied the grasses and occasional bare patches, thinking a print might show what direction he had headed.

The soaked grasses yielded nothing.

Inventory didn't take long.

Binos, jean jacket, blue jeans, hat, bra, underwear, socks and boots. There might be a Fig Newton tucked in a stray pocket, but she didn't want to look. Not yet. She found Colin's atlatl tucked in an inside pocket, didn't realize she'd been carrying it.

And no arrows.

Water? Real food? Horse? None of the above.

Cell phone? In Sunny Boy's saddlebag.

Miles to cover? Seven or eight.

Hours of daylight left? Three at the most.

Rain re-doubled its lashing, added weight to her hat and dripping onto the back of her jacket.

The moment was tailor made for one of Colin's favorite lines.

Welcome to the suck.

THIRTY:
WEDNESDAY, LATE
AFTERNOON

"He's a fugitive," said Jerry. "You can't harbor a fugitive. I don't know why they call it *harbor* but, you know, protect. Hide."

"It doesn't sound like any kind of justice system I know," said Trudy. She was ready for him, had predicted this reaction. She tried to stay calm. "He needs a few days of hot soup. He's banged up."

Jerry sat in the office like he ran the place, which he did. It was his desk, his chair, his place to be comfortable.

"I can tell that much," said Jerry. "And you know it hurts me too, to see him like this."

Even in fresh jeans and a new blue Down to Earth T-shirt, anyone could see Alfredo was a beaten man. He kept his left palm over his left eye and his head was drooped. This was a brief stopover on the way to the Flat Tops and her house, where Alfredo could get well and where Duncan Bloom would come soon for the full interview. Diaz had negotiated every detail and had talked Alfredo out of catching the next ride south.

"Whoever they are," said Jerry. "You don't want these folks to find Alfredo at your place. Or here."

Jerry's tone was relaxed. He understood the need to make Tomás feel unthreatened.

In bits and pieces, Trudy had picked up the story of Alfredo's terrifying day and night. Before she told Jerry the whole story, Trudy took a moment to corral her emotions. If she showed too much, she knew Jerry would be all the more likely to stay on the fence or, worse, disagree with her plan. But she thought his empathy would grow once he heard the details.

Alfredo had been plucked from the street on the way back from fishing with his brother. He was blindfolded, shoved down low on the floor of the van. He was cuffed. They had driven at high speeds, certainly on the highway. Not too long after they slowed down, maybe ten minutes, they put him inside a windowless room, removed his cuffs and told him he could take off the blindfold only after he heard the door shut. He was given water and three small slices of American cheese. When he needed the bathroom, he was blindfolded again. One of his jailers spoke fluent Spanish. After dusk, they told him he would be released. It was all a mistake. They had checked his background and he was fine. But Alfredo knew he was not legal, had no green card. Their claim made him nervous. On the trip back, the van blew a tire on the highway. He was still blindfolded, but not cuffed. He was sure it was night. When the van stopped for the flat, he half wondered if it was some sort of trick. He had heard the van's sliding door open, but not close. From the voices, the three men were all outside the van and even with the blindfold he risked wriggling out from the back seat and running for it. He slammed into the guardrail and fell over and rolled down a long hill. He ended on some rocks, heard the men shouting and thought he'd landed on a riverbed. He guessed he was between New Castle and Glenwood Springs. He remembered the train tracks. The men came down the hill with flashlights and Alfredo had to make his way downstream until they gave up. He waited an hour in a river-bank bush, soaking wet and growing colder until he felt safe to start working his way back to Glenwood, occasionally waiting for a freight train to pass.

"Sounds like a bunch of vigilantes," said Jerry. "He never got told anything official, was never shown an immigration badge, an ICE ID, nothing?"

"Blindfolds?" said Trudy. "Secret rooms? I have this friend with the newspaper and he called every official agency out there and there was no report of an escape. Nothing."

Alfredo was their employee. They were responsible. She couldn't flush him from her mind. Stray dogs and cats were treated better than Alfredo.

"Did Alfredo tell them where he worked?" said Jerry.

"He told them he was here on a visit, that he was a legal visitor and could produce his passport if needed," said Trudy. "It was a lie, but that's what he told them."

"So you don't think they can put two and two together, ask around, and come for you?" said Jerry. "They might know where he lived."

"Crossed my mind," said Trudy. "But then they would have to show their faces."

"And if they are legit—you know ICE powers seem to shift every few weeks. What then? I'm only trying to think this through."

He was the logic. She was the instinct. It was a successful balance, though at times she translated his "help" as stiff reluctance to change. It was easy to see he wasn't enthusiastic about any of this.

"All I know is he needs my help," said Trudy. "He's agreed to tell his story to a reporter—"

"A reporter?" There was an edge this time. "The same one?"

"Yes," said Trudy.

In reality, Duncan Bloom had heard all the details. He was going to come up for a more formal interview and review all the details. Alfredo had final approval on what went in print. She might need Juan Diaz to help as interpreter, although maybe Bloom would bring his own.

"Using his real name?" said Jerry.

"No names," said Trudy. "Or identifying pictures."

Jerry found a loose paper clip on his desk, started torturing it.

"Big leap of faith."

"The reporter is a good guy," said Trudy.

"Sometimes the reporter has editors who aren't so hospitable."

"We'll see," said Trudy. "You've got to trust at some point. Don't you?"

"I trust the reporter more than the government," said Jerry. "But that isn't saying a whole heck of a lot. So how long are you going to take care of him?"

"Until he gets his legs back under him," said Trudy. "It's like he's been dragged by a truck down a rocky road."

Ever so slightly, Alfredo moaned, let out a breath of pain.

"He might need a hospital," said Jerry. "What if he has internal injuries?"

"If he gets a fever, maybe," said Trudy.

"Okay then," said Jerry. "What can I do?"

"Give me a few days to stay with him," said Trudy.

Jerry sighed. "You're awfully popular around here," he said. "You know that. People are always asking for you. They think being around you will rub off in a good way. You inspire them."

"Couple days," said Trudy.

Alfredo sat in the front seat of her pickup. He slumped over like he was asleep. She balled up an old flannel shirt for a pillow, went back in the office to fill a bottle with water and put it in his left hand. "*Agua*," she said. "*Agua fría.*"

She drove through Glenwood Springs realizing that the last thing she needed would be a traffic stop for any reason, big or small. Crossing the bridge, she felt queasiness return as she drove by the spot where Lamott had been shot, now the site of a thick wall of flowers, signs, and banners. She wished she had the nerve to take Alfredo to the hot springs. He could use a soak.

Trudy pointed the pickup east, up the canyon. She drove like she had a precious egg rolling loose in the back and she couldn't afford to break it.

Which, in some ways, was exactly the case.

THIRTY-ONE:
WEDNESDAY, LATE
AFTERNOON

PERSON OF INTEREST.

Bloom hated the phrase, something so unofficial about it. Wyatt Earp wouldn't have gone looking for a *person of interest.* He would have picked up on the bad guy's trail and tracked his ass down.

Person of interest for someone who shot a U.S. Senate candidate with a high-powered rifle from three hundred yards? The label was too wimpy. Bloom decided he wouldn't use it, no matter the headline in the police department's news release.

He had made it to the department in time for the assembled phalanx of cops to announce that they weren't taking any more questions. DiMarco wasn't there, but Bloom had tailed Kerry London back to his news truck and begged for a favor. Between the replay of the eight-minute news conference footage, the news release and a quick call to DiMarco to gauge the cops' degree of certainty about the suspected bad guy, Bloom was making up time like the cartoon roadrunner.

"Glad to help," London had said. "That's what friends are for." London had started to tell him about something that happened up on the Flat Tops with Allison Coil but as much as Bloom wanted to hear it, he waved him off. No time.

Now, it was all about speed—getting the sucker on the web fast enough to make Coogan feel that newspapers based two thousand miles away weren't beating them to the punch on stories in their own backyard.

Bloom finished a three-hundred word recap, four long paragraphs, in four minutes flat. It wasn't pretty, but no one would be expecting a sonnet. When he hit send and gave the news desk a shout, he looked at his watch. It had been 53 minutes since he left the mobile home park and the story of the missing Alfredo Loya. The *Post-Independent* wouldn't be the first, but it also wouldn't be the last.

Undoubtedly, Coogan would want Bloom's full attention on the ensuing manhunt and every inch of progress—or lack thereof.

The cops were looking for a man in his mid to late thirties. He was average height, 5' 10". He was trim, about 160 pounds. He had wiry red hair that curled down over his forehead and ears. When he had been spotted at Glenwood Manor, he had been wearing a dark blue baseball cap. The man had an elongated nose. It was long and it flattened against the rest of his face like he'd run into a brick wall. In the drawing, he had a three-day stubble on his narrow, under-slung jaw. From right below his cheekbones to the corners of his forehead, an art teacher would have drawn a perfect rectangle in demonstrating how to analyze face shapes. From right below his cheek bones to the tip of his jaw, a triangle pointing down. If a drawing could convict, Bloom would have no problem with the legal system. This dude had a brooding, sinister look.

But all other details about his face were subordinated by the face tattoo. The police department news release cautioned that the rendering of the face tattoo was an approximation, but the impression on their sketch was that the man had asked the tattoo artist to draw a grid or spider web over his face. The overall look said *outcast and I know it.* Certainly somebody would recognize the drawing, unless the suspect had been in hiding for the past couple years and only now emerged for the purposes of this shooting.

The cops wouldn't say much about how the composite drawing was produced, whether it was from one eyewitness or several. Bloom had no trouble imagining it came from someone at Glenwood Manor—or several *someones* at Glenwood Manor—who had put two and two together and realized they had seen the shooter and had fallen for a repairman or building inspector ruse or a "friend of a guy on the second floor" story as his ticket into the building.

As if the drawing wasn't enough, the release said he was armed and "extremely" dangerous.

"Thank you for the helpful tidbit," Bloom told the email version of the news release on his computer screen.

Bloom's phone buzzed with a new text—an alert from the *Denver Post* about the cops' announcement. Pulling up his newspaper website, Bloom smiled. His story, albeit brief, was already posted.

DiMarco answered on the sixth ring.

"Playing hard to get?" said Bloom.

"I'm busy," said DiMarco. "Surprised you weren't the lead lemming at the rodent festival."

"Like being there would have added anything," said Bloom. "Maybe I could have experienced in three dimensions what I get electronically from your PR shop. Almost nothing."

"You don't like our drawing?"

"You talking to tattoo artists too?"

"In this country and twenty others," said DiMarco. "For starters."

"The guy could scare the stink off a skunk," said Bloom. "Who spotted him?"

DiMarco laughed. "Same thing the guy from NBC asked. You guys share a certain level of obvious."

"Whoever spotted him got fooled by some set-up, some scheme to get into Glenwood Manor. You're trying not to embarrass."

"We got feelings to consider," said DiMarco. "It's true."

"So they spotted him at the apartment building?" said Bloom. "You're confirming that?"

"What apartment building?" said DiMarco.

Bloom could hear the straight-face snicker in his voice. He let utter silence tell DiMarco he wasn't playing.

"Okay," said DiMarco at last. "How can I help you if you won't tell me which apartment building?"

"Give me a break," said Bloom. "Okay, on background, do you know anything more, where he's from?" The phrase *person of interest* flashed but Bloom refused to utter it. "Seems to me there aren't too many dudes on the planet that look like that."

The shift to chat mode might work. On the other hand, DiMarco knew all the tricks.

"In order," said DiMarco. "No. I don't know. And I agree."

"Guess I have to go down to Glenwood Manor and talk to the residents one by one," said Bloom.

"Knock yourself out," said DiMarco.

Browsing the web as he talked, Bloom found an alert on the NBC web site—Tom Lamott had allegedly responded to a question by squeezing his wife's hand. The doctors were urging caution.

"But I need a favor, too," said Bloom. "You can get my editor's bulldog teeth out of my butt."

"Maybe I think that's a good thing," said DiMarco.

The owner of the bulldog teeth sat at his desk behind a waist-high partition talking with a large man who now had his back to Bloom. The man's shoulders were wide. He had short, carefully-cropped hair. His shirt was blue, but more of a work shirt than business. Coogan's gaze looked submissive. Less bulldog, more puppy.

"Because you don't want me to get fired so you can continue to control the media," said Bloom.

"Right," said DiMarco. "Almost forgot my motivation. At your service."

"I need you to run a license plate," said Bloom. He pulled out his notes, including details Trudy had relayed.

"No magic word?" said DiMarco.

Bloom sighed. "Fuck you," he said.

"That's better," said DiMarco. "Whose plate?"

"I'm trying to find out the *who*," said Bloom. "It goes back to this ICE thing."

"Call ICE," said DiMarco.

"Yeah and then call the Pentagon and ask them how many bullets they own," said Bloom.

"Give me the context," said DiMarco. "Where'd the plate come from?"

"Someone who saw a van in action," said Bloom. "Moving illegals around, I suppose."

"What are you going to do with the information? Don't you have enough to do?" said DiMarco.

"I can multi-task," said Bloom.

"Lay it on me," said DiMarco.

"It's only a partial," said Bloom. "Wouldn't need you if it was a full."

"A partial?" said DiMarco.

"The first half," said Bloom. "CL9."

DiMarco paused. "Could be hundreds," he said.

"Registered in Garfield County or out here somewhere? Eagle County? Connected to a van?"

The man talking with Coogan—talking *to* Coogan—stood. He had world-class jowls and the kind of wide, proud belly that made Bloom think of steakhouses and steaming piles of heavily-buttered mashed potatoes. He had a dark moustache. He didn't smile as he shook Coogan's hand, but something about the space between them said Coogan had lost.

"Might narrow your options," said DiMarco.

"Can you run it for me?"

"What are friends for?" said DiMarco.

"And when you corner Lamott's shooter in some back-alley hell hole, don't bother calling anyone else but me."

"Of course," said DiMarco. "I'm always thinking of you."

Coogan's visitor departed and Coogan had covered half of the ten steps to Bloom's desk.

Bloom hung up.

"What's the afternoon look like?" said Coogan. It wasn't a real question.

"Big question in my mind is how'd they get the composite—who described the man they're after? Thought I'd go to the apartment building, Someone's gotta know who gave the cops the info."

"Keep on it," said Coogan.

"And if it was the apartment building he had to have had help, getting in and out," said Bloom.

One of the whacky theories a conspiracy theorist might concoct was that perhaps the shooter had help diverting the cops to Lookout Mountain—delivering convincing accounts of the shots coming from farther east, up the hill.

"Everything we can get by deadline," said Coogan. "Blow it out. Somebody must have seen this dude."

Coogan's words didn't have the usual zing. He looked like he had been dressed down a notch or two. Bloom was dying to ask for the identity of Coogan's visitor and then thought better to leave well enough alone.

Everyone's got problems, thought Bloom. *Everyone.*

THIRTY-TWO:
WEDNESDAY, LATE
AFTERNOON

Download the spirit of Devo. Be tough, find food, stay hydrated.

Another day, another slog.

The distance wasn't that bad. At the end of the trudge would be Trudy and her kitchen.

Hunger nagged at Allison's insides, but it wasn't true hunger, just a body grumbling about lack of routine. She wasn't that tired, just pissed off she didn't have a horse. She wasn't that wet, but her bone marrow was starting to slosh around.

Sunny Boy.

The dogs.

Dillard.

And company.

Why didn't they come after her? Was she being followed now? Doubtful. She gave an occasional look over her shoulder, but the woods were too wet, too inhospitable.

So why cut the horse loose—or steal it? At least she'd have some good leads for the cops, if they could be bothered.

Allison snaked her way through dense woods, picking her way up slopes packed with dead trees, soaked barkless trunks as slick as black ice. Keeping a straight line was dicey. Continually checking on her bearings, maintaining a set distance from the open valley, was exhausting. She would stick to the cover for another hour or so and then maybe risk making better time in the open, back on the trail.

Allison's legs screamed from the uphill work and her feet, thank you very much, would rather be settled in a pair of stirrups. She didn't take horses for granted, did she? Even at walking speed, they were faster than a human and they made the work look easy. At least, they rarely complained or balked, didn't ask for much in return.

Allison slipped into a semi-trance. Legs moved, brain evaluated the course for the next few steps, legs moved, eyes checked the trajectory against the open field to the south, legs moved. All negative thoughts were banished, cancelled, forbidden. At the mere first syllable of mental complaint, she slashed at the body of the word with a hot sword fresh from the fire. Bad thoughts were not allowed to gain traction. Every step, in truth, was easy. Putting all the steps in a row in one compressed effort was the hard part. She could use a quart of water but she wasn't utterly dry. She wasn't marching off a landing craft at Omaha Beach. She wasn't scaling K-2 without oxygen. She was walking in the Colorado woods in the rain and she'd be home, pending a random mountain lion attack, for dinner. The trance sucked her down, pulled her under into a quiet, small zone where problems were identified, run through triage for a quick and precise evaluation of their true risk factors, and just as quickly dispatched to the back of the waiting line and told to get real.

She pictured in detail, down to the order of the drawers in her dresser, her Iowa childhood bedroom. She went step by step through helping her mother prepare a Sunday roast. She saw the lumps of butter in the mashed potatoes. Allison remembered names from her senior high school class, 73 in all. She made it to 29 when the names went fuzzy and blank. She switched to working on a list of her hometown streets and then thinking with obscene clarity about her parents and the terrific gift they had offered by allowing her to disappear, essentially, into a broad and rugged landscape and step away into another world where her basic functions consisted of riding a horse in the mountain woods of Colorado, helping hunters set up camp after riding a horse in the woods of Colorado and helping hunters pack out their kills by riding a horse in the mountain woods of Colorado.

Except, of course, no horse.

Not this time.

She thought about the half-corpse, went over every detail in her mind, replayed arriving at Lumberjack Camp. She pictured the teenagers. She thought about the half-corpse and the sticks and the houndsman and the trail and then the trail vanishing. She wondered if the Lamott shooting investigation might be closer to done and would that mean they might shift their attention to the half-corpse? She wondered if they gave a shit about the half-corpse, a sad body from the woods with no name and no witnesses and no dramatic cell phone video. The half-corpse had no constituency, no advocates. She wondered if it was fair that certain celebrity shootings and celebrity attempted murders and celebrity murders drew more cop resources than others. If you are going to get murdered and you want your killer caught, she thought, make sure you've got some good public relations buzz before you get whacked.

The trance eased. The rain, too. Sun chewed its way through the raindrops and lit up a high ridge. The footing turned less spongelike. Her body caved to the steady pace of work. She was so tired she might turn Colin down if he asked. But a meal by Trudy and drinks by Mr. Hornitos might put her back in the mood, as long as she wasn't required to perform any Twister-style positions. Why shouldn't every body part end up the day as sore and ready for rehab as all the others? As Colin liked to say, *it doesn't count unless it hurts.*

Allison moved to the open valley. She had seen nobody all afternoon. It was time to declare herself, at least for the moment, unpursued.

She allowed a ten-minute break on a high spot. She scanned the view behind the binoculars, the only useful manmade object in her possession. No elk, no deer, no mountain lions. If all went well, she figured to reach Trudy's front door by 10 p.m., time for a fashionably late dinner in Paris or Athens, if not in the U.S.A.

She scanned ahead too—and quickly found a lone rider on horseback.

Apparition.

Mind playing tricks.

She was in the Sahara and this was a Bedouin in search of his next oasis.

Just because she had thought of Colin in the past ten minutes didn't mean she could conjure him up. The figure was a bouncing dot on the trail, but his riding style was unmistakable, as tall as he could sit and as natural, as one-with-horse as a man could get. The combination of living things was a magical meld. He was coming down a long, straight draw. He was moving in earnest.

The horse had the muddled colors of a dirty roan, like Merlin. Horse and rider disappeared from view as the trail pulled them down out of sight through a thick stand of aspen, shimmering and drenched in the spackled bits of sunlight.

Suddenly, they were right there, the pungent sweat of a horse happy in her nose.

"What the hell—"

With the apparition taking on three-dimensional form and sounding like Colin McKee, every repressed ache came roaring to life.

"You came," said Allison.

"Of course," said Colin.

"How did you know?"

"How did I know what?" Colin's embrace was the hug of the century. "Are you okay?"

"But how did you know?"

"Sunny Boy," said Colin. "He showed up a couple hours ago, winded and worn out. Lead rope had been sliced clean. There was a group out hiking, came across him walking down the trail. Like he was out for a Sunday stroll. They couldn't tie him up or leave him so they turned around and started heading back and when I came across them—"

Colin stopped.

"You were out," said Allison. "Looking."

"I've got some sandwiches," he said. "And water. Plenty. The hikers took Sunny Boy back."

These words were being said over her shoulder. She had his neck in an elbow-powered vice grip.

"Come on," said Colin. "We can ride double."

Inside, her body was singing or dancing. Or smiling. If non-verbal expression was possible, say, by bones.

THIRTY-THREE:
WEDNESDAY EVENING

ALFREDO SLURPED TOMATO-BASIL SOUP with the slow appreciation of a patient monk. He let each swallow settle before taking the next. Three basil leaves floated on top of the hot, creamy slurry. A home-made cheddar scone was ready about the time he had finished half the soup. The next course was a large bowl of gluten-free rigatoni and a simple garlic sauce with chopped zucchini, eggplant, roasted red pepper, and oregano. He would apparently keep eating and drinking as long as she produced food and kept his glass full. His devotion to the task—eating every scone crumb on the plate, leaving the pasta bowl empty except for a glistening sheen of sauce—made her smile inside.

"Full?" Trudy patted her stomach. "*¿Más?*"

"*No más*," he said with a shake of his head. "*Gracias.*"

"*¿Café?*" she said. She remembered somewhere the Mexican word sounded like the French.

"*No, gracias*," he said.

She showed him the front bedroom where he would stay, handed him a fresh set of towels and clothes, selected from the small stash of Jerry's stuff that had accumulated over time. The fit was reasonable.

Alfredo nodded. *Sí. Gracias. Comprendo.* His nerves were obvious. He was still unsure. When he walked, he favored his tender ankle, still swollen. The weak foot's sneaker, a brown running shoe, was loosely tied.

Trudy washed his clothes while he showered and by the time she had cleaned the kitchen, Alfredo was lying down on the couch. She poured a shot of tequila from Allison's stash and he smiled at the smell, offered her a toast. He took a polite sip of the India Pale Ale in the brown bottle but it was not to his liking. Five minutes later, his eyes were closed and he fell asleep on the couch.

Trudy steeped a cup of chamomile spearmint tea and took it to the front porch. A late-August shower had stopped, though another might be gathering over the ridge to the west. For now, the air was refreshing. She felt as if she had snatched someone back from the brink of a black hole. She didn't know precisely what the black hole *was* but it wasn't good. *Let them try to come and get him now*, she thought. Let them come and explain who they were, what government organization they belonged to, or claimed to be with, and then they could have a detailed conversation about their legal basis for pulling Alfredo Loya away from his work, family, and home.

The telephone rang and she tip-toed back inside through the living room, as if footsteps would have been louder than the shrill old-school ring.

It was Jerry.

"Checking on you—and Alfredo."

"Everything's fine," said Trudy. Alfredo, in fact, hadn't moved an eyelash since he had stretched out on the couch. "All that stress. He's sleeping it off."

"And his first decent meal in a long time," said Jerry. "If I know you."

"He's had some food," said Trudy. "Are you coming up tonight?"

"Not at the rate I'm going," said Jerry. "As long as you're okay and as long as you don't think you need me."

There was a chipper attitude to his voice that didn't seem right.

"You're the one who said they might track Alfredo up here."

"Is Allison around?" he asked. "Or any of her crew?"

"They should be, I suppose. Maybe working late up at the barn."

With the long cord on her phone, Trudy could talk and drift into her greenhouse, two steps down off the back of her kitchen. She pinched a dead leaf from a Weeping Fig.

"I'll be up later," said Jerry. "Now that I think about it. Looks to me like we had a great day, based on how tired everyone looks around here."

Daily receipt fluctuations. A favorite topic. In his perfect world, every day would be better than the next, a steadily rising line of income and profits like no other business in history.

"I'll button up here and head your way," said Jerry. "But don't wait up. Might take a while."

THIRTY-FOUR:
WEDNESDAY EVENING

"Turn around," said Allison.

They had gone a half mile, her tired body clinging to Colin as she sat behind him on Merlin.

"What?" said Colin. He turned to face her as much as he could. She had her arms around his waist. Her chest pressed against his back. He used an old-fashioned western saddle with a low cantle so doubling wasn't too uncomfortable.

"Let's go back," she said.

Colin's look was to see if she was serious. "You're soaked," he said.

"We'll build a quick fire, dry these things out."

"That'll take an hour or two, it's almost dark already."

"The better to sneak up on them."

"It's four miles back. You need a shower, real food," said Colin. "And a beer."

"The voice of reason," said Allison. "I'm fine. Now that you're here. Feeling better."

"What are you going to see?"

Colin sighed, turned back to face forward. Light was on its last legs. A broad meadow around them slipped toward darkness.

Allison thought the answer was obvious but said it anyway: "If I knew, I wouldn't need to go."

"And what are you going to do?"

Colin's tone was conversational. They could have been discussing a supply list for the hardware store.

"It depends," said Allison. She tried to match his quiet approach.

"Depends on what?"

"On what's happening when we get there," said Allison.

"Probably a whole lot of grown men hanging out and, if anything else, hanging out some more. It's already dark in case you hadn't noticed and it's at least two hours back, maybe more since we're doubling up here and can't exactly push Merlin too hard."

"Okay, then, modified plan is we go most of the way back, find a place to settle in for the night and we'll be there first thing in the morning, when it's light."

Colin didn't say anything, which was its own form of response.

"I've got one blanket," said Colin.

"All we need," said Allison.

"I've got about five or six of Trudy's granola bars." Her version included cranberries, dates, and apricots. Nutrition bullets.

"I know a pond back off the trail," said Allison, noting the talk had moved to a *how to make this work* mode.

"Build a fire, dry your clothes, boil some water so we can drink it later. You'd be *nekkid* for a while." Pronounced it like a hillbilly.

"You could keep me warm," said Allison. "But only until the clothes are dry."

The plan was a jolt to her spirits. Going back to mess with the campfire jerks pleased her to the core. A chance for rest, food, and a fire put the situation in an even sweeter spot.

"What about Trudy—or Jesse. Can we call?"

Colin dug into a jacket pocket. "Pulled your phone out of Sunny Boy's saddlebags," he said.

"You are even smarter than you look," she said.

Allison flipped open the phone. Low battery, no signal. They were down in a broad, flat-bottomed valley. Ridges and obstacles stood between them and civilization's mysterious cell grid.

"Jesse knows you're out looking?" said Allison.

"And I told him not to worry until about this time tomorrow," said Colin.

Which meant that Jesse wouldn't really start to worry for two or three days. He was as stoic and carefree as your average rock and one of the hardest workers she'd ever met.

"The Oklahoma group called again today," said Colin. "They were out buying supplies and made up some excuse to call. The guy made a crack about whether they should plan on buying an extra freezer for all the meat they would need to store."

"Another blood-thirsty realist," said Allison. "My favorite."

Time was an issue. Allison's only positive thought was her standards for cleanliness and organization were so much higher than the average outfitter that she was ahead of the game based on her own baseline. Few clients would notice an off year. The new clients would think she was average. But wandering into an elk herd and filling a tag or three would make any hunter overlook whether her ship was tidy.

They found a flat spot on the north side of the pond, guarded on two sides by trees. The other two sides appeared open, though it was solely an impression. They picked a spot to sleep with the aid of a flashlight. Colin found a place to lead Merlin to the water and the horse slurped noisily.

"I'm going back," said Colin.

Allison gave him a look, but he couldn't see it.

"Two hours each way," said Colin. "Back by 1 or 2, maybe a little later. We need another horse."

The plan made sense, much as Allison wanted to dispute it. "I'll go with you."

"You rest up. You need it." The idea of stretching out, putting her head down, sounded delicious. "I'll leave you everything I've got. Flashlight, matches, blanket."

It wouldn't be like her to complain about being alone. Going so quickly back to being alone, if only for a few hours, felt too abrupt. But Colin was right.

"Got any fire starter?" said Allison.

"Fresh out," said Colin. "But you know all the tricks."

Allison liked to think she could start a bonfire in a driving rainstorm, but every bit of the terrain was dripping wet. They were setting up camp on a soaked sponge.

"Don't need any merit badges," said Allison. She'd been a Brownie once but after graduating to Girl Scouts had only lasted a year. Something about ranks and mottos and preparing herself through prescribed tasks was unappealing. The checklist approach to conquering the home, the outdoors, and personal improvements didn't sit well. Neither did selling cookies.

"I'm not awarding any today anyway," said Colin. "No such authority has been vested in this particular cowboy. However, if you complete your task I do have a different sort of reward, depending on your point of view."

Colin rummaged around in Merlin's saddle bags. Like a magician plucking a fat gold coin from behind a stranger's ear, held up a pint of tequila. He blasted the bottle with the flashlight. Hornitos.

"Okay," she said. "Now get."

Allison cracked the bottle and took a swig, passed it back to Colin.

"One for the road," he said. "Though I shouldn't drink and drive."

She kissed him hard, touched tequila tongues, and then for a moment let her head rest on his shoulder. Releasing her weight into his grasp was as good as an hour-long massage by a pro.

"Hurry back," she said. Kissed him again.

Colin climbed up and headed off without another word. He wasn't born to linger.

If all went well, she'd have a fire hot enough to dry clothes within twenty or thirty minutes. Another forty minutes to an hour for the clothes to dry, or close. First thing she'd need was a downed dead aspen. Right under their bark, the wood would stay dry in a hurricane. She followed her flashlight beam back toward the woods, counted steps as she went. Tipped her head back to the sky, rolled her neck around. One faint star winked hello.

THIRTY-FIVE:
WEDNESDAY EVENING

The old woman was about the last person he was going to engage. She had emerged from an old Buick a half-block from Glenwood Manor and ambled along the sidewalk. Each arm lugged a stuffed-full shopping bag. She stared at the sidewalk as she moved, her head bent over. She was the picture of someone minding her own business.

Bloom was expecting the big blow-off, maybe a grunt or "go away." Instead, she set down her load as if she'd been hauling bricks, and smiled as if there was no difference between helping a reporter and helping a lost child. She had to be pushing seventy. She was small. She wore bifocals in heavy dark blue frames with a flourish Elton John might have designed. Her hair was pulled back and taut. Her eyes focused like a house cat eyeing a bird through a window. Her name was Marsha Painter.

"How well do you know this neighbor, the one who was arrested?" said Bloom.

"Being held," said Painter. "That's what I heard. Not arrested. Being held for questioning."

"So, how well?"

It was night. A streetlight gave him enough to see his notes and show her lined but pleasant face.

"About a year ago," said Painter. She thought it through, wanting to be accurate. "My LeSabre wouldn't start. The battery went click, nothing. He helped me jump it and we got to talking. It didn't take much. Scratch the surface and off he'd go on how miserable he was with the government, the price of everything. I specifically remember him mentioning the crimes being committed by illegals and how they're ruining our country. As if Bonnie and Clyde, Al Capone, and Timothy McVeigh were all from Juarez, for crying out loud."

It was such a great line, Bloom took extra care with his notes.

"That was it? The last time you saw him?"

"Yes." Painter was emphatic. "I mean, to have a conversation. Saw him around every now and then."

"Did he ever say anything else?"

Painter smiled. "I didn't want to engage."

"You're sure it was the same person they're holding?"

"No question," said Painter.

"What's his name?"

She inhaled, studied Bloom's eyes like a drill sergeant. "You're going to use my name?"

"I can talk to my editor," said Bloom. "Might make an exception in this case."

"What if he's a racist goofball and the police let him go, for some reason. If he comes back."

"I don't have to use your name," said Bloom. "At least, I won't use your name unless I call you back and get your permission on what we want to print."

Marsha Painter pursed her lips, looked down, sighed. "He told me to call him Frank but his real name was Emmitt. Emmitt Kucharski. After the cops questioned me, I went and looked on his mailbox."

Bloom couldn't imagine growing up with such a mouthful of a name. No wonder he went by Frank.

"How old? You know, roughly."

"Mid-thirties. Might be pushing forty."

"Big guy?"

"Oh no, the opposite. Slender, slight though he looked plenty strong too."

"Were you at home, in the building, on the day of the shooting?"

"Right there," said Painter. "I was half tempted to walk downtown and at least lay eyes on Mr. Lamott, even if I knew for a little old lady like me it would be a struggle. But I stayed home, let the great world spin on its own."

"Did you see your neighbor that day? Was there anything that morning that made you feel something was unusual? Out of sorts?" Bloom didn't want to seem too over-eager or let her know she was a fountain of gold. "Did you hear the shots?"

Painter gave him a sideways look. The smile was gone.

"Easy now, big fella," she said. "One question at a time. I've seen him before, like I said, but not recently."

"How about since the morning Lamott was shot?"

Painter took a full breath, looked like she was working hard to keep her story straight.

"This is the part the police were most interested in, too."

Bloom let her find her own way into it.

"I wonder if the police really want all this in the newspapers," she said. "I guess I can kind of see why they asked me to not talk about it."

Bloom opted for low-key and a touch of flattery. "I'm sure the police have a million leads."

Painter pursed her lips, squinted. "I've got ice cream," she said. "It's melting."

Bloom waited.

Glenwood Manor had become a hub of police activity since the crime scene had shifted—or, more accurately, lurched—from the hillside to the rooftop. An all-white vehicle like an oversize UPS truck had become a fixture on the street. The van was a mobile crime lab, no doubt on loan from a rich-uncle law enforcement agency.

Bloom wanted Marsha Painter to think he had all night. Her feistiness wasn't a streak of her nature, it was her essence. Being concerned about her name's visibility gave credibility to the story, though of course he would want corroboration. Coogan would, too.

"The cops will figure it out," said Bloom. "But it's not a small coincidence. The shooting. Your neighbor. The fact that you haven't seen him lately."

"Yes, but look how easy it is to convict in the papers before one single day in court. That poor guy in Atlanta who they thought bombed the Olympics? That French finance guy visiting New York they thought had raped the hotel maid."

"Did he have friends?" said Bloom, more than a bit impressed with her memory for the wrongly prosecuted.

"Didn't see him enough to know."

"Did you notice anything at all unusual?"

"You asked me that already."

She smiled like a stern English teacher. Barely.

"And I don't think you told me," said Bloom. He smiled back enough to say he wasn't being confrontational.

"It wasn't that day," said Painter. "It was the day before."

Bloom waited.

"I was up at some ungodly hour. Used to be able to sleep regular, but not anymore."

"What time was it?" said Bloom.

Bloom took notes as she talked. He found himself oddly calm.

Five a.m. Maybe a train woke her up. Went for a walk. Us old folks don't sleep so well.

Usually I walk for an hour. Came back, it was still dark.

This guy Frank—Emmitt—is out front but he's down on the corner. Standing there. Doesn't see me. Streetlight. I can tell who it is.

He's impatient. Looking around. I go to my room, right on the corner, looking down. He's unloading all this stuff from a car. Car is in the middle of the street.

Painter took a breath. She was reliving the fact that she had seen the would-be killer. No doubt she had given the cops the same detail a dozen times. Now she had the highlights down cold.

Loading in cases of some sort. Two cases, maybe three. One looked like the right shape. A rifle case.

Some rifles snap together. You never know. Not duffle bags. These were cases. The look of equipment.

"And his friend?"

Painter paused again.

"Never forget him," she said. "I sat for two hours telling the police artist yes or no over and over as he drew. And that face tattoo, like a scream to the world. One big tattoo. Hideous. Now, I must tend to my ice cream soup."

Bloom watched her go.

Bloom hadn't been to church since the early days of high school, but journalism appeared to have its own god-like entities. Sometimes those gods dropped off an easy-to-open gift on your front door. They knocked gently and then left. You had to go open the door, unwrap the package and figure out what the gods wanted you to do.

Other times, and it only happened rarely, the journalism gods opened the front door and dropped the gift in your lap.

When you opened the gift, you felt like your bank account had magically doubled in size or that the prettiest and smartest girl had purposely waved you over to the bar for a chat, her phone number already scrawled on a napkin.

THIRTY-SIX:
WEDNESDAY, LATE NIGHT

THE SLOW CRUNCH OF tires on the dirt road cut through the night like a gong at a Buddhist monastery.

The sound was unnatural, grinding. A pair of yellow parking lights led the way and, as the vehicle came into view, the lights snapped off. At the same moment, a light popped inside the cab, bringing shape and definition to the truck. The light came out of the driver's side window and it moved. A flashlight.

The beam stabbed the night, jerked around on the treetops and field and the clouds and came to rest on Allison's A-frame, several hundred yards to Trudy's left. The beam whipped across the open space and Trudy ducked and held still on the porch. The beam stopped on her door, three feet away.

And snapped off.

Trudy's heart tried to crawl its way up the back of her throat. She tightened her grip around the gun, the only one she kept from ex-husband George's cache. It was meant for bears, if needed.

Her mouth went dry. She sat up, but barely, and tucked herself down by the wicker chair on the front porch. She had an angle on the car. The parking lights snapped back on and the car turned toward her and stopped. Doors opened and the interior light popped on, enough to see two figures stand up, one from each side. The vehicle was a pickup or SUV.

The motor cut. The doors slammed. *Boom-boom.*

Footsteps headed her way at a deliberate pace. A low mumble rippled across the night. The mumbler was male. Three or four words. The speaker was confident, relaxed.

Trudy moved her butt to the wicker, jabbed her elbows on her knees, perched the gun in two hands. The wicker chattered slightly. The gun shook in Trudy's hand and she realized now she was stuck. She should have headed inside at the first sign of their lights and started moving away, away, away. Here, she was cornered. Jumping back into the house now would be too noisy, too obvious.

Trudy risked a slow breath, tried to find a place back on the dial toward cool and calm. She flashed on Allison—what would she do? And then Jerry—where was he? And then realized these two walking up the road to her house might have had to go through Jerry to get here and she realized, suddenly, that Jerry might be hurt.

Or worse.

She cocked the gun.

The sound, in this setting, was like a car crash.

"What the—"

The words gave away the distance—close.

Silence.

Trudy aimed high and to the left, pulled the trigger. Her body jerked, the recoil rippled every muscle in her arm and shoulder. Her ears ignited with a high-pitched whine.

She counted to four, aimed high and pulled the trigger again.

This time she was up and at her door, heading inside as the echo faded.

She flashed the light on and Alfredo was already up, eyes ready to kill if needed.

Trudy pointed at his boots as if she had always pointed at everything with the barrel of a gun. He scooped up his boots and she flipped the overhead light back off, her breath coming now in inefficient bursts. She yanked on his wrist with her free hand. They ran through the house in the dark, headed to the back door by the greenhouse.

Twenty yards of clearing separated the house from the woods. She ran expecting a tackle. Her eyes screamed for a scrap of light. She reached the first line of trees, her hand gripping Alfredo's wrist.

She squatted, pulled him down alongside.

"Your boots," she whispered. "*Los botas.*"

They waited.

The shots weren't enough. Trudy knew it.

Two shapes. Two presences. Right there. Closer to the house, but there. Trudy heard a step. Two. *Three-four.* One bumped into something, a metallic ring. The pole for her clothes line.

"Fuck me." Like a growl.

The *ping* hung in the air.

The back door opened and they were both inside.

She hoped.

Trudy jerked Alfredo again by the wrist and started up around to the front, staying clear of the house. A light flashed on in the corner of her view. Alfredo stayed close.

She hoped there wasn't a third who had stayed with the car.

It was possible they faced a long night. It wouldn't take her visitors long to figure out she wasn't in the house and she could have gone one of 360 directions, all pretty good cover in the night. It was her turf, her advantage.

Their vehicle was a presence, a hint of a shape.

She slowed, eyes straining, free hand up. She let Alfredo go, but he hovered close.

Her hand found the car—SUV.

If there was a third inside, she and Alfredo were dead meat.

Trudy took a breath.

The sound behind the house was an angry slam of the door, ten times the needed force. No words could be plucked from the general guttural wrath.

Time was fleeting, but that depended on whether her visitors thought their prey sought refuge in the woods.

More low grumbles and curses, but they were from the far side of the house.

Trudy turned the gun around in her hand, held it by the barrel, found the smooth plastic casing of the tail light and gave it a firm whack.

Another.

Her finger felt the jagged sharp plastic where she had hammered. "*Vámonos,*" she whispered.

She flipped aside the scrap of plastic.

She led the way up the slope on the far side of the pickup from the house. Trudy climbed for two long minutes and stopped, her chest tight from panic and exertion. Alfredo sat next to her, put an arm around her shoulders.

Alfredo was already Zen-like frozen, a cool customer. Waiting roadside at night and wondering about the intentions of strangers wasn't a new experience.

The driver side door on the SUV snapped open and the light caught the driver's general size—large—and a flash of dark shirt. The cab of the vehicle obscured his face. The driver climbed in and the light snapped off for a second before the passenger's side opened.

This guy was in no rush. He stood looking back across the truck at the house. He was heavy set too, or at least bulky. He looked to be shorter than the driver.

"Fucking, fuckin' A," he said. "They've gotta come back."

Trudy couldn't hear the response, but the passenger wasn't in charge. The light caught his thick neck and nearly chinless profile. If it came down to a foot race, Trudy wasn't worried. But now that she had put bullets between them, she doubted it would come down to speed or stamina.

"You know—"

The car door slammed with an odd sound like the frame was bent. The motor came to life and the truck started a three-point turn until the headlights pointed back the way they had come.

"Now," said Trudy.

She led the race back to the house.

Keys. Handbag.

They hadn't tossed the place. They weren't after stuff. They were only after Alfredo. The cats were stirred up, but okay.

Back outside, the SUV's tail lights were far ahead, climbing a low rise. Trudy would close the gap between them when they got closer to Dotsero and once they were on the highway. In a half-hour or so, she'd be right on their tail, the busted light leading the way.

"I know," said Trudy to Alfredo. She kept her eyes on the dimly lit road. "Oldest trick in the book."

THIRTY-SEVEN:
THURSDAY MORNING

THE HOWLS WERE PART of her dream. They triggered a line from college days or an old boyfriend. The words surfaced in the gray fog of morning thought.

"*The grief you cry out from draws you toward union...*" Rumi. *Love Dogs.* "*Listen to the moan of a dog for its master. That whining is the connection.*"

Was the howl real?

Or it was her dream turned three-dimensional, bridging the journey from subconscious to reality.

Allison blinked, confirmed to herself she was awake.

The sound was way off, on the distant fringe of what was audible. She listened, concentrated.

Nothing. As much as the arrogant pricks around that camp gave her all sorts of creepy vibes, the dogs had made her blood boil. They had no place. Ptarmigan hunters? Dusky grouse hunters? Their look was too savage.

And now the howls again. And now she was awake. Fully awake.

The sound was like a train passing through town in the next county, the noise carried on a lazy breeze.

But there it was.

And it wasn't going away.

Allison popped an eye open. She was tucked down completely inside her sleeping bag, one of Colin's gifts upon his return. She saw only darkness but turtled her head out to find a one-ray touch of dawn. Their camp was in a clearing from an old burn. Blackened tree stumps, fresh grasses, a pond with a surface so inactive every fish, bird and bug must be sleeping, too.

Colin's eyes were open, but barely.

"You hear it, too," he said.

"Yeah," she whispered. She didn't want to make any noise that would prevent her from hearing the next round.

"The hell," said Colin. A whisper.

"Exactly," said Allison.

It took five minutes to pack, sleeping bags jammed into stuff bags, blankets rolled. Another five to saddle the horses. All speed work.

Juniper was an imposing filly, a blue roan with an all-business demeanor who never balked at a hard day. She was a feisty girl with teenage kicks. Her added inch or two of height didn't seem like much but Allison felt it in the climb up and the view, an unmistakable sense of more control. The emotional alteration made no sense in a practical way, but it worked every time. Riding Juniper was like pulling on a new pair of all-business boots.

"She took no convincing," said Colin.

"How's Sunny Boy?"

"Sleeping it off," said Colin. "He's fine. Not like I was there for more than a few minutes. Jesse was still up. He'll get her treats."

"He'll never forgive me," said Allison.

The howls again. Dogs were allowed in the Flat Tops, but hunting dogs were only needed to follow mountain lions and the only time to pick up a cat's trail was after a fresh snowfall. The howls offered up a touch of the English countryside in Western Colorado, as alien as crumpets.

Colin led the way back through the narrow strip of forest that separated their camp from the main valley floor. Allison banished all thoughts of a much-needed coffee injection.

Morning light brushed the sky slate gray. Grasses chirped happily with their morning feeding, a fresh splash of morning dew.

Now in the open, Allison slowed Juniper.

If the gap here in the forest was shaped like a weirdly elongated melting watch dreamed up by Salvador Dali, the dogs were at eleven o'clock and they were at five. The gap in the forest widened in the middle and tapered down to a narrow funnel at each end. To the east, the gap rose in elevation back over a high ridge. To the west, the land dropped slowly away. The south side of the long meadow was guarded by a long, high ridge that climbed abruptly, its long top so intently and perfectly horizontal that you had to wonder if the glaciers had gone to carpentry school.

Binoculars up, she saw nothing.

Mist. Dampness. Greens. Stillness.

"No elk, either," said Allison.

"Not too surprised," said Colin. "Given the dogs."

"A girl can dream, can't she?" said Allison.

"No law against it," said Colin. "At least, not up here."

Still, the howls.

Fainter.

They stepped their horses across the meadow, cutting where there was no trail and wary for loose stones and chuck holes. They picked up the trail straight up the spine of the valley while dark gray skies turned light gray and then the sun slashed its way through the mist.

Allison kept Juniper on the quick side of first gear. She fought off that growing unease in her stomach. If her guts were responsible for logic as well as such intangible traits as determination and certainty, she would no doubt be making a beeline or horse-line for home and let everything sort itself out on its own. But the howls were foreign. They didn't belong. Even in mountain lion season, relying on a dog's powerful abilities to track didn't seem fair, though where they placed on the "fair hunting" scale alongside rifles and scopes that made it possible to drop an elk from 800 or 1,000 yards, Allison wouldn't want to say.

Fifteen minutes later, Allison pulled Juniper to a stop. Her mind's ear had drawn a line from their overnight camp spot diagonally across the valley and this was the spot on the trail that intersected it.

The horses stood on a trail as straight as a gun barrel, due west. They needed to veer off to the south about thirty degrees. Curiously, Allison noted, the forest bulged here and the line she had in mind would allow for a fast crossing of the open meadow. The way across was dense bunchgrass. Allison thought she could see a route where the grass had been disturbed, but couldn't be sure.

"Don't hear 'em now," said Colin.

"It's been awhile," said Allison.

Colin had once heard an elk scraping its antlers on a tree and it wasn't for another ten minutes of careful stalking in the woods that the sound came within range for her. Ah, tender ears never exposed to the crushing noise of the city.

"You have a bead," said Colin.

"If I was being chased, animal or not, and if I was somewhere around in here," said Allison. "I'd want cover pronto and I'd head straight for the woods—right there."

"Makes sense," said Colin. "About as much as anything else."

He had parked Merlin next to Juniper, haunch to haunch. With the early light, Colin didn't need his sunglasses yet. His eyes revealed the short nights and his hard work. Despite the obvious fatigue, his gaze held a permanent look that was one part sly and reserved, one part utter enthusiasm for whatever is next.

"I don't like that the howls have stopped," said Allison. She pointed Juniper off the trail.

"We can shoot the dogs," said Colin. "If they've got wildlife cornered, we can shoot them."

"And first go through the assholes I ran into yesterday?" asked Allison. She turned around in the saddle to look at Colin as Juniper picked her way. "They aren't going to appreciate the interference. They aren't expecting an audience."

"Call the game warden?" said Colin.

"Haven't seen a good cell tower in some time," said Allison.

"You prepared to shoot Rover or Lassie?" said Colin.

"If they've chewed up a deer or cornered a bear, I won't be thinking of them as pets," said Allison. "I'm not dying to shoot anything. But hell, with the howls all the elk and deer that were here are long gone and I'm mad enough about that to shoot anything in sight."

She thought again that she should be back at the barn getting ready for her clients. Depending on what the next hour held, she told herself, she could be back by noon and then work late or pull an all-nighter.

Dense fir greeted them at the forest's edge. They went back in time, at least using daylight as a clock, as they entered. The dim sunlight from the open field wasn't enough to light up the interior of these dark, wooded caverns.

The horses snaked around trees. Without discussing it, Colin separated about thirty yards on her left flank, deeper still in the woods, and matched her pace. She heard him, caught the occasional flash of Merlin's nut brown coat. They held their bearings, heading southwest. The terrain rose and fell in tame undulations like a gentle swell, the weakest tide the moon could manage. The forest floor was clear. This old stand had never suffered a blowdown or fire. All the saplings had grown up and grown old together with minimum family trauma. The footing for the horses was premium carpet, almost spongy. It was spooky quiet although Merlin's tack or something in Colin's gear clacked with a dull metallic rhythm like a quirky European waltz.

One, two, *clack*. One, two, *clack*.

Dogs would have had no problem, of course, keeping at top speed in these woods but Allison had to give credit to the riders who could keep up or at least stay close on a horse. Keeping a straight line presented a challenge at a walking pace, let alone moving at a faster clip.

Had they both dreamed it? Had they both heard an odd elk bugle as howling dogs? Had she been mentally tricked by the power of suggestion, seeing the dogs yesterday?

Allison shook off the notion, although the library-like hush of the inner forest fueled her self-doubt. It was hard to imagine a pack of howling dogs had torn through and torn up this much serenity, though maybe the sheer lack of bugs, birds, and woodland creatures was evidence enough that the fierce canine whirlwind had frightened the entire animal kingdom into deep hiding mode.

Ahead, a pattern of dark scuff marks in the pine-needle floor. Allison halted Juniper and slid off. Something had ripped through here, indents that exposed a nick of dirt in an obvious pattern. Horses.

Back on Juniper, Allison scanned the forest ahead. She veered to the right. To the left, Colin and Merlin cut through the densely packed timbers. She caught strobe flashes of horse rump, a glimpse of Colin's jean jacket.

It felt she was skimming breaths from the surface of her lungs. Her chest seized. Fear wormed into her and squeezed a python. The sensation came on in a flash. It wasn't born of logic. Nothing in her sight, smell, or lack of sound suggested she should hit the button of internal panic and basic dread. She didn't believe in ghosts, had a hard time with mystics who could read the color of your aura or the meaning of the creases in your palm, but she also knew enough to not ignore strange, unexplainable hiccups of attitude, emotion, or sensitivity. If dogs could sense an earthquake minutes before the real thing, there might be a more animal part of her that had already moved up ahead, tapping the vibe, touching the untouchable and sending up flares.

If she had a gun in a holster, she would have drawn it.

She stopped.

She listened to her heart thud.

She scanned left for Colin, but he had dropped out of formation. He was gone.

Nothing.

She was alone.

Then the soft *clack,* distant, of Merlin's tack and she spotted Colin up ahead.

Colin looked back and through an opening in the trees he must have seen her expression because he looked startled and tense.

He mouthed one word:

"What?"

She shook her head, shrugged.

Colin turned Merlin and headed her way.

She held up her hand palm-out like a stern traffic cop and he stopped.

She looked at Colin but suddenly realized it was her ears that were straining and picking something out of place.

A breath.

A groan.

Allison slipped off Juniper in a flash, tied her loosely to the closest low bush.

Colin was on his feet too, stepping her way like he was on a bomb squad dealing with a motion-sensitive trigger.

That breath again.

That groan again.

Soft.

Desperation and resignation buried in the mix.

Allison thought: *last gasp.*

Four steps from Juniper, the sound floated in on a cloud. She couldn't get her bearings.

Again, the breath and the groan and then she spotted the dark splotch that at least confirmed why her guts boiled.

Wet blood. A misshapen pool about the size of her boot heel.

And another.

Now the direction was a snap. She turned and gave Colin a wave to hustle and he was quickly alongside her and then on the far side of the next spruce—there was the source of the groans, curled up around the trunk like his grip was saving him from a fall off a cliff.

Maybe it was.

His face was covered in blood.

Most of his shirt was saturated in blood.

His eyes were closed. His mouth quivered. His body shook.

"Damn it," said Colin. *Pissed-off.*

The man was on his side, facing away.

"Blankets," said Colin, already on the run to Merlin.

Allison's heart ached. Her mind flashed back to the wet, sleek dogs she'd seen at the camp. Then the howls and the long quiet.

His head looked like he'd smacked a windshield. If the head gash was only to the scalp and no deeper, he might have a chance. Head wounds were notorious bleeders. The worst of his wounds appeared to be right below his rib cage.

The third spot was the other side of his top thigh. His jeans had been ripped neatly by two punctures. Blood oozed in a soggy mire.

There was no way of knowing if there was damage underneath. Allison could only hope that he had instinctively rolled to put the weight on his good side, to minimize the pain from added pressure.

"Keep breathing," she said. "Stay here, stay here, stay with me."

Maybe somewhere deep down he'd register the human contact.

The thought that dogs had been trained for this kind of manhunt—and that the dog handlers could do this to another human being...

Fuckers.

She felt her innards wobble, fought the urge to hurl. Her stomach was empty.

Colin was back, blanket in hand.

"We have to get him warm," he said. "Fast."

It was hard to imagine moving something that appeared so fragile, but Colin was right. It had to be done.

"Let's get his feet elevated," said Colin.

There was a small voice inside Allison that whispered "hopeless, hopeless" but Colin's actions rang a note of hope.

"Look what I found," said Colin.

He held up a stick the length of a bread knife. The tip came to a point that would give a gem cutter pride.

"Looks like our guy might have found a way to fight back," said Colin.

The stick was red and bloody.

There was hope.

THIRTY-EIGHT:
THURSDAY MORNING

THE INSIDE OF HIS Camry felt as warm as a walk-in freezer in Siberia in the long lonely days of March. It was August in the Flat Tops Wilderness, or at least smack on the border of the designated wilderness, and Bloom simply had not calculated how cold the inside of a car could get sans heater, at elevation.

Chilly? Sure. He could have handled a chill. He had found a light jacket in the trunk and curled up on the back seat. He thought that would be enough to fend off whatever punch the night might throw. Instead, the car magnified the cold, about the same as it might do with sunshine on a hot summer day in an asphalt parking lot in the city.

Now the sun was up. The broad, beautiful meadow was coming to life. The temperature might not provide any relief for an hour two, but relief was on the way.

Three fingers tingled with numbness. His chest shuddered of its own accord.

Dawn told him what he already knew. Trudy's house and Allison's A-frame, tucked off in the corner of the field, were empty. He'd knocked on both doors at 11 p.m., when he had arrived. Then, he had hopes he would have perhaps woken Trudy. It would have been a tad awkward, but Trudy would have taken him in. His plan had been to interview Alfredo, maybe get lucky enough to chat with Allison, or perhaps catch her where they could talk, really connect. These were G-rated fantasies involving whiskey and beer and some genuine bonding. That was the dream.

It didn't happen.

His breath formed wispy clouds that quickly evaporated. He yawned so hard his eyes watered. His breath and body odor had curdled into an inhospitable stench. His neck throbbed from the awkward sleeping positions. Each position had held its own tortures, a hard spot in the bench seat or a cramped place where he had to wedge his foot. He hadn't really slept.

And he was in the wrong place. The trip up had been useless.

Where was everyone?

Where would Trudy have taken Alfredo?

Why hadn't he turned around last night and headed back down the hill? He'd be waking up in his bed and he wouldn't be giving Coogan a fresh chance to question his ability to set priorities.

Bloom started his car. It answered with a tinny cackle. The mechanical sound in this serene meadow sounded like a Harley revving for a drag race.

7:47 a.m. He must have fallen asleep—*somehow*.

Bloom backed the Camry to the road. He remembered the stables and barn another mile or two west. Maybe he'd take a quick cruise around up there, see if anyone was stirring. If not, he'd take the long drive down to Glenwood and get back on the rails.

Bloom's cell phone sounded. The number looked familiar.

"Hello?" he said. He barely recognized his own raspy voice.

"Duncan, it's Trudy."

The signal was weak and choppy.

"Am I calling too early?" she said.

"No," he said.

"Where are you?" she said.

Bloom looked around. A shot of sun nicked the top of Allison's A-frame.

"Why? What's going on?" he said.

A pause. Too long. Bloom thought maybe the signal was dropped.

"Two men came to my house last night. They were after Alfredo. We got out and followed them."

"Jesus," said Bloom.

"I know," said Trudy.

"They didn't see you?"

"Don't think so," said Trudy. "But here's the deal. Alfredo wants to bolt for home. Like, now. If you want to talk with him—and I'm barely hanging onto him by a thread—can you get here soon?"

Bloom started a one-handed, three-point turn. "Maybe," he said. "Where are you now?"

Bloom gave the Camry some juice. He felt like the lone kid at camp who thought it was time for arts and crafts when everyone else had hiked the half-mile down to the lake for swimming.

"We're outside the Hotel Colorado," said Trudy. "On the west side."

A massive buck, straight off the insurance company logo, stood in the field off the road, its head up and chest broad and proud. His antlers were so large Bloom wondered how he held his head up. The sight took his breath away. In the sun, the deer's tawny hide made brown the new red.

Bloom had the car moving at a clip that was slightly reckless, especially given the one-handed steering. In spots the washboard grooves threatened to shake him off the road.

"Everyone okay?" said Bloom.

"Well ... sort of ..."

Words from space.

The line went black-hole dead. He was holding a rock to his ear. The Camry flew up over a short, blind rise and it was a damn good thing nobody was coming from the other way.

THIRTY-NINE:
THURSDAY MORNING

"Lost him," said Trudy.

She dialed him back, immediately heard: "Hi, this is Duncan, leave a message…"

"Where is he?" said Jerry. "Did he say?"

Jerry was in the front seat with her. Alfredo Loya was in the back with Juan Diaz.

"He didn't say," said Trudy. "For some reason, it didn't sound close."

"But he's coming?" said Jerry.

"I think so," said Trudy. She wanted Duncan badly, to change up the vibe in the dark car, full of brooding and worry. "But he knows where we are."

They had chosen the Hotel Colorado, a grand old operation built in the 1890s. It offered hide-in-plain sight protection and it sat north of the pedestrian bridge. They had found a spot to park where they could see anyone coming from three directions, overlooking the corner of the hot springs complex.

All of Trudy's senses were on high alert, the lack of sleep a contributing factor. They had been the followers, not the followed, but she was worried, shaken.

"What now?" said Jerry.

"I'm not sure," said Trudy. "Wait."

"And you still don't want to the report the break-in?"

"And that will get straight back to the whole deal with Alfredo and him staying at my place and it gets messy in a hurry."

"Plus, you're a terrible liar," said Jerry.

"Thank you, I think," said Trudy. "I'd have to tell them everything."

"Including why Alfredo was with you."

In the back seat, Alfredo mumbled something to Diaz. Alfredo looked strung out but his eyes were busy. He made no pretense about looking over his shoulder every now and then. Diaz and Alfredo talked for a minute, low and fast and on top of each other. Diaz' tone sounded argumentative.

"He asks for a ride close to Riverside Meadows or he'll walk from here," said Diaz. "He would rather not have to walk across the bridge and right through town."

"And then what?" said Trudy.

"And then he sees his girlfriend and baby and then he leaves," said Diaz.

Trudy turned sideways so she could look directly at Diaz, who was sitting behind Jerry. "Leaves?"

"Heads back," said Diaz. "Home. All the way home to Mexico."

If Alfredo took off now, this would have all been a waste.

"Can he wait for the reporter?" said Trudy. "At least?"

Diaz turned to Alfredo and translated.

Alfredo popped open the back door, climbed out and shut the door behind him. He walked to the intersection to cross the road in front of the hotel. He didn't wait for the light but jogged between oncoming cars, one of which felt it necessary to deliver an irritating honk.

"Can't say I blame him," said Jerry. "Not sure I'd stick around waiting for another chance to be yanked off the streets and taken to some jail."

Alfredo headed down the steps to the pedestrian bridge. He didn't look back.

Trudy gave Jerry a look, but he didn't seem to notice. Why didn't he see the bigger picture?

FORTY:
THURSDAY MORNING

HE WAS CLINGING HARD to the non-dust version of himself, but Allison couldn't be sure.

Every minute was precious. He'd lost a lot of blood.

Each breath came with a gasp and shudder. He was unconscious or deep in shock. His forehead sprouted beads of sweat.

Allison made sure the blanket stayed loosely tucked around him. If he was about to go to his grave with the big questions unanswered, maybe he was getting close to the details now.

They hadn't really decided who would go. Colin was up on his horse without discussion. Colin would climb high as fast as possible, get a cell signal, call for a rescue and call the state division of wildlife, National Forest, county sheriff and anyone else interested in a case of attempted murder and illegal hunting with dogs. There was a helicopter based out of Aspen and if she remembered right Rio Blanco County Search and Rescue had access to one, too.

They would need some luck, starting with a quick cell signal.

Ninety minutes since Colin left. Maybe right about now he would be talking to someone, maybe the help was already on the way.

Maybe.

Maybe.

Too many maybes.

Waiting sucked.

Allison left her patient for mini scouting missions. Two minutes, three minutes. The longest was five. She was looking for a small clearing and found one that would work.

The spot was flat, round and clogged with blown-down trees. On her second reconnaissance, this time with matches and a starter stick, she had a fire going in a safe spot.

Locator smoke.

She shuttled between her patient and the fire, building the fire on each trip until it was in bonfire category, about chest high and as wide as a dinner table for eight.

She rushed armloads of old pine needles, still damp from last night's rain, to the fire to generate thick white smoke.

Check on her patient, chop some branches, jog to fire.

Build it up.

Repeat.

She fell into a rhythm, took a break every other trip for water and something to munch.

On one round-trip, her eye spotting a head-high branch thick with dead stuff and looking bone dry and fire-ready, she found elk scat and, nearby, a whole bedding area where elk had taken siesta. The scat was fresh, most likely from that morning and no earlier.

"Just fine," she said to the scattering of poop. "Be that way."

It wouldn't be good if the nurse collapsed. She wasn't consciously hungry or thirsty, but knew that her own system was cranked up and not necessarily taking care of its own basic needs.

Every trip back, she expected to find he had taken his last breath. On each circuit, she approached with that idea, that the rescue would become recovery and that her patient had taken that last step off the stairs and was gone.

But he was stubborn. He was a fighter. Shock was a fascinating feature of the human system, the ability to shut down every other sensory intake and focus relentlessly on righting the ship.

If he recovered, this time between attack and waking up in a brightly lit hospital bed would be relegated to a fuzzy, near-mystical storyline that would take shape over time, the result of bits and pieces of what he truly remembered melded together with fragments and details from the perspective of others.

She knew that score.

Her patient's brain was now hibernating. It was doing itself a favor. It might be deleting files from before the attack. Some survivors of spectacular crashes and collisions recalled nothing of the moments that led up to impact, even though they watched it all happen.

That was another reason Kerry London could go fuck off. For him to think that she would be a reliable narrator of her own story, after years of processing, was ludicrous. And for her to pretend to recount those events as if they were crisp photographs or HD video, when in fact they were now a set of feelings combined with the fuzzy flash frames of memory, was absurd.

But now Allison chided herself. All she had to do was tell Kerry London "no thanks" a dozen times, smiling the whole while, until he got the message. The result would have been the same as letting him witness her meltdown. And tantrum.

Her punishment, of course, was to relive the accident. The turmoil she had added to the conversation with Kerry London transformed the sleepy, distant memories into vivid colors and smells. The images had climbed down off the high, dusty shelf and come down for a party on the living room floor, as if the accident had happened yesterday, without the shock or the salt water or the hospital stay. Her uncontrolled thoughts—*who was in charge here anyway?*—didn't run to the aftermath, those odd minutes after the crash when they were suddenly back on earth and the fuselage belly-flopped oddly and ripped apart, jettisoning its contents and cargo and passengers in a wicked game of seat-assignment fate. The thirty-one who died were concentrated in a section just ahead of Allison's row. Allison didn't know precisely what had happened other than she was one of eighty-eight survivors suddenly swimming and bobbing and she understood instantly that her attachment and connection to this earth dangled by one brittle hair. And she simultaneously knew, given that she wasn't one of the ones screaming or floating upside down, that she'd never be that fortunate again.

All these thoughts, of course, benefitted from years of retrospection. She was now able to layer into the scene in her head the thoughts she *hoped* she had in the moment. Because the moment didn't contain thoughts or decision-making or anything that would truly bolster Kerry London's book. The moment only contained a dark whirl of numbness and bewilderment where logic was an outcast.

Allison's uncontrolled thoughts focused mostly on the few airborne seconds when they all knew in their guts that something wasn't right. The moment was pure, utter uncertainty. The moment was a collective gulp, coated in dread. They were all so utterly trapped. Optimism had been sucked from the cabin. The laws of physics dictated what was next. And the savvy, perhaps, of a couple unknown pilots up front.

Allison stood, took a deep breath—stared at one particular towering spruce to make it more real. She had no idea how long she'd been gone. Now, she was the unknown pilot and her patient depended on her talents. Allison banished the accident from her thoughts, concentrated on the moment, her current mission.

Two hours.

Three.

Her routines settled in. The fire was now a hungry beast, pumping up flurries of white smoke in a shaft so straight and thick it would have worked fine as a column for the ancient Greeks. Smoke shot from the roaring blast furnace like it was on a mission.

There was half a chance the dog runners would see it and she hoped they might be having a *what-the-fuck* moment. If they were anywhere in the main valley, they likely would have spotted it, but perhaps they were also long gone, racing their injured dog or dogs for help.

It was at least a mile or more from the fire to their camp, most of it open tundra west and northwest. Their camp was closer to the edge of the forest. She was in much deeper, although once or twice she pondered leaving her patient for an extended scouting mission straight north, to see how close. But it was too risky and unnecessary.

Her own *what-the-fuck* meter spiked past the red zone. The mountain lion scenario hadn't made sense, but this?

Her patient had been the prey.

The dogs were the weapon.

A million *what ifs* might be out there to fill in the background, but Allison didn't care. Around the world, hell had more names than there were for good but she would march deep into each one in order to track down Mr. Muttonchops and his oversized buddy. Maybe the dogs had died and the men were digging their graves.

No matter.

As soon as the helicopter came or as soon as whatever was going to happen next happened, they were first on her ever-broadening, fast-changing list.

FORTY-ONE:
THURSDAY, LATE
MORNING

A FAST SHOWER DELIVERED the kick of re-birth, although it might take a day or two for his back and neck to loosen up from the awkward sleeping arrangements in the Camry.

His e-mails included one from Coogan.

Nice job on Marsha Painter interview. Expand and get cop reaction by print deadline. Load as much on the web as you can as it comes in.

Turning last night's interview into "more" would be a snap. He called Coogan.

"I'm on it," said Bloom.

10:30 a.m.

"Where have you been?" Coogan's tone suggested a hint of kindness.

"Following stuff."

"You're sure your source is credible?" said Coogan. "Good get, though."

Coogan's highest praise was a "good get." It meant enterprise.

"I'll run everything she said by the cops. She was stable, articulate. I'll have reaction by mid-afternoon or at least comment."

"Stay on this," said Coogan.

Bloom weighed the pros and cons of laying everything out—Trudy's visitors, Alfredo's story, what he was going to do next with or without Coogan's blessing. It was too much to run through.

"Deal," said Bloom.

Coogan hung up.

Trudy smiled. She was holding a mug of Earl Grey tea. He'd found a box of tea bags in a back corner of a cupboard. His apartment was the antithesis of Trudy's mountain-fresh, plant-magnet home. Except for the hours when he dropped by his own place, Bloom's quarters were devoid of any living thing.

Trudy didn't appear to be on edge. She had settled into Bloom's armchair like she belonged.

"Jerry was okay?" he said.

Trudy shrugged.

Bloom had arrived at the Hotel Colorado after Alfredo had left. Jerry was getting ready to head to the office. Bloom had heard Jerry's admonition to Trudy to take everything—*everything*—to the cops. Then he had broken formation, saying someone had to run the business. The mood had lightened.

"Are you sure about not going to the cops?" said Bloom.

He sat down in a small, armless chair next to Trudy. Both seats had been full exactly twice in his year in Glenwood Springs—two dates that got as far as watching a movie in his apartment. One long make-out session, nothing more.

"And do all that explaining about Alfredo?" said Trudy. "I don't think so. Not yet."

"Maybe you don't tell them that part," said Bloom. "You heard someone breaking in, you made your way out the back, drove down the mountain."

"And got to my car fully dressed and they never caught up to me or ran me off the road."

"You hid in the woods until daylight, they left, you came down to Glenwood," said Bloom.

"I'm not a good storyteller," said Trudy. Her eyes were clear and her skin was flawless, the result of a daily dose of mountain air and, no doubt, a daily mountain of vegetables. If someone looked that healthy on the outside, he thought, the insides must be happy, content, and stress-free. Bloom had a notion to restrict his diet to what was good for him, but he'd need a year-long quarantine to kick the occasional yearning for a juicy cheeseburger.

"All right then," said Bloom. "Tell me again where you ended up last night?"

"Four Mile Ranch," said Trudy. "We had to really hang back at that point. It was us and them, far up ahead. There's only a couple dozen houses back in there."

Bloom put his laptop on the dining room table, a stability-impaired yard sale number. He opened a browser and grabbed a bookmark, IRB, and logged into his account.

"Those houses are spread out," said Trudy. "One of my best customers had me stop by her house back in there to help locate a vegetable garden. The houses are big, the lots are bigger. All perfectly spaced. And it was too damn open to follow anyone."

Bloom pulled the table close so Trudy didn't have to move, pulled his chair closer to her.

"So I turned around and parked down by the side of the road, off to the side," said Trudy. "I figured there was a chance these two weren't, you know, a couple."

She smiled.

"The marauding random gay midnight burglars who steal nothing gang," said Bloom. "Probably a fair assumption."

"My thinking exactly," said Trudy. "Though at the time I thought maybe they had spotted me and they were leading me back into the dark neighborhood—I mean, the whole thing is one big cul-de-sac—so they'd have a spot to corner me. My heart was doing funny things and Alfredo, well, he was sweating and I could feel his agony. He kept making these little gulping noises like he was at the top of a rollercoaster or something."

Trudy caught her breath like she was re-living it.

"And?" said Bloom.

"I had stopped in a small pull-out a quarter-mile from Four Mile Ranch. I hid off the side a bit like a cop might do, you know, watching for speeders. I had my lights off and we both slumped down. Two minutes later, the pickup goes by, broken tail light, you know, obvious. Tried to look for the license plate but it was moving too fast. No way. I couldn't exactly pull out right away but by the time I do, I see him turn right to go back across the bridge at 27th Street to go downtown and I follow right along and then he's back on the interstate."

Tension grew in Trudy's tone.

"I figured this could be bad," she said. "What if he lived in Grand Junction? I wasn't running out of gas, but I was getting low. Anyway, he pulled off in New Castle and I followed along enough that I saw what street he lives on. At least, I know where he went. I waited twenty minutes, to see if I could spot his place by where he parked, but he must have a garage or something. His car wasn't on the street."

"And how do you know he stopped anywhere on the street?" asked Bloom.

"The street is a dead end with five or six houses on either side. He went down, didn't come back. Thank my lucky beans for the "No

Outlet" sign at the end of the street so I didn't follow him at first but went down later and looked around. Then I went back to the highway, bought gas, and drove back to Glenwood Springs, rousted Jerry and called you. Where were you, anyway? Not that it's any of my business."

"Chasing my tail," said Bloom. He sighed. "What street in New Castle?"

"Red Cloud Court," said Trudy.

Bloom kept an active IRB account in part for moments like this, when speed counted. "Information Exclusively for Investigative Professionals" was the IRB tag line. In a separate browser, Bloom opened Google maps, zoomed in on New Castle.

Bloom followed Trudy's finger—a functional, gritty-looking finger but no less feminine—as she pointed out Castle Valley Boulevard that led off the interstate and up to Red Cloud Court. The Google data vacuum would get there eventually with its image-snapping trucks, but so far Red Cloud Court remained an inert gray line on the map.

Back at the main search engine page, Bloom entered "Red Cloud Court New Castle + street addresses" and immediately was given information about a home for sale at 41 Red Cloud Court via the real estate site Zillow.

"A start," said Bloom.

"Nice," said Trudy.

For a woman who spent most of her time at 9,000 feet above sea level and who surrounded herself with soil, plants, herbs, flowers, and cats, Trudy Heath's determination to get things right with Alfredo—and understand what had happened to him—created a healthy energy. As part of the profile he'd written about Trudy, Bloom remembered her ex-husband's crimes—multiple murders weren't that hard to forget, neither was rigged big-game poaching and more— and he imagined that having lived so long with a wildly duplicitous man had created this need to make sure she never missed another secret. Her determination was better fuel for his gas tank than any editor breathing down his neck.

Next Bloom pulled up the Garfield County Assessor's Office, found the draw-down for residential and entered "41 Red Cloud Court" in the search engine. The results revealed a legal summary of the property sale information, a description of the tax area, tax history, assessment history, owner address and owner information.

A Chicago bank.

"Smells like foreclosure," said Bloom.

"Smells empty," said Trudy.

"But we've got double-digit numbers in the forties," said Bloom. He went back to Google Maps. Red Cloud Court was a teardrop-shaped loop, the teardrop falling southwest. "I see ten houses in all, all with driveways from Red Cloud Court."

"Doesn't matter," said Trudy. "The car didn't stop right away. He kept going down the street."

"So eliminate the ones on the corner," said Bloom.

"And the next one on each side, maybe two," said Trudy.

"That would leave four," said Bloom.

"Minus the foreclosure," said Trudy, pointing to the web map where Zillow had placed an icon on 41 Red Cloud Court at the tip of the teardrop.

"Three," said Bloom.

"Maybe," said Trudy.

"It's possible it's still being lived in," said Bloom. "True."

Back at the assessor's site, Bloom punched in a series of numbers until he started getting hits off the database. 47 Red Cloud Court, 44 Red Cloud Court, 53 Red Cloud Court. The search engine needed a minute or two each time to process. "I've got broadband," said Bloom. "But I think the regular clerks are out and Google must have hired a senior citizen who doesn't walk too fast. It's taking her an awfully long time to shuffle down the stacks of data."

"I hope she's not the only one working," said Trudy. "I believe there are one or two others out there who use Google too."

The slow search time didn't match Bloom's mood, but sitting with Trudy was a perfectly fine way to spend the morning and Bloom worked to embody her minute-at-a-time vibe. Already he was starting to think about what Coogan would expect from the day's production and how he should make an appearance in the newsroom. He needed to call DiMarco, who he hoped would be good for an hours' worth of advance notice that a break in the case was imminent.

He needed another tack. Back at Google, Bloom punched up the image search and entered "New Castle Colorado Zoning Map." The results returned dozens of options, including one series of PDF images for the neighborhood and a marked Red Cloud Court and all four house numbers at the bottom of the teardrop—36, 38, 40 and 42.

Back at the assessor's site, Bloom began entering street numbers and Trudy wrote current owners.

36—Maximillian T. Waters
38—Robert M. Bailey
40—Emilio A. Perez
41—Victoria C. Day

"What were her parents thinking?" said Bloom. "Was she born on V-Day?"

"Maybe it's an unfortunate married name," said Trudy.

"We'll find out," said Bloom.

On the IRB database, Bloom entered names and addresses. They were soon swimming in data and details on Maximillian T. Waters. The categories included Names Associated with Subject, Possible Criminal Record, Motor Vehicle Records, People at Work, Voter Registration, Hunting and Fishing Permits, Bankruptcy and more. The data revealed a list of previous owners of each property as well as a list of current residents, which might indicate a renter if that was the case.

"What kind of truck was it?" said Bloom.

"A Chev-*role*," said Trudy. "In Glenwood Springs, when we got off the exit, I was two cars behind at a light and I tried to stay left in the lane, still trying to get a look at his license plate. The *t* was missing on the rear emblem. A Chev-*role* Blazer, I'd say at least five years old, maybe ten."

Max Waters owned a Dodge Durango and a Dodge Caravan, both 2011.

Bloom entered names and checked motor vehicle registrations of all the owners. No Chevy Blazers. But at 40 Red Cloud Court, Emilio A. Perez was the owner, not the resident.

Bloom entered the name of the renter, or at least the name of the other person who said the address was his current home. The data didn't distinguish. The data didn't care.

The renter was Ricardo Reyes and the car registered to his name popped right up—it was a 2004 Chevrolet Blazer.

"It says Chevro-*lay*," said Bloom. "They need to adjust their records."

Trudy nodded agreement. "And he needs a new taillight."

FORTY-TWO:
THURSDAY MID-DAY

HALFWAY BACK TO HER patient, walking the quiet woods and away from her roaring fire, Allison heard the distant throb. Allison knew they would see the smoke, as thick and dense as she could make it, but she headed to the open valley and watched the odd beast land.

Allison led three of the four—two men, one woman and all business—into the woods. One of the men carried a yellow plastic spine board.

The fourth, the pilot, stayed with his ship and let the engine idle, perhaps an indication that this wouldn't take long. The whistling engine followed them into the woods like a pair of determined mosquitoes. The whine suggested it was strong enough to cause flight. The whine was macho, obnoxious, and, she knew all too well, living a lie.

Allison stood back while the three worked. Their line of work required considerable time in the zone where that slippery little thing called life was moments away from going *poof,* like a candle blown out by a hurricane. The medical dance among those able to hold off gale-force winds at bay was well-rehearsed and highly synchronized.

The trio pulled on blue rubber gloves that snapped and squeaked. Giant rolls of cloth and bandages emerged from silver cases and high-tech backpacks. Scissors clipped, tape creaked. A mask was slipped over the patient's face and oxygen started to flow from a green tank the size of a Thermos. One of the men used a penlight to check the eyes, another wrapped a blood pressure cuff around an arm and started listening with a stethoscope. The scene was instantly home to colors—bright blues and yellows and dark blacks—that didn't otherwise belong in the woods. Allison told them every detail she thought was relevant.

Suddenly they moved their patient in a well-choreographed routine and strapped him gingerly to the spine board.

She followed them back to the edge of the forest and stopped. Conversation past this point would require shouting, given the helicopter's grinding, impatient clatter.

"You coming with?" The woman asked. She was short, trim and wiry. She was eye-to-eye with Allison and carried a seasoned gaze. "There's room."

"No thanks," said Allison. "My horse."

"Whoever called it in said you could leave your horse—they'd send somebody up for him."

"Not going to happen," said Allison. She might never leave a horse alone again.

"Okay," said the woman.

"How is he?" said Allison.

The men with the stretcher had gone ahead to the helicopter.

"He needs blood and we won't really know until we get X-rays. One more chance to come with us. You sure?"

"Positive," said Allison. She offered a knowing smile to reinforce it, ground her boots into the earth as thanks to the sensation of solid ground.

"You did a great job," said the woman.

"I told to him to keep fighting. Where's he going?"

"St. Mary's in Grand Junction," she said. "He needs everything he can get."

One of the others was running back toward them. He was carrying a cloth bag that looked heavy.

"Supplies for you," he said. "Water, snacks, a sandwich. We've gotta go. I know the sheriff wanted information and Parks and Wildlife passed a message along, too. Sure you'll hear from some folks."

The soft-sided lunch cooler must have weighed ten pounds. They hustled back to the helicopter, which then roared and shook and lifted straight up and headed due west, nose tipped down like a charging bull. The thundering wake took a full minute to subside.

Allison wanted to leave quickly, too.

But couldn't.

The fire roared like it could burn for a week.

FORTY-THREE:
THURSDAY MID-DAY

TRUDY STOPPED AT JERRY's house for a quick shower and one-hour power nap while Duncan took care of "keeping up appearances," as he put it, and "keeping his job." He had smiled broadly when he said it. "Doesn't matter where you've been before, what you've done in this business. It's all about today and tomorrow's editions. It's a treadmill and the treadmill never stops."

Jerry was at work so when she stretched out on top of his bed, warm and lulled by the shower, she was asleep in mere moments.

Allison had taught her the self-alarm trick and it worked, even from the near-comatose depths of her nap.

She dressed with a strange but relentless thought in her head. She had been thinking about Ricardo Reyes and his broken taillight and his house in New Castle and imagining what the next steps might be, how this was going to play out, when she suddenly realized how much she had been thinking about Duncan Bloom and his cool, capable demeanor. She couldn't help but contrast it with Jerry's general attitude and she fought the urge to think about their relationship, which had reached a state of maintenance. Jerry was a stellar example of the old saying that ex-hippies make the most zealous capitalists. She wasn't sure she shared his thirst for bottom-line business viability. Everything was *viable this* and *viable that.*

Yet she had always been fascinated by news. Before her brain surgery and back when the epileptic seizures kept her confined, the news networks had become her lifeline to the world. She was intrigued by reporters who buzzed from assignment to assignment and she was interested in how ideas and issues took hold—or didn't. And here was a reporter and he was engaging and personable and unassuming. And he knew how the world worked. Or, at least, he knew how to ask the right questions and dig for information.

The thought was hard to shake. The drive to Down to Earth offices was out of obligation. She knew Jerry would read the contradictions on her face. Duncan Bloom understood the human struggle in Alfredo Loya's predicament. To Jerry, Alfredo Loya was a business complication.

Jerry stood up from behind his desk and gave her one of his too-long, overly purposeful hugs, as if she might crack unless he held the pieces together. The hug said more about him and his needs.

"You look refreshed," he said. "Smell great, too."

"Showered at your place," said Trudy.

"I can smell the shampoo," he said. He circled back behind the desk. "It's already a busy day around here, practically an invasion."

The implication was clear. *Get to work.*

It would be unlike her to ask for time on the computer. She wanted to muck around on the websites Bloom had shown her, see what she could find out about Ricardo Reyes and the company he listed on a car loan application as the place where he worked. They had the company name, Pipeline Enterprises, but no solid information about location, service, products, or purpose.

"Anything new?" said Jerry. "I assume you haven't been talking to the police."

The space between them felt dead. Trudy sat in the chair for salesmen and visitors.

"No police," said Trudy.

Jerry took a swig from a quart-size cup. She could smell Jerry's custom roast. "You're tense," he said.

"Hard to feel settled or centered," said Trudy. "People in your house, you know. Creepy. I don't want to be here, in fact. I feel like we're a target."

She had a right to a healthy streak of paranoia, given the late-night intruders.

"They won't come here in broad daylight," said Jerry. "I hope. I think. If they were broad daylight types, they would have official roles, specific powers. Names, too."

The words came tightly, with restraint. They had the air of instruction. He tapped twice on his keyboard with one hand, glanced briefly at the computer screen, picked up his coffee and leaned back.

"You still want me to go to the cops," said Trudy.

Jerry paused like he was thinking, but Trudy knew better. "What I want is for you to be out mingling with our customers and showing them how to turn Roaring Fork clay into power-packed loam."

Jerry took a drink from his coffee. He could work on the cup all day, didn't mind it tepid.

"And, yes, a quick trip down to the police," he added. "Would it hurt? Put it on the record? Forget about everything that led up to it, but someone broke into your house and they drove a long way to do it. Let the cops decide what they want to do with the report, but give them the option. What if they come back tonight, still looking?"

Trudy's thoughts drifted to River Meadows Mobile Home Park and she imagined their home now bare to the walls, their lives blown apart.

"At some point Alfredo must have told them where he had been working," said Trudy. "So when he ran from the van they knew where to come looking."

Minor businesswoman celebrity good for sales, bad for every other reason. Her late-night visitors had probably figured out where Tomás or Alfredo had lived, asked around enough with their quasi-ID's to find his home and then they put the screws to his girlfriend or one of the others who coughed up the fact that Alfredo had been squirreled away by his boss. "No cops. Not yet."

Jerry folded his arms. Trudy could feel the admonishment before it was uttered.

"There's more at risk here than you think," he said. "The business is an extension of you and when the business doesn't play by the rules, it will come out. If they both came to your house, this spot is next. Everyone in town knows I sold the grocery store to work with you. Any ten-year-old with an old phone book could find my home address and the *I'm-Feeling-Lucky* button on Google would fork it over in nanoseconds."

He had rehearsed this pitch. Trudy felt every ounce of his logical fretting but what came through his look had more to do with his disappointment in her, like she was the feisty renegade who didn't know her limits.

"All this is at risk," he said. "Somehow or someway it will all get dragged out. Businesses are not immigration authorities. The humanitarian gestures, getting Alfredo back on his feet—it's all well and good up to a point. But we're not in a good position to sit here and wait for their next move. It would be a public relations disaster if this hits the news."

Actually, thought Trudy, the newspaper in this case sees the bigger picture and knows that her business had been working in the murky waters of the immigration issue, like virtually every other firm out there that depended on physical labor.

"One more day," said Trudy. She tried to hit a tone somewhere in the general neighborhood of non-inflammatory, but she was sure it came out argumentative. "Maybe two. And maybe you turn off the lights here for a day or two and spend time at the store or the herb stand, where there's lots of people around."

"And after one day or two?" he asked.

"I go down to the police, lay it all out." Trudy had a hard time picturing it, but she said it. Her head was already thinking ahead to when she was back with Duncan Bloom and they were studying the dirt on the underside of every rock they could find.

FORTY-FOUR:
THURSDAY MID-DAY

THE FIRE WAS HOT enough to melt steel. It was cooking hard. It was pleased with itself and looked like it could go strong for days without another twig. Unfortunately, there was no water anywhere nearby. No creek, no stream, no spring. Had there been one, she also had no pail. A couple gallons of water on this blaze would be the equivalent of mist. She wished the helicopter had come with a giant Bambi Bucket and an hour to spare.

The only idea she had was lame but it would have to do. She unpacked Juniper's saddle bags and remembered from her wood gathering a patch of undergrowth where the soil was loose enough—and pleasantly damp enough—to scoop by hand.

The fire laughed in a mocking crackle at the first loads of dirt. By the fifth, it was starting to sit up and take notice of the attack. Allison emptied her new lunch cooler and used it to haul dirt, too. By the third trip, she had rigged a rope from Juniper's saddle and walked him to drag the loads from the dirt mine to the fire. An hour later, her skin slick with sweat, the fire was coughing and sputtering. The next-to-last attack was fueled by the rage prompted by the howling dogs and her inability to make sense of anything. The final attack was double the pace so the fire didn't have time to think it could regain the upper hand. Allison's goatskin gloves took a beating. Her hunger was exquisite, but it was no time for a break. Her thirst hit new depths. She chased all the aches away until the fire receded to a gently-smoking mound of dirt only capable of a non-poisonous hiss from an old, dying snake.

Saddle bags repacked, Allison walked a mile across the valley and let Juniper slurp and satisfy himself in a mosquito-bite pond. It was three o'clock. Allison found a spot in a grove of Colorado Blue Spruce, its silvery blue cast shining in the afternoon sun, and downed her sandwich, homemade ham and cheese packed in its own Tupperware, complete with freezer pack. There were fresh red grapes and a packet of peanut butter crackers in her gift pack of reinforcements. In her package of manna from the mechanical bird.

Sleep tempted but she shook off the notion, sat up with her arms around her knees. A flicker cut a jagged line across the sky, a pair of ducks paddled the edge of the pond and, to the south, three fat does and a healthy buck walked out of the woods, well upwind. The does picked at the grass and shrubs, the buck played guard. He sensed something. All four animals were plump and prime. The buck's rack was a wide-beam affair that would make trophy hunters drool. On top of the fresh elk scat, she could declare her scouting task done.

The deer bounded off when she climbed back on Juniper. She felt satisfied, transformed by the nutrients in her lunch, though a nap would be the capper on refreshment.

Once more back to the main east-west valley. Once more a choice. Four o'clock now, barely four hours of daylight left. This stretch of the Flat Tops was a no man's land of sorts—too far for day-trippers coming from any direction. She and Juniper were alone.

An hour later, she found the spot that would lead into Dillard's camp. There was a break in a dense thicket of gambel oak where horse tracks funneled in from all directions. Allison dismounted, let her breathing subside.

On foot, Allison led Juniper into the woods. She hadn't approached the camp from this side, but knew that it should be within a hundred yards, tops. She approached with care, peering intently for a flash of movement and listening for a voice. Or voices.

The trail was distinct, well-worn by a month or two of horse and foot traffic this summer and maybe five years prior. The clearing came into view and Allison stopped to watch and listen but the eerie quiet and lack of horses at the rail screamed *empty*.

The fire was out. The tent was zipped tight.

Rocks around the fire radiated heat. Ash in the pit smoldered. A wisp of smoke curled up from the ash. Allison squatted by the fire and waited, Juniper still on the rope.

The camp was a mess, as if it had been quickly abandoned. A short-handled spade leaned against a tree, a brown sleeping bag drooped on a makeshift clothesline. A pile of plates and bowls looked like they contained enough food scraps for a chipmunk feast. Scrambled eggs and some grease, by the looks of it. A fat fly was working on his share. A white all-plastic spatula sat upside-down nearby, dusted in a coating of fireside dirt and pine needles. One pile of horse manure near the hitching rail sported a shine. She guessed an hour old, no more. A feed bag hung off the back of the tree nearby and, tapping the bottom, she could tell it held cups of oats. Above the oats, hanging from a branch in a bear-proof manner, a dark green trash bag dangled. It was tied to a rope that had been slung over a branch as a hoist. The bag strained under the weight like it would burst at any second.

Allison hitched Juniper to the rail and circled the wall tent. An open window would have been convenient, but no such luck.

Opening the outer door of the tent involved unfastening a flap, penetrating the inner layer meant tugging down a tent-high zipper as wide as her forearm that gave way only after much fidgeting and fussing. By the time the zipper was up, if anyone had been in the tent, a warning shout or shotgun blast would have already identified her—guilty as charged—as a trespasser or intruder, take your pick.

The inside of the tent was another unkempt mess, more like frathouse untidiness than anything else. Either the crew wouldn't be gone long or nobody in this camp knew the definition of shipshape.

The smell was of impacted sweat and smoke—a smoking lodge inside a high school boy's locker room. There were six cots. If they all came back at once, she was in trouble. If one or two came back, same thing. On her left, a simple table and three fold-up camp chairs, the small ones that supported your butt and nothing else. On the right, in the middle of the tent, a stove. Stone cold. There were plastic tubs with dried food inside—graham crackers, cans of pinto beans and corn, tomato sauce and pasta. One day pack coughed up T-shirts and a pair of jeans. The pockets were empty except for one piece of white paper, half an envelope with a telephone number scrawled in blue ink. A 970 area code. Allison stuffed the envelope in her back pocket.

A soft-sided suitcase hiding underneath one cot turned out to be a messy cache of tools and archery-related gear and gizmos, from a spray bottle of fox urine to a feather repair kit, cans of green greasepaint and a pack of high-tech broadheads that looked menacing enough to kill without being fired. "Stainless steel instant cut tip." "HexFlat design for exceptionally stable flight." "Body machined from aircraft quality aluminum." There was that whole aircraft thing again, chasing her around. The tips were designed to create fast blood loss on impact. The package of tips was wrapped in a white plastic bag with a receipt inside from a Wal-Mart in Rifle.

Allison thought the suitcase was empty but ran her hand along the bottom anyway, hoping for some scrap of something with useful information. The back of her hand touched something soft and light and she pulled it out.

A blindfold.

A professional, real-deal model—the kind you imagine for firing squads or kidnap victims being held by back-alley terrorists in Afghanistan. It was black, padded and big enough to cover half an average face—not only the eyes. It appeared well-used, with a faded line of jagged white streaks, maybe dried sweat. The elastic strap was tired.

She wondered how long it might take them to realize the blindfold was missing, if at all.

Back outside, Allison walked the perimeter of the tent, hoping for anything dropped or windblown or lost. Nothing. She walked around the camp for the same reason, here and there poking into the woods to look and listen. Except for the occasional bits of camp junk—a dirty plastic fork, a scrap of aluminum foil, a dried-up apple core—nothing.

Back on Juniper, feeling a rising bit of panic that she might be lingering too long, she took one more walk around, this time studying everything from horseback height.

The trash. She lowered the bag easily and decided to sift through the waste at home. The bag was knotted tightly. It weighed about fifteen pounds. She didn't want to cut it open here, lacking another bag or container. After rearranging Juniper's load, the trash was securely on board and Allison headed for home, trying to think of innocent reasons for why anyone would need a blindfold in the woods.

She reached the valley and turned east, the sun dropping like a cannonball. She might have an hour of good light left, but that was it. There was really no point in riding in the dark, she thought, when she could make camp here and hope to catch sight of them in the morning.

Dillard and his pals.

And the dogs.

Them.

FORTY-FIVE:
THURSDAY, LATE
AFTERNOON

"YOU'VE GOTTA HELP ME," said Bloom.

"How's that?" said DiMarco.

"When I talk to my editor, I want to come bearing a few fucking gifts."

Marjorie Hayes looked around quickly. She frowned on use of the F-bomb in the office. Bloom had an image of her working at *Sunset* magazine or *Highlights for Children*.

"A bottle of good whiskey might do the trick," said DiMarco.

Bloom let the sarcasm die without a laugh, waited.

"How big a gift does it have to be?" said DiMarco.

On the phone, standing, Coogan stabbed the air with his finger.

"Size doesn't matter," said Bloom, cradling the phone tight to his lips. He turned to put his back to Hayes. "Preferably shiny. Gold is good."

"And remind me again why I'm helping you," said DiMarco. "I need my motivation if you want an Oscar-worthy performance."

Bloom wanted to say the truth—that there is always a cop or two who get their limelight jollies by trying to be friends with the media. DiMarco enjoyed being the dark whisperer, relished the feeling of influence.

"You don't want your reporter pal to have his fingernails harvested one by one via dull scissors," said Bloom. "That's your motivation."

"Oh, thank you," said DiMarco. "I was losing my focus."

"Glad to help," said Bloom. "Now don't make me beg."

"Okay," said DiMarco. "First, that partial plate you gave me. My guys here said it only took an hour of crunch time on a supercomputer but they narrowed it down. Registered by a private corporation called Pipeline Enterprises. Out of Rifle."

Two Pipeline Enterprises hits. That was enough. Bloom drew a mental dotted-line from Trudy's house in the Flat Tops, through Ricardo Reyes' rental home in New Castle to a place of business in Rifle.

"Some company names are pure genius," added DiMarco. "You know? No messing around with cutesy."

"What do you mean?" said Bloom. The connection made sense. The same people who had lost Alfredo Loya had come back to look for him.

"I mean you'll do all your investigative reporter things with that name."

"But you've already looked," said Bloom.

"Why would I do that?" Self-mocking.

"Because you're curious. Your middle name should be Alice."

"And *you* deserve the thrill," said DiMarco. "It's your lead. Chase it down."

"The name of a meaningless company in Rifle is not going to mollify, satisfy, or pacify my editor." Bloom heard his own terribly white voice doing a Jesse Jackson impersonation. Weird.

"It won't take you long," said DiMarco.

Bloom inserted "Pipeline Enterprises" and "Rifle" into the search engine and retrieved a batch of hits. One looked likely. He'd have to check each link one by and one as well as the incorporation papers with the Secretary of State.

"Clean? Dirty? Legit?" said Bloom. "And let's say it was a Pipeline Enterprises van that grabbed an innocent pedestrian off the street. Wouldn't you want to talk to them? Isn't that your old-fashioned, straightforward kidnapping?"

Bloom knew he had to play along, but leaving the office and reconnecting with Trudy couldn't happen fast enough. She had stayed in Glenwood Springs for the night with Jerry but she had sounded tense and couldn't talk long. New ideas were occurring to Bloom that didn't involve enigmatic Allison.

"It depends," said DiMarco. "What if we don't have a complaint? Or a *complainant*?" He hit the last 't' like a speech coach.

"It happened," said Bloom.

One of the links from the Pipeline Enterprises search turned up some sort of bid notice on a purchasing process in Mesa County, one county west and home to the Western Slope's largest city, Grand Junction. The type of contract was embedded in codes and bureaucratic jibberish.

"Oh, so you were there?" said DiMarco.

"I talked to the guy who got snatched. You don't make this shit up."

"Really?" said DiMarco. "Nobody ever pretends anything to serve their own purposes or needs? Ever?"

"I could smell the credibility," said Bloom.

"How about we move on?" said DiMarco.

"You got something else?" said Bloom. "The drawing of that creep has to be bringing some hits."

"Hits, sure," said DiMarco. "Everyone thinks they've seen him. Everybody's in show biz. Everybody's a star."

"So other than the usual pack of eyewitness wannabes, anything useful?"

"Each tip takes time," said DiMarco.

"Let me put it to you this way," said Bloom. "Are you on someone's trail right this second?"

Bloom heard the rising intensity in his own voice. Marjorie Hayes shot him a look and now Coogan was off the phone and staring straight at him.

"No," said DiMarco. "The answer is no. Would I tell you if we had someone cornered right now? Maybe not. But we've got nothing. It's as if the shooter rode a transporter beam to the roof and escaped the same way."

DiMarco's image would have made for a dynamite quote. Bloom might be able to use it, even without DiMarco's name. But if DiMarco used Star Trek imagery around the cop shop, it might give him a way.

"Later," said DiMarco.

"That's it?" said Bloom.

DiMarco hung up.

Bloom followed one of the Pipeline Enterprises links. The dull world of drilling rigs and all the related equipment, fluids, pumps, hoses, saws and bits came at him. Pipeline Enterprises, from what Bloom could gather from the lingo and the obtuse array of photographs, specialized in horizontal drilling and could help you get there faster, farther, and cheaper. 'Fracking R Us,' though the service was not specified. The website was an ugly mess. The design was a decade old. "*Moderate drilling costs often $300,000 or less before casing point, 3-D* *seismic based exploration, a high occurrence of stacked pays on structural features.*" The company touted "*straightforward deals.*"

Names of owners or any staff didn't exist. The trucks drove themselves, the equipment loaded itself, the corporate office was run by robots. It did not seem like the kind of firm that needed a big passenger van, unless it was used to shuttle crews into the woods.

Marjorie Hayes packed her all-in-one bag, ready to head out. Each story was its own production and came with the needed rituals.

Coogan was back on the phone. It appeared World War III had been averted.

There had been an undercurrent to DiMarco's tone. What had he been trying to say? *You won't have any trouble.*

Bloom's thoughts ran to Thomas Lamott in the hospital and around to Allison Coil and back to Trudy Heath. There was some spark with Trudy, no question. She lived in a bubble of tranquility. She was a wellspring of health and her smile was the antidote for any poison. It was another case of Bloom overlooking the obvious. He had picked up on an unmistakable vibe. Among all the rubble and puzzles in front of him, this was the only one with a clear path, though the footing might be treacherous.

Pipeline Enterprises.

Bloom stared at the computer screen.

The company names are *pure genius.*

Bloom studied the address: 1649 Airport Road. He flipped to Google Maps and switched to satellite view. The company was located in an industrial thicket south of the interstate and west of the Garfield County airport. The company's home base looked to be a large metal box. Pipeline Enterprises had one of the biggest facilities on the block. Bloom switched to street view, but the street didn't light up. No street-level pictures to go with it.

He would have to run out to Rifle. There was work to do on Ricardo Reyes and his Chevy Blazer. Maybe Trudy would want to go for the trip to Rifle but, in reality, Bloom couldn't imagine ducking out of sight for an hour or two to Rifle. Coogan expected him to be covering the Lamott investigation like he had a hidden microphone on the wall inside the cops' war room.

Coogan was now crossing the ten steps of office and, with Marjorie Hayes gone, there wasn't much question who he was gunning for.

"Got a phone tip in," said Coogan. "Search and rescue pulled someone off the Flat Tops. Injured hiker, something like that. Took him to St. Mary's in Grand Junction."

Bloom flashed briefly on the body Allison wanted him to track. He needed to check back with the cops on that one, too.

"As if there wasn't enough already," said Coogan. "Plenty going on. Sounds like it was a touch and go situation all the way."

FORTY-SIX:
FRIDAY MORNING

BLOOM WORKED HIS PHONE, grabbed tidbits off the web. Trudy kept her eyes out for cops and the speedometer a steady ten miles over the limit.

They had talked about a quick buzz through New Castle to circle the house of Ricardo Reyes, or waiting there, but the odds of success were low.

If the Rifle tour was quick, they might stop on the way back.

Bloom called the hospital in Grand Junction but Trudy could tell he'd hit a brick wall.

"Used to be they'd give you detail," he said, "but the whole health care privacy stuff now, about all they say is they are a hospital and they do treat people with medical needs, in case you thought you were calling a used car dealership."

The valley broadened, following the Colorado River on its descent west.

"All I know is they pulled someone off the Flat Tops with search and rescue," added Bloom. "Nothing more."

A dozen or so men and women worked a roadside alfalfa field, their necks covered in white kerchiefs. All wore matching wide-brimmed hats, pixilated dots of humanity in the corner of a heat-soaked field of bounty and beauty. Trudy imagined Alfredo hunkered down in the back of a pickup or waiting for his next connection along a back road.

At the Garfield County Airport exit, Trudy turned the pickup back across the I-70 overpass. The frontage road on the south side of the highway snaked west past a field of horses tucked against a high bluff, where the airport was built. A private jet was on final approach, bearing down straight at them. Its landing gear was down and so close Trudy could make out the pattern in the oddly motionless tread of tire under the plane's nose.

The road led them to an industrial park, a stretch of hefty warehouses and prefab buildings for businesses and operations that required heavy equipment and big storage spaces. Despite the scale of the buildings—some with doors the size of a three-story house—there wasn't much human activity. An oversized hauling truck, wheels higher than their pickup, rumbled past. Two men chatted by an idling bulldozer blowing black puffs of exhaust.

Trudy turned onto Buckthorn Drive and stopped.

"What are you doing?" asked Bloom, still busy searching on his phone.

"Coming up with a plan," said Trudy. "And waiting for you. This road ends in about ten seconds. You can see it dies right up there. I'd prefer not to slide past Pipeline Enterprises without a plan."

"Go down to the end and turn around," said Bloom. "We're a couple of lost tourists looking for Rifle Gap and we turned the wrong way. Something."

"And if Mr. Reyes is out front or his truck is parked there? Do we have a plan?"

"Do we need one?" said Bloom without a hint of judgment.

"Drive down, turn around?" said Trudy.

"And see what we see," said Bloom. "Based on the inert website, could be an empty lot or fake scenery for an old western movie. All front."

By Trudy's estimation, there were eight businesses before the dead end, four on each side.

"And if we get recognized?" she said. Bloom appeared invigorated, unworried.

"Then I don't think our lost tourist story will work," said Bloom.

"The sign on the pickup," said Trudy. "They might be looking out for it."

"Then we'll have our conversation sooner than I thought," said Bloom.

He smiled as faintly as a man can smile.

"I wasn't exactly thinking ahead," said Trudy. "Should have taken your car."

Trudy put the pickup in gear and tried to squelch her gnawing fear. She felt as if a giant spotlight hung in the sky, tracking her every move.

Some of the operations were devoid of external information about the nature of their purpose or function, but Pipeline Enterprises looked to be about pipes, drilling rigs and, simply, enterprise.

"Son of a bitch," said Bloom.

The giant doors were opened wide, as if to say, "no secrets." The doors faced straight west. The interior looked well-stocked and well-stuffed. Workers outside buzzed around a truck that sported a tall, dense thicket of pipes and blue hoses, twice as thick as the versions at the quarter-powered car washes. Four more trucks stood in a neat row

270

nearby. There was order to the place, perhaps military blood in the family.

Trudy did an unhurried three-point turn and crawled back in front of Pipeline Enterprises.

"Pull right up in front like we mean business," said Bloom. "Got anything to deliver? A bouquet or something? Roses?"

"Nobody has basil or rosemary delivered," said Trudy. "And we are not florists."

"I need a rose, a prop of some sort," he said. "Or not."

Trudy pulled up alongside the broad apron of concrete that served as the industrial front porch. Bloom wasted no time opening his door.

"What, what are you—?"

"I don't know," said Bloom. "Sometimes you just have to ask."

"I'll go with you." She heard herself say it, but it was the last thing Trudy wanted to do.

"Stay here," said Bloom. "I might come running."

There was an element to Duncan Bloom that was relaxed and unflappable. The world owed him information. Simple.

Bloom smiled. "If I'm not back in three hours, send help because I might be bored to death learning more about well casings and pressure gauges than one man can stand."

Trudy watched him walk away, a fine stride with purpose and an appealing, well-rounded quality.

The men around the repair project stopped in unison, looked up at Duncan's approach.

Suddenly a dog jerked to attention, standing its ground, no chain in sight. Its bark was a baritone and dark. Trudy shuddered. Bloom kept walking, didn't look back.

FORTY-SEVEN:
FRIDAY AFTERNOON

THE BOUNTY IN TRUDY'S refrigerator gave up a wedge of eggplant lasagna, fat red grapes, crackers and homemade hummus laced with roasted red peppers.

It wasn't exactly typical breakfast fare, but worked fine. Delicious. Allison had broken camp at 7 a.m., certain that Dillard and the dogs would return as soon as she left but also certain she couldn't wait forever.

More than Trudy's food, she needed her phone. This was no time for lame-ass cell signals and wimpy phone batteries. Allison needed the full artillery.

Trudy first.

"I'm eating your leftover lasagna," said Allison as a greeting.

"Dig in," said Trudy. "Might need salt. See if you spot anything missing from the house, will you?"

"What do you mean?"

Allison ate but her thoughts turned sour as Trudy told her the story of Alfredo, bringing him up to her house, avoiding the prowlers, following them down, losing Alfredo and working alongside the reporter to start to figure out who was on their tail. The reporter was the one Allison remembered after coming down from the rooftop of Glenwood Manor and Allison thought Trudy went on a bit too long and with a touch of giddiness in her voice. *Duncan this, Duncan that.*

"We're in Rifle now," said Trudy. "Duncan just walked into a warehouse to ask a few questions. Pipeline Enterprises—that's the name of the company."

"And anything new on the shooter?"

"They're looking for someone. A woman who lives in the apartment building saw two men carrying rifles or equipment. Now there's a drawing all over everywhere. Flip on the TV. I'm sure they'll show it."

Trudy's TV was a twenty-year-old number connected to a satellite system and all Trudy had to do was switch on the power button, no inscrutable remote involved. A Denver news station came on and the first view was an aerial of a thick clog of cars, eight lanes wide in the hot summer haze. Allison toasted the Flat Tops, and its utter lack of traffic jams, with a swallow of orange juice.

"What's going on with you?" said Trudy.

Allison took a breath. Dogs. Injuries. Fire. Helicopter. Camp. Blindfold. Telephone number. The worthless exercise of spending the night camped nearby. Allison spared no detail or any conclusions. Trudy listened without comment but uttered "oh my" at the appropriate moments, quizzed her for a few more details when she was done.

"I'm horrified," said Trudy. "It's inhuman—beyond belief."

Trudy's voice was small. She was seeing everything Allison saw—staring into the abyss.

"Give me the number," said Trudy, perking up. "You won't believe what Duncan can do with a telephone number. Turn one telephone number into someone's life story."

The half-envelope had been transferred to her clean pair of Cruel Girls. "I guess that last nine could be a four," said Allison. "Handwriting is like scratches."

"Can you find out if the guy they flew out of there is okay?" said Allison. "How he's doing?"

"I suppose," said Trudy. "If they're saying. What did he look like?"

"What do you mean?"

"Describe him more," said Trudy.

Flashes came. "Hispanic," said Allison. "Darker skin, anyway. He was contorted and it's not like I ever got a full-on view of his face, but I'd say Hispanic. Medium-height, trim. If he was more than one-fifty, I'd be surprised. Short hair, black. He kept it short."

There was silence on the line, but Allison knew the moment for what it was—pure Trudy instinct, something beyond intangible forming itself into words and taking its own time to render.

"It's connected back to where Alfredo was being held," said Trudy. "Somehow connected. The holding cell or whatever it is."

Allison let the idea settle, rolled it around.

"How did he look?" said Trudy. "I mean, really look?"

"Borderline," said Allison.

"We've got to get that blindfold looked at."

Allison didn't realize she'd been staring at the television news when the drawing flashed full screen. Prime suspect number one had a heavy, round face and a thick neck. He was bald. Two thick clamps squeezed his ears. A tattoo like a maze for rat experiments covered his face—forehead to chin, cheekbone to cheekbone.

"Holy shit he's ugly," said Allison.

"They're showing it?" said Trudy.

"You've either seen him," said Allison, "or you hope you never do. His mama must be so proud."

"He better be in a hole in the Grand Canyon right now if he doesn't want to get caught," said Trudy.

The sketch, in fact, made Allison queasy. The look alone said hideous things.

"Think you're the last person on earth to see it," said Trudy. "What about the blindfold?"

"DNA?" said Allison. "Possible. Some sweat. Or lots of sweat. Dried sweat now."

"You need the cops," said Trudy.

"My next call," said Allison. She had a hunch they would want her to drive down to Glenwood Springs, something she didn't want or need.

"Will you talk to Duncan?" said Trudy.

Suddenly Allison could see where her discovery of the injured man would grow too big, too fast and possibly get too ugly. "You mean to be quoted?" said Allison.

"It's going to be a story," said Trudy. "You were there."

"The next time they come up here they won't be the genteel, steal-nothing burglars," said Allison. "We may as well put a target on our backs."

"No names," said Trudy.

With Kerry London still buzzing around, the last thing she needed was her name splashed around in the papers. Having shared some quality time with the fine gentlemen of Burning Fire Camp, ditto.

"Not yet," said Allison.

And, she hoped, never.

"Can I tell Duncan then?"

The other end of the telephone connected to a jumbled, uncontrollable world where information transformed from a single sheet of paper to a million bits of confetti within the first nanosecond of its arrival. Each consumer latched onto the scrap that matched their view of the world and held it up like a 24-carat version of Dewey Defeats Truman.

"You trust him?" said Allison.

Lightning couldn't have flashed in the time before her answer. "I do."

"You haven't known him long—"

"Going on what I feel," said Trudy. "Good heart."

"Okay," said Allison. "But only to help with the bigger picture of what happened. And no names."

"We'll start on that phone number," said Trudy. "Are you going to come down with the blindfold?"

"Have to get it to the cops somehow," said Allison. "Since I don't have a dog to show them."

Wasn't there a carrier pigeon that could save her the trip? The thought of a day trip to Glenwood Springs and waiting her turn in the world of the officialdom held zero appeal. She might have to succumb, given the importance of the blindfold. If she was playing by the book, or at least pretending to, it was her obligation to provide her side of the story, probably the only "side" the cops would ever hear.

"If I have to come down, I'll let you know," said Allison.

"I hope that goes without saying," said Trudy.

Allison smiled, said good-bye and hung up.

She zapped a secular prayer in the general direction of the Grand Junction hospital. She needed her patient to live and tell the story of being hunted, for sport, by other men. And to see if he could identify any of the hunters.

FORTY-EIGHT:
FRIDAY AFTERNOON

"We don't talk to reporters."

"Glenwood Springs," said Bloom. "Not Rifle."

"The difference is?" He was tall and fit. He had a densely-forested moustache that curled down so the whiskers obliterated his upper lip.

"I'm looking for a passenger van."

"Try a dealer."

"A specific van. Registration lists it here." Bloom was in no position to study the surroundings with care, but Martha Stewart might have been in charge of the cleaning and organizing. A neat freak reigned. In general terms, the inside of Pipeline Enterprises was a cavern of equipment and trucks and heavy gear. There was ample room to hide a passenger van. Or ten.

"You're on private property."

"The cops know about the van, too."

"We will give them a tour," he said. "When they get here."

The dog that had greeted him so warmly was now tethered to a corner of the industrial office on a lead that looked no stronger than well-boiled spaghetti. The dog's snout was short, somewhere between Rottweiler and Boxer. Its size and thick chest were closer to the Rottweiler, but its hair looked longer.

Off to Bloom's right, two men had closed ranks. The timing of their arrival—and their bouncer-like presence—would have made synchronized swimmers envious. Each stood three feet back. Bright yellow earplugs dangled near one guy's ears; the other wore safety goggles. Bloom had no trouble deciphering the message.

He realized immediately he'd seen the one on his right before. He was older, calmer but glaring like he practiced the look at home. Or maybe it was permanent.

"Does Pipeline Enterprises own any vans?"

Behind the men, off and to the side, stood a pallet stacked high with green bags, probably fifty pounds each. The bags were held in place by giant sheets of pink-tinged shrink wrap. The shape of the bags looked familiar, but not the brand.

"Did you happen to hear what I said about reporters?"

"How about if I tell you about this story I'm working on? See if any of it rings a bell?"

Somewhere, he'd found the nerve. Maybe it was standing near the open doors. Surely they could see the pickup. They must have known he wasn't alone.

"You're working on a story, go dream some shit up."

"It's about immigration," said Bloom. "It's about the cops not doing their job, being lax about letting the illegals go."

"Really?" said the man.

"We've been following them around, long before the shooting," said Bloom. "It's obvious they know when they're talking to someone who doesn't belong here."

Maybe he could sucker them in, pull them over.

"The fuck." The man took a step toward Bloom, leaned forward. "We like the cops."

"This isn't going to look good, you know," said Bloom. "The fact that you wouldn't even answer a few—"

"Get the fuck out of here."

Bloom held the stare. The man's two buddies hadn't budged.

"Okay," said Bloom. "We'll go with what the registration shows and put you down for no comment. Can I get your name?"

Trudy's pickup fired up when he was twenty steps away. He tried to walk normally, but his knees shook. He half wondered if each step was his last.

Reporter Gunned Down.

Hey, it happens.

"You okay?" said Trudy when he'd closed the door.

"Is it that obvious?"

"You're white."

"You're supposed to say 'like a ghost.'"

"Like a ghost," said Trudy.

"Funny," said Bloom. "I may as well have been talking to one in there."

"What did they say?"

"Not much," said Bloom. "But we've got the right place."

"Meet Reyes?" said Trudy.

"No names on the first date," said Bloom.

Trudy pulled away and Bloom glanced back. His friendly Wal-Mart greeter was now joined by four others, a blur of heft and muscle. A new dog, no leash in sight, barked in staccato triplets.

"So how do you know?" said Trudy.

"I don't," said Bloom. "Not really. But the overall vibe suggested one thing—score."

Trudy turned right at the end of Buckthorn Drive, retracing their route back to the highway.

"Your instincts are probably right," said Trudy.

"And the craziest thing. You know, there are dogs around of course, but they either ordered a lifetime supply of food for him and all his puppies and grand-puppies or there are a whole lot more dogs somewhere."

"Dog food?"

"A pallet like the ones you see in the warehouse stores. Could have come straight off a semi."

Trudy edged over on the narrow shoulder and then pulled a slow U-turn, inched back to the top of Buckthorn Drive, looked back down the street. Stopped.

Bloom didn't need another encounter with the friendly Welcome Wagon from Pipeline Enterprises. But Trudy's expression read complete determination.

"Allison just called—while you were inside," said Trudy. "The guy they airlifted to Grand Junction from the Flat Tops. She and Colin were the ones that found him."

"They just *found* him?" Bloom didn't know the Flat Tops well, but what were the odds?

"He was attacked by dogs," said Trudy. "Allison and Colin heard the howls."

"The hell," said Bloom.

"And I've got a phone number that Allison pulled from their camp. She went to their camp, which was empty, but she got this phone number off of something."

"It's not the only lead," said Bloom. "Hang on."

Bloom punched in Coogan's number, knew Trudy would follow along on speaker.

"Two days ago," said Bloom. "Late afternoon. A man in your office, not very happy."

"Tell me the cops are getting close," said Coogan. "That's all I really I want to hear."

"Who was he?" said Bloom.

"What's going on?" said Coogan.

"Let's say I ran into him."

"He's in the energy business," said Coogan. "Drilling. Name is Adam Paxton."

"And why was he talking to you?"

"What's this got to do with anything?" said Coogan.

"He's smack in the middle of the whole immigration business," said Bloom. The statement wasn't a stretch as far as he was concerned. "There's money being made. Pipeline Enterprises—does Paxton own it?"

"Don't know the name of his business," said Coogan. "Think he's involved in several."

"Then it's more than drilling," said Bloom. "Why was he in your office?"

The brief pause meant that Bloom had pushed too hard. Or that Coogan was thinking.

"Marjorie saw a fight," said Coogan.

"Marjorie Hayes? Our Marjorie?" said Bloom.

"She was down at City Hall for a story around those zoning issues with the library and parking structure downtown. She was coming out of a hearing and, completely unrelated, Adam Paxton was going at it with Troy Nichols. I guess Adam had his hands around Troy's throat, practically nose to nose."

Nichols' post-shooting quote came rushing back to Bloom—the same quote he had discussed with Marjorie Hayes and that Hayes had failed to recognize as incendiary.

"A certain inevitability to the shooting."

The phrase had rattled around in Bloom's head since he'd read it. It had been uttered by the Chamber of Commerce board member, Nichols.

"Marjorie had stepped out of the hearing to make a call," said Coogan. "They're scuffling, fighting—hands on each other. She starts asking questions since she knew Nichols, who was rattled but not hurt. Paxton stormed off but Nichols told Marjorie he was glad there had been a witness, told Marjorie he was the one who had been attacked."

"So Paxton wanted you to keep it out of the paper," said Bloom.

"Nichols didn't press charges," said Coogan. "It was a close call."

"Any word on what the fight was about?"

"Not from either of them," said Coogan. "But Marjorie did some digging."

Digging? Maybe in her garden.

"I know," said Coogan, reading Bloom's mind. "I gave her a few pointers. But she said something didn't seem right. Then she got intrigued. I don't discourage it when a reporter gets p.o.'d. So anyway Paxton had his name on a contract over in Mesa County, a contract to run a detention center for ICE."

Trudy shook her head slowly.

"I know of only one, in Aurora," said Bloom.

"Marjorie is checking into it," said Coogan.

"And where does Nichols come in?"

"Paxton only asked to keep the scuffle out of the paper. Couldn't get much out of him on the substance of his fight with Nichols, though I did try."

"Maybe Nichols wanted in on the action," said Bloom.

Trudy nodded, mouthed: "I know." Something had clicked.

Bloom suddenly wanted off the call.

"Where are you now?" said Coogan.

"Rifle," said Bloom firmly. "Near Paxton's business. At least, one of them."

"And nothing going on with the cops?" said Coogan.

"Checking every minute," said Bloom. A lie.

"Hound them," said Coogan.

"I'll check in now." He needed more slack, not less. But there was no margin in hinting at disobedience. "Where's Marjorie?"

"She's down at the courthouse pulling records and then she's going to check the Secretary of State's office online, Motor Vehicles—all that good stuff," said Coogan.

Imagining Marjorie Hayes sifting through a stack of folders or cruising databases online was like picturing Mary Poppins in a dark parking garage getting details on the Nixon White House from Deep Throat.

"Call me if she gets any hits," said Bloom. "I'll check with the cops on Lamott."

Bloom punched off the phone.

"Troy Nichols?" he said to Trudy.

"Always coming around Jerry's old store before he sold it," said Trudy. "Always trying to get Jerry to carry these Mexican cheeses and Mexican products—avocados and other things. Later, Jerry went strictly with local products but for a while there he was taking some goods and Nichols had shipments from the border twice a week. Straight from El Paso."

"I don't mean to be dense," said Bloom. "But, so?"

Trudy took a second, dialing in a thought. "He was really putting the pressure on Jerry, especially after Jerry stopped taking the shipments from Mexico. He kept coming around."

"Trying to fill his trucks," said Bloom.

"So maybe Paxton and his crew from Rifle thought they had the Glenwood Springs turf covered," said Trudy. "Somehow they find out

Nichols has a dark side of his business, transporting illegal immigrants, and there's some sort of clash and fallout."

"Maybe Paxton wanted a piece of Nichols' action."

"And maybe Nichols' wouldn't crack," said Trudy.

DiMarco must have known about the expanded version of Pipeline Enterprises.

Some company names are pure genius.

"Alfredo said it wasn't that long of a drive," said Bloom. "Rifle would fit. But where?" said Bloom.

Trudy gave him a look like he should try adding two plus two.

"Where the dog food is," she said.

FORTY-NINE:
FRIDAY AFTERNOON

DEPUTY SHERIFF CHADWICK SOUNDED weary.

"Heard about Search and Rescue up your way," said Chadwick. "Think they've got an investigator assigned and should be calling you pronto."

"I'm available," said Allison. "But one lone investigator isn't going to cut it. You need a whole pack of cops up here now—there are people hunting other people. *With dogs.*" She paused. "*For sport.*"

"What the hell?" said Chadwick.

"I know," said Allison. "But this isn't a case for a lone investigator. You're going to need some troops."

Carefully, Allison walked Chadwick through the same details she'd given Trudy.

"Do you think those guys are coming back to that same camp?" said Chadwick. "And you can find it again?"

"On a moonless night walking backwards," said Allison. "I spent last night waiting for them, but they didn't come back before I left this morning. If their dog is injured or worse, you could check with some of the vet clinics down there. Track who brought the dog in, you're on your way."

Chadwick asked her to double back over key parts of the story one more time. "We need the doctors to work some magic in Grand Junction," he said, speaking with about as much urgency as a cop might ever let on. "A witness would change everything. And I need that blindfold as soon as possible."

Allison didn't want drive it down—shouldn't the cops come get it? But another idea was brewing and she was the lone candidate to do what needed doing.

"What's new with the hunt for Lamott's shooter?" For a second she thought the call had dropped.

"Manhunt," said Chadwick. "Picture your big Hollywood movie manhunt and quadruple it."

"I've seen the sketch," said Allison.

"If you've even uttered the word immigration in the past five years, we are in the process of tracking you down to find out if you've seen this guy."

"That's a lot of people," said Allison.

"That's a whole heck of a lot of people," said Chadwick.

"And so far?"

"Still looking."

The news station switched back to a live shot of a reporter standing on the pedestrian bridge. He appeared to be college-fresh. But he already had the appropriate reporter face: weighty dejection.

The mug shot sketch replaced him on the screen. If you wanted to attempt assassination in broad daylight, it was about the least advisable look you would want to adopt.

The mug shot stared back with fury. In her mind, she converted the sketch to flesh. "What time of day?" asked Allison.

"What do you mean?"

"Was it high noon when this guy was spotted?" said Allison. "Broad daylight?"

"Pre-dawn," said Chadwick.

"And he had help, right?" said Allison.

"From one Emmitt Kucharski," said Chadwick. "Resident of Glenwood Manor."

Allison had the sound down on the television but knew that was the other mug in heavy rotation. This wasn't a drawing of Kucharski, but a photo from a previous arrest.

"A third-rate tire mechanic is about Kucharski's highest professional accomplishment," said Chadwick. "He had about thirty-five lives and as many jobs before he moved here fifteen months ago. He's got some backcountry experience, by the way, so maybe he slipped off into the hills."

An uplifting thought.

Kucharski's mug shot from an earlier burglary arrest showed a man with serious issues. He had short, disheveled hair groomed by scissors and mirror. His gaze could have been that of a stoner, but there was something clear-eyed and calculating about his stare.

"Can't find him either?" said Allison.

Silence answered her dumb question and then he said: "We have some leads."

"I need two things," said Allison.

"And I need two *people*," said Chadwick. "But, fire away."

"I need an ID or some indication or whatever you've got on that body we found."

"Thought I saw that we got something back on that," said Chadwick. "Nobody called you?"

This time Allison let Chadwick decipher the silence to his own satisfaction.

"I'll get the initial finding and call you back but I remember Hispanic male, approximate age of twenty. A pretty youthful coccyx bone from what I remember. There were traces of cocaine in his jacket or what was left of his jacket. More than traces. Enough to suggest he was transporting."

"Cause of death?"

She heard her own sudden hesitance, like she didn't want to know. Not really.

"Still not clear. Too much of him was gone. An animal of some sort got to him and might have consumed some evidence but he was healthy and fit from the internal organs they had to work with."

"And the sticks? His clothes? DNA?"

"Nobody called you?" said Chadwick.

In this conversation, silence was the equivalent of saying "dumb question."

"I had a retired cop friend who was headed for Mount Rushmore," said Chadwick. "With his family. August and all, and they delivered the material that day on the way through Wyoming. I guess maybe they thought the evidence was somehow all tangled in the Lamott mess so they put a rush job on it and they e-mailed a report back to the office here two days ago. I asked that you be called. The only thing on them is fingerprints—one set of fingerprints over and over."

A firm knock on the door.

"—I haven't checked my e-mail yet today but they were supposed to send down images of the fingerprints, too," said Chadwick.

"The people who found him—at first there were kids, then the adults—might have moved the sticks."

"One set of prints," said Chadwick. "All I know."

A firm knock again.

Allison flashed on Trudy's intruders, felt her breath shorten at the thought.

Colin would let himself in...
The door was unlocked...

"Okay, thanks," said Allison. "Can I call you back?"

She was ready to yell "it's open."

She didn't want to lose Chadwick.

And it wasn't her house.

"Of course," said Chadwick. "And I need that blindfold."

She hung the phone back in the cradle, stepped lightly to the door. She could sure use a peep hole but that was a city touch, not common out here.

Cracked the door.

Smiled.

"Colin—why didn't you just—"

Something in his look. Downcast.

Message in his eyes.

Bad news.

Trouble.

He didn't move, but shifted his gaze slowly left.

The gun came from that same direction, gripped by a hand attached to a forearm like a four-by-four. The gun pointed at Colin's temple.

"Trudy Heath?" came the voice.

Allison took a step back, held the door open, focused on the gun.

"Don't fucking move," said the voice.

Silence, in fact, was golden.

FIFTY:
FRIDAY AFTERNOON

TRUDY PARKED ACROSS AND up the road from Pipeline Enterprises, maneuvered the pickup in between a cluster of flat-bed trucks that looked unused since the shale boom went bust about six years ago. Trudy's pickup joined the industrial cemetery.

If they had stirred the hornet's nest at Pipeline Enterprises, all the hornets had flown inside to buzz and huddle. Bloom pulled a pair of fit-in-your-palm binoculars from a jacket pocket.

"Free with my subscription to *National Geographic*," he said.

If the men from Pipeline Enterprises weren't happy with Bloom's questions and related interruption to their day, they certainly would be none too thrilled to look up the road and see the same pickup still in the vicinity and a pair of binoculars pointed back at them. Trudy felt her breath tighten.

"The buildings are connected—or at least related to each other for sure," said Bloom. "Two men walked between them and there's a top to a chain link fence behind the buildings where the ground slopes away."

Bloom passed the binoculars to her. The smaller building filled her entire field of vision, but Trudy couldn't get the image to settle.

"Take a long, slow breath," said Bloom. "Or prop your elbows on the steering wheel."

"That obvious?" said Trudy.

"Hey, my heart is jumping, too."

Bloom's voice was reassuring.

The view steadied. Trudy adjusted the focus. The binoculars packed more power than their size suggested.

"Couple guys walking back to the bigger building," said Trudy. "Maybe the same two. And two dogs on leashes."

Golden sun drenched the men. One wore a blue work shirt over black jeans and brown work boots. The other wore a green hoodie over blue jeans and dark running shoes. Green hoodie was taller. The dogs kept the leashes taut. Halfway between the two buildings, the men put their backs to Trudy's view, disappeared as the land sloped away to the east.

"I want to go down that hill," said Bloom.

"But you're not," said Trudy.

Trudy handed the binoculars back. Without magnification, the smaller building was a dwarf. Easy to overlook.

"If I was Paxton I'd want my detention center hopping." Bloom lined up his smart phone with the camera app up. He attached a pencil-thick tube like a miniature telescope. "Telephoto. We need a witness who has been inside—like, say, Alfredo, if he could identify it."

Trudy was surprised Jerry hadn't called to check on her. She knew she wouldn't answer if he did. "How long are we going to wait?" she said.

"Don't know," said Bloom. He snapped pictures. "Unless I get a call and something is happening back in Glenwood with the cops. We don't have reinforcements, do we?"

"While you were at the newspaper," said Trudy. "I made a trip to the store."

From behind Bloom's seat, Trudy produced a lunch-size cooler with slices of prosciutto and Muenster from Rocking W Cheese. "Made in Olathe," said Trudy. Crackers, a bag of plump grapes, two bottles of cold water.

Bloom laughed. "Did you wave a wand or something while I wasn't looking? I was just thinking it was time to see if we could do something with the telephone number Allison found at that camp."

He started tapping on his phone with two thumbs. Finally he pressed one last key and held up the screen for inspection.

"Good old IRB account again," he said. "Of course I could dial the number and pretend I'm selling home security or carpet cleaning."

"Too easy," said Trudy. "And what if they have Caller ID?"

"Now you're thinking," said Bloom. "Come on, IRB, spit it out. How long will it be before we have a powerful cell tower within ten feet no matter where you go? Is that asking too much?"

He smiled. He was open to the world, still thinking it through.

"Patience?" said Trudy. Tried to keep a straight face. "No reporter classes on patience?"

"In fact, they go in and surgically remove that trait," said Bloom. "Not a virtue in my business."

"Maybe we stop, use a computer at a library or ask at a hotel or motel at the Rifle exit," said Trudy.

The exchange of warmth and friendship with Duncan felt a bit like she was cheating on Jerry. Oddly, it gave her a lift. It was as much danger as she wanted to taste but there it was, like a perfect pinch of salt.

"Here we go," said Bloom. "The electronic device speaks."

He peered at it, scrolled, peered at it some more and scrolled again.

"That number belongs to a Joseph C. Harbor. Hometown of Colbran, Colorado. Address on Spring Street. A friend took me fly fishing once in Buzzard Creek. We were hoping for bullheads or brookies but got a bunch of pumpkinseed sunfish."

Colbran was another hour west. It sat back up off the highway to the south, toward the Grand Mesa. It was on a list of second-tier towns where Down to Earth didn't yet have a retail outlet. Jerry had a list of untapped markets.

"And looks like Allison's got a winner. Lists his company as Pipeline Enterprises Inc. Lists a wife, Abigail Harbor, and five little Harbors." Duncan looked up, stared out at the highway. "Not made for the big ocean liners, those little Harbors."

"Not a problem in western Colorado," said Trudy. "Could they handle a kayak?"

"Possibly," said Duncan. He returned to his screen. "The five little Harbors are Sarah, Eunice, Joanna, Ruth, and Mary. I bet they've got a Bible in the house, maybe one for each room or exposed surface."

"All roads lead to Pipeline Enterprises," said Trudy.

"At least, the scrawled telephone number that Allison finds at a camp up in the woods and a van that plucks unknown illegals off the streets both track back to the same company."

"Better call her back, give her a heads-up," said Trudy. "You or me?"

"I'll do it," said Bloom.

"But no questions about finding the body," said Trudy. "Not a peep."

"Promise," said Bloom.

Bloom dialed, waited. He held the phone away from his ear, shook his head.

"Allison Coil's probably never known for instant accessibility," he said. "She's already slipped back into the woods and gone off the grid."

FIFTY-ONE:
FRIDAY AFTERNOON

"WHERE THE FUCK IS Alfredo Loya?"

The tip of the gun pressed the back of Colin's left ear.

"I don't know," said Allison.

Trudy's phone rang. That was one call that would have to wait.

"He's your no-good illegal wetback motherfucker and we know you had him up here."

The man was all shoulders and chest. He towered over Colin. He had a head like a block, face like a pinched turnip and the creased-up rough skin to go with it. Needed boiling. The flesh on his cheeks flashed red—a touch of youth. Gin blossoms. Was he even thirty? Allison held his stare. His dark eyes jumped. She didn't study what he was wearing, but the basic message was black.

"I don't know what you're talking about," said Allison.

"Don't give me that crap," he said. He moved the barrel off Colin's ear and jabbed it in the soft spot under his jaw. The tip of the barrel disappeared in Colin's neck.

"There's nobody here," said Allison. "Nobody. Maybe you got the wrong—"

"The hell," he said. "You're Trudy. This is your place."

Colin was wide-eyed.

"I can say it again," said Allison. This guy hadn't studied his brief. Nobody would mistake her for her best friend.

"Alfredo was here last night," he said. "Why don't we have ourselves a little look around?"

"Why don't you put the gun down and I'll give you the grand tour?" said Allison. The man moved the gun to Colin's temple. "How do you know he was here last night?"

Maybe there was something about Trudy's absence she needed to know.

The man's cheeks flared a fresh coat of scarlet. He was plenty mean-looking but might still be carrying rookie status.

"I am not, as you may notice, in a position where I am the one who has to answer questions. You are the one—"

Patience, if that's what it was, evaporated. The man flicked Colin aside with a shove. Colin stumbled sideways and slammed into a floor lamp, which did nothing to break his fall. Colin tried to cushion the fall with his outstretched arms, but his chest took the blow on the hardwood floor and the lamp crashed next to him. He rolled over and groaned, facing away.

The gun switched targets in a flash. She stared up at the barrel, inches from her nose and an unwavering extension of his locked-elbow grip.

Colin moaned, turtled up on his hands and knees. The unwelcome intruder had made a big mistake by letting Colin go free.

She stole a glance. There was blood on Colin's face.

The gun didn't budge.

"Doesn't change anything," said Allison.

"Alfredo fucking Loya," said the man. "Now."

"I'm telling you," said Allison. "Let's have a look—"

Colin used the couch as a launching pad. He was mid-air when the man turned to defend himself. Too late. Colin was airborne and had aimed at the man's right flank. Colin came feet first. His left boot jammed into the man's torso with a crack. The man reeled back. Allison figured his fists would clench in reflex and she turned and ducked, ready for the gun to fire. No shot. The man's head snapped back on the wall with a thump. Colin whacked the man's right wrist like karate on a woodblock and the gun hit the floor with a clatter. The man staggered like a drunk and Colin kicked him hard in the groin and he let out a powerful bellow, all agony. As the man reached to protect himself, a flash of Colin's fist went straight to his face and the man's nose exploded in a gusher. He landed with a thud, blood pooling as quickly as if a bag of maroon paint had been slashed open from the bottom.

The man brought his legs up in a curl, out of reflex, to protect his balls. As if that would ease the pain.

Allison picked the gun off the floor.

They took in an angry bleat of epithets in a multitude of colorful combinations, fucker this and fucker that.

"You okay?" said Allison.

An inch-wide gash oozed blood on Colin's right cheek. He panted hard as she spread the gash with her fingers, knowing it would hurt, and Colin yelped. A piece of glass—no doubt a bit of light bulb—shined back at her from the wound. She handed Colin the gun so he could watch their visitor and she went for a cup of water and a wet wash cloth. She poured water over Colin's tipped head and the wound came clean. Colin never complained, though the same couldn't be said for the man still writhing on the floor.

"Son of a fucking bitch," he said.

On her next trip, Allison found a bandage in Trudy's bathroom. She hoped Colin didn't need stitches.

Colin put the gun down, his former captor was seriously focused on the pain and nothing else. Colin jerked his arms around behind him to tie him up.

"Watch him," said Colin and took off for the kitchen where Trudy kept a magical always-be-prepared drawer of wonders.

"My pleasure," said Allison. "Your cheek okay?"

"Stings a bit," said Colin from the kitchen.

"Fuck you," said the man. "What about me?"

His nose looked broken. It throbbed purple-red.

Allison said a quick thanks to Trudy's oak floors. Though they had a rustic finish, most of the blood would clean up.

"Who the hell are you?" said Allison.

Colin returned with long leather shoelaces and duct tape.

"Fuck you." The enunciation was lacking, given the problems in the nose and mouth area, but the spirit was there.

"Watch him while I call the cops," said Allison.

"Wait."

"Your name," said Allison. She cocked the gun so he could hear it, pointed it to the ceiling. Colin produced a clean kitchen towel and tossed it over the pool of blood.

"I came for Alfredo." Each word was followed by a painful breath. "Give me a second."

"A name," said Allison. "Yours."

Allison would have no problem with a swarm of cops. An even dozen should do it. Perhaps they could arrive by helicopter, pronto.

"Let me go," he said. "Pretend this never happened."

"Cops it is," said Allison, heading off.

"Wait."

"I'm short on time," said Allison.

"It's Boyd."

"First or last?" said Colin.

Boyd was on his side, head tipped away. "Junior Boyd."

"Given name?" said Colin.

"Carl," he said.

"Who the hell is Alfredo?"

"Thought he was your dude, your worker," said Boyd.

"I'm not Trudy," said Allison.

Boyd rolled over as far as he could go, looked at her hard. "You ain't Trudy?"

"I was lucky enough to be the one to be here. Who the hell is Alfredo to you?"

"Actually, you don't match the description," said Boyd.

"Who is Alfredo to you?" said Allison.

"What's your name?" said Boyd.

"My questions," said Allison. "Tell me about Alfredo."

"I'll be on my way," said Boyd. "Soon as I can walk. Pretend this never happened."

"Hard to do," said Colin, daubing at the bandage on his cheek. The blood was coming through.

"Alfredo," said Allison. "Tell us."

Colin gave Boyd's boot a kick.

"Bounty."

"Bounty?" said Colin.

"He's an illegal. He was on his way back to that shithole country he comes from and he slipped away." Boyd took a breath. "Hell my nose hurts."

"Why the gun?" said Allison.

Boyd continued: "This guy tried to play dumb." He meant Colin. "He wanted me to think I was in the wrong county. Knew I wasn't. I want Alfredo, wherever the hell he is."

"Who's paying bounty?"

Boyd looked down like he hadn't heard the question.

Allison came down close to his side, put her face up close. "If I have to ask you again, I am going to be on the telephone to the cops faster than—"

"The detention center," said Boyd. Choosing his words carefully.

"What detention center?"

"I don't know," said Boyd.

"Whose?"

"Same answer."

"How much bounty are we talking?" said Colin.

"Enough," said Boyd.

"How much?" said Allison, with more bite.

"A thousand," said Boyd.

Boyd strained like he wanted to sit up. Colin pulled him by the shoulders and he slumped against the side of Trudy's couch. Boyd winced. His nose would be puffy and sore for weeks.

"So there are others looking, others who know about the bounty?" said Colin.

Boyd rolled his head around. "Everyone who knows is looking and helps."

"Helps with?" said Allison.

"Helps with keeping a lookout for the fucking illegals. Help with getting their asses off the street. This guy escaped. He needs to go back."

"Where to?" said Colin.

Boyd let his broad chest rise and fall. The question brewing for Allison was what they were going to do with Boyd once this exchange was over.

"I don't know," said Boyd.

"Hell," said Colin.

"I got a number to call. I call it. They come."

Boyd was out of gas, defeated. His tone was matter-of-fact.

"I don't think they want me to see it," said Boyd.

"And who pays you?" said Allison.

"I don't need an ID," said Boyd. "Bye fucking bye is all."

Allison stood up straight, walked outside. Boyd's Taurus stared back, its doors flung open and the interior dome light on. The last thing anyone needed was a dead battery and the need to jump a car. Swift kicks delivered to each door and the doors slammed shut with authority. The inside of the Taurus looked like a hoarders' exhibit, the back seat piled to the gills with papers and junk. If Colin had been forced to ride in the car, even for a minute, he'd need the equivalent of a Karen Silkwood hose-down.

"Whatcha doin'?"

Colin stepped outside on the porch. Boyd was behind him, only his legs visible.

"Thinking," said Allison.

"Noisy way of thinking," said Colin.

"It helps," said Allison.

"Can I get you a sledgehammer or maybe a crane and a wrecking ball?" said Colin.

"You're not pissed off?"

"I was the one with a gun to my head," said Colin.

A mumble came from inside the house. "What did he say?" said Allison.

"He said he wasn't going to use the gun," said Colin. "If I had known that, I would have hit him earlier."

"Hey!" said Boyd. And then another mumble.

"What now?" said Allison.

"He said he was helping his country. He's a patriot in case you didn't know."

"Patriot?" said Allison. "He said *patriot*?"

"His word," said Colin.

Allison was up on the porch and she passed Colin in a flash.

"You know anything about hunting dogs?" she said.

"Seen them in movies," said Boyd. "Brits chasing the fox, that sort of thing. Blowing horns."

"Around here?" said Allison. "Ever seen them? Heard them? Heard about them? Nasty games with hunting dogs?"

Boyd's face was a dull dead blank. "No," he said.

"Then how about this?" said Allison. She pulled the half-envelope from her back pocket. "Is this a number you recognize?"

Boyd studied it like an algebra problem. "I don't know," he said.

"Look at it." Her order was an uppercut.

"I don't know," said Boyd. "I never could remember numbers. But I've got a cheat sheet in my wallet."

Colin helped Boyd to his feet, gingerly pulled the wallet out of Boyd's back pocket.

Like Boyd's car, the wallet was an overstuffed home for crap. Worn papers jutted from the main billfold compartment, notes and receipts and newspaper tidbits.

"Not much of an organizer," said Boyd. "I can find the paper if you—"

Colin opened the wallet upside down. Papers and junk fluttered down on the couch like confetti.

"Hell," said Boyd. "Never going to find anything again."

"Where are your numbers?" said Allison.

"I laminated the card," said Boyd. "It's still in the wallet in an inside flap."

The business card encased in plastic sported a list of phone numbers.

No names.

No instructions.

A dozen or so numbers altogether, handwritten.

All 970 area code.

The fifth number down was a dead match.

FIFTY-TWO:
FRIDAY AFTERNOON

BLOOM CALLED COOGAN, LET him know the cops were still dead in the water. He logged into IRB again and scoured for any detail he could find on Troy Nichols. Trucks passed, cars passed, nobody looked over. Trudy listened and followed along. She could blink and sense Bloom's calm. She could blink again and dread was right there, shot up from the depths. The two lived side by side.

"Troy Nichols' business is InterWest Distribution," said Bloom.

"That's the one," said Trudy. "He pressed Jerry to open an account—several times. Nichols wanted his business badly."

When she spoke, she worked to add to the confidence. And calm.

Bloom punched the name of the business into Google. "Big operation," said Bloom. He stared at the screen like a watchmaker.

"Here's a link about InterWest down in New Mexico," he said. "Truth or Consequences—the town, that is. The local paper is called *The Herald.* According to their slogan, there is nothing more powerful than the truth. In case that's news to you."

Bloom's phone buzzed. A 212 area code.

Bloom put the caller on the speaker so she could hear.

"To what do I owe the pleasure of a call from television's most intrepid reporter?" said Bloom.

"Well, since you're an old pal and not really competition, I wanted to make sure you have your eyes on the right national evening news broadcast."

Bloom didn't seem to mind the voice's flip tone.

"I'm not near a television," said Bloom. "But I can watch best-of-Kerry-London videos on YouTube, right on my phone. It's how I spend most of my spare time."

"You make it sound like you might be working," said London.

"If I was on the East Coast and the piece had already run, what would I know by now?" said Bloom.

"It's much more dramatic on tape," said London. "Hard to describe."

"Try me," said Bloom.

"Well, we have access to a former FBI profiler," said London. "That's a network budget for you. We got him to sketch out the profile of Lamott's shooter. And we also, as you might not be surprised to learn, get tips all the time. There are visible anti-immigration groups but there are also invisible ones. Those are the really dangerous ones, the groups that don't need a brand or a slogan."

London stopped as if that explained it all. Bloom shrugged, gave a puzzled look and smiled. Trudy wanted to blurt out: "And?"

Bloom covered the same ground. "So, connect the dots here."

"You might want to find a hotel or bar or a good Internet connection somewhere," said London. "The show starts out here in forty-two minutes and your editor might want you to file something, get some local reaction—"

"Tell me," said Bloom.

"We found a guy who knows the shooter. Of course we had to promise all sorts of protection, put him in a silhouette for the interview, modulate his voice. And now the cops are all over us, but that's another story."

"You mean he claims to know the shooter," said Bloom.

"If you want to get technical about it," said London. "Okay."

"And?" said Bloom.

"And the shooter is a damn good shot," said London. "That's a given. But he's also extremely quiet, someone who doesn't say much or brag much and might be a straight-and-narrow guy. He hasn't gone out and waved his virtual dick around in the Internet chat rooms. But in this case the profiler thinks it's someone who was avenging an issue for someone else, possibly a father or a close friend. The shooter wasn't getting the recognition he needed, not necessarily from the world or from the anti-immigration crowd, but from one or possibly two other people."

"And that explains why he's dropped into a hole," said Bloom.

"Mission accomplished and pride restored," said London. "Cops have been checking all the hate groups, which makes sense. But they aren't coming at it from the right angle. The shooter might be right under their noses, a former Eagle Scout type who has taken the whole red, white, and blue thing into his own hands in order to prove a point. And it might be as much about himself or a relationship as much as it's about what Lamott tried to promote."

"Whoa," said Bloom, like he meant it. Bloom turned to her, shook his head slightly.

"Told you," said London.

"Dang," said Bloom. "I'm screwed."

Trying to imagine the kind of personality London had described, Trudy had to agree—it all clicked. She could almost picture the shooter, had a fleeting image in her head.

"But you didn't get any names on camera or off?" said Bloom.

"Nope," said London. "Of course, not on camera. And I wouldn't tell you if we got them off camera."

"And how did you identify your main source, the guy you put in silhouette?"

"A local businessman is all," said London. "He's credible. See for yourself."

London said good-bye and hung up.

Bloom lifted the binoculars, going back to the routines. "One thing about being a reporter, you never know if you're poking around in the right dredge full of muck."

"You're in the right place," said Trudy, but didn't know if it was true. "I'm scared sitting here, so that must mean something."

"I had the feeling all along the national news teams would get the edge," said Bloom. "So hard to keep up."

Like a shift change, three pickups and a gleaming SUV roared up Buckthorn and sped past. None of the drivers looked over.

"You've got Truth or Consequences," said Trudy. "You had something there."

"Almost forgot," said Bloom. "Wallowing in my own misery over here. Hard to imagine somebody won't identify a suspect or two once London's piece runs."

"What happened in New Mexico?" said Trudy. "Forget about Kerry London. We've got stuff right here."

Bloom went back to his phone. "Here it is," he said. Read for a minute, then summarized. "A truck registered to InterWest Distribution was stopped to fix a flat tire on I-25 eight miles north of town. It's one of those service vans, not a passenger van. Cops pull up to help. The back is crammed with illegals. Van impounded. The illegals are taken away and the driver is held—and here's the controversy—they didn't charge the driver. All the lawmakers down there are in an uproar. One of the illegals was carrying a decent amount of cocaine."

"Nichols kept his InterWest trucks full one way or another," said Trudy.

"Playing both ends," said Bloom. "A contract up here to ship them out to ICE and they ensure a fresh supply of warm bodies by hauling them north."

Trudy pictured the huddled bodies in the back of the van. No windows. She pictured the bodies bouncing around, not knowing why they had stopped or possibly sensing the flat tire, and then the back of the van flying open. And cops.

She pictured the hope on their faces.

"It's perfect," said Trudy. "It's a self-cultivating garden."

FIFTY-THREE:
FRIDAY AFTERNOON

"Let's start with the name William Sulchuk. Mean anything?"

Everything she'd been told needed to be put in a shaker and jacked around like a bartender making a drink.

"Sounds sort of familiar, but I'm not good with names or numbers," said Boyd.

"Goes by William," said Colin. "Not Bill."

The entrails of Boyd's wallet sat jumbled in a large plastic bag, worn-down scraps of cards and notes and receipts.

"I'm a peon," said Boyd. "They don't let me into the tent where they keep the whiskey and the battle plan."

Boyd sat up. Colin had loosened his restraints.

"The other guy was Larry Armbruster," said Colin.

"Good memory," said Allison.

"When I saw the size of his arms, I remember thinking arm bruiser," said Colin, by way of explanation. "Don't ask me about the Larry part."

"How about that name?" said Allison.

"I'm a nobody," said Boyd. His posture confirmed his self-worth. Long gone was the first impression of towering tough guy. Dejection coated every word. "There are lots of us, far as I can tell."

"Answer the questions."

"You calling the cops?"

"I'll bet they'll have questions."

Mountain lion, *hell.*

"Larry Armbruster," said Allison. "Come on, give it to me."

"It's not like we know everyone," said Boyd. "We all have our roles."

"But you know the name," said Allison. "So tell me who he is."

Boyd sighed. "He's a truck driver."

"And?"

"They pay by the head," said Boyd. "You deliver, they process."

"Process?" said Allison.

"I only know my end of it," said Boyd. "The more Mexicans you bring in, the more you make."

"But you know Armbruster?" said Colin.

Boyd felt his jaw with his hand. "It's numb," he said. "I'm going to need a doctor."

"The ice is all you get for now," said Allison. "What about Armbruster?"

"Times are tight," he said. "Economy is down, border gets tougher to cross. There isn't as much business. Armbruster got squeezed out, which meant things had dried up for lots of us, too."

It was like she'd been working on a jigsaw puzzle of Monet's lily pads but at the end she blinked and it was a splotch abstract by Jackson Pollock.

"Know anything about a body up by Lumberjack Camp?"

Boyd shook his head. "I don't do woods."

"Do you know anything about it or hear anything about it?"

"No," he said.

The dog camp.

The *trash.*

"Wait here," said Allison.

She hustled back across the meadow. Her thoughts churned through detail again. She retrieved the plastic bag of trash from her front stoop, hustled back with her load.

She used her pocket knife to slash open the bottom of the bag. The viscera poured out on Trudy's porch.

Styrofoam cups, plates, plastic utensils, paper towels, granola bar wrappers, empty cans for beans and chili and beer. The trash stew coughed up a repulsive odor. Allison kicked the items around with her boot, picked up a ripped-open plastic clamshell with two fingertips like forceps and flipped it over.

The package label: Wicked Ridge Crossbow Bolts, Spitfire Mechanical Broadheads.

"Know anything?" she said, holding them up.

"Larry loves his crossbows," said Boyd. "But you couldn't say those are his."

"Illegal during archery season," said Colin.

"And no mechanical broadheads in Colorado," said Allison. "Even during rifle season."

Allison speared each bit of junk with her pocketknife, stabbed one strip of paper. The receipt dangled from the tip of her blade. It was smeared with ketchup or chili. $75.99 for the bolts and tips, purchased at Rifle Sporting Goods.

The receipt carried an image of the purchaser's signature, the first name starting with an L followed by a snaking squiggle. She shoved the receipt in Boyd's face.

"Recognize it?" she said.

Boyd studied it. "Hell," he said. "Course not."

"The hell you don't," said Allison. "How well do you know Armbruster?"

Boyd stood up, grabbed his plastic bag of wallet confetti. He took a breath, handed the ice towel to Colin. "Am I free to go?"

"How well did you know him?" said Allison.

"Pretty well," said Boyd. "He's my uncle."

That sinking feeling. "So it's a family business?" said Allison.

"Oh no." Boyd tried to sound helpful. "Hardly. Uncle Larry's always had a bug up about the Mexican mooches, that's what he calls them. For some reason I don't know, that was his thing. He got in a fight once at a family reunion, got himself so worked up that he turned over a whole picnic table. He picked up a can of beer and flung it. Only problem was the can of beer hit a child. Cops came, you know, the whole bit. Ended up in a big lawsuit. About ruined him."

Allison gave him space but he didn't go on.

"Seen him since the shooting?"

"No," said Boyd. "But Larry hated guys like Tom Lamott. *Hated.*"

Allison scrambled back over the scene at Lumberjack Camp in her mind. She replayed the day the body had been discovered—allegedly *discovered*—and the next when she had gone back.

The scene had been a stage.

Audience of one, front row center. She hadn't bought a ticket, hadn't read the program.

But it was all theater.

Perhaps Uncle Larry had been forced out of the round-up-the-illegal-Mexicans bounty plan. Perhaps there were degrees of empathy for the illegals. On one end of the scale, mere loathing. On the other, kill the occasional Mexican for sport. Maybe Uncle Larry came up with a way to get back in the business. Maybe he thought of exposing whatever was happening to some of the illegals up in the woods would take down one whole end of the ring. The mountain lion ruse worked. Maybe Sal Hickman and his hounds were all part of the act. It wasn't going to fool anyone for long, but all it had to do was suck her in, start stirring stuff up.

"So who else do you know besides your uncle?" said Allison. "Others in his group?"

"It's not like we're all friends," said Boyd. "Don't have to be."

"Who else?" said Allison.

Boyd appeared to give it some thought. "Like I say, I'm just a—"

"Who else?" said Colin.

Boyd looked at his sneakers, wide black ones with the laces tied but barely. "We each have our areas to patrol. Our routes. It's like checking a trapline. Making the rounds."

"You must have people you report to, check in with."

"Numbers to call," said Boyd. "The pick-ups, the drop-offs."

"Such as?" said Colin. "Give us one example—how it works."

Boyd thought, shook his head.

"The city has all these places where they hang out. Once you start seeing them," he said. "Like this one guy out fixing a flat on a bicycle over by the new Target, up there on the ridge. I gave him the old '*como está?*' bit and did a two-handed gesture like I'm gripping the wheel and I'd drive him to get a new tire. I called Uncle Larry to find out where he wanted him taken. Uncle Larry was busy with something, couldn't meet me. I was smiling the whole time, this Mexican right there in my front seat. Larry said take him to this address in West Glenwood, across the highway. A big old operation with trucks and of course it didn't look like a bike repair shop. I'd never been there before, but okay. The office had maps on the wall, red lines on the highways showing all the routes. All Glenwood Springs and south to the border, down through Texas and Arizona."

"That's where you left him?" said Colin.

"I used the word '*amigo*' and made it sound like everything was good," said Boyd. "A smile goes a long way. But within minutes my Mexican buddy was gone and I had a wallet full of cash. Plus, I got to meet Troy Nichols, who is always being quoted in the paper. Nice guy."

Allison had never heard of Nichols, which meant nothing. That was the same for most of everybody.

"Anyone else?" said Allison. She tried to ignore the acid churning in her system, already focused on her next call, thinking it through. "Or should we go down the list of numbers on your cheat sheet?"

"Can if you want," said Boyd. "I don't have names to go with them."

"So that's where you left him?"

"Yeah, that time. He had a worried smile in his face, like maybe they were going to offer him a job. He had a job all right, to get the hell out of our country. But my job was done." Boyd paused, looked at each of them with the sincerity of an earnest choir boy. "You sure he ain't here?"

FIFTY-FOUR:
FRIDAY AFTERNOON

ON THE HIGHWAY, BLOOM's phone buzzed.

"A cop friend," said Bloom before answering. "Cop for sure. Friend I think. His name's DiMarco."

Bloom put DiMarco on speaker.

"Find what you're looking for?" said DiMarco.

"And then some," said Bloom. "Cops are looking the other way on this stuff?"

"I have no idea what you're talking about," said DiMarco.

Bloom shook his head, rolled his eyes for her benefit.

"Our friendly engineers at Pipeline Enterprises," said Bloom. "Social engineers, in a way."

"And you want to know if the cops care about a few less illegal Mexicans on the street?" said DiMarco.

"They're being kidnapped," said Bloom. "Where's the due process?"

"Where's the due process when they sneak across the border? Criminals and low-lifes, most of them," said DiMarco. "You think we enjoy having them here?"

"I get the picture," said Bloom.

"Are you close?" said DiMarco.

"Close to what?" said Bloom.

"Glenwood."

"Fifteen minutes," said Bloom. "Maybe less. You're making me think something's going on."

DiMarco paused. "Let's say there's some excitement."

"Shit," said Bloom.

Trudy's eyes widened. They were over the speed limit, but she pushed it a notch.

"Announcing a name? A suspect?" said Bloom.

DiMarco hesitated. "Going to bring him in first."

Bloom could go straight back to the newspaper, put something on the web, start working his way back into Coogan's good graces. If such graces existed.

"And you can't do anything with this," said DiMarco. "Nothing. I don't want you off on some wild goose chase."

Trudy's cell phone rang.

"What the hell was that?" snapped DiMarco.

"My other cell," said Bloom.

Trudy fumbled for her phone as she drove, tried to put it on vibrate. It rang again.

"No lowly Glenwood Springs newspaper reporter carries two fucking cell phones," said DiMarco. "Who else is there?"

"It's my personal cell—"

"Give me a break," said DiMarco. "Give me a fucking break."

Bloom scrounged for his next counter punch, came up empty.

The pop-up message on the cell phone screen in a gray box read: Call Ended.

"Damn it," he said.

"Sorry," said Trudy. "Just sorry."

Now on vibrate, her phone buzzed.

"Jerry," she said.

"Take it," said Bloom, switching his cell off the ringer.

Trudy answered. And listened. "Rifle," she said after a minute. "My newspaper friend found something he wanted to check out. Almost back. Why?"

She listened for another long stretch. "I'm on the way," she said. No niceties. Hung up.

He knew Trudy would share what she could.

Trudy waited, took a breath.

"Our office is having a visit by the sheriff," said Trudy. "They are going through the records. They showed up right at close of business, had a truck waiting at the fields as the workers came off, though I guess a few saw what was going on and ran for it. Jerry is freaking out."

"Damn," said Bloom.

"Didn't need this," said Trudy. "And out of the blue."

"Or not," said Bloom.

FIFTY-FIVE:
FRIDAY AFTERNOON

OFFICER CHADWICK MET HER in the front lobby and she handed him the blindfold, now in a plastic bag.

He wanted her to sit down, but she declined. She was hoping to find Trudy and the reporter and then make one more stop on the outskirts south of town. In all, she hoped to be heading back to Sweetwater in an hour.

"And here's a receipt I found up there for illegal hunting gear and it's got a signature. Found it at the same camp," she said.

She handed him an envelope, where she had carefully placed the receipt.

"I see," said Chadwick. He said it like she'd was a speeding driver with a weak excuse.

"Look, the whole mountain lion thing was a *ruse*. A stage littered with props. Somebody wheeled that body into position for our entertainment. And then there's the poor guy in the Grand Junction hospital and the dog bites all over his body, you should have plenty to go on."

Chadwick dragged the spiral binding on his notebook across his upper chin like he needed a scratch. "We'll need to establish chain of possession on the blindfold. And your statement about how you came into possession of it and who else might have had a chance to handle it, contaminate it—that sort of thing."

"You should have plenty," said Allison. "There's a company in Rifle that's all tangled up with this, too. And I can give it to you but I don't have much on it. Forget the blindfold, but keep it if it will help round out your case."

"I'll make a note," he said. "And I'll take the name of the place in Rifle."

"Pipeline Enterprises," said Allison. "Shouldn't be too hard to find. And one other thing."

She handed him a piece of paper with Carl Boyd's particulars— name, address, telephone number. "And I'm going to email you with a photo, too."

It had been part of the deal of letting Boyd go—checking all his particulars, having him pose for a reluctant photo next to his trashed-out Taurus.

"He's right in the whole nest of snakes running their own round-them-up network," said Allison. "I'd file an assault report against him, too, if I had the time right now."

"Assault?" said Chadwick.

"And felony menacing," said Allison. "Something along those lines."

"Where?" said Chadwick. "When?"

"No time now," said Allison. "I've got to run."

There were bigger worries on her plate than Carl Boyd, at least for now.

Trudy was climbing out of her truck with the reporter as Allison came up to 8th Street. They were on the sidewalk walking toward Grand Ave. Allison jogged in her boots to catch up.

Trudy delivered one of her powerful, signature hugs.

"I'm dropping Duncan at the newspaper and I'm on the way to my office." Trudy looked tense. They huddled in front of the Haute Plate Bistro. "The cops are at my office going through all the paperwork and I can only imagine Jerry is a bit freaked out."

"Not the kind of publicity you need," said Allison.

"At all," said Trudy.

"What else happened in Rifle?" said Allison.

Trudy was careful, detailed. Bloom listened, filled in a gap here and there when Trudy needed the right word.

Trudy's version was understated. How the number on the envelope from the camp and how her late-night visitor had led them to Pipeline Enterprises.

Bloom told about going into the Pipeline warehouse and recognizing somebody who had been in the newspaper offices. Then, a story about a newspaper account in Truth or Consequences. The call from Kerry London.

"Kind of a smug tone to his voice," said Trudy, which made Allison smile. "But it was him."

"And there's a pen behind the buildings," said Trudy. "Dogs. Lots of dogs."

Allison heard a click like a trigger being pulled. A shiver bloomed from her neck to shoulders. "If it's the same pack, I'd recognize a couple of them. The wanted posters are in my head. Dog faces."

Trudy kept on with her story, somehow calm and precise. When she mentioned Troy Nichols, the name Boyd had mentioned, Allison held up her hand. "Whoa," she said.

"Say again how you know that name?" she asked.

"Some sort of rupture in the business," said Trudy. "At least, based on the fight the other reporter saw at the courthouse."

"And he's some sort of business bigwig?" said Allison.

"Chamber of Commerce," said Bloom. "He's the equivalent of a quote machine as far as most reporters are concerned."

Allison tried to imagine a distribution truck heading north, full of illegals, and remembered Chadwick mentioning traces of cocaine on the half-corpse.

"They supply their own raw material," said Trudy. "So to speak."

Allison hoped enough dirt had come to the surface that now it was a matter of the institutions—say, journalism and law enforcement—taking care of business.

Trudy's phone beeped. "Jerry again," she sighed. "Wondering what's taking me so long. Not a happy camper. Not a happy anything."

"Want me to go with you?" said Allison.

"Just something I've got to go through," said Trudy. "How about you? And is Colin okay?"

"All fine," said Allison.

"The cops have something brewing," said Bloom. "They're close."

"We're going to get back together later this evening, pull up more information on all these people," said Trudy. "You should see what's out there online about people, about everyone."

"One more name for you to run," said Allison. "Larry Armbruster." She spelled both names for Bloom. "And I don't know about this other guy who was there, William Sulchuk, I know he's from Glenwood Springs. You may as well run it, too."

"He lives here?" said Trudy.

"I'm headed to his house," said Allison. "That fancy development south of town. Four Mile Ranch."

Trudy shook her head, disbelieving.

"What?" said Allison.

"That's one of the places my guy headed to when I followed him that night. One guy got dropped off and then the other went on to New Castle."

"Did you follow them in? See the house?"

"No," said Trudy. "I would have been too exposed. You're going up there?"

"By yourself?" said Bloom.

Allison gave it a moment. "I think this was Armbruster's stage and his props," said Allison. "I only want to ask Sulchuk a few questions face to face, see what he knew."

"Jesus," said Bloom. "Be careful."

"And I've got two more names for you. First one is Dillard. I don't have a first name, but it's Dillard. He's one of the guys in the camp with the dogs."

"Got it," said Bloom.

"And the second name is Carl Boyd. Also goes by Junior Boyd. Nephew of Larry Armbruster and connected to the whole racket."

"Writing it down," said Bloom.

"And tonight?" said Trudy.

"Tonight I'm going to check on my hunters who are getting ready to head up in the woods tomorrow and then I'm going to get a good night's sleep," said Allison. "A helluva good night's sleep."

FIFTY-SIX:
FRIDAY, LATE
AFTERNOON

ONE POLICE CRUISER SAT next to Jerry's pickup and a white, un-marked sedan parked askew nearby. It had a government-issue vibe. As raids went, it appeared to be a civilized affair.

Inside, Jerry introduced Trudy to three men—one city cop, one from the Colorado Office of Homeland Security and one who was a contractor working for the state, "an identification specialist."

Trudy didn't try to remember names. They were huddled around two laptops and a stack of manila folders in a cardboard box.

Jerry gave her a "follow me" head nod and they stepped back outside.

"Weird timing," said Trudy. "Did they say why?"

"They don't need a why."

Jerry's scowl appeared to be hours in the making.

"Are they finding anything?" said Trudy.

"They aren't giving me a blow by blow," said Jerry. "Lots of muttering. Worse than the dentist while they're poking around in there, jabbing one tooth for an hour. No idea what they're finding."

"They haven't been asking questions?" said Trudy.

"A few," said Jerry.

"Maybe it's all fishing," said Trudy.

"I don't think they'll find anything," said Jerry. "But we need to be ready."

"For what?" said Trudy.

Jerry looked at her like she was a high school graduate who didn't know how to read. "For any major problems," he said.

"And then we'll deal with them," said Trudy. "Totally on the up and up. We aren't trying to get away with anything and so we'll deal with it."

"You're not worried?"

"No more than any other business that depends on labor," said Trudy. "We'll see what they find, have a conversation about it, and move on."

Jerry wanted her to panic, wanted the "raid" to bring her back in closer orbit. He shook his head, ever so slightly.

"I can't stay," said Trudy.

"What?" said Jerry. "This is your business. They are poring through the records of *your* business."

"My name is on it," said Trudy. "Sure. I'll answer any questions. I'll be around."

"You're going to leave me?" said Jerry.

Trudy took a second to process the fact that he meant *alone with the cops.* She had been thinking how to answer the same question, only on a much bigger scale.

"There's nothing for me to do," said Trudy. "And if you've been through the records they probably aren't going to find an undotted i.

It's a scare, that's all. It's a *scare*. Somebody saw my truck where they didn't think it belonged, called their cop friends to see if they'd put a jolt of fear in me. In us. In the business."

Jerry didn't believe a word. He shook his head. "Where were you?"

Was it worth going into it all? Did she have the time to go into it?

"A place in Rifle. Trying to figure out who had come to my place. We're close. Duncan is close. The reporter."

She was having trouble with full sentences, knowing where to start. She was sure it showed.

"Well, you must have created some conversation," said Jerry. "You got someone's attention."

Trudy took a step down toward her pickup, took a breath, turned back around to face Jerry, knowing they both had reached the same conclusion. She couldn't imagine sticking around long enough to watch it all explode. The finality of it was sad, but she would never be okay with Jerry's world view. It was as if there was a whole layer of the city he didn't want to see. Accusing him of anything, leveling charges, made no sense.

One of them would have to utter the words hanging in the space between them and, knowing Jerry, it wouldn't be a quick conversation.

FIFTY-SEVEN: FRIDAY, LATE AFTERNOON

"I WAS WATCHING FOR you," said William Sulchuk. The heavy-looking, tall front door had opened slowly when Allison was halfway along the flagstone walkway.

Four Mile Ranch. The only thing being ranched here was another addition to residential U.S.A. There was no sneaking up on anybody in this neighborhood, unless it was by foot on a moonless night.

She had called ahead to let him know she wanted to stop by, found her voice caught. Her uncertainty was closer to the surface than she would have preferred. If Sulchuk had any knowledge of the dog hunts, whether that knowledge was remote or intimate, she was walking into the house of a monster.

His easy smile belied all the implications to date. He led her into a gleaming, oversized kitchen with high ceilings and a five-seat breakfast bar. The kitchen was showroom ready, except where Sulchuk was preparing food in one small section of the available acre or so of counter space.

"Elk tenderloin," said Sulchuk. "About the last from the freezer. Last year's cow—she was a beauty."

So was the tenderloin—a roundish strip, not a scrap of fat on her.

Sulchuk wore an Oxford button-down like a lawyer on the weekend at the country club. His blue jeans were crisp with a manufactured fade. He had that uncanny ability to look like he was mere minutes from his last shower. She couldn't say the same for herself. The adrenaline that flowed when Boyd had showed up was equal to about a week's worth of routine sweat in the woods. She wished Colin could have come along for the trip to Glenwood Springs to deliver the blindfold and have this chat with Sulchuk, but the Oklahomans had showed up, three matching black Dodge Ram pickups tugging three behemoth camping trailers.

Sulchuk offered her a barstool at the kitchen counter. "And it's close enough to five o'clock so around here that means a cock-a-tail," he said. "If I'm not mistaken, you are partial to tequila."

"Good memory," said Allison, trying to think when she might have ever revealed that fact.

"I have some Alquimia," said Sulchuk. "Ever had it?"

From a top cupboard, Sulchuk produced a wide-bottom bottle about three-quarters full. A seductive brown liquor sloshed inside. "One hundred percent organic tequila in hand-blown glass bottles," said Sulchuk. "From Jalisco. How do you take it?"

From a Nalgene flask, she wanted to say, with a hint of Triple Sec and a squirt of lime. Sitting near a lake in the Flat Tops watching the light fade. Alone.

"Neat," she said.

Sulchuk ran through the ingredients in his tenderloin marinade—red wine, soy sauce, balsamic vinegar, rosemary, garlic and honey—

and asked her why he had the "honor" of her visit. "Aren't things getting busy up your way?" he said.

"Matter of fact, yes," said Allison. She pictured Colin running around answering questions for the crew from Oklahoma. They had looked like they might be needy. Polite, probably, but needy.

She wished she could trade places. But Sulchuk was her connection. The initial Lumberjack meet-up had been his request.

"That was no mountain lion," said Allison. She made sure to say it when she could watch his eyes. He stopped chopping garlic and looked up. His reaction suggested bewilderment, but the acting was amateur.

"Finally and for sure?" he said.

"No question," said Allison.

"You don't hear about too many lion attacks. But how do you know?"

"Cops," said Allison.

"What did they find?" said Sulchuk. "Was it some other animal?"

"Yeah," said Allison. "Human."

"Well, we were all around that poor guy," said Sulchuk.

He looked like he was trying to help. The look of a befuddled professor.

"More than that," said Allison. She sipped the smooth tequila. Not bad. "I'm not exactly sure. Surprised they haven't talked to you."

"No. Not me." Sulchuk put down his knife. Folded his arms thoughtfully. "Of course, as we all know, they've been busy."

"They'll probably get around to it," said Allison. "But can I ask you one question?"

"Of course," said Sulchuk. He had poured a healthy shot of tequila for himself and splashed in some store-bought Margarita mix. Poor tequila, she thought.

"Tell me how you picked Lumberjack Camp to meet up," she said.

He gave it a moment. His drink glowed an artificial green.

"Just an easy spot to find," he said. "You said you'd be up in that area and there's not much else I really know as both a place to wait, you know, it's perfect. And pretty easy to find."

"I'm packing in a crew from Oklahoma that's heading up that way. Crack of dawn tomorrow, as a matter of fact. I'm sure they'd leave at midnight tonight if they could."

"Lucky you," said Sulchuk. "Think of me. I'll be in the office working, even on the weekend."

"Has to be one of the most beautiful spots around."

"Seemed like an easy place to find each other, like Times Square in New York or the D&F Tower in Denver," said Sulchuk. "Why?"

Allison ignored his question.

"Lumberjack was your idea?" she said.

Sulchuk shrugged. "The others were along for the ride. It was something I put together and, as you know, was kind of a last-minute deal."

"Hey, Dad!"

Gail bounded into the kitchen. She looked fully two years older, almost mature, without the sobs and worried face Allison had seen at Lumberjack. Her hair at Lumberjack had been pinched in pigtails but now it shined and bounced, shoulder length and blond. Full-blown beauty waited right around the corner.

Her mood darkened at the sight of Allison. "Whoa," she said. "What's—?"

Gail put her arm around her father's waist. He pulled her in for a quick hug.

"Finding out more about, you know—" said Sulchuk.

"Don't say the word," said Gail. "I didn't sleep for three nights."

Allison offered a warm, not-too-worry smile.

"Stick around," said Sulchuk. "It's about the investigation."

"I don't watch *Bones,*" said Gail. "Too gross."

"There's nothing to see here," said Sulchuk. "Just talk."

"But then I'd have to think about it again."

"Try," said Sulchuk.

Gail took a seat at the bar next to Allison. "I'll try," she said.

"Where were we?" said Sulchuk.

"Lumberjack," said Allison. "Meeting there—was your idea."

"Yes," said Sulchuk. "Well, Neil and Dusty had never been up on the Flat Tops before so they didn't have a clue. Their jaws were on the ground most of the time, like most people who get up there for the first time."

"And?" said Allison.

"And now you're wondering about Army?"

"Army?" said Allison.

"Larry Armbruster," said Sulchuk.

"Rejected by the U.S. Army," said Gail as if she was talking about her best friend. "And his name is Larry *Arrrm*bruster. So, Army."

Sulchuk shook his head slowly. "He wears it on his sleeve. Still angry about it. He didn't survive boot camp. A medical issue surfaced. He won't talk about it. He was none too happy. This was during the first Gulf War. The U.S. Army had been his dream."

"That's how I learned the word ironic," said Gail. "Nickname Army, but he's not."

"Call him that to his face?" said Allison.

"He likes it," said Sulchuk. "Or claims he does. Says he wants to be reminded every day that the whole military operation is a bunch of clueless fools."

Allison dampened her lips with tequila. She had to put aside her general resistance to Sulchuk's corporate flair and realize, from Gail's perspective, that William Sulchuk was just another dad. This was Gail's definition of dad.

"So how about Army?" said Allison. "Did he go up with you?"

"No," said Gail, blunt like that boot camp drill instructor. "We brought Hank with us."

"His son," said Sulchuk.

"I remember Hank," said Allison. The unflappable one. All boy. "So where was Larry?"

"Larry's a big time hunter," said Sulchuk. "Obsesses about it—bowhunting, black powder, and regular rifle too. You should see his barn, back in a deep canyon halfway to New Castle. Put it this way, he has a storeroom full of rifles and bows. He trades, fixes up, deals some more. We first met at the Lake Catherine shooting range. He was admiring my new Sako. Hank was with him. When we got to talking, it turned out Hank was the same age as Gail and then I saw Army at a school function. This was a couple years back. We hunted together twice. The man is a bulldog, predawn to after dusk, no weather bothers him. The rougher, the better. He's got something to prove. I don't know who he's proving it to, but that's his thing. He put the T in tenacious."

Gail nodded knowingly. "He's nice though. He'll help you with anything. Teaches you how to survive and stuff."

"Big on survival," said Sulchuk.

"And where was he before we met at Lumberjack?" said Allison.

"Don't know," said Sulchuk. "He said he'd meet us there and a guy like that, there's not much question or doubt—he had a little fire going and some beef stew bubbling away when we got there. I guess he'd been scouting and said he'd found some big old bulls. First time he'd drawn a bull tag in a long time."

Allison let the information settle. She wanted to see if Gail would fill in any blanks or if Sulchuk would know to do some calculations on his own, maybe pick up the thread.

"Holy shit," muttered Sulchuk.

"Daddy!" cried Gail. "You owe mom a dollar."

"Sorry. I suddenly realized—" Sulchuk looked at Gail. "You know, I've got some things to say about the body."

"*Ewww,* don't say that word," said Gail. "Okay, I'm leaving."

With Gail gone, Sulchuk took a slow tour of the kitchen, drink in his right hand and his left rubbing his neck as he cranked his head around, working out the kinks. He came back to his starting position, stood at the counter and stared at Allison. A full minute passed. Sulchuk looked worried.

"Does he spend a lot of time in the Flat Tops?" asked Allison. Giving him a nudge.

"As soon as it opens up," said Sulchuk. "He knows it like he knows his house. Army was the one that pointed up the hill and wanted us to all try that area for some mushrooms."

"Not exactly prime mushroom terrain," said Allison.

"I don't know mushrooms," said Sulchuk. "But he almost pointed to the spot."

Allison held his gaze. Nerves fired inside. She hoped they didn't show. "Let me ask you this," she said. "Did he ever talk about illegal aliens? About immigration?"

Sulchuk took a deep breath.

"Holy fuck," he said. "And that's going to cost me ten bucks. How did you know he's got a bug up his ass about immigration?"

FIFTY-EIGHT:
FRIDAY EVENING

DINNER WAS THE BEST the convenience store had to offer—two slices of warmed-up cheese pizza and a giant energy drink that tasted like no natural flavor on earth.

The newsroom was empty. It was almost 9 p.m. A check with DiMarco tilled no fresh ground, though he conceded the whole department was on high alert.

Bloom found a fresh tablet of lined paper and wrote down a name across the top of ten sheets of paper. Below each name, he jotted notes.

Troy Nichols.
Chamber of Commerce. Shooting "inevitable."

Adam Paxton.
Pipeline Enterprises. Dogs. Fight with Nichols. In Coogan's office.

Joseph C. Harbor.
Phone number from Allison. Leads to Pipeline Enterprises. Colbran. Mesa County.

Ricardo Reyes.
Chevrole. Was at Trudy's house; came after Alfredo. At least, his car.

Emmitt Kucharski.
Glenwood Manor. Helped shooter.

Emmitt's Partner (the shooter) ??
???

Larry Armbruster.
Was at Lumberjack Camp (via Allison & Trudy).

Carl "Junior" Boyd.
Came to Trudy's house looking for Alfredo.

William Sulchuk.
Was at Lumberjack Camp (via Allison). Connections uncertain.

____ Dillard.
At camp with dogs and others (via Allison).

On another set of pages, Bloom wrote two company names:
Pipeline Enterprises
Joseph Harbor – Mesa County.
Rifle. Paxton. Dogs.

InterWest Distribution.
Glenwood Springs. Nichols. Chamber.

Bloom cleared his desk of all extraneous papers and books and old newspapers, made a sloppy pile on the floor. After five minutes with a bottle of spray cleaner and a rag, his desktop revealed itself as a fresh canvas.

Bloom placed the sheets of paper on the desk next to his computer in neat rows.

He moved Ricardo Reyes next to Pipeline Enterprises.

Troy Nichols with InterWest. He put Adam Paxton near Pipeline Enterprises and then put the Paxton and Pipeline sheets on the other side of InterWest to show some kind of dispute.

Joseph C. Harbor went with Pipeline Enterprises along with Armbruster and Boyd. The two men who came after Alfredo were connected to Pipeline Enterprises so that meant Boyd was, too.

Sulchuk was unclear. Maybe nothing. He could or could not be connected to Pipeline—there was no proof that Ricardo Reyes, assuming he was the driver, had any direct connection with Sulchuk even though Reyes had dropped somebody off in the Four Mile Ranch development after his visit to Trudy's house.

Suddenly Bloom realized that he had not searched for basic details on Ricardo Reyes, just as an individual.

On his desk computer, Bloom used his IRB account to develop a picture of Reyes. He was forty two. He was born in Pueblo. Reyes had three arrests up and down the Front Range—disorderly conduct, failure to pay child support and possession of a minor quantity of cocaine. The drug bust was a decade old. Reyes had one daughter, who would now be fourteen, and he was married.

His wife's name was Juanita Reyes, maiden name Tovar.

Bloom studied the surname, shook his head to discount the coincidence with her last name and Bloom's friend and the Hispanic studies professor, Luis Tovar. He told himself to keep moving. Any search could open up new rabbit holes to chase down.

Ricardo Reyes had no loans. He had worked at a variety of odd jobs, heavy labor around railroads, trucking and warehouses. He hadn't worked anywhere for long. No current occupation was listed.

On Zillow, Bloom checked the houses for sale in the neighborhood where Reyes rented. One was listed for $290,000—three bedrooms, two baths—and 1,492 square feet. Bloom figured rent must be close to $1,500 a month or maybe more, a steep monthly tab for somebody not pulling a regular paycheck and no indication he had previously mined or found gold, unless his wife came with a fortune or had a great job.

For the heck of it, Bloom checked his notes for the owner of the house Reyes was renting and let IRB have its way with the name, Emilio A. Perez.

A picture of modern-American stability emerged. Perez had bought the house when it was new, in 2003. He had moved from Glenwood Springs, where he had lived for a dozen years before that, in an older house downtown.

Emilio Perez was listed as the co-owner of Delta Holdings, a name that quickly went on another new sheet of paper.

And his wife's name was Yolanda Tovar.

Bloom shook his head in dismay, heard a soft tap at the front door.

Bloom might have ignored the sound on most nights, but he'd been hoping for it, too.

This greeting came with a deep, meaningful hug. This hug came with her breasts pressed against his chest and her scent, something lemony.

"You okay?" he asked.

She looked disheveled.

"I will be."

"The raid?" said Bloom.

He led her back to his cubicle, stepped around the pile on the floor.

"All theater," said Trudy. "The raid was lightweight from what I could tell. Half-hearted."

He rolled Marjorie's chair closer.

"They must have seen you, called their buddies while we were waiting."

Trudy tried on a half-hearted smile. "Talk. Talk. Hours of talk," she said. "I tried to leave. Jerry wants me back tonight. I told him I was going out for some fresh air."

"What more is there to say?"

"He wants resolution," said Trudy. "That's what he calls it, *resolution*. I almost wonder if Jerry didn't ask for the raid so he could make his points. Crazy. I know."

Bloom wanted to give her space, but was eager to know where things stood. It wasn't too hard to imagine Trudy defending to Jerry her right to run things in her own free-form way. Follow the law, sure, but don't be a slave to it.

If Jerry had created an opening, Bloom wanted to be at the head of the line for "next."

"And?" said Bloom.

The tear fell from the inside corner of her left eye. She didn't try to hide it. "I don't know," she said.

Bloom waited. He knew one thing for sure—silence is never inaccurate or off-point.

"I wanted it to work," she said. "It seemed like a good fit for a long time. But I think my heart's been aching for a while now and I've been ignoring it, trying to will the pain to go away."

"I'm sorry," said Bloom. "Not what you needed right now."

"Or it's exactly what I needed," said Trudy. "Someday, I'll know which."

He knew not to rush. There would be plenty of time for follow-up, for mentioning his feelings or finding a way to make them clear. A week or two down the road might be about right. The thought of Trudy's availability was a straight shooter of hope and brightness.

"I was looking for connections," he said. "Try this—the guy who owns the house being rented by Ricardo Reyes, the one in New Castle?"

"Red Cloud Court—sure," said Trudy.

"He has a wife named Yolanda Tovar and Ricardo Reyes' wife is another Tovar. Juanita."

"And?"

"And there's this guy I know, Luis Tovar. He's kind of a guru of sorts, the wise old sage. He's a professor at Mesa State in Grand Junction, commutes down there I suppose but lives here. He's the observer, the commentator. I interviewed him on the night of the big candlelight vigil. The guy is as mellow as they come. He's the guy with the view from the sidelines, putting things in perspective. But—"

Bloom was already on the IRB site, studying details about Luis Tovar.

Trudy watched while he followed leads.

"Luis Tovar does have a sister named Yolanda and she's been married to Emilio Perez since 1984. Juanita is one of two children, married Ricardo in 2006."

Bloom muttered as he went. He grabbed another sheet of paper, put a line connecting Ricardo Reyes and Juanita Tovar and added the names of her parents above, then the name Luis Tovar next to Yolanda.

"So the parents are renting to the kids," said Trudy. "Not unusual."

"But that means Luis Tovar has some kind of role in all of this mess—or that he might," said Bloom. "Not the kindly professor we think."

Bloom flipped on the Denver news station at 10 p.m. to make sure there was no breaking news. He called DiMarco.

"Past your bedtime."

"Nothing?" said Bloom.

"You think I'm talking to you?" said DiMarco.

"What?"

"Who was on the speaker phone last time? Earlier?"

"A friend," said Bloom. He stared straight at Trudy. "Trudy Heath."

Trudy nodded her assent, let out a breath.

DiMarco took it in, didn't respond.

"So, anything going on?" said Bloom.

"Lot of hurry up and wait," said DiMarco.

"Nothing tonight for sure?" said Bloom. Trudy stood up, studied the sheets.

"I'm not in the business of guarantees," said DiMarco.

"What do you know about Luis Tovar?"

"Dr. T?" said DiMarco.

"He's got a nickname?"

"Guy who has been around that long, sure," said DiMarco. "If you've got some questions about Dr. T then join the club. Membership is free."

"Even *you* don't know what he's up to?"

DiMarco paused. "Sometimes. Then he pops up in a new place. He's like that game at the arcade. Whack-A-Mole. You smack him down in one hole and he pops up in another. With a silly grin on his face."

FIFTY-NINE:
FRIDAY EVENING

"THE HERD WE'VE BEEN watching is doing some funny things this year."

Allison could have said anything. Didn't matter. In their minds, she was describing a magical, far-off place they only dreamed of reaching, like the Himalayas.

"We were thinking Lumberjack Camp for you guys, but something has spooked them off the area and we saw fresh sign two days ago near Button Down Camp. Two miles north from Lumberjack and over on the other side of Triangle Peak. Whole different drainage," said Allison. "Jesse is going to take you up first thing, you'll be all set. I'll be over to check on you the next day or day after and hopefully we can pack out some kills."

The Oklahoma Gang murmured approval.

"So how long a ride tomorrow?"

This question came from the ostensible leader, Matt. He gripped a worn paperback of Rick Bass' *The Lost Grizzlies* in one hand, took a sip of wine from a plastic cup. The bottle nearby carried a fancy French label. Some of the others were drinking what appeared to be small-batch India Pale Ale and she spotted a bottle of Hornitos, too. The mood was relaxed, serene. They stood around a knee-high, mood-setting fire near one of the crews' pop-up trailers. The men sat in fold-up lawn chairs in a tight circle. They scared up two more chairs and she and Colin settled into the ring as welcome new friends.

"Four hours," said Allison. "Straight uphill for one hour, easy and flat for the next three."

"And you've seen elk?" said Matt.

"Elk, deer, and a lot of sign," said Allison. She wasn't lying. He hadn't specified a time frame. She smiled to add emphasis. "Fresh sign every day," she added. *Now* she was lying. Or misleading them.

"Good deal," said Matt, the walking antithesis of what she was expecting. "We really appreciate your hospitality and letting us crash a bit early. Our main goal is to just get a good chance, get a good look. I know we've been talking big, but when it comes right down to it, we know they call it hunting for a reason."

There were six of them in all. The youngest looked to be in his early twenties, the oldest about fifty. They were a blur of dark, un-shaven cheeks but where Allison expected a wall of camo print base-ball caps and camo print hunting gear and camo-perfect boots and packs, these guys could have been sitting around a campfire on a casual weekend getaway.

One of the older guys was patching an elbow on a jean jacket with needle and thread. One of the younger ones had a novel tucked under a thigh, with the spine out: *Nature and Selected Essays* by Ralph Waldo Emerson. A man after Devo's heart. Who were these guys?

"If you want to hunt tomorrow evening, or at least scout, you'll want to leave at dawn or no more than an hour after," said Colin.

"Love it," said Matt. "One more drink and I think we're all going to turn in and get some rest." Matt had a gentle sparkle to his eyes.

Someone handed Allison two fingers of Hornitos in a plastic cup. Neat. She liked it better than Sulchuk's fancy brand. She took it with a *thank-you* smile and a toast. Everyone smiled back. Colin took a shot, too, and it was good times all around.

SIXTY:
FRIDAY, LATE NIGHT

"THOUGHT I MIGHT FIND you here."

It was Marjorie Hayes, a laptop clutched to her chest like body armor. She looked breathless and focused, like she'd jogged for the first time in her life.

"You heard about Adam Paxton," said Hayes. "I talked to Coogan and he said he told you. You know, it's not every day you see a guy's hands around another guy's throat. Made me so angry, to think one man could do that to another."

Bloom handled the quick introductions, felt a bit stunned by the interruption. He had imagined pleasant hours ahead with Trudy, alone. Marjorie Hayes didn't do overtime.

"I know you," said Hayes when Bloom introduced Trudy. "Oh my, I know you. I buy all your products and one of your staff delivered two big loads of peat one day and he was so nice, gave me about ten minutes of suggestions about the garden, how to lay it out."

Trudy offered a smile like she was hosting a summer cocktail party. "A pleasure to meet you," she said.

Bloom gave her a quick tour of their working outline. "We already have a sheet for Adam Paxton, but it's blank," he said.

"Not for long," said Hayes.

Hayes had spent the last hours at the library and more time at home.

"And then for him to come here and think he could talk the newspaper out of writing up the assault," said Hayes. "I mean, I saw it with my own eyes. Troy Nichols' face was beet red, ready to burst. Never seen so much anger and Paxton, I'm telling you, he had a death grip on him."

Hayes shuddered, remembering the moment, then launched into what she'd found. "Have you heard of Pipeline Enterprises?"

Bloom exchanged a look with Trudy.

"Paxton is vice-president," said Hayes. "And one of the original owners. I can't tell you every entanglement, but Pipeline is connected to another company, a new one, that works over in Grand Junction that's the operating business in Colorado for a string of for-profit prisons around the country. They have contracts with ICE. When ICE started talking about putting a detention center in Glenwood Springs, another company named InterWest for some reason thought they already had an edge. That's where Nichols comes in."

"Truth or Consequences," said Trudy. "They were already part of the trafficking."

"They were delivering Mexicans north," said Bloom. "Keeping the supply fresh to ship warm bodies south."

Hayes absorbed the new information like a seasoned analyst. "This goes back to when ICE was looking to expand, before the economy tanked. There must have still been some bad blood between InterWest and Pipeline. InterWest felt they had a commitment of some sort that had been broken."

Hayes reached in her oversized purse, nearly as big as a beach bag, a thick wad of papers held together with a giant binder clip. "Ran out of ink on my home computer," she said. "But after ICE changed its collective mind, InterWest filed a big lawsuit. Not here, but over in Mesa County. There was a reference to the suit in the Grand Junction paper, but we missed it. The case is still on track for a trial but the depositions lay it all out."

Bloom grabbed his phone.

Kerry London answered on the first ring.

"What did I miss?" he said.

"What are you doing?" said Bloom. "Care to lend a hand?"

If London was staying at the Hotel Colorado, it would take him no more than ten minutes to walk across the bridge.

"Wrapping up my last round of calls before ordering late room service and a massage," said London. "You know, these expense accounts. Hate to see them go to waste."

Negotiations didn't take long. No doubt London could hear the seriousness in Bloom's tone. London said he'd get out of his silk robe and head over.

"You are hired help," said Bloom when London showed up. London looked more relaxed than a national news reporter should look after a week on a story that needed around-the-clock updates. "Not hired, because we have no expense account, but on loan."

It was nearly 11 p.m.

Marjorie Hayes was utterly unimpressed by the arrival of a national news television celebrity, but Trudy took a minute to chat and shake hands and offer a gushing smile. Bloom and Trudy flanked London while Marjorie snapped a picture with Bloom's phone.

"I better not see that on the World Wide Web," said London. "Consorting with the ink-stained wretches might ruin my reputation for perfect hair and shallow sound bites." He laughed.

Taking the "no-surprises-for-the-boss" approach, Bloom called Coogan and laid everything out.

"We have a mountain to climb," said Bloom. "In the dark. London is an old Denver friend, so he's coming over to help with the route finding. He's not going to represent the paper."

Coogan asked questions about what Hayes had produced and for any details Bloom and Trudy knew. "Hang on," he said. "I'm coming down."

Bloom called for a huddle when Coogan arrived. He reviewed everything they had learned, including the information from Trudy and Allison.

"The story is those dogs being used to chase men like foxes," said London. "That's national news. Tonight. Top of the show. Lead item. If they find the shooter today, that's the only other thing that would top it—or you'd have to mention both in the same sentence. It's unbelievable."

"Hey," said Bloom. "On my schedule, not yours."

"Agree with you both," said Coogan. "We need our version up pronto."

"We only have the outline," said Bloom. "The rough picture."

"There's enough," said Coogan. "If Allison is the source."

"That's all information via Trudy," said Bloom. "And she's only putting two and two together."

"Allison Coil actually heard the hunt?" said Hayes.

"She heard the howls, found the man who was badly bitten—and they got him flown to the hospital," said Trudy.

"Sure it was dogs?" said London.

"If Allison said it was dogs," said Trudy, "believe me, it was dogs."

London shook his head. "Thought I'd seen everything."

SIXTY-ONE: FRIDAY, LATE NIGHT

COLIN SAID: "PRETTY SMOOTH."

"They've got as much at Button Down as anywhere else."

"You sold them," said Colin. They were in bed, Allison on her back but propped up by a plump pillow. Colin sat on the edge of the bed facing her, a bedtime beer still in one hand. "They've been thinking Lumberjack for weeks and weeks and you got them switched and you made it look easy."

"Those are terrific people, it turns out," said Allison. "Just not what I'd been expecting. I mean—Ralph Waldo Emerson for crying out loud."

Colin took a sip of his beer, passed it over. This brew tasted like a hearty loaf of bread compared to the fizzy swill preferred by the Oklahomans. Good thing Colin was sharing. The beer was going down smoothly on top of her tequila; she'd taken the generous offer of a second shot.

"So Lumberjack is empty," said Colin. "Now what are we going to do?"

"Get up in that area on our own," said Allison. "If you know a back way or a side door into Lumberjack, some way to approach it other than the main trail, tell me."

"I might," said Colin.

"Good," said Allison.

"And how are you so sure this won't be more than we can handle?"

Allison gave it some thought and another tug on Colin's beer. "I don't."

"But?"

"But what?" said Allison. "We lay low. We circle. We sniff around. We go in real slow. Observe. See what's what. It could be empty. But only three people know I'm going to be there in the morning—you, William Sulchuk and Trudy."

"You talked to her?"

"After the stop at Sulchuk's, on my way out of town," said Allison. "Definitely wanted her to know where I'd be."

Colin looked puzzled. "So you think they'll be at Lumberjack—"

"Might be no *they*. Maybe it's just Armbruster all by his lonesome."

"But you said Sulchuk said all the right things."

"He was sending me a message that he was clueless," said Allison. "But I'm not as sure as I'd like to be."

"And we'll be coming in with a big target on our backs, wide open."

"We did what we were supposed to do," said Allison. "We were sucked in and we followed through. And now we have the upper hand—Armbruster doesn't know we know."

Allison sounded more confident than she felt. If Armbruster was there and if they could get close enough for conversation, her loose plan was to assure Armbruster that they would help expose the "sporting" aspect of the game and, somehow, they could keep his name out of it.

"We've got to come up on Lumberjack on our own terms," said Allison. There was really no sneaking up on Lumberjack, but she liked to think it would help. "See if the trap worked."

SIXTY-TWO:
FRIDAY, LATE NIGHT

THE NEWSROOM CARRIED THE feel of a war room. Bloom relished the determined hum of the place and his odd, disparate team.

Kerry London, putting his own IRB account to use, focused on Troy Nichols.

Bloom showed Marjorie Hayes one of the better people-finder web sites and Pacer, the federal court database, so she could work on Adam Paxton. Hayes also did general Google searches, looking beyond the first hits, in combination with Joseph C. Harbor and Ricardo Reyes.

Coogan worked on Dillard and the nephew-and-uncle combination of Larry Armbruster and Carl "Junior" Boyd.

Trudy took William Sulchuk.

They would all keep an eye out for Dillard, Kucharski, and any of the company names.

"Dillard is probably connected to Pipeline," said Bloom, "since Allison heard that name in the camp and also saw the dogs in the camp, but we need a first name and occupation and all the other details. And I'll take Luis Tovar but keep an eye out for him showing up. Put his name in combination with the others in searches too."

"Tovar?" said London. "The professor? We interviewed him two days ago. So mild-mannered. Not that his words amounted to anything."

"That's him," said Bloom. "If it's the same clan, he's got a sister and she and her husband rent out the New Castle house to their daughter and her husband, Ricardo Reyes."

They needed a week in the courthouse. They needed to get lucky.

Bloom started poking around in Mesa County records. Luis Tovar taught in Grand Junction. Maybe the 85-mile commute allowed him to keep some of his interests quiet.

"This Troy Nichols dude is squeaky clean," said London. "Married for nearly thirty five years now. His house is paid off. Chamber, church and chicken for dinner three times a week. Check, check, check. That Truth or Consequences story you already found is about the only scrape with the law Troy Nichols has ever had and from what I can tell it kind of got swept under the rug in the media coverage down there—another sad saga from the immigration wars. Driver let off easy."

"Not exactly squeaky clean," said Bloom. "One of the sardines in that truck had swallowed a brick of cocaine," said Bloom.

"So he's good at keeping his dark side quiet," said London. "His online presence is a yawn—and maybe the truck was in his fleet but that appears to be an isolated incident—nothing ever implicated the larger business and nothing happened up here. Nichols is dullsville."

"Keep looking," said Bloom.

Hayes' digging put Adam Paxton in deep with Pipeline Enterprises and she found that Pipeline was a subsidiary of the second largest private prison network in the country.

Coogan's efforts turned up a bite on Dillard. Coogan had tried entering the surname Dillard in a variety of search engines in combination with the company names and other individual names floating around. Suddenly he found a Lonnie Dillard who lived in the area and was active, he said, in the CBA.

London gave a little shrug and turned his head. "Continental Basketball Association?"

"The Colorado Bowhunters Association," said Coogan. "So I popped his name in Facebook and he's right here in Glenwood Springs. A bowhunting expert who runs Rifle Sporting Goods. He was quoted in the Rifle paper when the Wal-Mart opened, complaining it would destroy downtown Rifle. His shop is known as a bowhunters' mecca in Western Colorado. So then I ran a search for Lonnie Dillard, Adam Paxton, and bowhunting, and Google Images coughed them right up. They are both in CBA."

Bloom went to his sheets and put Dillard near Paxton and Pipeline Enterprises.

"Pieces falling together," said Bloom. "We need the Tovar shoe to drop."

An hour slipped by, keyboards clacking.

"And now Armbruster," said Coogan. "I thought that name rang a bell."

Coogan stood, leaned on his knuckles as he summarized. Armbruster and his family were at Two Rivers park. At the time, he worked the loading dock at a grocery store. He gets in an argument with someone in his family over immigration. He gets mad, throws a full can of beer. The flying can hits a seven-year-old boy who is playing Frisbee with his dad. The seven-year old is Arturo Anaya from an All-American family, third generation. Little Arturo doesn't speak a lick of Spanish. The Anayas are from Denver. Dad is a big-time eye doctor. The family was in Glenwood for the day, relaxing.

Arturo had to be taken to the hospital. He was treated for a badly bruised leg and released.

Bloom took a swig of a flat energy drink, tried to picture the scene.

"All this comes out later in the lawsuit," said Coogan. "One thing led to another. A prominent leftie lawyer from Hotchkiss moves in on the case, to make a statement. Filed a civil suit and one year later almost to the day, Armbruster writes a check for $28,000. Not an enormous sum but it was more than Armbruster had on hand. By now, he's divorced."

"Sounds like a peach," said Hayes.

"It gets worse," said Coogan. "The reporter covering the trial was thoughtful enough to throw in some detail about Armbruster. Ironically enough, he had applied with the U.S. Border Patrol and hadn't made the cut. He had also formerly enlisted in the U.S. Army but had been given a bad-conduct discharge, no stated reason given in the article but maybe that'll be in the court record, the transcript."

"I remember that trial now," said Hayes. "Before you and Duncan both got here."

"Wait," said Trudy. "Allison said the kids she met that day at Lumberjack were all roughly the same age—twelve or thirteen."

"IRB," said Bloom. "Let's run Larry Armbruster through IRB."

"Got him," said London.

Bloom circled London's desk while he combed the data.

"Two kids," said London, ten minutes later. "Woodrow, twenty six and Hank, twelve."

"We need his deposition from the trial," said Bloom.

"Courthouse opens in about eight hours," said London.

"Unless we can find it online," said Bloom. "Try Smoking Gun and try Gawker. Both sites love that kind of detail."

"I'm on it," said Hayes.

"Got a picture of Woodrow Armbruster," said Trudy. "This from El Paso, Texas. Two years ago."

The shot showed a solid young man holding an over-sized trophy. Safety glasses propped on his forehead. The trophy consisted of three, one-quarter scale rifles leaned together, tips of the barrels touching.

Woodrow Armbruster held the trophy with one arm, clutched like a bouquet of flowers. The other balanced a long rifle, butt on the ground and the barrel almost to his waist.

SIXTY-THREE:
SATURDAY, PRE-DAWN

STONE COLD AWAKE. THERE wasn't a tired thought in her brain. Her body felt alert, ready.

Colin slept peacefully. It was 3:00 a.m. She didn't need a clock.

They had agreed to wake at 3:30 a.m., be on horses and on the way a half-hour after that.

What was the point in grabbing a wink now, even if it came?

Allison rested on her back. She replayed the first day at Lumberjack with Sulchuk and Armbruster, tried to slow the scene down step by step in her mind.

Inflections. Gestures. Indications. Anything.

She replayed the scene at Burning Camp.

Inflections. Gestures. Indications. Anything.

Tried to picture what happened *before* she arrived. *Long before.* Armbruster seeing the opportunity, planning it out. Had Sulchuk suspected anything when the body had been discovered? Did he sense anything? Wonder?

Allison's mind ran in disorganized snapshots.

She remembered the delicate, faint tracks she'd found. Had Armbruster wheeled a body over on a sled? He would have had to work all night before the rest of them arrived.

She remembered looking for drag marks—no wonder there were none. Had Armbruster wanted to create some fake drag marks—and ran out of time?

How could he be that certain she'd follow through? The proof was in this moment, wasn't it? And in every question she'd asked since last Sunday afternoon.

Would Armbruster show at Lumberjack? Had Sulchuk done what she'd hoped—pick up the phone?

The questions came. No answers followed.

SIXTY-FOUR:
SATURDAY, EARLY
MORNING

"THAT'S A McMILLAN," SAID London. "Tactical weapon. Perfect for long-range shooting."

"I think I saw a YouTube link, too," said Trudy. She clicked back. London had some smugness to him, but she was impressed by his array of knowledge, dusted with a fine coating of bullshit.

On the video, Woodrow Armbruster pumped a shot with a loud pop, stayed focused on the target and prepared for his next.

A caption popped up: Winning Shot at Six Hundred Yards. The screen split in two and the right half revealed the target as a neat hole ripped a hair's width from the bull's-eye.

"The recoil reducer on those has a gas piston inside that cushions the blow," said London. "Like a shock absorber for the shoulder. It's sophisticated."

"But we don't know if he's moved up here from Texas?" said Trudy.

"Maybe that's who the police are looking for," said London. "If there's an alert out, maybe he's it."

The man on the screen looked sad and lonely. "He's a bit odd looking," said Trudy. "Shouldn't he be smiling, at least a little?"

"You'd think," said London.

There was a general similarity to the structure of the police sketch but the lighting wasn't good in the photo or the video. And no face tattoo, though Trudy knew that could have been added in the interim.

"He could have arrived up here two months ago, six months ago or two weeks ago," said Bloom. "Who wants to take Woodrow Armbruster, add it to the list?"

"I've got it," said London, back at his computer.

Trudy said she had a stray thought about William Sulchuk and started poking around.

"Gawker's got the deposition," said Hayes, breaking the silence. "Forty five-page deposition with Armbruster. He's got two kids but never married. He grew up in El Paso but moved here seven years ago. At the time of the trial, Woodrow lived in El Paso but he brought his other son Hank with him here. Both exes live in Texas."

"In his case," said London. "That's all his exes. He was inspired by George Strait, no doubt."

"So Hank was the one at Lumberjack that day," said Trudy. "Fits better."

"And not too much more about his life after that," said Hayes. "Although there's a long grilling about his views on immigration. He doesn't see much gray area, that's for sure."

"Print out the whole thing," said Bloom. "I want to read it. Nothing turning up on Luis Tovar? Nothing at all?"

"Not here," said Trudy. "But I've got a problem with Sulchuk."

"Shoot," said Bloom.

London stifled a yawn, snapped open a can of soda. Hayes stood to stretch, came to Trudy's computer. Despite hours of work, Trudy still looked steady and comfortable.

"I thought I'd check on Sulchuk's kids," said Trudy. "I checked Sopris Elementary School but of course the school doesn't publicly list student names. But when I put the last name Sulchuk and Sopris Elementary in Google, nothing. Tried the same thing as an image search and up pops an image and that image is connected to a school newsletter in a PDF. An article in the newsletter shows the star of the school play as Gail, with her mother Page Wright and her father, William Sulchuk. Gail's last name is Wright. And that's the name Allison gave me—Gail."

"So the daughter kept the mother's maiden name or maybe it's a second marriage to Sulchuk," said London. "Married the mom, got the daughter, and she keeps her original surname."

"Or maybe try William Wright on the search engines in connection with all this," said Bloom. "Maybe Sulchuk borrowed his wife's surname for a legal paper. Or two. What the hell are we missing?"

"That unlocked it," said London. "B-i-n-g-o. William Wright and Luis Tovar both come up together and they go straight to a holding company in Nevada. G.A.O.L. Inc."

"More initials," said Trudy. "Great."

"That's not an acronym," said Hayes. She smiled, wondering if anyone else would get it. Even London was shaking his head.

"It's the British word," added Hayes. "Originally interpreted as little cage. Pronounced like ours. Jail."

SIXTY-FIVE:
SATURDAY, EARLY
MORNING

BLOOM'S SHEETS OF PAPER filled up. Wright, the correct surname, unraveled the tightened threads.

William Wright was up to his neck in G.A.O.L. and, by association, Pipeline Enterprises.

G.A.O.L. was an office address in Nevada, a holding company on paper.

Sulchuk had a lot at stake and Professor Luis Tovar appeared to be Sulchuk's silent partner.

Kerry London dug up a thorough history on the Tovar clan—a generations-old, all-American family that started in the sugar beet fields near Greeley and moved to the mines near Cripple Creek and then to the underground coal mines near Paonia. The Tovar family was expansive. Luis Tovar was the grandnephew of the patriarch and, in London's words, "there are more Tovars than drilling rigs on the Western Slope of Colorado."

At dawn, Trudy made a run for coffee, rolls, juices, fruit. The digging continued for another hour. A fresh injection of sugar and caffeine did the trick. The sheets of information grew dense. A diagram started to take shape.

"Tovar and Sulchuk look like they're above the fray," said London. "They're corporate, not operations. Sulchuk might not have known squat about what was happening down on the ground."

"So Nichols might be worth pressing," said Bloom. "He'd know all about the company trying to muscle its way onto his turf."

Coogan volunteered to call Nichols.

"Who's going to find Allison? Warn her?" Trudy's look established the priority. She was focused on only one thing, one person. "We've got to warn her about Armbruster and Sulchuk—she didn't think Sulchuk was involved. Allison thinks she's got Armbruster biting on a hook to come meet her today at Lumberjack. This morning, I mean. Now."

"That's a problem," said London. "What was her rush?"

Trudy closed her eyes, looked down. Bloom thought he saw a flash of Trudy as a young girl. Piercing certainty was one of her strengths but it was wrapped in such a gentle spirit that the whole package yearned to be held, celebrated, and enjoyed.

"She thinks Armbruster might be okay," said Trudy. "But she has no idea about the older son, I'm sure of that. And if Armbruster is part of the whole racket that snatched Alfredo Loya, he's got to be more trouble than she thinks."

The Flat Tops Wilderness map came up online and then they switched over to the Division of Wildlife version for the more detailed game units, with the camps marked.

"Got it," said Bloom. "Practically due north of here and not very far if you've got a big enough crow and one's that trained to follow directions. Based on the topography, though, it looks like it's in the bottom of a hole."

"Maybe a large crow?" said London. "Or how about an ultralight? Devo's pal Ziggy. Flies out of Glenwood Springs. There's a chance we get lucky, maybe he's over here somewhere getting ready to do a run."

"Police helicopter?" said Bloom.

"On our say-so?" said London.

"A bit safer?" said Bloom.

"Cops stop massive manhunt for assassin to honor reporter request," said London. "I'm writing the headline now. I've got Ziggy's number in my contacts. I was going to call him if this thing dragged out another day."

London went back to his phone, flipped through his directory.

Bloom studied the map, wondered what kind of terrain an ultralight needed in order to put down.

London punched in the numbers. "Is this Ziggy?" he said. Waited. And drifted away, phone to his ear.

"I'm sure there's a liability issue in here somewhere," said Coogan. "But I don't give a fuck. I got your notes and with Marjorie's help we can piece this together but you have to come back—like quick."

On the map, Bloom figured Lumberjack was eight miles due north, maybe a couple degrees to the east. Driving to Sweetwater and getting up on horses and riding in would take all day. Too long.

"An ultralight?" said Trudy, concern on her brow. "Not much better than a lawn chair and balloons, is it?"

"He's got to be an experienced pilot," said Bloom. "Knows the terrain—"

"But still," said Trudy.

"Compared to the trouble Allison's in?" said Bloom. "Might be in?"

London returned. "Ziggy is on the road between Carbondale and Glenwood Springs right now and was on his way up here for a Devo run. But he's willing and he knows Lumberjack, thinks we might be able to find a spot."

Bloom looked at London to see if this was all a joke. He wasn't fond of roller coasters or single-engine prop planes, let alone this.

"I know there's a rush, but—" This time Trudy came to Bloom, brought her hands up to cover her nose and mouth. She shook her head. "I know, nothing I can say."

"You or me?" said Bloom.

"Oh no," said London. "I'm the last person Allison Coil would want to see hopping off that flying contraption."

SIXTY-SIX:
SATURDAY MORNING

THE ASPEN GROVE, FULLY leafed, held secrets. A dozen horses could be tied to trees on the far side and be easily obscured.

"You'd think something would move," said Colin.

They'd been glassing it for ten minutes.

"Maybe they come later," said Colin.

"Maybe I'm way off here," said Allison. "Wouldn't be the worst thing."

The binoculars pulled the view up so close she could only fit half of the grove in her field of vision.

They lay prone, side by side at the edge of the forest, three hundred feet above the valley floor. The only approach to the camp without being noticed would be by parachute. Merlin and Sunny Boy, fully recovered from his ordeal, though no horse ever forgot, were tied to trees behind them.

"How long do we give it?" said Colin.

"If they are up and about, we would have seen something by now," said Allison. "Maybe we take our chances, go right on down. If we're still alone, we make a bee line to Button Down and help out Jesse. You know he's got his hands full."

Allison lowered the binoculars.

"Looks peaceful enough," said Colin.

"So we expose ourselves?" said Allison.

"Unless we wait until dark."

"Maybe they'll be watching the main trail," said Allison. "Not the back door."

"We could leave the horses," said Colin. "We could split up, lay low. There's some scrub oak might give us a chance, a bit of protection."

"Not leaving the horses," said Allison.

Colin lowered his binoculars. "Then we go down, straight up, riding high. See what's what."

It was hard to ignore the powerful feeling that crossing the half-mile of open terrain could amount to target practice for whoever was lying in wait.

"We could wait them out," said Allison. "War of attrition. If they're there, they won't stay all day. They're thinking it's a waste, too. If they aren't there—"

She stopped. She didn't have a *then*.

"Yes?" said Colin.

"Then we are alone again," said Allison.

"This could all be over when we're halfway down."

"A rifle shot up here? During archery season?" said Allison.

Colin rolled on his back, stared up at the dense fir trees overhead.

"Who exactly is going to come running? All those others we saw this morning?" he said.

"Yeah," said Allison. "They'll all come running to see where I got shot and how far I fell from my horse. By the way, wherever it is that

I fall, bury me right there. Dig a hole next to me, push me in, call it good. Don't drag my body all over the place, okay?"

"Whatever," said Colin. "Nobody is stupid enough to fire a rifle up here today."

"An arrow then—*pfffft*. Old school."

They were delaying the inevitable—climbing on their horses and walking down to Lumberjack.

"Then it's fifty-fifty," said Colin. "Whoever doesn't get plunked first has got a chance."

"Unless there's more than we bargained," said Allison.

She stood up, led the way back to Sunny Boy, whose ears pointed forward. He'd been listening, knew something was up. His eyes looked relaxed, however. Trust was back.

They waited at the edge, Merlin and Sunny Boy shoulder to shoulder. Based on his look, Colin could have been preparing for a summer joy ride. Allison worked to mimic the resolute attitude, but feared the bubbles of uncertainty were popping in her eyes, lungs and nerves.

She took a deep breath.

"Better?" said Colin.

"Better," said Allison.

Colin and Merlin obediently stepped out into the sunlight. Sunny Boy was a half-step behind.

SIXTY-SEVEN:
SATURDAY MORNING

BLOOM THOUGHT IT MIGHT be good to know the full name of the last person who would see him alive, but Ziggy was just "Ziggy."

He looked like he walked off the set of the Broadway musical *Hair,* or time-warped in from Altamont. He had long dreads, a full red-brown beard that came to a natural point and a long, thin face with brown, happy eyes. A plain leather necklace held a small metal peace symbol. He smelled of Patchouli and weed.

"Ever flown in an ultralight?" said Ziggy.

"Nothing smaller than a 737," said Bloom.

Ziggy smiled. "If that's like being on a bus, this is like being on a motorcycle. Same basic principle, though. It's all lift. What do you weigh?

"Roughly one-seventy," said Bloom.

"Scare easy?"

"Not until right now."

"We don't go more than about 70 miles per hour but when you're buzzing treetops it can get a bit hairy." Ziggy was doing pre-flight, literally kicking the tires, studying the wings, checking the fuel and oil levels with dipsticks.

The plane looked like a couple of backyard armchairs sitting on an aluminum base that might double as a canoe rack for a mid-size SUV.

For the most part, Bloom concentrated on the story he'd write when he got back and worked hard to ignore that he was putting his life in the hands of a stoner hippie from Paonia and an "aircraft" that looked like aviation's answer to whatever would be produced if an early VW bug and a recumbent bicycle had babies. "How's Devo doing?"

A change in topics might help.

"Fine as far as I know. Still big on YouTube and last I heard he's got more than a few folks with him now, starting some sort of encampment."

Ziggy picked up the ultralight by the tail, gave it a spin around. He handed Bloom a helmet, showed him how to work the built-in headset so they could talk in flight.

Ten a.m. If there was fatigue building, it had been chased away by white hot fear.

Bloom's cell phone chirped.

"Do you mind?" said Bloom.

"Hey, it's cool," said Ziggy.

DiMarco calling back; Bloom had left a message.

"Does the name Woodrow Armbruster mean anything to you?"

DiMarco paused. "That's pretty good," he said. "Pretty damn good."

"He's your guy," said Bloom. "And lives in a ramshackle house back in the canyons before you get to New Castle."

"Funny," said DiMarco.

"Funny ha-ha or funny coincidence?" said Bloom.

"We've been watching that house since dusk last night."

"So I'm right," said Bloom. "And obviously he's not there because you'd stop watching and start questioning."

"Correct," said DiMarco.

Which meant if the house was empty, Allison was likely in deep trouble.

"You know about the detention center in Rifle?"

"What about it?" said DiMarco.

"How come you didn't tell me about it? When I was asking about ICE?"

"It's not our deal," said DiMarco.

Bloom cut him off. "Yeah, private contractor. Did you look at people associated with them?"

"We checked everything," said DiMarco. "And beyond."

"There's a few in that group took it to a whole other level," said Bloom. "At least, the feeder system—rounding up Mexicans that looked like they didn't belong. And using them for sport up in the woods, too."

"Now you're beyond me," said DiMarco.

Ziggy climbed into the front seat of the ultralight.

"I've got to go," said Bloom. "But the whole private prison thing—"

"Not something Glenwood cops or Garfield County cops are going to give a rat's ass about," said DiMarco. "Only makes our job easier."

"But there wasn't always enough supply," said Bloom. "So they played both ends of the system, trucking them north, working with coyotes, let them get settled up here and then snatching them back."

"Helluva story," said DiMarco. "Hope you've got it air tight."

"Find Larry Armbruster," said Bloom. "Find his son. The rifle that shot Tom Lamott is in the Armbruster place if it's anywhere at all."

"I'll pass it along," said DiMarco.

"We think Armbruster and maybe his son too are in the Flat Tops," said Bloom. "Can you send some manpower?"

"We?" said DiMarco. "Who is 'we?'"

"My editor and Marjorie Hayes. Been working all night," said Bloom.

"Marjorie Hayes the knitting and gardening queen?" said DiMarco. "That one?"

"Can you send someone?" said Bloom, ignoring him.

"You make it sound like I control the National Guard," said DiMarco. "If we had spare troops, where should they go?"

"Start at Allison's place at Sweetwater," said Bloom. "Ask for directions or a guide to take you to Lumberjack. The main trail goes west from there. All the help they can bring. Or send the helicopter to Lumberjack Camp. If you're looking for Woodrow Armbruster, it's a better bet than anything you've got going right now."

This time, Bloom hung up first.

The seat behind Ziggy in the ultralight had less substance than a bleacher at the ballpark, plus seat belt.

Ziggy taxied to the end of the runway and revved the motor, his hands on a horizontal bar that was the sole barrier between him and the wide open air.

The plane lurched forward, spun right and then left and then lifted off the ground. Bloom gripped his knees.

"Yee haw," said Ziggy in Bloom's headset. "Here we go!"

Ziggy circled to climb up out of the hole where Glenwood Springs sat at the mouth of Glenwood Canyon and as they banked and climbed,

Bloom spotted the Riverside Meadows mobile homes and two boys in the street, playing soccer.

The sky opened up. Ziggy pointed the craft north to the vast sea of woods. Bloom tried to ignore the fact that he was dangling in the air.

Literally, on a wing.

And a prayer.

SIXTY-EIGHT:
SATURDAY MORNING

OTHER THAN THE CHATTERING squirrels, the lone resident of Lumberjack Camp was a large, ungainly man perched on the Official Camp Sitting Log.

On foot, Allison hung back behind a fat aspen, within earshot but back from the camp circle. Sunny Boy was tied up on the edge of the grove, far back.

Colin had gone in on Merlin, came around the side to suggest he was alone. He wouldn't have looked right without a horse—he didn't have enough gear on his back.

The man sat watching a cup atop an eight-inch tripod over a fire so small that Sunny Boy could have put it out with one painless stomp.

The pint-size fire reminded Allison of the old Indian saying—*Indian build small fire, sit close. White man build big fire, sit far away.* This guy ran against stereotype.

He sat on the camp log where a hundred Boy Scouts and Girl Scouts and hikers and hunters had sat before. Nearby, a loosely-folded sleeping bag lay on the dirt next to a sturdy backpack and a five-arrow quiver, an open rack with pre-cut holes for standard broadheads.

"I figure the less smoke, the more elk," he said.

The man's voice resonated. Purposeful. Over-eager. A voice for theater.

"Been hunting since dawn. Where's your rig?"

Colin replied from the saddle, but he had his back to her. Allison made out the tone—casual. There was a breeze no stronger than a kiss you'd give a newborn. She was downwind, which might be helping.

"Didn't see anything," said the man.

The lone hunter had a two-day red-brown stubble and a camo baseball hat with an extra-long bill. He was fair. He hadn't stood up on Colin's approach, but he appeared to be a healthy XL. He reminded Allison of fluorescent lights and indoor video games.

Allison was semi-pleased not to find Larry Armbruster lying in wait, but there was something unsettling about the scene.

How long had he been sitting here? How come they hadn't spotted him from the ridge, coming in?

The camper's water bubbled and he picked the cup from its spot over the fire, dropped in a bag attached to a string.

"It's coffee," he said. "Make you some? Gets to a point I come back to camp and start over."

He took a scalding hot slurp. The tag from the coffee bag fluttered in the breeze. The backpack was scuff-free. The guy didn't look like he'd slept outdoors and been on a five-hour hike that started pre-dawn. If he had camped here, there was no sign of last night's fire.

"I got this enzyme spray. I can be straight upwind of a fat buck, forty yards away and he doesn't have a clue I'm there. Like a cloaking device. I know it ain't me that's scaring them all away."

Colin muttered something.

"Say, you wouldn't happen to have instant glue and a superfine nozzle?" He set his cup by the puny fire, stood up, giving her a better view of his face, more square on. "I ripped the fletching on three of my arrows. I was ducking through some scrub. When I went to my kit, I realized I'd forgotten the glue."

That face …

Her insides wobbled and she knew, hot waves of prickly panic shuddering from shoulders to calves and back.

Colin don't …

She scanned left, scanned right.

Colin don't …

The man couldn't be alone.

The man held up his quiver. Torn fletching, yes.

More show.

"These old school recurves. The only way to hunt," said the man.

The bow was dark, elegant and classic. Five feet high, tip to tip.

Allison focused on the man's face.

Colin don't …

But Colin felt some inner kinship.

Always wanted to help.

He slid off Merlin.

Colin was glancing at the ankle-biter fire and when he looked up he was facing a large, shiny gun that glinted in the grove like a diamond.

"Right there," said the man.

Elbow locked and arm shoulder higher.

He was taller than Colin. The gun barrel looked big enough to store quarters in a stack. It gaped long and dark, like the opening to a coal mine.

"Where is she?"

"What the hell?" said Colin, like he meant it. Louder for her. "Where is she?"

He kept the gun on Colin, stole quick looks around.

"Who?"

"Motherfucker, come on."

Come awwwwwwn.

Colin took a step back. Two.

She put her hands in her pockets, hoping to find a Ninja five-star throwing blade.

Nothing.

But throwing something...

"Where is she?" he said. "I got all day. You, on the other hand. Care to see this thing work?"

Held the gun like it was no heavier than a toothbrush.

"I'm on my way back—"

"Fuck that." He let Colin stare down the barrel for a couple of painful seconds. "You did not come alone."

She'd been scanning the ground, spotted a stick with a nub like a thumb jutting up at the end. The length of a mini-baguette, but thinner.

She'd need an arrow.

The mini-baguette was a couple strides away, across a gap in the trees.

Down like a crab, scampering low, she came up with the stick in her hand and gripped it like a club, nub out.

Tingle in her shoulders, an infusion of panic like a booster shot.

"How about if you wait right here," said the man. He took two steps toward Colin, who recoiled before being pushed back and plunked down on the Official Camp Sitting Log.

"What the hell—"

Allison peered up, hand around the stick. Thought about giving herself up. Two on one. It had worked with Boyd. Two on one, let Colin find his moment.

The man had his head down and Allison moved one tree closer. Stayed low.

Colin's hands were tied behind him at calf-roper speed. He was face down. A moment later, his legs were bound at the ankle and the rope went around Colin's neck, pulling his head off the ground. It was a hog tie, torture style. Colin would need every bit of strength he could manage to keep his neck up and avoid strangling himself.

"She can't be far, can she?"

Rhetorical. He was looking around now, choosing a direction.

Pocket knife out, Allison whacked the tip of a new stick. Six quick strokes.

A flash came of her patient from the dog attack. He must have made his weapon in a rush, too. But with what knife?

It was no time for perfection. No time for feathers. No time for pretty things.

No time for a nock in the butt end of the arrow, either, but it fit pretty snug against the protruding nub.

She grabbed a stone and flicked it deeper into the woods but to draw him toward her.

"Nice," said the man. "Thank you."

Allison slithered up against the tree until she was standing, back to the tree and to him. Waiting.

Heard him approach.

She walked clear of her spot, stood there, hands low and hands trying their best not to shake.

"Right here," she said.

He was ten steps away, but stopped.

Shook his head.

"Told you," he said. Turned to Colin. "Told you so. Well, that was easy. Now, come join your buddy."

Colin groaned. Saw his neck bulging and red.

Mini-baguette gripped low, behind her leg. Clamping the arrow down with her hand, too.

"You're a little thing," he said. "My god, causing all this trouble. Shit."

Sheeeit.

He relaxed, lowered the gun.

She gave her best sigh, her best *I surrender* body language. Slumped, defeated.

Took two steps forward, showed complicity.

Cleared the trees.

In the open.

"Come on now," he said.

One more step and then as naturally as if she was stretching she lifted the mini-baguette stick, gripped it hard, flung it forward, and whipped the arrow-dart with a snarl.

He jumped like he'd walked into a juiced electric fence and his body collapsed, a stun-gun effect and his hands flew up high around his right eye, where he'd been stung.

Bitten.

Hurt.

The gun dropped.

He writhed on his knees, his hands bloody and wet.

She needed both hands to untie Colin. Started with the legs, let his head down gently, and then the wrists.

They sat on the camp log, Colin still gasping for a bit of air and rope burns on his neck.

Two on one.

"I wouldn't last long in that nasty sling," said Colin.

She showed him the crude atlatl, at least the mini-baguette piece of it.

"My eye." The guy writhed in pain. "My fucking eye."

"Now what?" said Allison.

Her heart worked its way back to even keel.

Felt a prick on her neck like a hot match.

Grabbed Colin's leg, started to look around.

"Oh no," said a voice. "Drop the gun right now and then don't— don't move. Either of you."

Blood trickled down her spine where she'd been pricked.

"Stay right there," said the voice.

The voice she recognized. A recent voice.

He sounded like he was struggling, straining at something. The voice was stressed, but it was him for sure.

She heard another layer of grunts and the prick in her neck kept telling her to not look around but Colin had turned and he shook his head, just enough.

And now the shape came around in the corner of her eye as the voice came front and center.

Sulchuk.

With Larry Armbruster in a head lock.

SIXTY-NINE:
SATURDAY MORNING

SULCHUK HELD A CROSSBOW, loaded and cocked. The limb strained. The string was taut.

With a mean shove, Sulchuk body-checked Armbruster out of his grip toward Woodrow, who was still bent over and focused on the wound to his eye.

Armbruster went sprawling, an awkward somersault of tumbling big man. He issued a grunting gasp as he came to rest in the dusty earth by the campfire ring.

Three against two, Allison figured, and the three might be in sweet harmony.

Three against two.

Sulchuk put the tip of the arrow inches from her face. The arrow was a three-wing broadhead fat enough to drop an elephant.

"Quite the little fucking mess," said Sulchuk. He was breathing hard. His chest heaved. His hands were pristine clean like a secretary's but any hint of corporate control had vanished.

"So Armbruster was setting you up?" said Allison, as cool as she could muster. "The so-called mountain lion attack was designed to bring you down—at least, your end of the operation. Did you know about the dogs? Was that the kind of hunting you were going to show Gail?"

Naming the daughter added extra pleasure, might make him pause before his next rash move.

"Hell," said Sulchuk. He spat the word.

Armbruster made his way up to his knees, his back to them, but facing Woodrow.

"The hell did you do to my boy Woodrow?" he said.

My boy ...

Armbruster turned to look at them. His jowls were puffy and red. His eyes didn't settle on anything for long. He was jacked up.

"What else was I supposed to figure out?" said Allison. She'd take an answer from any source, whoever wanted to talk. "That there are two groups of hunters chasing Mexican immigrants out of the country?"

Armbruster stood slowly and turned, launched a prodigious loogie high and off to the left.

My boy ...

Woodrow ...

Wounded Woodrow ...

Woodrow stood, gasping and making awful noises from the pain. He covered his bloody right eye with his bloody right hand, trying to staunch the flow. It wasn't working.

There was something in the eyes and fat nose, a resemblance.

"Fucking mooches," said Armbruster. *Mooches* like a growling bark. He walked back toward them, watching Sulchuk. "Mexico's finest, crawling all over and taking our work."

"Shut up," said Sulchuk to Armbruster, showing him the cross-bow. He gave Armbruster another shove back toward Woodrow, but Armbruster didn't lose his footing this time. "I told you to shut the hell up, this is my deal now and we're going to sort this shit out."

Sulchuk must have surprised Armbruster and waited for his moment to get the upper hand.

Allison stole a quick glance at Colin, who was looking around for something useful. An angle. Anything.

"But Armbruster, your team or your side—whatever—didn't approve of the whole hunting dog thing?" said Allison. She was trying to provoke Armbruster into talking. She wanted Sulchuk focused on him.

"That was beyond your standards?" she asked. "Beyond your level of acceptable? Or were you just trying to expose one operation so your so-called business could take over everything?"

"Hell," said Armbruster. "Does it matter?"

"Shut the hell up," said Sulchuk. He turned to her. "And you."

"I can't" she said. "I have to know—why me?"

Armbruster managed a laugh. "Come on now," he said. "Your reputation. Knew you'd be compelled. Like a dog to a squeaky ball. You wouldn't be able to resist."

She'd been hoisted, so to speak, by her own curiosity. Coupled with a desire to keep the Flat Tops free of crazy shit.

"What about William Sulchuk?" she asked, looking straight at him, pronouncing the name right. Just the thought of it was enough to keep her riled up inside. "I still don't have a clear picture."

"I think everyone can just shut up," said Sulchuk. "Just keep a lid on—"

"Yeah, tell 'em," said Armbruster. "Go ahead."

"Hell," said Sulchuk.

"I think we are about out of time for questions," said Sulchuk.

Colin looked like he was searching for an edge. He turned slightly to face her.

"Easy," said Armbruster.

Colin shrugged, used his elbow to tap hers. He gave her a look like she was missing something.

"So Armbruster, how far did you have to bring the body? Two miles? Three?" said Allison. "Did you have a sled or a cart? And you couldn't be heading down the main trail in the middle of the valley in broad daylight so you had to do that all at night. Long night, I'm sure. Who was he?"

"Another Mexican," said Armbruster. "One of millions. One of hundreds of millions."

"But you didn't like—"

"No, you're right. He didn't like the sport of it," said Sulchuk. "For crying out loud, him of all people, drawing the line. He didn't think it was fair. As if it was fair when they all came across the border and jacked up our crime rates, starting milking the government hand-out system, made sure their babies were born here—all of that."

A mocking tone.

Sulchuk cradled the crossbow like precious cargo, left hand too close to the trigger for any comfort. He scowled.

"From the moment they cross our border, they're targets," said Sulchuk. "They *asked* to be targets. So they get one last chance to run for it, one wee bit of hope. The illegal loser of the day gets picked by lottery—righteous, isn't it?"

"But Armbruster wanted to expose it," said Allison.

Armbruster shook his head. "Just business," he said.

"Fighting over a government contract?" said Colin.

"Contract to manage the jail or help fill it, too?" said Allison.

"Does it matter?" said Sulchuk. "Armbruster wants a bigger slice of the pie so he looks for the tender bits and squeezes hard like a mother fucker. That's all."

Was Colin planning anything? He turned to look at her again and then he slowly looked back across the campfire ring.

Woodrow's hefty handgun.

Sitting there, inert.

The new arrivals had overlooked it and Woodrow was too focused on his injury to retrieve it.

Woodrow had managed his way to his feet so he stood side by side with Armbruster. Woodrow's face bugged her. Simultaneously homely and creepy.

"I'm bleeding," said Woodrow. "It won't stop."

He doubled-over again at the waist, one hand over his wound. Blood ran down his wrist, streamed down his arm and dripped from his elbow.

Armbruster turned back to Sulchuk. "He needs a doctor."

"Now," said Woodrow. He tried standing up straight again, but it didn't last long. "*Shit*. My fucking eye!"

"What are we going to do with them?" said Armbruster. "Here, give me my crossbow back and we'll take care of these two first."

There was no *second* or *next*.

"You know some spots," said Sulchuk to Armbruster. "You know every inch up here."

The whole thing came together, the curtain yanked back faster than twenty men pulling on the rope.

"So that was a temporary tattoo?" She said it casually. "Henna or something?"

The question caught everyone off-guard.

"Damn," said Colin.

"The fuck you talking about?" said Woodrow. He spoke in full growl.

"Helluva shot from there," said Allison. "I found your shells in the bushes. A flat-shooting load, right? Shot by a left-hander."

Woodrow stood up, turned to face her with one good eye. Blood continued to gush.

"Hell," said Armbruster. Looked at his boy. "For real?"

"Of course it is," said Allison. "Face tattoo threw everyone."

Armbruster turned to his son, not pleased.

"Was that henna? Few hours in a sweat lodge and a good scrub will take it right off," said Allison. "Right?"

Woodrow smiled faintly—sheepishly—at his father.

"Shit," said Armbruster.

"You hated Lamott," said Woodrow to his father. "Much as anyone on the planet."

"Hell," said Armbruster. "You know what the fuck this means?"

"It means with your help they aren't going to find me," said Woodrow.

"Holy shit, we've got problems," said Sulchuk.

Colin stood, sighed.

"Sit down," said Sulchuk, showing him the crossbow.

"You don't stand a chance," said Colin. "Not a flipping chance."

"Don't make it worse," said Allison.

There were plenty of spots in the Flat Tops that were so remote no random fisherman or hikers or hunters would ever discover their bodies.

Or bones.

Or ashes.

"You were taking a stand about the dog hunting—big point in your favor," said Allison.

"Hell," said Armbruster. "Now Woodrow here has gone and made sure every cop in the land will be on our trail. All that work. Nothing."

"Think it's already over," said Colin. "If you think we came alone…"

"I've been watching this valley since dawn, don't give us that crap," said Sulchuk. "Shit."

"It's true," said Allison. "They're right behind us."

Sulchuk held up the crossbow, the front of the industrial weapon like a Hammerhead Shark.

"Let's get them out of here," said Sulchuk. "First things first."

Armbruster must have read Sulchuk's intention. He went back to the rope, tied Colin's hands behind his back, cut another length and then tied her wrists, giving an extra yank and pinch. Her skin burned where the rope dug in.

She tried not to look at the handgun, so close.

The horses…

If they left Merlin and Sunny Boy, it was too much of a giveaway.

But taking the horses was no easy solution, either. They could dispatch the horses in some remote location—perhaps—but you couldn't exactly bury a horse the way you could two smallish-trim wranglers.

"We gotta take the horses," said Sulchuk, a step behind her thought process. Crossbow in her face. "Where's your horse?"

"Back," said Allison, gesturing sort-of in the right direction. "Edge of the woods."

Were Colin and Allison supposed to walk? Putting them up on horses would be faster, to get off the main routes, and they would all look more normal. But it would be hard to climb up on a horse with your hands tied behind your back.

They would have ten minutes or more in the broad open meadows around Lumberjack Camp. It was a beautiful, clear day. Lumberjack Camp was a tough place to be stuck with two hostages on the first day of archery season.

"Fuck," said Sulchuk, perhaps realizing the same issues or perhaps not wanting to take the time needed to fetch Sunny Boy.

Armbruster and his boy stared at each other, loathing their mess. "What the hell," said Armbruster, all his anger at his boy, squaring off, realizing the impacted dilemma. "You fucked this whole thing up."

"No," said Sulchuk, "you fucked things up with your whole scene up there in the woods."

Father and son glared at each other and Sulchuk raised the crossbow and started walking toward Armbruster, who turned his attention to the bigger threat.

Colin gave Allison a minuscule high sign. He stood, hopped rabbit-like over the official camp sitting log and he was at a dead run into the thickest part of the woods, zig-zagging around trees. Allison was right behind him, but headed off and away at an angle, her last glimpse of Colin through the trees as she heard a crack and she turned sharply and weaved her way and heard the men call and she saw the edge of the woods coming up, wondering if it was better to hit the open country and give either one of them a chance to test their accuracy—or to stay in the woods and try to hide, buy time.

Maybe the sound was an echo lingering in the woods.

But there it was, a high-pitch buzz.

Steady. Purposeful.

The sound came from a bloated mosquito, circling down.

Allison stayed low, looked back over her shoulder on the edge of the woods and suddenly Colin was at her side like he'd slid down the tree.

"What the hell is that?" he said.

"Don't know," said Allison.

There were two people wedged on board the airborne apparatus, wingspan no wider than a standard-issue couch.

The person sitting in front wore dark sunglasses and his long dreadlocks flapped in the breeze. He was focused on the narrow trail that would be their landing strip. He feathered the nose up, slowed the flying bug even more.

The one in back she recognized.

Duncan Bloom held out his arm and popped up a thumb like he'd seen the whole show and approved of the outcome.

In the distance, cresting the ridge to the east, four backlit black dots and she caught the heavy *whock-whock* shudder of helicopters and they looked like they were coming fast.

SEVENTY:
SATURDAY, LATE
MORNING

"Señor Bloom," said Tovar. "¿*Como está?*"

He stood behind the screen door, face in shadow and dark. His house had a wide porch, clean and sharp, fronting a large stone house on the edge of the downtown streets, south of Lookout Mountain.

Tovar opened the door a crack and filled the space like he'd been watching something inappropriate.

"*Muy bien,*" said Bloom. Bloom was hoping to sense a touch of fear, some recognition of trouble. He wanted this over quick. "¿*Y tú?*"

"Bit of excitement today," said Tovar. No glasses. He looked tired. No Guayabera shirt. Just a sweatshirt. He looked ordinary. No *schtick*. "Helicopter traffic makes it difficult to watch the game. What can I do for you?"

Bloom had rehearsed this a hundred times but still wasn't ready. He hadn't caught up with himself. The run to the Lumberjack Camp and back had taken three hours. The police helicopters and an air ambulance landed five minutes after Ziggy put down. Allison said one of the helicopters was familiar. Last seen, the Armbrusters were in cuffs and growling at each other. After an interview with police, Allison and Colin were riding their horses back to Sweetwater. Ziggy had made a run for his ultralight and got it airborne before he could be arrested—at least, for now—about flying a motorized vehicle into the Flat Tops. Bloom had taken the option of returning to Glenwood Springs via trained police department pilot. It was the only option.

"I was wondering if I could ask you a couple quick questions," said Bloom. "Won't take a minute."

Tovar sighed.

"This really isn't a good—"

"Three questions," said Bloom.

Wondering if Tovar would be able to tell he was nervous.

"Aren't the police arresting someone?" he said. "The TV reporters aren't saying exactly, but can't confirm, you know."

"I'm in the same boat," said Bloom. "Sketchy at this point."

A complete fabrication.

"What I want to ask you about is a holding company, pronounced *jail* I believe."

Tovar froze. He sighed, stared at Bloom.

Finally, he ran his fingers through his black hair. "Señor Bloom. You have been a busy boy."

"G-A-O-L," said Bloom. "Yours, correct? And Mr. William Sulchuk too. Or as you know him, William Wright. How long have you known each other?"

"I think I'll ask you to leave," said Tovar.

"And GAOL owns Pipeline Enterprises," said Bloom.

Bloom had left the voice memos app on his phone in record mode. He was holding the phone tucked underneath his notebook, but not trying to hide it. He had his pen out, too, but hadn't taken a note yet.

"We have your sister Yolanda and her daughter, Juanita?"

Again, more sharp breathing.

"We know Juanita's husband, Ricardo, and his role, helping round up illegals for the detention center, tracking them down when they slip away."

"I don't think this is a fair conversation, Señor Bloom," said Tovar.

"So a big, powerful Hispanic family wants to keep the Mexican riff-raff off the streets?"

"Illegals." Tovar was ready for the bait. His eyes tightened. "You know, they damage our reputation. We are upstanding Americans. We are legitimate. We have worked hard. We have put in our sweat, we worked our way up. We have been here for decades, helped build this country. We accumulate resources, like good Americans are supposed to do."

"And the dogs?" said Bloom. "Did you know about them?"

"I am going to close the door," said Tovar.

"Do you know about the dogs? Hunting Mexicans for sport?"

Tovar looked exasperated. The door opened wide and Tovar backed away.

Bloom held the screen door open.

Bloom stayed on the porch, knew he hadn't been invited in.

"Give me a minute," said Tovar.

Bloom could see Luis Tovar moving quickly toward the back of his house.

Bloom turned around and gave a small head nod.

DiMarco climbed out of an unmarked car and from the cars parked nearby, another dozen cops were right behind him.

SEVENTY-ONE:
SATURDAY AFTERNOON

TRUDY SHOOK HER HEAD. "Damn," she said. "Sanctimony meets arrogance."

Bloom was still rattled. Felt jacked up all over when he played the recording for Trudy, Coogan, and Hayes. He hadn't turned the record button off when the cops came up the steps, warrants in hand.

"No time for chit-chat." Coogan smiled. He was one happy editor. "The others have the arrest. We've got the whole story. And we've got Kerry London to beat."

"Which we're going to do," said Bloom. "With sheer, utter pleasure."

"I want my byline on that one," said Hayes.

"You got it," said Coogan. "If I have the whole piece in an hour, you got it."

Trudy sat next to Bloom at his desk. She had given him the hug of a lifetime when he'd returned. It wasn't too much of a stretch to imagine regular trips to Sweetwater, and it wasn't too much of a stretch to imagine being invited into the Sweetwater fold. Trudy's vibe was unmistakable. Allison's too.

Trudy was relaxed. The whole town had relaxed—or was about to. Bloom pictured the bars and restaurants filling up, strangers greeting each other again with a smile, the handshakes and back-slapping at police HQ. The sigh of relief.

"There was no resistance?" said Coogan.

"No," said Bloom. "I think he was tired. He tried to make his way out the back, but they were waiting."

Bloom smiled.

"And while you were out," said Coogan. "Got a call from a Ms. Stacey Trujillo, who is at the hospital in Denver with Tom Lamott."

Bloom flashed back to the pedestrian bridge, remembered Stacey's sobs—knew he'd lost track of what had happened to her. Remembered her beautiful smile, too.

"Apparently, unknown to any other media outlets so far, Lamott has been conscious since yesterday morning and this morning our new pal Kerry London immediately jumped on the network and claimed that he was aware there was about to be a big break in the case and he credited the work of the local newspaper and named the two of you."

"Holy crap," said Bloom, imagining his name even being mentioned on national news. "A moment of magnanimity as big as his ego."

"He credited inside sources but said an army of cops were headed into the Flat Tops based on your work," said Coogan. "London has been breaking in all morning with updates."

"London is a hard boy to figure," said Bloom.

"The best thing is that according to Ms. Trujillo, Lamott wants to give the first interview to you."

"Now we're taking generous and forgiving to a whole new level," said Bloom. "Today?"

Denver wasn't in his plans. He only had eyes for Sweetwater.

"I asked. Ms. Trujillo said whenever you're ready," said Coogan. "And she also said something else."

"What was that?" said Bloom.

"She said Lamott said he'd answer any question you had about what happened in Glenwood Springs or anything before that, too."

"Remarkable," said Bloom.

Bloom's well-trained streak of cynicism immediately surfaced one thought. What better time to discuss old sins than when you were the nation's current favorite victim?

"When?" said Bloom.

"Tomorrow would be fine." Coogan handed Bloom a scrap of paper. "Her cell. Go get 'em."

Hayes went back to packing up—headed to Grand Junction. The dog bite victim Allison had found on the Flat Tops had woken up after surgery and might be willing to talk. They were two for two. Bloom to the east, Hayes would head west.

"Wait as long as it takes for that interview," said Bloom.

"All night and all day," said Hayes.

"Marjorie?" said Bloom, looking straight at her. "I know for a fact I underestimated your abilities."

Marjorie gave a pursed smile. "Thanks—and I probably thought you were only here long enough to work your way back to the big city. Never thought you'd care so much about little old Glenwood Springs, never thought you'd put your back into something up here."

"We wouldn't have made it to this point without you," said Bloom. "You know that for a fact—and Coogan knows it too."

"Thanks," said Marjorie. "Then you and me have a whole new deal." She packed her all-in-one bag, ready to head out. Her rituals wouldn't change, but Bloom had a whole new view.

"Got a problem," he said to Trudy.

"What's that?" said Trudy. Looking concerned.

"There is no way I can write with you sitting right there." He said it low-key, took her hand, felt her fingers fold with his.

She studied his face.

"You want me to go?"

"Not what I want," said Bloom. "What I need."

"Go where?"

"You go home," said Bloom.

"Can you come up? Remember the way?"

"I'd love to," said Bloom. "I'll stop at home and get cleaned up. Leave here in an hour. Two at the most." And he pictured leaving early the next day for Denver, filing an exclusive story that every reporter in the country would be required to credit.

Trudy smiled. "Okay. If that's the way it's going to be."

"What can I bring?"

She gave him an earnest look, thinking things through.

"If you want, bring your toothbrush in case you have an extra glass of wine." She smiled. "Or three."

SEVENTY-TWO:
SATURDAY, LATE AFTERNOON

THE ELK STEPPED OUT the clearing like she owned the meadow, which she did. The plump cow made quick work of aspen sprouts and a patch of milkweed. From what Allison could tell through the binoculars, she didn't have a care in the world.

"Let's hope the view is as good as this for the Oklahoma Boys," said Allison.

They had briefly discussed taking a detour to Button Down Camp, opted to head home in hopes Trudy might be back. Allison wanted to hear every detail.

"You doing okay?" said Colin.

"Whipped to the core," said Allison. "Inside and out. Other than that, fine."

For the last hour, riding quietly, she wondered where the anger had gone. It was there, but it was stuck to her bones. Stubborn. They were taking a break, sitting cross-legged side by side on a high ridge looking east. They had an hour left to ride. They were sitting as close as two people could sit, her knee tucked under his, sharing water and Fig Newtons. At this pace, they would arrive back exactly at dark. For now, the light was a golden kiss of serenity and order.

"Mighty quiet," said Colin.

"Mighty got-a-lot-to-think-about," said Allison.

"You recognized Woodrow right away?" said Colin.

"Hardly," said Allison. "Like reverse-space drawings. You finally blink and see it the other way."

"Think Sulchuk was above it all or you think he was out there hunting Mexicans, too?" said Colin.

"It might not be his style to get his hands dirty at that level," said Allison. "But it will all come out."

During one lull in the police interviews at Lumberjack, Duncan Bloom had given her a rundown from their night of research, more than a few mentions of Trudy along the way. She was happy for Trudy. Allison's interviews with the police had taken two hours. No doubt she wasn't done.

"So Armbruster was working against a friend?"

"A business partner," said Allison. "Armbruster was hoping the whole hunting with dogs thing would be exposed and he'd have room to move in."

Sunny Boy exhaled as if to say *look at the time, look at the time.* She was sitting on his lead rope. He had hay buffet on the brain.

"Armbruster was a soldier in the operation and wanted to find his own way to get promoted," said Allison. "Best I can figure."

"Kind of a long shot, do you think?" said Colin. "That somehow he could bring down the empire and keep his fingerprints off it?"

She was worried how she had reacted to everything, beginning with Kerry London. Maybe the arrival of the reporter and the helicopters had interrupted any chance for the emotions to erupt.

"As a way to stage a coup, it wouldn't have been my first choice," said Allison.

She found her heart focused on the half-corpse, his journey north, his hopes. Snagged in the wrong snare.

She thought of her patient in Grand Junction and sent another bundle of secular prayers his way.

She put an arm around Colin's shoulders, kissed his sweaty cheek. She felt as if she took too deep a breath that she might sob on exhale.

The cow stopped eating, stood up straight and, for no reason that she could see, bolted into the woods. She tipped her forehead on Colin's shoulder, reached an arm up and around his neck, pulled him close. He couldn't hold her hard enough.

The weight suddenly enveloped her and it came shuddering up through her system. The half-corpse. Her patient in the woods. The dogs. *Trained* dogs.

She felt it now. She let the weight press down, let it crush her.

I see the workings of battle…

The thought came and she cried, anger right there.

I observe the slights and degradations…

She pulled Colin closer.

… cast by arrogant persons…

She couldn't get every line, but recalled the essence.

All these—all the meanness and agony…

She exhaled. The dogs, the hunt, impossible inhumanity.

… without end.

© KENTMEIREISPHOTOGRAPHY.COM

ABOUT THE AUTHOR

Mark Stevens lives in Denver. He worked as a reporter for *The Christian Science Monitor, The Rocky Mountain News, The MacNeil/Lehrer NewsHour* and *The Denver Post*. He has also worked in school public relations. He is a member of the Mystery Writers of America, Sisters in Crime, Rocky Mountain Fiction Writers, and the Colorado Authors League.